W9-AVR-689

Suddenly, the Garage Door Blew Apart . . .

Atlanta Police Detective Swift dropped to the ground but kept his eyes leveled on the door. A large, heavy sedan blasted through. It slammed into gear and was gone.

Noiselessly, Swift charged into the building. Hugging its wall, he found a shoulder-level window. He shattered the glass and ripped out the cardboard, wielding his flashlight with the ferocity of a cutlass, then dropped under it and listened.

He heard the sound of water, gurgling as though spilling over rocks.

The wrecked garage door in front was twisted and torn, as though opened with a grenade. He dove through and rolled to his feet, tucked in a crouch and looking for cover. There wasn't any. The cavernous room appeared empty except for a table and lamp near the back. Light from a small-wattage bulb was muted with a heavy shade. He saw what looked like a gurney with a body on top, shoved headfirst into a closet. With his flashlight he probed the room. An office in the back jutted into the room and a sink hung off a bathroom wall. The platform—it wasn't a gurney—held the shoeless body of a man. It had been thrust into a shower stall. The water was on . . .

THE
WATER
CURE

Books by Warwick Downing

A Clear Case of Murder
The Water Cure

Published by POCKET BOOKS

Most Pocket Books are available at special quantity discounts for bulk purchases for sales promotions, premiums or fund raising. Special books or book excerpts can also be created to fit specific needs.

For details write the office of the Vice President of Special Markets, Pocket Books, 1230 Avenue of the Americas, New York, New York 10020.

THE WATER CURE

WARWICK DOWNING

POCKET BOOKS

New York   London   Toronto   Sydney   Tokyo   Singapore

This book is a work of fiction. Names, characters, places and incidents are either the product of the author's imagination or are used fictitiously. Any resemblance to actual events or locales or persons, living or dead, is entirely coincidental.

An *Original* Publication of POCKET BOOKS

 POCKET BOOKS, a division of Simon & Schuster Inc.
1230 Avenue of the Americas, New York, NY 10020

Copyright © 1992 by Warwick Downing

All rights reserved, including the right to reproduce
this book or portions thereof in any form whatsoever.
For information address Pocket Books, 1230 Avenue
of the Americas, New York, NY 10020

ISBN: 0-671-72219-0

First Pocket Books printing January 1992

10 9 8 7 6 5 4 3 2 1

POCKET and colophon are registered trademarks of
Simon & Schuster Inc.

Cover design by Corsillo/Manzone
Cover photo by John Farrell/FPG International

Printed in the U.S.A.

Hi, Mary

Thanks for your smile

Acknowledgments

A lot of people helped me in this effort. They might choose to remain unknown, but I like to spread the blame around. Please do not blame them for the mistakes, however. The mistakes are mine. Give them the credit for anything you find about the book that you like.

From Atlanta:
Wendy Shoob and Carla Young, of the Fulton County District Attorney's office, who—in a manner of speaking—prosecuted the case; Bob Joiner and Bill Gignilliat, who defended; and Robert McMichael, then a district attorney investigator and presently the Sheriff of Fulton County, who put it together. I am deeply indebted to each of you for your generous extension of friendship, time, invaluable criticism, and advice.

From Denver:
Bruce Mendelson of the Colorado Department of Health, Alcohol and Drug Abuse, who modeled expert testimony; lawyers Bill Wilson and Morgan Rumler, who tried to educate me but could not; attorney M. Katherine Bradley for her puckish humor and critique; and my good friend John Dunning, who made me keep working it until it was done.

From New York:
My agent, Bill Reiss, and editors, Jane Chelius and Dana Isaacson, for their friendship, support, and critique.

                                          Warwick Downing

Part
One

Chapter
1

Friday, October 4 • Bozeman, Montana

WHAT A STUPID WAY TO MAKE A LIVING, FRANKIE ROMMEL thought. When you win, you feel nothing. When you lose, you want to die.

A broad-shouldered, vital-looking woman in her early forties, Rommel had been raised on a ranch near Lander, Wyoming. Her trim body radiated fresh mountain air, spring water, and lean beef. She didn't look her age. She still rode horseback whenever she could and jogged in the morning because it felt good. She smoked for the same reason.

At that moment she felt far from good. She hooked her heels on the bottom rung of a bar stool and searched through her purse for a cigarette. She didn't even know the name of the bar. It was the closest drinking hole to the courthouse where she had been living for the last four days, and an hour ago, the jury had come in with its verdict. Not guilty. She had lost. She wanted to die.

"Say. You're that woman prosecutor, ain't you?" a man's gravelly voice demanded. Frankie looked in the mirror that lined the wall behind the bar and saw a grizzly bear standing next to her, peering with hostility into her

3

left ear. He wore a plaid wool shirt and denim trousers, both of which stank of urine and sweat.

She didn't like the tone of the man's voice. She found the cigarettes and, without looking at him, pulled one out and lit it. She looked at the strong-looking blond woman in the mirror staring back at her. A cowboy two stools down grinned at her reflection and lifted his glass in a toast. He had nice eyes, she thought, but he couldn't have been more than twenty-five. She smiled at him. It might be fun to flirt a bit, but she was not in the mood for anything serious.

"You people are all in cahoots, ain't you?" the grizzly bear growled. "Jason Berridge is guilty as sin. How much did he pay you?"

Frankie considered moving to a table. She didn't want to deal with this animal whose nose was in her ear. Berridge—a pudgy, balding psychiatrist—had been charged with killing his wife and two small children. But the jury had walked him. "I feel as bad about it as you do, partner," she said. "And I'll tell you something. I'm not in cahoots with anybody." She turned her back on him and drank her beer.

Frankie Rommel had lost her share of trials. As one of the lawyers for NASP—National Association of Special Prosecutors—she had tried dozens of cases, and she knew you don't win them all. NASP didn't get the easy ones, either. But she usually won, and this one hurt. Alena Berridge had been a decent woman who—like Frankie—had been brought up on a ranch. Her kids weren't angels, but they were good kids. Rommel pictured the photographs of their bodies: sprawled against blood-spattered walls, arms and legs at odd angles, dead eyes. A scene of awful violence. She shut her eyes to block out the vision.

Berridge used the "unknown intruder" defense, popularized by television, and the jury gobbled it up. Somehow they ignored the fact he had recently doubled his wife's insurance. They also were persuaded to believe the scum bag had slept through the whole thing. Frankie trembled as she thought about it. She wanted to get blind.

All at once she had a more immediate problem. "Don't turn away from *me* when I'm talkin' to you," the grizzly bear demanded. He grabbed her by the shoulder, spinning her around, then took a fistful of blouse in his large hand. He yanked her off her perch and shoved his menacing face into hers.

Frankie reacted without thinking. She lifted her knee powerfully into the man's crotch, then hit him as hard as she could with the beer mug. However, the move didn't work the way it was supposed to. His grip on her blouse should have loosened, but he tightened it in pain and fell to the floor, dragging her with him.

All the cowboys in the bar surged toward the grappling bodies on the ground, but the fracas was over before anyone could step in. Frankie got all of her 118 pounds behind a bone-crushing smash with her elbow, snapping the man's head back and breaking his nose. His grip relaxed with the suddenness of a switched-off light. She rolled away, and strong hands raised her gently to her feet. Her breath came in gusts, and she realized the buttons down the front of her blouse had been popped.

Blood gushed from her antagonist's nose, but the cowboys didn't care. They picked him up, carried him to the door, and tossed him out. Frankie's stomach and chest heaved with exertion, and she knew she looked a mess. "Someone stay with him, okay?" she asked. "I think I broke his nose."

"Don't worry about old Bill, ma'am," the curly headed hunk said, steadying her. "It's been broke before." The bartender mopped up the contents of the spilled beer and gave her a new one. "You okay?" he asked. "Old Bill tried to inflict some serious damage."

"*He* won't get my telephone number," Rommel said, tucking her blouse into her waist and folding it in on itself, covering her chest. She smoothed her skirt over her knees. "What got into him?" she asked, her hands shaking as she picked up the beer. "I wish I'd had him on my jury." She let some of the frothy coolness bubble down her throat.

"Alena Berridge, the murdered woman?" the cowboy said.

"Don't tell me. Old Bill's daughter."

"Almost," he told her. "His niece." He took a hit of beer and leaned on the bar. "Bill called her 'Punky.' Her kids thought he was their grampa."

*   *   *

5

Frankie spent the night alone in her motel room, waiting for the dawn and her flight back to Denver. She sat at the small desk with the lights off. Her depression numbed her to the bone. It went beyond the loss of the case. She found herself asking hopeless questions like "Why am I here?" That particular question—in addition to its sophomoric quality—was legally flawed. It assumed a fact not in evidence: that life had a purpose. If she were certain it did, she wouldn't need to ask.

She asked herself a different question: Am I letting myself down? According to her grandfather, the answer to that one was all that mattered.

He had died ten years earlier, but she still loved him as if he now stood beside her. Her parents had been killed in an automobile accident, and the old man had raised her from infancy. He provided her with a wonderfully wild childhood, with Shoshone Indian ranch hands for companions and the Bridger National Forest for a playground. She had been enthralled by life in all its violence, majesty, and seeming indifference. As a child she wanted to know whether clouds could feel, or trees or flowers. As a teenager she wondered how she could have become so totally absorbed in the life-and-death drama of the hunt, and whether it was awful to kill elk. Grampa Rommel—tough, fair, thoughtful, and loving—guided her as she grew up without trying to run her.

When she immersed herself in the freedom movement of the 1960s he even "gave her her head," as he would a horse on a narrow trail. Against his advice, but not his order, she dropped out of high school in Lander to march with Dr. Martin Luther King. The man and the movement set her mind on fire. The experience changed her, too. She was beaten by the police and raped by two of the marchers.

She never told the old man about the rape. He had a tough enough time dealing with the fact that she'd been beaten. He was not surprised when she talked about law school, but he told her what he thought: She would have to choose between a career and children. "A woman isn't like a breeder cow," he said. "She can't pop 'em out and then forget about them. She needs them the same as they need her."

6

But when Frankie dated a hardworking young banker in town and started attending the Baptist church with the man and his family, Grampa Rommel got the notion she was trying to conform her life to his desires. He was right. He offered more advice: "Don't worry about whether or not you disappoint me. Only worry about whether you disappoint yourself."

Frankie smiled, sitting in the darkness with her memories. She studied law at the University of Wyoming and loved it. She grew with experience and took advantage of opportunity, but her focus narrowed. She quit searching for the answers to the huge questions, or issues to fight and die over. She traded those pleasures for the practical implementation of the ideal that made it all possible: The end does not justify the means. So simple to say, so profound in its implication. She truly believed that the law was the bulwark between self-appointed saviors, and freedom.

Eventually she became one of the hired guns at NASP. The courtroom filled her life with excitement and provided her exuberance with an outlet. She was very good at what she did, and she loved doing it.

Then why, she asked as she sat alone, do I feel so awful? The system worked, didn't it? The means and the process were not a charade, as they were in so many other countries. Occasionally a guilty man will go free, and that was as bad as it got, a sacrifice within a mostly just system.

The following Monday, as Rommel drove to work, she smiled at herself in the rearview mirror. The wretched feeling of emptiness remained in her guts, and she checked her reflection to see if her facade was in place. She wore a chic suit and a bow tie and was ready for the good-natured gauntlet she knew she would have to run after losing the trial. But first she was to meet with her boss in his office: a tradition of sorts, a debriefing exercise. He called it a critique, though generally it was a pat on the back.

She really loved James Trigge, the frumpy old bastard who headed NASP. He epitomized all that was good about prosecutors: hard-headed, cynical, tough but fair. The rumpled, bear-bodied, middle-aged man reminded her of her grandfather. Her love and affection was almost filial, even though he was but ten years older than she.

His office—formerly the master bedroom of an 1880s mansion that had been transformed into NASP headquarters—was decorated like an exclusive men's club. Its wood-paneled walls were lined with bookcases, a thick reddish rug covered the floor, and leather furniture stood about like cattle grazing in a mountain pasture. She sat down in a chair opposite him and pulled out a cigarette.

"Hey. If you're going to smoke, over by the French door, okay?"

Rommel got up slowly. A massive bruise had formed over her left hip. She could feel her lover's hands trying to massage away the pain. She slid back one of the French doors that opened onto the large balcony. "Did you quit smoking again, Jim?" she asked, lighting up and dragging down a huge wad of smoke.

"You should, too," he said, his hungry eyes glowing as he stared at her cigarette. "What happened up there?"

"Justice," she said sarcastically. "Everyone in town knows that creepy little shrink killed them, but I couldn't prove it." She pushed back a wisp of hair, exposing a slight discoloration on her right cheek. "The defense lawyer—one of those screaming assholes—hammered away at the obvious. Some very expensive stuff was gone, including an original Remington statue. A pillow case was gone, too. You know, the thief-in-the-night routine—absolute bullshit. Berridge stole it himself."

"Is that what you argued? Premeditation?"

"I tried, but it worked better for him than it did for me. The cops locked the little prick up right after finding the bodies. They went through everything he owned, even a house boat on Lake Powell, and came up with zip. So he argued, 'It was a burglar.' "

"Didn't he fail a polygraph?"

"Yes." She exhaled angrily. "Maybe I screwed up."

"How?"

"The judge wanted the little creep even worse than I did. He'd have let me put that in evidence."

"But you didn't offer it?"

"No."

8

"You didn't screw up, Frankie. We really are the white hats. Give me a cigarette."

"You quit. I'm not going to be the one who kills you."

"Come on, babe. What's the point in living if you can't smoke?" He stood up, feverish for a cigarette now that he'd decided to have one. He patted himself down and opened and shut all the drawers in the desk. He was looking through the wastebasket for a butt when she came to his aid. "Ah, my darlin', everything I own in this world is yours," he said gratefully, settling blissfully in his chair and dragging a half inch off the end of the stick.

"Everything?"

"Well, almost." He grinned at her. "What about something you could really use, like a vacation? We can get somebody to do that Ciccarelli thing in Phoenix. Let's put Reddman on it. He knows that country."

Rommel was tempted, but she shook her head no. "When I'm lolling on the beach at Cancun I don't want to be gritting my teeth."

"What is it, Frankie?" Trigge asked.

"What do you mean?"

"You're too quiet. You aren't bouncing off the walls, pissed off, threatening to quit. You haven't thrown anything at me. What's wrong?"

"I'm bored." Her statement surprised her. "I'll be damned. It's as simple as that. I'm bored!"

Trigge grinned at her. "Blood, bodies, gore, the chance to flail away in the pit like a gamecock—that bores you?" He pushed his chair back and stuck his feet on his desk. "You've only been doing it for ten years."

She ground out her cigarette and leaned back in her chair. "I used to think—I *still* think—what an incredible game. High stakes, drama, intellectual challenge. But something's missing."

"What?"

"They're never the same, but in a way they're all alike. Tell me, ladies and gentlemen. Are you going to let this baby-raping dog beater get away with murder?" Trigge laughed, then put out his cigarette. "Don't we ever get cases that involve more than bodies? The Scopes case. Remember that one?" she asked him. *"Inherit the Wind?"*

"The Monkey Trial. Sure. When Clarence Darrow peeled William Jennings Bryan of his beliefs."

Frankie nodded, feeling some of her old enthusiasm. "Instead of bodies all over the place, ideas. A case where *ideas* are in the closets and on the bedroom floors, along with the corpses." She spoke wistfully. "A trial that really means something, other than—you know—he'll pay for what he did, or he won't."

"You know what, babe?"

Frankie didn't quite know what Trigge meant when he called her "babe," but she let it go. He always said it softly, and with affection. "What?"

"Maybe it's time you moved on."

"Jim! Are you trying to get rid of me?"

"Hell, no, lady, I'd rather lose my wife. But you could make three times what I pay at Rowland and Rogers and only sweat when you jog. Or climb on the bench and make momentous decisions."

"Me, a judge?" She laughed. "The *last* thing I want is to sit in judgment." But something in her manner suggested she was intrigued by the thought. "I don't think so. I'm too much of an advocate."

"What do you want, then?"

"Ten thousand wishes! My youth! Grandchildren!"

"You need children of your own before you can have grandkids, don't you?"

"That's usually the way it happens. Do you know what I'd really like, Jim? More than anything I can think of?"

"What?"

"I'd like to make a difference. Do you know what I mean?"

Trigge smiled at her. "Yeah."

Chapter

2

Saturday, April 3 • Atlanta, Georgia

DETECTIVE DOUG SWIFT OF THE HOMICIDE DIVISION, Atlanta PD, stared at the strangely twisted body of the white woman at rest in the pile of dead leaves. She lay at the bottom of a wooded ravine, south and a little east of Five Points. The woman wore a starchy white blue-trimmed uniform with a "Woodhaven Rest Home" emblem stitched over the right jacket pocket.

For a moment Swift saw her through the eyes of the young black man who had found her early that morning. "You okay, son?"

The boy straddled his stump-jumper bike, clutching the brake levers as though trying to slow everything down. He nodded at Swift, but his eyes were stuck on the woman.

"Everything look the way it did when you first saw her?"

"Yes, sir."

"Okay. This man over here"—Swift pointed to a uniformed cop—"will take you home." Swift wasn't about to let the boy go home by himself. "He might ask you and your momma some questions, and I may be by in an hour or two to ask some more." He put his hand on the youngster's shoulder. "You go on now. You'll be all right."

"She so white," the young man said. "I never see anybody so white."

There were what appeared to be rope burns around the woman's neck, and her eyes had filled with blood. Evidently she had fallen backward after losing consciousness, one leg bent under her like a broken stick and the other one stuck out. She resembled a puppet whose strings had suddenly been cut.

An area around the body was cordoned off. The ID unit arrived, Lester somebody in command—Swift didn't know the man's last name. The team of two men and a woman took pictures of the body and carefully searched through the brush and grasses under the trees. Anything that looked fresh was tagged and bagged. A canvas purse was found in a bush a few yards from the body and photographed in place. Measurements were taken to show its proximity to the body, then Lester handed the purse to Swift.

The detective carefully extracted a billfold and opened it: two twenties, a ten, a couple of ones. He continued to handle the billfold by its edges even though he didn't think its surfaces would tell them anything. The contents of the purse hadn't been scattered all over the ground as if someone had been frantically searching for drugs or money. There was nothing to suggest the killer had even looked inside.

There were three or four "hits" each year like this in Atlanta, and although Captain Al Fiorello of the narcotics squad would never admit it, street talk usually developed a drug connection. Swift assumed she'd been "narking" for Fiorello and gotten whacked.

Swift located a driver's license and compared the photograph with the corpse's face. They matched. Thin-boned, white almost to the point of transparency, auburn hair, eyes—described as green—that seemed to reach for understanding in the photograph but were unreadable in death. Weight 103, height 5' 02", birth date not quite thirty years ago. Name, Melody Thralkin. Swift wrote down her address in his small notebook. He glanced at his watch: almost eight o'clock. "Medical on its way?" he asked, carefully folding the billfold and putting it back in the purse. He handed it to Lester.

The thin, light-haired man nodded an affirmative. He had the palest, bluest eyes Swift had ever seen, like a desert sky just above the horizon. "Hope they get here before she starts to smell," he said.

"You mind waiting for them?"

"I have to anyway. A new protocol. We shoot 'em in the bag."

"Ask them to give me a call on the autopsy, okay?" Swift asked. "If I can, I'd like to be there."

"Come on, man. She ain't that pretty."

The detective climbed out of the ravine and jumped into his small sports car, parked on the edge of the road. He marveled at the way it sank with his weight, then righted itself. It didn't seem to him that 165 pounds should make that much difference to a car. He drove to the address given on Thralkin's driver's license: a rooming house on North, near Moreland Drive.

Brown skin covered Detective Doug Swift's lean, muscular body like a coat of paint. His face, supporting three scars, had the appearance of one who lets it hang out there an instant longer than he should. His lips were thick and sensitive, his nose wide and flat, and his eyes—soft and eager—saw everything.

The landlady, with a housecoat wrapped around her thick body as though to protect it from evil influences, was first shocked, then unsurprised at the news. She signed a consent form for a search of Thralkin's room and, at Swift's request, helped him with an inventory.

The two-room unit was simply furnished with bed, dresser, and vanity table in one room, a small shower and toilet between, and a sitting room. The sitting room was comfortably furnished with a sofa and chairs, a desk and table surface, reading lamps, television, a compact disk sound system, and a small, expensive portable microwave oven.

All of the furnishings belonged to the landlady except for the sound system and the microwave oven. "Melody had a gentleman friend who gave her those things and, I believe, helped with the rent," Mrs. Nelson confided.

"Do you know his name?"

The woman shook her head. "A very handsome man,

rather slender, very fit-looking, although middle-aged." She frowned at that. "I didn't mind. They made quite an attractive couple. And she did seem to enjoy holding his hand."

Dresses, suits, and rest-home uniforms were hung neatly in the closet. Swift glanced at some of the labels: Neiman-Marcus, Saks, Neustedters. "Pretty nice stuff," he commented. "You mind leaving her things here, see if we can't find a relative?"

A tear rather unexpectedly appeared in Mrs. Nelson's eye. "Of course not," she said. "The poor dear is paid up to the end of the month."

Thralkin kept her drug stash in the bottom left-hand drawer of the bureau in the bedroom. It consisted of a pouch large enough to hold two or three ounces of marijuana, a clay pipe, and a Zippo lighter; a Sucrets box with three vials of rock cocaine; and a glass pipe. "I had no idea," Mrs. Nelson said. Swift bagged the drugs in a paper sack, labeled it as to time and place, and initialed it.

In the desk drawer they found an address book, a few letters, a picture album labeled "Memories," and an envelope that held some color photographs. Two letters showed a return address of Leonard Thralkin, B/N 695–375–08, PO Box 79857, H–950, PO Box 1000, Petros, TN 37845. Swift knew Petros. The Brushy Mountain State Penitentiary was located there. The "B/N" stood for "booking number." Swift wondered if Leonard was a father or a brother.

He ran through the names in the address book in the hope that Mrs. Nelson might match one to the gentleman friend. She did: Randolph Richardson.

"Huh!" Swift said. "Maybe I know him. Six feet tall, fifties probably. Wouldn't talk much, but you'd listen when he did. Eyes that don't miss much, and long legs."

Mrs. Nelson frowned as though unwilling to place Mr. Richardson in a room with a black man, but she nodded. "That fits him."

They placed the photo album on a table and opened it. Something about Mrs. Nelson's attitude suggested she'd seen the contents already. They were carefully labeled snapshots, mostly of the Thralkin family: Melody as an infant in the arms of her mother, later holding hands with her daddy Leonard. Mrs. Thralkin appeared to be a large

14

woman with a bit of a mustache. Leonard was short, pudgy, and blond. Swift flipped through the album, watching the faces of the adults age and their bodies thicken, and the girl grow from infant to young woman. Throughout her expression stayed the same: a wide smile that conveyed sheer delight at the fact her picture was being taken, but eyes that seemed to hide other feelings.

The picture chronicle ended during the spring of Melody's senior year in high school.

An unsealed nine by five manila envelope was taped to the inside back binder. Swift pulled out a collection of newspaper clippings.

They were from the Bristol *Times-Herald*. It had been several years, but Swift remembered the incident they depicted because the media in Atlanta had covered it also. Melody Thralkin had been the star witness for the state of Tennessee in a murder trial. Her father—the mayor of Bristol—had been charged with blowing her mother apart with a shotgun. In the course of the trial it developed that the man had sexually abused his daughter from infancy. "The poor child," Mrs. Nelson commented over Swift's shoulder.

The loose photographs were more recent. Swift flipped through them, looking for a picture of Richardson. He saw several of Melody in her work uniform, looking brighter than she did in the album; an attractive woman, a cute figure, auburn hair framing a thin face. But none of any men. He selected what appeared to be Thralkin's most recent photograph and dropped it in his pocket. Everything else from the drawer was dropped in another brown bag.

He thanked Mrs. Nelson for her help, asked her to keep the room locked, and told her not to allow anyone in without police authorization. He promised the investigation would be finished within a week so she could show the rooms.

He was not in a hurry when he left Thralkin's apartment. He drove to police headquarters across the street from Georgia State University and secured the items he had taken from her room in his locker. Propping her photograph against a coffee cup, he typed a report of what he had done to that point, knowing it would help him decide what to do next.

On the computer in the homicide division squad room he punched up the Randolph Richardsons in Georgia, comparing names with the address from Thralkin's book. A moment later he had a picture of the man's driver's license on his screen: Colonel Randolph D. Richardson, retired, USMC. Swift grinned at the photograph of the man who had been his platoon leader in Vietnam. "Hi, Captain," he said, writing down his date of birth and social security number. "So you came home, too." He ran Richardson's name and DOB through NCIC, GBI, and FBI locators, but there were no "hits," nor had he expected any.

He fed the computer Melody Thralkin's name and date of birth. She had been confined in Bristol as a material witness in the trial against her father, but other than that she had no record.

Woodhaven Rest Home was on Briarcliff Road in DeKalb County. Swift called the sheriff's office in DeKalb according to the protocol, received their authorization, and drove out. The facility was protected by a brick wall and an electronically operated gate. He identified himself through a speaker. The gate slid open, and he drove inside.

The head nurse at Woodhaven—a large, matronly woman with an efficient air—examined the nurse sign-in sheets and told Swift that Thralkin had been on duty until three o'clock that morning. She had no idea where the girl had gone after work. Thralkin had been a good worker, she told Swift: dependable, reserved, and very sympathetic toward their elderly patients. She knew of no one who disliked her, although no one knew her very well, either. "A shame," the woman said matter-of-factly. "Well. She won't be coming in tonight, then. I'd better see about a replacement."

It was almost noon when Swift parked in front of the address in Avondale Estates where Richardson lived. A wavy belt of town houses—connected to each other, but architecturally distinct—curved around a cul-de-sac. The smooth asphalt roadway leading in to the development was lined with a white cement gutter-curbstone-sidewalk, like the beveled trim around a floor. Beyond the border stretched a carefully cut, radiantly green lawn. Some of the houses were one-story, others two. Their angles and corners were different; the distances they jutted into the lawn also varied from house to house. But the trim around the windows and the rain gutters of the brick structures were painted with the same pale green, and the buildings looked as though they had come from the same box of Legos.

A copper-brown 1984 Chrysler sedan was parked in front of the Richardson residence. Swift checked the license number against the one his computer search had provided him, verifying that it belonged to Colonel Richardson. "Good. The old man is home." He parked his car and climbed out, walking up to the front door. Swift felt a surge of anticipation. The two men had soldiered together in Vietnam. He rang the doorbell, listened to the chime, and waited. There was no answer.

He pulled a card from his billfold identifying him as a detective, Atlanta PD, homicide division, and turned it over. He wrote a note on the back. "Hi, Captain, remember me? Please give me a call, sir. Little Mac." He stuck it in the screen door and walked back to his car.

He had turned onto Ponce de Leon, less than a mile from Avondale Estates, when the police radio in his car crackled on: "DH Three, Atlanta. Twelve oh four."

Swift picked the microphone off its hook. "Atlanta, this is DH Three."

"Were you just out in Avondale, residence of Colonel Richardson?"

"That's right."

"Go back, DH Three. He's there. Says he thought you was a salesman."

17

Chapter

3

THE TALL, LANKY FIGURE OF DETECTIVE DOUG SWIFT'S FOR-
mer platoon leader stood on the lawn in front of his Avondale townhouse. Swift jumped lightly out of his car and
grinned at the man. Richardson's hair was tinged with gray,
there were lines in his face, but his skin still looked young,
and his thin body remained as taut as wire. His eyes poked
holes in whatever they touched, too. "How are you, sir?"

"Well, I'll be damned." Richardson had on a comfort-
able-looking old-fashioned smoking jacket. He moved with
a natural and easy confidence, as though he were the only
lion in the jungle. "Corporal Swift, the war machine! One
mean Marine!" What started out as a handshake turned
into a warm, affectionate embrace. "Come in, you old
hound dog."

Swift found himself full of questions. "What are you
doing for yourself now, sir? Shoot. You look just the
same." He let the man guide him toward the open door.
He became aware that his accent had moved back in time
to the 1960s. "You look like you could still fit the same
uniform, go out and do battle in the same old grungies."

"You look better, Corporal. You smell better, too. I
guess we all smell better, but you in particular." He
grinned. "You were spectacular, Mac. When you stank,

you really stank. Like a drink?" He shut the door behind them and guided Swift into the living room.

"I'd take some coffee." Swift glanced around the room: inexpensively furnished, magazines stacked neatly in piles on the hearth, the television set aimed like a cannon at a comfortable, somewhat worn recliner. He wondered why Richardson lived in a townhouse in Avondale Estates. The location suited a retired enlisted man more than an officer.

"Coffee it is. Black?"

"Yes, sir."

"You can dispense with the 'sir,' Mac," Richardson said. Swift could hear the rattle of cups and saucers from the kitchen. "Of course, I expect you to stand at attention, and you probably ought to snap off a few salutes, but I don't expect you to call me sir. Makes me feel too blasted old!"

Swift grinned. "I'd better call you 'sir,' sir. Be awful hard on me to call you 'Randy.' "

Richardson handed him a white china cup filled with coffee. "Suit yourself. Don't expect me to return the favor, though. I don't intend to call you anything decent." He smiled with pleasure. "Sit down."

Swift did, basking in the charismatic glow that Richardson still managed to generate. The old man had always done it "his way." He was no ordinary Marine. He had been awarded the Medal of Honor for heroism in Korea, but fifteen years later in Vietnam he was only a captain.

What Swift remembered most was how his troops had loved him, even if the brass didn't. Richardson refused to take unnecessary risks with his men, and because he was a certified war hero he could get away with it. Yet when opportunity knocked he would hit hard. A band of glory surrounded the platoon like a halo, and his oft-decorated men enjoyed the distinction of being live heroes rather than dead ones.

"Remember when you got knocked down in that bunker, Captain?" Swift asked, smiling with the memory. "Ceiling bent clear down to the floor, then moved back up to where it belonged."

Richardson's eyes were alive with recognition. "That

was before I made you a corporal, wasn't it? Terrible mistake, that, but too late to change it now. Of course I remember." He drained his coffee and set the cup and saucer on the arm of the couch. "What's this all about, Mac? I haven't killed anyone for two or three days."

Swift set his cup down, too. He did not want to get down to business. He started to pull a photograph out of his pocket but saw a five-inch-by-eight-inch color glossy of the woman on top of the bookcase. "Did you know Melody Thralkin, Colonel?"

"Yes."

"She's dead, sir. She was murdered early this morning."

"I see. Well." Richardson's tone was conversational. He started to stand, but then dropped back as though losing his balance. He covered his eyes. Swift leaned forward, wanting to help but unsure what to do. Richardson's mouth was twisted in pain, and his face seemed to lose control, as though trying to do too many things at the same time.

Swift put his hand on Richardson's shoulder. "Are you all right, sir?"

"Of course." Richardson brusquely shrugged off the contact and leaned back. His hands rested firmly on his knees. "You're sure about this?" he asked.

"Yes, sir."

For a moment Richardson's face hardened into rock, like one of the heroes who rode across Stone Mountain. Then it relaxed. "Tell me what you know, will you, Mac?"

The hell with the manual on investigative procedure, Swift thought. He told him when it happened: sometime between three A.M. when she got off work and seven that morning when she was found. He described the crime scene, too, like a point scout reporting on an enemy location.

"How did you get my name?"

"The landlady. Matched you up with a name in Miss Thralkin's address book."

"I see." Richardson sat like a statue, not even breathing. "Then you know of our relationship?"

"The landlady said you were a gentleman friend."

"We were lovers. Does that make me a suspect?"

"According to the book you are," Swift said, wishing he could help. "Not according to me. She was hit."

"What do you mean?"

Swift told him of his suspicions. Richardson listened with the intensity Swift remembered but made no comment. He got on his feet. "D'you suppose I could see her? One last time?"

"If that's what you want, sir."

"It is."

The manual called for a positive identification, and the drive would give them time to talk. "Use your telephone?"

"It's in the hall."

Thralkin was still in the cooler, Swift was told. The pathologist from the medical examiner's office wouldn't do the autopsy until the following Monday.

When Swift walked back to the room Richardson looked older. "It could be a mistake, right?" he asked.

Swift hooked his arm through Richardson's as they walked across the lawn to Swift's car. "It could be, sir, but I don't think it is." He wished he could think of something more to say.

Late that afternoon Swift parked on the street in front of his apartment. It was on a shady street near the Atlanta University campus. He let the dispatcher know where he was, locked his car, and went inside.

The sparsely furnished apartment was simple, neat, and clean—as was the man. Swift cleaned his three rooms every Saturday. The idea of having someone do it for him was repugnant. It had nothing to do with money. Perhaps it was that his mother had cleaned homes for a living. He peeled off his coat, hung up his pistol, and began the routine.

Swift wished he had looked the old man up after the war. Of course, they hadn't traveled in the same social circles. But seeing him brought back memories—not all of them bad. As he wiped off the bathroom mirror he grinned at the face in the glass, remembering how long it had taken him to like it.

A black face named Douglas MacArthur Swift. In rural Georgia, after the war, that particular name had some definite drawbacks.

His daddy hadn't thought so, though. On a burial detail in New Guinea during World War II MacArthur had patted his father on the head. So five years later a little baby got draped with a whole set of hard-to-handle baggage.

"Your name *what?*" Swift's first grade teacher had said. Like most black people, she considered MacArthur a racist. "Well, sit right here then. At attention."

Lots of young blacks were named after famous whites in those days. There were two Roosevelts in Swift's first grade class and one Lincoln. *They* didn't have to sit at attention. It got worse when he went to boot camp at Parris Island. The drill instructor said, "We got us a *Douglas MacArthur Swift!*" That's when he found out the Marines hated MacArthur as much as the blacks.

But in Vietnam Captain Randolph Richardson told him that MacArthur was the greatest soldier who ever lived. The old man seemed to know what his problem was and bent over backward, explaining to Swift why he should be proud of his name. As Swift thought about his tall, wire-thin, sardonic company commander, goose bumps formed on his arm.

The man would stand up during a firefight, shit flying everywhere, just like John Wayne in a movie, grinning at death. And somehow—like in the movies—you knew he would make it through to the end. He would stick his ass out there against all regulations, leading recon patrols, just as liable to get fragged by his own men as blown up by the VC.

Except every jarhead in the platoon idolized the man, although none of them knew how he stayed alive. Maybe he wouldn't have if he hadn't been the central character in his own book.

Swift's daddy had worked on the garbage truck while his momma cleaned houses for white folks. When Swift enlisted in 1965 she could still stand up, but his father couldn't. He was all bent over with smiles, having been twisted into a corkscrew by fear and hate. How different his father was from the captain.

Swift didn't know what he wanted from life in those days, but he sure as hell knew what he didn't want. He didn't want to be like his father. He would rather be dead.

That may have been why he became a good soldier. It was easy to blow up animals and people and buildings and bridges because he hated everything: whites, blacks, gooks, his Uncle Tom father—even himself. He fought with a savagery that impressed even Richardson.

Officers weren't supposed to develop personal relationships with enlisted men, but Richardson didn't care about the rules. He would send for the young Marine, and they would talk a "ton of shit." Both of them were Georgians who knew where the invisible lines were drawn. They role-played their parts. The captain was the decent white southerner who treated the negro with dignity and respect. Swift did the trusted manservant. He cringed slightly now, a dust mop in his hand, as he thought about it. Then they got tighter, as though the captain realized he was Swift's father and had to struggle with the duty to do what was right by his bastard son.

"If you survive this ordeal—if I don't manage to get you killed—show them for me, will you?" Captain said.

"Show them what, sir?"

Captain stuck his hand on Swift's shoulder like a king who could transform a footsoldier into a knight with the magic touch of his sword. "Show them how wrong they are about you, my young soldier friend. Show them you are a man."

White man guilt trip, a brother had told Swift later when he tried to explain how he'd gotten over his hates. As Swift pulled out the vacuum cleaner he knew it had been Richardson—not his father or mother or even Martin Luther King, Jr.—who had given him a sense of personal pride.

But as he pushed the nozzle of the vacuum cleaner across the floor he saw, in the patterns of the rug, the faces of those little tiny soldiers he had killed. He remembered how confused he'd been when he realized he didn't want to kill anymore.

The first time was when he watched the interrogation of a prisoner. It was daytime, a little village not far from Dac To. Two ARVN intelligence officers had tied the boy up by lashing him to a couple of poles and laying him on the ground. The information they needed was vital, and Richardson asked the questions. It was awful to witness. They tested the answers by burning holes in the boy's foot with cigarettes, then dripped water from a hose over his face and into his nose and mouth, making a game out of catching him when he breathed.

Richardson turned it into a joke. He said the little gook had a disease, but water would cure it. Finally they were satisfied with what the boy said. The ARVN officers untied him and took him behind a hut where they shot him. The doctors must have decided the gook was contagious, Richardson said.

Later they caught another Cong soldier hiding in a hooch, trying to look like a straw mat. The boy's eyes were too much. They darted all over, real quick movements, and saw so much, as though they could see the meaning of life. They "cured" him, too. An hour later his eyes were covered with flies.

Swift didn't like being a soldier anymore. When Martin Luther King, Jr. got fragged the blacks in the platoon stopped talking to the whites, and Swift cut it off with the old man. All he did was grin cynically at him when he rotated out, although he gave him a real snappy salute.

That hadn't been a good way to end it, Swift thought, putting the vacuum cleaner away. He showered and shaved. He was supposed to referee a Little League game that night but thought of calling the old man instead. They had talked a lot on the way back from the cooler, and maybe he needed a friend.

Swift found out about Richardson's mother, who lived the life of a Southern belle—in part on Richardson's retirement income. The old man even joked about his two childless marriages and how he'd made a couple of lawyers rich. But he didn't mention Melody Thralkin. Yet the sight of her body jolted him like the touch of a hot wire. Swift had felt it himself.

He decided not to call. A man like Richardson had all the friends he needed or wanted. Probably more than anything, he would like to be left alone.

Swift promised himself to check the old man out in a few days.

Chapter
4

Wednesday, April 14 • Denver, Colorado

JAMES TRIGGE SLID QUIETLY INTO THE COURTROOM, HOLD-
ing the door so it wouldn't slam. A jury trial was in progress. The judge—an old friend—nodded at him as he
walked down the center aisle and took a seat in the front
row behind the defendant.

Frankie Rommel stood at the lectern. Both sides had
rested. The defendant's lawyer had finished an impassioned
appeal. When Frankie was done the case would go to the
jury. "Those of you who have hunted deer will know what
I mean," she said. Her slim figure moved with natural grace
to the table by the court reporter where the exhibits were
piled.

"When you first hear a rattle in a bush you don't shoot,
do you? Because you don't know what's back there. You
have a reasonable doubt." She picked up a small plastic
bag that held a cartridge casing. "So you wait. You probably wouldn't even take the safety off at that point. For all
you know, the sound you hear in the bush is another
hunter, not a deer." Then she hefted a .41-caliber Smith
and Wesson revolver that was also encased in a clear plastic sack. "But this is an unusual weapon. It belonged to

25

the defendant. And there can be no question that this casing—found near Witherspoon's body—came from this
gun.''

She put them back on the table and moved back to the
lectern. "Wouldn't you, at this point, take the safety off?
You know where the gun was found. But you might still
have a reasonable doubt. Before you pull the trigger you
would want to be certain you're shooting a deer.''

As Trigge listened she piled incriminating fact after
incriminating fact into her argument, skillfully weaving
them into her analogy. "Can you see the animal now?" she
asked the jury. "Aren't these his antlers?" She held up
some documents: a statement from the defendant, an insurance policy on the life of the victim. "Isn't this his long
neck sticking out in plain sight?" She picked up a pair of
gloves that had been found in the defendant's car. The
evidence had shown that the gloves had traces of the victim's blood on the fingers. "Ladies and gentlemen, can
there be any reasonable doubt in this case? You can see
the animal clearly, can't you?"

She moved away from the lectern to her chair at counsel
table. "The evidence is there," she said. "You know it's
a deer. It's okay to shoot." She sat down.

After the jury had been excused to deliberate, the judge
declared a recess, doing his stage exit behind the bench.
The defense lawyer—angry about something—snapped his
briefcase shut and stormed into the hallway, followed by
the defendant's family and friends. Trigge pushed through
the swinging gate in the bar to counsel table. "Hey, lady,
I saw *Bambi*," he said to Rommel. "Are you telling me I
should shoot Bambi?"

Only the court reporter was close enough to hear Rommel's throaty and vibrant voice. "Right. Blow his fucking
head *off*."

Trigge grinned at her. "You're a sketch. Do you want
the good news or the bad news?"

Frankie continued packing her briefcase. "Good news,"
she decided. "Keep the bad news to yourself."

"You're in the running."

"What?" Then the meaning of his statement registered.
"I am! Really?" She flung a file full of papers into the air.

"I could kiss you, you old bastard!" she shouted, grabbing him and smearing his face with her lipsticked mouth. Until that moment she hadn't realized how much it meant to her. "Who else?"

Trigge named the other two successful candidates for the appellate court judgeship that Frankie had applied for. She collected all the papers and neatly packaged them with the rest. "That must be the bad news," she said. "I didn't know Mary applied. She'd be my choice."

"Too radical," Trigge said. "Besides, she's black, and so is Marten."

"I hope *that* doesn't matter," Frankie said. "If she's the best person for the job—"

"Yeah, well get your head out of your ass. The only way a black woman would get the nod is if all the candidates were black women."

"Don't be such a cynic," Frankie said. "This governor is very popular. He can actually do the right thing and get away with it!"

"Won't even occur to him," Trigge said. "Old habits die hard."

Frankie took Trigge's arm and started walking down the hall. "Now the bad news."

"Remember Berridge?"

"That slime ball. How can I forget?"

"Guess what, babe, the jury was right. He didn't do it."

Frankie stopped in her tracks and stared at him. "You're kidding. He couldn't have slept through that! All that new insurance on his wife, and he failed the polygraph! I don't believe you."

"Straight goods, Frankie. Remember that Remington statue he claimed the killer took? It turned up in an art gallery in Sacramento. The cops traced it to a little sneak thief who burgled it out of Berridge's home. They got a confession out of him."

"Who confessed? Berridge?" Frankie asked, still clinging to her belief in the man's guilt.

"No, the burglar. Wallace Sinclair III. A third-generation pill popper."

The news angered her. "That doesn't change a thing,"

she said. The hallway was practically empty, as though there was a lull between trials.

"Slow down, crazy woman. What do you mean it doesn't change a thing?"

"The jury should have convicted him anyway."

"*What?* Why?"

"Because," Frankie told him, "the evidence was there."

Chapter

5

Friday, April 23 • Atlanta, Georgia

DOUG SWIFT TURNED INTO THE DRIVEWAY OF A NICELY LAND-
scaped residence off Briarcliff Road. He snapped off the
headlights of his Japanese sports car, yanked a long black
flashlight out of its cage, and jumped out. The car bounced
up as he cleared the door.

Although it was eighteen minutes after midnight—a late
hour in a quiet neighborhood—the house was ablaze with
light. Neatly trimmed bushes tossed long shadows that
faded into a circle of darkness. It looked like a party after
the last guest has gone but before the lights have been
turned off. In the middle of the lawn, about forty feet from
the porch, lay a shapeless lump covered with a bedspread.
Swift let the beam of his flashlight illuminate the grass
around it.

A uniformed officer—small, white, young—approached
Swift from the side of the house. "Detective Swift?"

"Yeah."

"I'm Office Mobley." They shook hands. "I'm kind of
new, but I think the crime scene's pretty secure."

"How'd that blanket get on him?"

29

"Happened before I got here, sir. Mrs. Williams, the victim's wife? Well, she covered him up."

"You look around the body?"

"I didn't get very close. You know, didn't want to disturb anything."

Swift nodded his approval. "Mrs. Williams in the house? Anybody with her?"

"Just her daughter and Officer Hughes."

"Okay, I know Hughes. What can you tell me?"

"Not much, sir. Me and Hughes on patrol, dispatch said respond to this location, 911? Everything out here just the way it was when we got here—"

"How long ago?"

"Twenty-three fifty-two."

"Then what'd you do?"

"Well, no light on—no porch light, anyways—but lots of light from the house, and we see the body. Martha—well, she went over to it? Just lifted a corner of the blanket, you know, seen what it was? Then we kind of eased up to the door, and it opened, and Mrs. Williams asked us to come in."

The two men stood on the path to the porch, facing the house. "What'd she say?" Swift asked.

"She's cryin', you know. Martha could talk to her, though. Said she's comin' home from a visit with her mother?" Mobley had the Southern habit of ending sentences as though they were questions. "Saw a body on the lawn, you know, kind of unusual, turned out to be her husband? Said at first she thought he was drunk, but then she realized he was dead, so she called the police."

"She say anything about how come? I mean, what'd she see on the body? Bullet hole? Blood? Knife?"

"Said he was just wet, his face and head all wet, but nothing really wrong with him, except he was dead."

"How'd she know that? She a nurse?"

"Don't know, sir."

Swift walked over to the body, probing the ground in front with a beam of light. He removed the bedspread and, as he did, observed faint depressions on the lawn that might have been heel marks. The man lay sprawled on his back, eyes open, an expression of annoyance on his face. He was nicely dressed, wearing casual clothes and expensive shoes. His hair—short, tight waves—had a peculiar matted appearance, and his shirt clung to his muscular shoulders as though pasted on. Otherwise he was dry.

You been bobbing for apples? Swift wondered, finding the man's carotid artery. He held his fingers over it long enough to satisfy himself there was no pulse. Just want to make sure you don't get up and walk off, he said to himself, addressing the dead man. Then, carefully, noting where his own feet were, he drew back the way he'd come.

"You wait out here, okay?" he told Mobley. "Keep the dogs off, you know. ID been called?"

"Yes, sir. Martha did."

Swift was searching for the doorbell when the front door opened. Officer Martha Hughes, big brown eyes, smooth brown skin, real nice smile, but about forty pounds more than she needed. Swift had worked with her before. "Hey, sweet stuff, how you doin'?"

"I'm all right. How's yourself?"

"Everything under control here?"

"About what you'd expect," Hughes said. "The woman's got a hurt on, you know. So does her daughter. You know the dude?"

"Huh-uh. Man was related to Marcus Williams is all I know."

The house was tastefully and expensively furnished: deep yellow carpet, sunken living room, Chippendale desk set in an alcove, sofa and matching chairs near a large fireplace. Mrs. Williams sat alone in the adjacent dining room, which was filled with burnished hardwood surfaces. She was an extremely attractive woman in her thirties with straight black hair styled nicely along her temples, which complemented a luxuriant cream-brown complexion. Her head barely moved, and her hands comforted her face. She had been crying. Her teenage daughter, huddled on the sofa, sobbed miserably.

Swift hesitated. He didn't want to intrude. "Uh, Mrs. Williams, I'm Doug Swift, homicide division, Atlanta police." He searched for her eyes. "We talk?"

"Yes. Of course."

"Martha, find out if ID's on its way, okay? Better call

the lieutenant, too," Swift said, giving Officer Hughes something to do. He didn't want her looking over his shoulder. "I'm sorry this happened," he told Mrs. Williams after Hughes was gone. "I pulled back the cover. He looked like a nice man."

"He was a nice man."

Swift balanced the flashlight on the floor and opened a small notepad. "You know where your husband was earlier?" he asked, keeping his voice as matter-of-fact as he could.

"He called home just before seven and told me he'd be late. Something about a reporter who wanted to take pictures." She brushed moisture away from her nose. "We waited for him until nine and then got tired of waiting." She stared hard at the floor, her eyes wide open in an obvious effort not to cry.

" 'We'?"

"Felicia and I. My daughter."

Swift nodded at the girl on the sofa. "Then what did you do?"

"We went over to my mother's. We watched a movie and came home."

"That's when you found him?"

"Yes." Her eyes were glazed with disbelief. "I thought he was drunk."

"He drink a lot?" Swift asked.

"Not anymore. He used to."

"Where'd he call you from, Mrs. Williams? When he told you he'd be late?"

"His office. At least, my impression was his office."

"Remember anything else about what he said?"

"I don't, really. Just that a reporter was going to take pictures."

Swift nodded. He hadn't paid much attention to the latest scandal in which the city administration found itself embroiled, but he knew who the players were. The victim, Charles Williams, was one of the players. "Your husband have any medical problem you know about, Mrs. Williams?"

"No."

32

"Like heart disease or diabetes? Anything along that line?"

"No."

"What about drugs?"

"What do you mean? Medication?"

"Really was asking, you know, did he do drugs?"

"No. Oh, sometimes, at a party, he might . . ." Her voice hurt. "But he hasn't done anything like that for years."

"Mamma, Daddy didn't do drugs! I *know* he didn't do drugs! Ever!"

"Be still, child. Go upstairs."

"No!" The girl pushed herself off the sofa. Swift was stunned by her beauty, and her pain. "Isn't it bad enough he's dead? Why do you have to tell lies about him?"

"Come over here, girl." The beautiful young woman draped herself over the older woman's legs. "He used to do some coke, honey, but that was a long time ago. Don't you think I know him better than you?" She stroked the girl's shoulders and soothed her neck with her hands.

Swift felt strangely that he was in the presence of something holy. Perhaps the healing has already started, he thought, even before the wound has been cleaned. "We can talk later if you want, Mrs. Williams."

"We can talk now. Felicia is a lot older than—well—than she knows herself. Why do you ask about drugs?"

"Like to know what he died of, you know."

"It wasn't drugs," she said emphatically.

"Your husband owns that contracting business, right? 'Build in Atlanta'?"

"Yes." She looked defiantly at Swift.

"He do anything else? A second job?"

"No. It's quite a successful business." Her lower lip quivered.

"How'd it work—him and his uncle, I mean," Swift asked, referring to the controversy in which her husband was involved. "Were they business partners?"

"Absolutely not," she said. "His uncle Marcus is the public works administrator, and Charles was the low bidder on a contract." Angry tears pushed into her eyes. "Should he be *punished* because he's related to the man who gives out city contracts?'' She wiped her cheek with her hand. "They still won't leave a black person alone."

"Sometimes it looks that way," Swift said. "But there's a lot of money involved in that deal. You think, any way you can think of what—"

Officer Mobley stuck his face through the doorway into the room. "Sir?"

"What is it, Mobley?"

"ID is here, sir. They're out there now."

Swift hurriedly excused himself and ran outside. Two of the ID units had reputations, and Swift didn't know who was on that night. "Hey!" he hollered when he saw what was going on. Two photographers were standing over the body, taking pictures. "Get away from my body!" He charged forward, scattering them, then frantically searched the ground. It was too late. Any trace of footprints had been obliterated. "Which one of you assholes—"

A large, very dark black man emerged from the ID van parked behind Swift's sports car. "Goddam, Swift, don't you start hasslin' my crew."

"Goddam," Swift yelled, "why don't you check with the detective in charge of the investigation before you start messing with the crime scene?"

"Because I expect the detective in charge of the crime scene to be *at* the goddam crime scene, man. If he so busy he can't be there when we get there, then we go to work. Goddam." He glared down at the little man. "You ought to know, Swift. The longer you wait, the more you gonna lose."

"Goddam, you *knew* I was around. You put your van right behind my car. You mean you don't have time to come to the house, look for me?"

"They don't pay me to look for anybody," Goddam Monroe said. "Just do, and I been doin' it longer than you been doin' it, and I do it by the book, and I do it right. Goddam. Now you got any more questions?"

"Yeah. If I kill somebody, how do I get you on the case?"

Monroe stared at the little man, then laughed. "Goddam."

The investigator from the medical examiner's office

arrived. "Y'all want an autopsy, right?" he asked, survey-ing the body. "Think an autopsy be a good idea?" The man smiled all the time, but his eyes wouldn't hold. They slid off Swift's face as though a negative force field pushed them away.

One of those Stone Mountain rednecks, Swift thought. The South will rise again. "Definitely need an autopsy," he told the man. "What do you think he's dead from?"

"Don't he look just like a drowned puppy?" the man asked, laughing. "Don't he look like he got fished out of the water just long enough ago to get dry?"

Swift nodded in agreement.

"But how come he's here?" the investigator asked. "How do you explain him on his lawn a way out here in Briarcliff? Got to be three miles at least from the Chattahoochee."

The light in Lieutenant Leon Webster's office on the fifth floor of the Police Building was often on at night. He had earned his reputation as a hard charger. The window looked across the street toward Georgia State University, and Web-ster often stared at the campus. He had graduated from the school in 1973 with a degree in criminology, the first mem-ber of his family to go to college. During the graduation ceremony the white students on either side of him treated him like a special friend. In her speech to her fellow stu-dents the valedictorian told how only ten years earlier Medgar Evars had been murdered in the cause of integra-tion. "The man did not die in vain," she insisted, her soft blue eyes wet with real tears.

Webster had been thrilled by her words. Everything moved so fast then, though at the time it had seemed so slow. His daddy had marched with Martin Luther King, Jr. in front of a mob of hooting whites, carrying a placard that proclaimed, "I am a *man!*" and less than a decade later Webster himself graduated from what had once been one of the most racist institutions in the South. Webster had wanted to touch the white girl's arm, to tell her everything was all right. Not even the dreams of his childhood had seemed to equal the promise of that night: a promise of

equal treatment, of the same chance, a promise as bright
as the stars, as enduring as all time.

"Shoot."

Doug Swift watched as Webster stared moodily out of
the window. "Hey, man, do you like the view, or are you
gonna jump?"

"I was just thinking about all the shit this case will generate. Why did it have to be Marcus Williams's nephew?"

"God did this to you, Leon," Swift said. "He wants to
see what you're made of."

The two men waited in Webster's office for the preliminary report from the pathologist. Normally Swift would
have attended the autopsy, but there had been too much
to do. They had awakened Major Noah Ralston at three
that morning, and the first thing the old man wanted to
know was what the fuck Williams had died of.

"Maybe we don't have a problem," Ralston shouted.
"Maybe he just fell over dead with a heart attack." He
told both of them to be in his office at seven A.M. so they
could see what they had before the mayor and the media
got in it.

Politics and power, Swift thought, relaxed and at peace
with himself. Bombs bursting in air, bright flashes all the
time, huge fallout. Though not like a real war, he thought,
breathing deeply, filled with gratitude for life. Real bombs
in 'Nam illuminated, exploded, and blew you to shit. Here
and now he and the lieutenant were just sitting and waiting,
breathing air, feeling blood in their bodies, alive.

For a moment the detective—who had been up all night
investigating a murder—exulted in the simple, wondrous
knowledge that he was alive.

"How old are you, Doug?"

"Forty-two."

"My older brother is younger than you are. How come
he looks older?" Webster squeezed the rolls of fat over his
hipbone. "He looks like a blimp. It's happening to me, too,
you know? It must run in families."

"What's happening to you doesn't run in families, Leon.
Molasses and grits'll do it to anybody."

Webster glared at the wide-shouldered, thin-waisted
detective. Except for the scars and lines on his face and

his patient eyes, the man could have been in his early thirties. "We can't all be monks."

Swift looked at the clock on the wall. The Atlanta PD squad rooms reminded him of the Marine barracks in San Francisco: slate-gray metal furniture, khaki-green walls, big round clocks with sweep seconds. You aren't allowed to feel comfortable when you're a Marine, he thought. You do everything by the numbers, so whatever you do can be measured. The clock showed 05:12:48. "Who's doing the autopsy?" he asked.

"German."

"No wonder it's taking so long. He probably hasn't even finished yet." Swift rubbed off an itch under his eye. "Old German just loves autopsies. He gets down there in all that blood, messing with all those parts, he'll have so much fun he could lose track of time."

"I'd better give him a call." Webster punched the telephone into the speaker mode so that both of them could listen, then dialed the number.

The pathologist spoke with a thick German accent. He'd finished the autopsy and had been dictating his report. Urinalysis and drug screens would have to wait until the lab opened in the morning. But the man hadn't died of drugs, he informed his audience. "Suffocation. Mr. Williams drowned."

"How could he drown?" Webster asked. "He was on his lawn when they found him."

"Yes. Curious. But there is no question. He drowned."

"What did he drown in?" Webster asked.

"Explain, please," the pathologist said.

"I mean, did he drown in his own juices, or a keg of beer, or a lake?"

"Water. But good point," German said. "I shall extract more fluid from his lungs for analysis. Perhaps the location can be determined. I make note." Webster and Swift waited. "There is something else of great significance," the pathologist said a moment later. All his "s" sounds were like the "s" in "snake."

"Let's have it," Webster said.

"The lungs are not for water designed. Lungs are insulted by the presence of water. Visualize please a valve

in the throat that can distinguish between air and water. It
will direct air to the lungs and send water to the stomach."

"The epiglottis, right?" Webster offered. "When it's up,
air goes down the windpipe, but when it closes, liquids and
foods go down the esophagus and into the stomach?"

"It is obvious you have studied well anatomy," German
said. "Do you appreciate the difference between drowning
accidental and drowning intentional?"

"That's a very speculative distinction," Webster said.
He sounded nettled.

"What are you guys talking about?" Swift asked.

"Permit me," the pathologist said. "In drowning intentional the lungs and usually the stomach are gorged with
water, filled to capacity, flooded with liquid. The victim
has been deprived of air for longer than he can stand, and
he will open valve in throat all at once, gulp in water with
voracious appetite, literally inhale water into lungs."

"That's drowning intentional?"

"Yes. Water is packed into lungs, often into stomach.
Density. Much more density."

"What kind of drowning was Williams's?" Webster
asked, as though prepared for the worst scenario.

"Under circumstances—body dropped on lawn after he
had apparently been murdered—I expected drowning intentional. But this was drowning accidental."

"How is it different?" Swift wanted to know.

"The water is not packed into the lungs with such density. The lungs are not bursting with water. Visualize: a
drowning man, bobbing up and down on the surface, gasp-
ing for air. Inhaling air and water in the same breath. Do
you see the difference?"

"No," Swift said. "Won't it pack in there anyway?"

"Not with such density. When the life processes stop,
they stop. When the victim no longer lives, the systems
cease to function. And in drowning accidental, they cease
before the victim can gorge with water."

Webster looked at Swift. "What he's saying is this,
Doug. The likelihood is that the man drowned accidentally,
as opposed to being dropped overboard with his feet tied
to a concrete block."

"Exactly," the pathologist said. "And I, of course, will be compelled to so testify."

"Which could screw up our case if we ever get one," Webster said.

"Why?" Swift asked.

"We have to prove a corpus delicti. We need criminal agency. If the drowning was accidental, we may not have it."

Swift rolled his eyes and grinned. "God still working on you, Leon," he said. "Okay for me to ask some questions?"

"Go ahead."

"German, Doug Swift," the detective said. "You undressed the man, didn't you? Went through his clothes, his pockets?"

"Yes."

"Find anything?"

"Loose change, a comb, implements for the fingernails."

"What about a billfold?" Webster asked. "Anything to suggest a robbery?"

"No, Leon," Swift said. "His wife took his wallet before we got there. More'n two hundred dollars in there. German?"

"I am waiting."

"He was kind of wet from the waist up, wasn't he? Like he'd been bobbing for apples?"

"Yes. His shirt was damp and wrinkled, yet his trousers held a crease, and his underwear, shoes, stockings, quite dry. Something most unusual I observed, however."

"What?"

"Before autopsy begins and after body has been completely disrobed a gross visual examination is first conducted."

"And?"

"The visual revealed recent—most recent—burns, cigarette burns, to the soles of the man's feet. They matched perfectly with his stockings."

Swift's face closed in concentration. "You mean the man took some burns to the bottom of his feet?"

"I believe that is precisely what I said."

"Yeah, German, just taking it in, you know." Swift

looked at Webster. "What does that mean to you, German? The man isn't gonna just hold his foot out, let somebody burn him with a cigarette, is he? Was he dead when he took the burns?"

"No. They were to living tissue. They occurred before death."

"What about other marks then, like rope burns?" Swift asked. "You know, was he tied up?"

"Mr. Williams is very dark. Mahogany dark. Visual reveals nothing, but perhaps spectrography will answer that question if you think it important."

"It's important," Webster said. "We'll need a spectrograph. Can you do it, or shall I call somebody?"

"I will arrange," German said.

Swift got up slowly, a thoughtful expression on his face. Webster watched him walk the floor, then ended his conversation with the pathologist. Swift also had a reputation in the department. Some of his insights were uncanny. "What are you thinking, man?"

"Maybe Williams got interrogated by intelligence."

"What are you talking about?"

"That's what they'd do in 'Nam. They'd take a Cong prisoner, tie him up, burn his feet, then 'cure' him with water." Swift rubbed his eyes, partly to block out the vision and partly because he'd been up all night.

"Why would they do that?"

"Find out what he knows. You know, nothing personal. War."

"A form of interrogation?"

"Yeah. No *Miranda* in 'Nam."

Webster settled thoughtfully into his chair. "That's good, Doug. The major might shit, though."

"Why?"

"He'll consider the ramifications. The newshounds'll be all over us."

"Huh. 'Murder Victim Questioned to Death.' Like that?"

Webster nodded. "It could make a great story."

40

Chapter

6

MAJOR NOAH RALSTON SAT RAMROD STRAIGHT AT HIS DESK, poring over the reports that Webster and Swift had just given him. He muttered as he read, blood throbbing in his temples. Occasionally he would stab a nearby legal pad with a ballpoint pen. "So Williams drowned, did he? Right on top of his lawn." He glared at the cops. "Men, this is not your ordinary homicide."

Webster laughed. "You're right, sir. We haven't had one like this for quite a while."

Ralston's facial features evidenced a typically mixed Southern ancestry, in this case Indian, African, and European. The result was a strikingly handsome man with a stained copper complexion, white wavy hair, thin lips, and piercing gray eyes. But his manner did not fit his appearance. One might expect this man who photographed well to be cool rather tham bombastic, objective rather than opinionated, predictable instead of completely off the wall. Yet his staff loved him. He could make fun of himself and would go to any length to protect his people, including blaming himself for their errors. "Any leads?" he asked.

Swift glanced at Webster, who signed him to go ahead. "You were IO in 'Nam weren't you, sir?" Swift asked.

Ralston had been an intelligence officer under General

Westmoreland during the latter stages of the Vietnam war. "Two years in Saigon," he said.

"Ever hear of the water cure?"

"A torture, right? Interrogation technique?" He snatched the autopsy report off his desk. "Need more data. You don't conclude a man fell out of an airplane and lit on his head just because he has a concussion, know what I mean?" But his eyes glinted with recognition. "I like those burn holes. Consistent with softening up your source. Anything to show he was tied up?"

"We're trying to verify that now," Webster said.

Ralston pushed back from his desk and jumped up. "You know who he is, don't you?"

"Marcus Williams's nephew," Webster said. "He just landed a fat contract with the city."

"That contracting business of his doesn't make enough to pay the rent!" Ralston declared, reaching for the telephone. "I thought you could access Narcotics, Leon."

"No, sir. Fiorello's screen has been wired by some real heavy-duty hackers. I can't get in."

Ralston dialed a four-digit number, indicating the call was to someone in the building. A moment later he had Al Fiorello on the line. "I thought you might be in early. Bullshit. You think the chief will allow the nephew of Marcus Williams to be investigated by Narcotics?" Fiorello's voice rose two notches, and Swift could pick out his New York accent but couldn't understand what he said. The major laughed. "Listen. I'm sending Leon Webster and Doug Swift over. I want you to give them everything you've got. We're together on this one. . . . It's *in* the fan, man. Me and the chief are meeting the mayor in ten minutes. . . . They're on their way now." He hung up.

"Got that?" he asked, standing up.

"Kind of quick for me, sir," Swift said. "What happened?"

"Tell him, Leon." Ralston glanced at his watch and put on his coat.

"The major just made an appointment for us to see Captain Fiorello in Narcotics."

"Why?"

"I imagine we'll find that out when we get there."

42

THE WATER CURE

They stopped in Webster's office for messages. A short memo from the pathologist described the results of the spectrograph examination. It revealed minor burns and abrasions on Williams's wrists, ankles, and knees, consistent with the man having been tied with a rope or cord. They boarded the elevator for the seventh floor and a few minutes later were ushered in to Captain Al Fiorello's office.

Fiorello ran Narcotics like J. Edgar Hoover had run the FBI: with an emphasis on voluminous records, in an atmosphere of secrecy, and from a firmly established political power base. The man even looked like Hoover. He had a short, square body, a large, square head, and protruding eyes that seemed to see everything of significance to a crime fighter, then suspected everything they saw. The tough one-time New York longshoreman had been a union organizer before becoming a cop.

Fiorello's office was no larger than Webster's, even though he carried the rank of captain. The ordinary symbols of rank carried no weight with him, which had the peculiar effect of enhancing his prestige. "Have chairs, fellas," he said as the two men walked in. The top of his desk sparkled. It was absolutely clean. "Close the door, Doug."

"How do you keep your desk so clean, Al?" Webster asked.

"The desktop is a reflection of the mind, Leon. John Locke said that. Mine is a clean slate."

"Locke said the mind is tabula rasa," Webster corrected. "He didn't say anything about desktops."

Fiorello grunted, then opened a pedestal drawer and pulled out a cigar. "You lads are about to write upon my rosy tabula, then." He lighted up and thumped an ashtray on the wood surface. "What happened to Williams?"

After glancing at Webster, Swift spoke. He described the attitude of Williams's body as it lay on his front lawn and how Goddam Monroe had screwed up by allowing his crew to stomp all over the scene taking pictures, destroying any evidence of footprints; wove in the pathologist's report, including the new information indicating Williams had been bound; and brought up the possibility that Williams had been given the water cure.

43

"Water cure! That's brand new shit." Fiorello tapped the ash off his cigar. "What is it?"

Webster told him it had been used to interrogate prisoners in Vietnam.

"What the fuck is going on?"

"Who is Williams, Al?" Webster asked. "Is he big-time bad? I've never heard of him."

Fiorello put his hands on the desk as though to say, I'm leveling with you. "You lads have heard this little litany before, so don't fall asleep. It's a procedure, and I'm big on procedures. As you know, I get information from all over, not just Atlanta. I'm a regional clearinghouse, and before I can release information on any person under investigation I have to get authorization from a drug council made up of the local DAs, sheriffs, police agencies, and feds. It networks and interlocks, and lives are at stake, as well as days, months, and years of intelligence gathering. So I'll tell you what I can, but I can't get specific and can't give you sources. Not at this time."

"Come on, Al," Webster said. "You work for the mayor and the chief, just like the rest of us."

"That's where you're wrong. I tell Noah what I can, but he knows I'd resign and destroy files before compromising my word. What I do won't work any other way. Sure it's an empire, but it has to be that way, or I wouldn't get jack shit." He stuffed the cigar in his mouth and filled the air with smoke. "Also, what you hear in this room stays in this room until I say otherwise. Dig?"

"Comprende," Webster said, as though trying to maintain a certain amount of cool.

"Doug?"

"Don't worry about me, man."

"Williams was a cocaine distributor. That contracting business, pure bullshit." Fiorello inhaled deeply. "It don't even pay his secretary's salary."

"What's going on, then?" Webster asked. "Do you know who killed him?"

"I don't know jack shit except that guys in the drug business don't kill that way." Smoke leaked out of his mouth. "It don't look like a hit, and I don't see torture.

44

When they do that, there's more to it than cigarette burns and water."

Swift frowned. A thought he had been fighting with bubbled to the surface. His old captain knew as much as anybody about the water cure. "Remember Melody Thralkin? She was a nark, right?"

Fiorello shrugged. "Yeah."

"What kind?" Swift asked. "Like, an informant? Or an undercover cop?"

"An informant. What a waste." Fiorello's mouth worked angrily, as though he wanted to bite off somebody's ear. "This goofball from Memphis, supposed to be one hot shit, he was gonna make Thralkin's pusher, right? After she got hit I took one look at the dude and thought, What the fuck have we done? I swear he was one of these guys if you put him in a gorilla costume, dress him up like King Kong, he'll *still* look like a cop."

"She had a boyfriend," Swift said.

"Yeah, I know, the poor bastard. Medal of Honor winner, retired Marine. He came down here with questions, we didn't have no answers."

"He came down here?" Swift asked.

"He do that often, Leon? I mean, what the fuck. I said he came down here, then A-1 homicide dick says, 'He came down here?' "

"The man was my platoon leader in 'Nam. He knows the water cure."

Fiorello frowned. "That's interesting, I guess, but what difference? Probably only a million guys know about it."

Webster was equally unenthusiastic. "Doug likes to confabulate," he said.

"This what you guys downstairs do? Define words? Crossword puzzles? What the fuck is confabulate?"

"That's where you have some facts, right? Then your mind makes up a narrative that fits them into a story." He gave Fiorello a wink. "It's a quirk of the human mind that studies show leads to belief in a lot of bullshit."

"Yeah, Leon, like E equals mc squared." Swift had bounced to his feet. "What's between Williams and Thralkin?" he asked, looking toward Fiorello. "Like, did they know each other? Did she get her drugs from him?"

"No way they knew each other. She made her buys from pushers, not distributors."

"Okay, Williams was a distributor. What about Thralkin's pusher? Did he work for Williams?"

"I don't know. All we wanted was a hook in him so we could make his distributor. Siddown, will you, Doug? You make me nervous."

"Don't bother me about sitting down. We got some stuff here." Swift stared with great intensity at nothing, as though he could see something that wasn't there. "Thralkin a nark, takes a hit, then her boyfriend Richardson starts nosing around. Richardson knows the water cure, and the next thing, a coke distributor drowns like maybe he'd been cured." He rubbed the back of his head. "If Thralkin tried to put a hook in her pusher, what if the pusher worked for Williams?"

"Wait here." Fiorello left the room. A few moments later he bustled back in and shut the door. "Could be A-1 homicide dick has a point, no pun intended. Thralkin's pusher's a dude called Dogwood, real name Benjamin Smith. Williams's territory included Little Five Points and east, most of DeKalb, which is where Dogwood pushes. So the answer to your question is yes.

"This just came in on Dogwood." He handed over a two-page Atlanta PD complaint report. Swift and Webster pulled their chairs together and huddled over it.

According to Officer Hugh Dawson, Buckhead Subdivision, an anonymous telephone call had come in at 17:25 Thursday afternoon, April 22. The caller reported suspicious activity in a vacant lot near Bankhead Road, Northwest. The responding officer drove immediately to the designated location, arriving at 17:31, where he located the subject—later identified as Benjamin Smith—in a shallow depression in the vacant lot. Smith was attempting to hide. His ankles and wrists were handcuffed. The subject was transported to the station house at Buckhead, and the irons were removed. The subject was extensively questioned but said it was all a joke. Since he refused to identify assailants and refused to press charges, he was released.

"We'd better find the lad," Webster said, looking at his watch. "We also need more information on Richardson."

46

"What's your protocol, Leon?" Fiorello asked.

"I assemble a team on the big ones. A DA for warrants, a couple of your cokeheads to guide us through the drug maze, someone from records for computer searches, and some footsoldiers for legwork."

"You got me from Narcotics," Fiorello said, flexing his hands. "I'm the only one I can trust. But what do you need a DA for? Never trust a lawyer. It's a well-known fact. The best way to fuck up an investigation is bring a lawyer in."

"I have no choice. Major Ralston says we do it that way. It's possible there's enough for a search warrant on Richardson."

"You're fulla shit, Leon. You don't have enough to scratch your ass with, let alone get a warrant."

"You think so?"

"I know so. DA'll say, 'Get outa here!' DA'll say, 'You need evidence!' DA'll say, 'What you got so far is a person with a possible motive, and that isn't evidence.' "

"Catch-22," Webster said. "We need evidence to get a warrant to get evidence."

"Do the warrants yourself, Leon." Fiorello's left hand stroked his right hand as he spoke. "Take them to old Judge Dinkins. He'll sign anything."

"I can't, Al. My major won't let me."

"Then have Doug talk to the man. You're his buddy. He'll ask you in, won't he, Doug? Maybe you'll see something."

The jaunty, sardonic expression on the face of his one-time platoon leader imaged in Swift's mind. "I'm supposed to go play 'I Spy' on my old captain?" He remembered Richardson feeding a small girl with no hands and kidding her about it, helping her to laugh. "The man saved my life."

"He risked it first," Webster said. "Come on, let's go."

When the two men were gone Fiorello found the telephone number for Colonel Randolph D. Richardson, Retired, USMC, Avondale Estates. He started to dial it, then changed his mind. Slowly he replaced the telephone.

* * *

Doug Swift stared at the spoonlike depression in the dirt, wondering how a grown man could have hoped to hide in it. Yet he'd hidden in smaller holes than that in 'Nam. "This happened yesterday afternoon?" he asked Hugh Dawson, the cop who had reported the incident.

Dawson was not in uniform and clearly wanted Swift to get on with it. "Yes, sir. About seventeen hundred."

Swift looked around. They were in Rockdale Park, an abondoned industrial area near the intersection of Elmidge and Bankhead. A railroad line ran north–south about a hundred yards east of them. The fence lines and backyards of shanty-looking houses were south. To the west and north he saw three buildings that were surrounded by weeds. "How did Dogwood get here? Ankles cuffed, hands cuffed, how'd he get in this hole? Where'd he come from?"

"The guy was a real asshole," Dawson said. "He seen me comin', and like he tried to pull dirt over his head, pretend I wasn't there."

"Yeah, but where had he been? Where'd he get all cuffed up? One of them buildings?"

Dawson shrugged. "Maybe he just got rolled out of a car."

"Who owns them buildings?"

"I don't know. That auto repair shop went out of business two, three years ago. I don't even know what those other buildings are."

"What about those houses? People live in them?"

"Far as I know."

Swift looked around on the ground, but nothing caught his eye. There were trails like cow paths all through the area. "This is a strange place. No trees. The only place in Atlanta without trees."

Dawson looked at his watch. "Do you need me for anything else? Glad to stay, you know, if I can do you some good."

"What about Dogwood? Your impressions, you know."

"He didn't smell like no Dogwood, I'll tell you that." He squinted into the distance. "He was wasted, sir. I would definitely have to say he'd been up all night."

"What did he have on?"

"Real nice shirt. Honest-to-God silk. Cost a lot more

than I could pay. Expensive pants, too, but he'd pissed all over them. Shoes weren't tied—shoelaces flopping all over—and he limped. His feet hurt, sir, like an old man with arthritis.''

"Like the soles of his feet were sore?"

"Could have been." Dawson glanced at his watch again.

"Thanks," Swift said. "I'll stick a letter in your file."

Swift walked over to the buildings. Two of them were open, doors kicked in and windows broken out, floors littered with refuse. But the third—Flanagan's Auto Repair—didn't look that bad. Some of the window panels were cracked, but all were in place. They were lined with cardboard, like a porn movie studio. The doors were padlocked shut. The dirt floor in front of the garage door bore the unmistakable mark of tire tracks. Someone had been there since the last rain anyway, Swift thought, studying the tracks.

They seemed suddenly to swim in front of his eyes. It startled him until he realized what it was. He hadn't slept for two days and one night. "Must be tired." After noting the name and address of the building he got in his car. "Dispatch, DH Three," he said into his microphone. "I'll be home for a while."

Later that afternoon, Swift parked in front of the town-house in Avondale Estates where Richardson lived. He didn't like his mission at all. It presumed on a friendship, like selling life insurance to an old buddy. He tried telling himself a search warrant could clear the old man as well as convict him, but the knot in his stomach refused to untie.

The sun tossed long shadows across the street. He hoped Richardson was out to dinner, but his large Chrysler stood in the drive. Swift looked in the windows as he walked by it. Nothing in plain view: no handcuffs, ropes, knives, guns. He felt dirty, like a private dick sniffing out a love nest. He glanced at the tread of the tires, realizing he might have made them with the tracks at Flanagan's Garage if he'd studied them more carefully. Then he squared his shoulders and headed up the walkway toward the front door.

His mind played back a dialogue, a ritual between Richardson and his troops, after a pounding. Listen up, you animals, the captain would shout. Count your appendages and report all losses to Corporal Barrett. Yes, sir, the men boomed back. The Marine Corps has a heart, Richardson told them. If it's a serious loss, you can go home. Corporal Barrett! Report!

Johnson and Dushane took hits in their legs, sir. One leg each, below the knee.

Below the knee?

Yes, sir, Barrett said.

Give those men the rest of the day off.

One finger off Hardesty's right hand, sir.

Is that all? Richardson scoffed. Tell him to take an aspirin.

Jackson can't find his whanger, sir.

What? Richardson shouted. That could be serious! How much is gone?

Six inches, sir.

Not enough, Richardson said. Less than half a whanger doesn't count.

Chapter

7

RANDOLPH RICHARDSON, CASUALLY DRESSED IN SLACKS and a golf shirt, opened wide the door to his home. "Well," he said to Doug Swift. "I thought you'd dropped off the face of the earth. Where have you been?"

"I came by three times, sir," Swift said, moving into the living room. "For a man who's supposed to be retired, you stay too busy." He looks younger, Swift thought. Stronger, too.

"Sit down, son. Coffee?"

"I'd take a cup." Swift walked with him to the kitchen, eyes unfocused, trying to soak up everything. Nothing jumped out. The surfaces were clean; some dishes piled in the sink; one of the cabinet doors stood open. "You look good, sir."

"I feel great." Richardson moved quickly around the room, rinsing out a coffeemaker and reloading it. "You get over things. And the spring this year—it still works for me, Mac. I can smell it."

"That coffee is all the smell I need right now. I been up all night."

"You used to manage without sleep." Richardson searched through a cabinet for a couple of mugs. "You're not complaining, are you?"

"Wouldn't do me any good to complain. Just a man got murdered last night."

"Aha." Richardson poured coffee into the mugs. "Then this isn't purely social. Am I right?"

"No, sir. I thought maybe you could help me."

"Corporal, you look like the cat that swallowed the canary." Richardson grinned and handed Swift one of the mugs. "Who got murdered? Why do you think I can help?"

They moved into the living room and sat down. Swift's eyes were drawn to a large Oriental screen covering a corner of the room. It hadn't been there a month before. "His name was Charles Williams, nephew of Marcus Williams, big juice in the city administration."

"He's the fellow they found on his lawn, right?"

Swift nodded.

"It's been on the news, but it doesn't interest me much. I've seen enough dead bodies in my time."

Swift forced himself to look Richardson in the eye. He was afraid his attitude would give him away. "I don't know if the media has it yet, but the man was tortured."

"You don't say." Richardson met his eyes calmly. "Well, let's just hope the fellow had it coming. He drowned, didn't he? Rather an unlikely place for someone to drown."

"The autopsy shows he'd been tied up first. He took some cigarette burns to the bottom of his feet." Swift tasted the coffee. "Remember those gooks got 'cured,' sir?"

"Of course I remember them. Hardly the kind of thing your forget. But they were soldiers, even though they looked like high school dropouts. Casualties of war."

"Are you at war, Colonel?"

Richardson smiled. "Mac. Are you accusing me of killing the fellow?"

"No, sir. Not at this point."

"*That* sounds ominous." Richardson's mood seemed to improve. "Those 'gooks,' as you call them, weren't drowned, were they?"

"No, sir, they were fragged."

"Williams wasn't fragged, was he?" Richardson spoke

quizzically, as though forgiving the detective an obvious mistake.

"No. I hope you can overlook my manners, sir, but you didn't answer the question. You got a war going?"

Richardson laughed. "You amaze me, Mac. Your dialect has improved—I guess it's an improvement—but you haven't changed at all. Your acumen is as brilliant as ever."

"Are you telling me—"

"Mac, it's peacetime!" Richardson opened the palms of his hands to the detective. "We're at peace, the last I heard. Of course, that was earlier this afternoon, when I came back from the grocery store. What makes you think I'm at war?"

A beam of light from the afternoon sun had worked its way from the kitchen into the living room. Some particles of dust danced in the shaft, shimmering like tiny flecks of gold. Swift watched the specks of light, engulfed with a feeling of sadness. Richardson would not answer the question. Was it because the man's ethic wouldn't allow him the luxury of a lie?

"Captain Fiorello told me you came down to headquarters after Melody Thralkin got killed. Did you get what you wanted?"

"Yes. I wanted to find out if they knew who killed her, and found out they didn't." His eyes twinkled.

"What do you think of drug dealers, Colonel?"

"Scourges. Carriers of a plague. Societal germs."

"What should happen to them?"

"Society should gargle a disinfectant and destroy them."

"How come you're down on them so bad?"

"Because they kill. They destroy lives."

"Melody Thralkin. Did you know she was a nark?"

"You told me that, didn't you? Or just that you thought she was because of the way she was murdered."

"Did you know Charles Williams was in the drug business?"

"I suppose it's possible. I might have heard about him while rooting around in Fiorello's pigpen." He opened his face mockingly. "Do I need a lawyer?"

"I don't know, Colonel. It probably wouldn't hurt."

Richardson laughed, then drank some coffee. "Do you suppose I'm the only person around who could be responsible for this apparent extermination of a germ?"

"No, sir."

"There must be—and I'm not exaggerating—a million people in the South who feel the drug problem should be dealt with severely, wouldn't you agree?"

"Yes, sir."

"But out of that million you have focused on me! What a tribute!"

Swift had the sense that Richardson wanted him to talk, as though to pump him for information. "Sorry, sir, it's just—you know, a man—tied up, feet burned, drowned—like my major said, 'This is not your ordinary homicide.'"

"Your point?"

"What does it look like to you, sir?"

"If you mean does it look like an interrogation, I'd have to say you're taking a mighty leap." Richardson smiled with real pleasure. "If I were the judge, I'd toss you out of court."

Swift made a movement to go, hoping Richardson would say something more to keep him there. "Maybe you're right, sir. I like seeing you again anyway."

"That won't stop you from sniffing around at my feet though, will it?" Richardson asked. "Your problem, Mac, is that you have a conscience about such things."

"It's more than that. I don't like killing except if it's legal." He looked earnestly at his old commander. "This will sound strange out of a black boy from rural Georgia, but the law should set the limits, right? If a person kills within the law, that's one thing, but killing outside the law is murder."

"Don't serve me any more portions of 'poor black boy' soup," Richardson said. "You're the most intelligent man I know—which doesn't say much. When your life is spent in the military your opportunities for meeting geniuses aren't exceptional. But I don't accept your premise." He stuck the mug on the arm of his chair. "Isn't the law designed to protect people? Unfortunately, it's been twisted into something that only protects those the rest of us need protection from!" He leaned forward, smiling thinly. "Tell me something, Mac. If the law won't do what it was designed to do, what chance do the rest of us have? What can be done about these awful societal germs when the law refuses to apply the necessary disinfectants?"

This is the way we used to talk, Swift thought. About our own selves, but we'd tie it to the stars. "An attitude like that takes us back to lynch-mob justice, doesn't it, sir? We didn't fight the war for that."

"I haven't the foggiest idea why we fought the war. I don't care, either. But I agree that the excesses of vigilantism—at least in the south—were awful. However, there were places in the West where it worked well enough. Would you concede there are times when vigilantism is necessary?"

"Is now one of those times?"

Richardson smiled, then glanced at his watch. "I have the feeling we are at a philosophic impasse, Mac." He stood up. "I don't want to seem impolite, and I hope you'll be back and rather expect you will. A bit like bunker talk, right?"

Swift got up and stuck out his hand. "Thank you, sir. I appreciate your courtesy." He let his attention be drawn to the screen. "That's a pretty thing." The three-paneled screen was covered with silk. Outlines of mountains and trees had been sketched on its surface. They stood out with stark clarity, like a haiku poem. "Japanese, isn't it? Can I look at it?"

"Go ahead." Richardson walked beside him, his hand resting lightly on Swift's shoulder. "The depth and the simplicity of Japanese art remind me of you, as a matter of fact. Do you remember any of those long, pointless instructional discussions I inflicted on you about Douglas MacArthur?"

"Sure do. I hated my name until you came along, Captain."

"He was a great admirer of the Japanese. It's odd, isn't it, Doug, the way a true warrior can love his enemies."

Swift peered through the crack between the panels. What he saw startled him. The portrait of Melody Thralkin he remembered from the previous visit stood on a platform no higher than a desktop. A flag was spread over the platform like a tablecloth. He moved his head, letting his eyes soak up what they could. "I don't know, sir." He could feel Richardson's speculative eyes. "I'm just a civilian."

As he drove away he tried to make sense out of it. He was sure he'd seen a sword behind the screen—of the kind knights fought with—jammed behind the portrait, with the hilt and part of the blade exposed like a cross on an altar. Weird, he thought, wondering what it meant. Twenty minutes later he parked in the lot behind the Police Building and rode the elevator to the fifth floor.

"Go see the lieutenant," the receptionist told him when she saw him. "Says go in. Never mind the door." She was crying.

"Hey, sweet stuff, what's wrong?"

The heavyset woman tried to rub the wetness off her lip. From the neck down she spread out like a tent, but from the chin up she was the most beautiful woman Swift knew. "Why can't they leave us alone? What we do to them that they treat us that way?"

"What happened?"

"Maurice Brown. They just pull him out of a ditch in Gwinnett."

Swift was stunned. Brown—widely known in the black community—had a reputation locally that rivaled that of Martin Luther King. He had great political influence that he never used. He did not have a high school eduction, yet he had the intellectual respect of the city fathers, black and white.

Swift pushed into the empty squad room. Through an adjoining glass wall he could see the crowd in Webster's office. The door was shut. Usually that meant "Do not disturb," but he stumbled in.

He nodded at Fiorello and a couple of others, including the deputy DA, whose name he couldn't remember. Nobody looked very cheerful. "Doug, somebody took out Maurice Brown," Webster said from his chair. "Did you know him?"

"Just, you know"—Swift realized he wasn't breathing—"who he was. What happened?"

"Someone tied him up and shot him through the right temple with something big."

56

"Drug hit?" Swift asked, looking at Fiorello.

"Not a chance. We got absolutely nothing on Brown." Fiorello squared toward Swift with as much dignity as he could muster. "It looks like a hate killing, Doug. What can I say?"

Swift opened his eyes as wide as he could and stared at the ceiling. He had learned how to do it as a kid, to keep his eyes dry. "You want me on it, Leon?"

"I don't. Ralston does. He thinks you can work with those cowboys over in Gwinnett." Swift started to leave. "Wait a sec. What did you get out of Richardson?"

Like a zombie Swift reported everything he could remember, including the conversation. The deputy DA—the only woman in the room—wrote it all down, making him stop and repeat. "I can make a story out of this," she said, "but I don't know if I can torture it into a search warrant." Thoughtfully she pressed her fist against her cheek. "What are we looking for? Anything specific?"

Swift suddenly hated her. She was young, pretty, and white. He let the feeling wash through him, which was the only way he could let go of it. "You know. Implements of murder, like water and cigarettes." He knew he hadn't kept the sarcasm out of his voice. "Okay if I go?"

"If I come up with something, you'll have to sign the affidavit." She spoke softly.

Swift had the sudden awareness that she felt as awful about Maurice Brown as he did. "Dispatch'll know how to bring me in."

Webster waved him out of the room.

Swift knew the sheriff in Gwinnett would rather work with a white detective, but killings with racial overtones were assigned to blacks. When Swift got in his car he switched on the radio and picked up the microphone. "Dispatch, DH Three," he said. "Plug me in to the SO in Gwinnett?" He fell in a line of cars waiting to loop onto the freeway. Rush hour traffic. It would probably take him two hours to get there.

"You're on band four, DH Three. Do you copy?"

"Yeah." He switched to band four. "Doug Swift, Atlanta PD. Who've I got?"

"Howdy, hound dog," a voice drawled lazily at him. "Remember me? We had a flap over a pit bull killed a little girl two years ago."

Swift remembered the man's voice but couldn't think of his name. "Hard for me to remember when I can't see you."

The man laughed. "Ives. Raleigh. You coming out on Maurice Brown, ain't you? How about first thing in the morning?"

"Let's get started now, Ives. You know who he was?" It occurred to Swift that two prominent black men had been murdered in the space of a couple of days. Like a lot of cops, Swift believed disasters were bundled in packages of three. He wondered who the next one would be.

"Come on ahead if you want, dude, but you won't get here till after dark. We got the location secure, you'll see it better in daylight. Tell you what." Swift heard the pop of a match and its flare. Ives smoked one of those pipes that looked like a saxophone, and Swift was treated to the sound of him sucking and blowing. "He's all bagged up and on his way to the butcher shop. Whyn't you ID him for us? Get him sawed on tonight? He's kind of rank, and the sooner the better."

Swift shut his eyes. "The man's got kin."

"Yeah, I know. We was thinkin' a formal ID later, after he's been sewed back up and his face cleaned and his ears put back on, know what I mean? That family's gonna shriek and holler even when his ears is on right."

"Okay, I'll ID him, then," Swift said quickly. "Any reports?"

"I'll fux 'em over." He laughed. "Them little fux machines sure save us lovers lots of time."

"Where did it happen?"

"That Sugarpine Creek Road, east end of the county? Know it?"

"The one that runs through the marshland?"

"Well—the developers been workin' it," Ives said. "It's better than marsh now. More like jungle." He laughed. "He's about forty yards off the road, his face in the water. One shot, pretty close, behind his right ear."

"Do you know why?"

Ives pulled on his pipe. "We know it wasn't robbery because the man had a billfold on him with about sixty dollars in ones and fives. His hands was tied behind his back with a rope, so it looks like he might have offended somebody, but we don't know who. Swift?"

"Yeah."

"I'm really sorry, dude. I mean it."

Swift signed off quickly, knowing he was close to losing it.

He got off the freeway at the next exit and looped back toward the hospital. Over the radio he confirmed that Brown's body had arrived. It was in the cooler.

The words on Martin Luther King's tombstone formed in his mind. Free at last, free at last, thank God Almighty I'm free at last.

Swift logged out at 22:31. He hadn't eaten and wondered if there was anything—even a raw potato—in his fridge.

"Ooooooh," he groaned as he unlocked the door to his apartment, anticipating the feel of flannel sheets. Except for a one-hour nap earlier that afternoon he'd been up since Thursday morning looking at bodies.

The shot that Brown had taken was a real brain sucker, Swift thought dispassionately. No blow-back, but close enough to tattoo him. The bullet punched a small entry wound behind his ear, then tore a dollar-size hole out of his head. What it didn't pull out it rearranged.

Maybe it's time I became a monk, Swift thought. They're all starting to look the same. Maurice Brown's eyes, with no life in them, were no different from those of the gooks he'd seen in 'Nam: as if they were contemplating the mystery of the universal soul.

Chapter

8

Saturday, April 24

IN SPITE OF THE IMAGES THAT FLOATED IN HIS MIND, SWIFT fully expected to sleep like a rock. But his body kept twitching awake, as though it knew there was something he should do.

At three o'clock in the morning he found himself sitting up in bed with his eyes wide open. Jumping to his feet, he started putting on clothes. "Come on, man," he encouraged himself, shoving his left foot in his right shoe, then having to start over. "Come on, baby." Part of his mind had yielded to what the other part had known. He wondered if it wasn't too late.

He splashed water on his face, tucked in his shirt, pulled a coat out of the closet, and put it on. As he trotted toward the door he broke open his revolver, checking to see that the weapon was loaded and the safety was on. He slipped it in the holster beneath his armpit, shut the door behind him, and ran to his car.

He turned his radio on but decided against reporting himself on. Too many people could listen in. Traffic was light, and within minutes he cornered onto Bankhead, heading west. He yanked a right onto Elmidge, then spun off at

Jefferson. The black outline of Flanagan's Auto Repair loomed ahead like a ship in the night, and he cut off the lights. Driving slowly along the dirt road, he parked next to one of the vacant buildings he'd seen earlier that day and eased out of his car, locking it. He went inside.

The beam of his flashlight swept through the room, touching the corners. No one there. He hadn't taken the time to urinate before leaving his apartment and did so now, relieving himself against a wall.

Flanagan's was two hundred yards from where he stood. Flashlight in one hand with the light out, pistol in the other with the barrel up, he approached the building.

Risking the glow of his flashlight, he quickly studied the ground in front of the garage door. The fresh imprint of tire tracks over the ones he had seen earlier was unmistakable. A crack—less than an inch—ran between the surface of the ground and the bottom edge of the door. Swift snapped off the beam. If that old soldier is in there, his body organs alert, he'll feel that light like a beacon, Swift thought.

He dropped to his hands and knees and tried to look through the crack but couldn't get low enough. He needed a piece of flat glass that, pressed against the ground, could be a mirror. In the vacant lot he found a square Jim Beam whiskey bottle with flat sides. You be quiet when you break, he told it, softly hammering it against a piece of cinder block. When it came apart it sounded like thunder.

He remained absolutely still, all the pores of his body open and listening. In 'Nam, moving through a village at night, he had learned to focus on each hooch as a living thing. When they were awake he could hear them resonate. He tried it now. "You are awake," he said softly.

Swift felt overmatched, as though he had challenged his fencing master to a duel. He's better at war than I am, Swift thought, knowing he'd never take his old captain by surprise. If that's him in there, he knows I'm out here. And there's no way I can catch him in there. He's too good. He'll have an escape hatch.

Swift had come to the conclusion he needed help when the garage door blew apart. He dropped to the ground, ready for a firefight. A large, heavy sedan had blasted through. Something interfered with the tires, and the car shifted into reverse, shaking itself free of the impediment, then slammed into gear and was gone.

Noiselessly Swift charged the building. Hugging its wall, he found a shoulder-level window. He shattered the glass and ripped out the cardboard, wielding his flashlight with the ferocity of a cutlass, then dropped under it and listened.

He heard the sound of water, gurgling as though spilling over rocks.

The wrecked door in front was twisted and torn, as though opened with a grenade. He dived through and rolled to his feet, tucked in a crouch and looking for cover. There wasn't any. The cavernous room appeared empty except for a table near the back holding a stand-up lamp. Light from a low-wattage bulb was muted with a heavy shade. He saw what looked like a gurney with a body on top, shoved headfirst into a closet. With his flashlight he probed the room and the car pit in the center. An office in the back jutted into the room, and a sink hung off a bathroom wall. The platform—it wasn't a gurney—held the shoeless body of a man. It had been thrust into a shower stall. The water was on.

Moving quickly, he checked out the office—nothing inside—then approached the body of a man dressed in a tuxedo. It was on a hand truck, modified with a large post in the middle that thrust obscenely upward between the man's legs. His white face, slack-jawed in death, stared at the stream of water from the shower head. Swift pulled the truck out and checked his carotid pulse, confirming the obvious.

He was off the charts as far as protocols were concerned; a never-never land where a pitiless review board would second-guess his actions. He pushed the man back under the water, positioning him as he had first seen him. Then he ran outside and hotfooted it for his car.

Jumping inside, he turned on the engine and clicked on the radio. "Dispatch, DH Three, I have an emergency," he said softly into the hand mike, imbuing his voice with the accents and timbre of a white man. "Send a unit out to Flanagan's Auto Repair in Rockdale Park. Immediately. There's a dead man inside."

"Location again, DH Three?"

"Flanagan's Auto Repair, Rockdale Park. Nearest sub-station the one in Buckhead. Also telephone Lieutenant Leon Webster that he should roll out there with his team. Over and out."

"DH Three, Dispatch. Will you be at the location?"

Damn it, Swift thought. With half the people awake at that hour watching the Playboy Channel and the other half tuned to the police frequency, she should not have asked. "Approach with caution. I'm off the air, Dispatch."

He cradled the mike, eased into gear, and let the clutch out. There was no question in Swift's mind: The car he had seen blasting through the door was that of Colonel Richardson.

There was virtually no traffic, and it took less than twenty minutes to drive to Avondale. Swift drove softly through the village, turning left off Ponce de Leon into Avondale Estates. A couple of porch lights were on; he could see people moving in a lighted kitchen in one of the units. No one else in the long, looping avenue appeared to be awake. Richardson's car was nowhere in sight.

A few doors beyond Richardson's house, on the other side of the street, Swift saw a For Sale sign planted in a yard that needed mowing. The porch light was on, but a couple of newspapers had been slung on the sidewalk in front of the steps. No cars were nearby. Silently he backed into the driveway, all the way to the garage door.

He waited a few moments, then slid out of his car, extinguished the porch light by unscrewing it, and crossed the street. The old man could be in the alley, if there is one, Swift thought. A dog started barking. "Hi, pup," Swift said quietly, exuding friendliness. "How you doin', dog?" he said, not seeing the animal and hoping all it wanted was to say hello. He found a break between buildings and slid into it. A high board fence waved between small backyards. Good, Swift thought. No way for Richardson to drive back there. He'll have to come in the front door if he comes home. Swift saw the dog—tail wagging and crowding toward him—whining for attention.

"You're okay, dog. Wish people were as nice as you." Swift spoke softly, reaching over the fence and letting the animal sniff his hand. He ruffled his ears. "You be good."

A car started up, and Swift let it go by before crossing the street and getting into his.

He could see Richardson's yard, driveway, and front door. He turned his radio on, the volume low, and listened to the terse, occasionally good-humored interchanges. He had monitored enough to know that a unit had arrived at Flanagan's Auto Repair. All he could do now was wait. He knew how tired he was and tried to keep himself from getting too comfortable.

But his head kept drooping, then snapping up. Fifteen minutes drifted by. Was the old man watching him? he wondered, easing out of his car and squatting beside it. Still his head drooped. He tried to visualize the inside of Richardson's car, to see the radio. He could not. An occasional car drove by; the neighborhood started to stretch itself before waking; the sky to the east began to lighten. It was after four o'clock.

"DH Three, Dispatch. Come in, DH Three."

Swift scowled, wanting to kill the dispatcher. He didn't want to give himself away.

"DH Three, you have a visitor. A Colonel Richardson."

Swift stood up, reached in his window, and grabbed the mike. "Dispatch, DH Three. Where is Richardson?"

"DH Three. So you *are* out there. He's at HQ. Your office."

"Is he tuned in?"

"Negative. Unless you have a radio on in your office."

"Dispatch, don't mess with the man. Get somebody up there and arrest him for murder." He signed off and moments later was on his way.

The elevators were too slow, and Swift ran up the stairs to the homicide squad room. "Doug! Nice work," Leon Webster said.

"Where's my man?"

"Fiorello's got him upstairs. He's spilling his guts."

"Does he have a lawyer?"

"Sure." Webster grinned. "The deputy DA."

Swift ran up to the seventh floor and pushed his way into Fiorello's office.

Fiorello, a dead cigar in his hand, stared in surprise from a chair in front of his desk. The deputy DA—wearing a different dress, but the same frown—glanced at him, then continued making notes on a legal pad. Richardson—impeccable in a tuxedo—sat easily in the high-backed swivel chair behind the desk. A court reporter, planted out of the way in a corner of the room, was in a position to take it all down.

"You look tired, Mac," Richardson said pleasantly. It was just before five o'clock in the morning. "I hope you're still taking your vitamin C."

"You have a lawyer, sir?" Swift blurted out.

"I don't need one, Mac."

"Captain, before you say anything more—"

"Do you want him out of here?" Fiorello cut in.

"Hell, no, I don't," Richardson said. "I want him where I can see him. I've seen him in action."

"Get a lawyer, sir."

"Mac, I'm not confessing to anything. I'm merely telling Al Fiorello here about a conversation I overheard only this morning. He tells me the information might be useful to him, and I'm a good citizen and want to help."

"Al, what are you doing to this man?"

"Power down, Swift. Do you know who that scuzzball you found at Flanagan's is?"

Swift glanced at Richardson, who looked innocently in another direction. "No."

"Andrew fucking Boatwright the Third!"

Swift's eyes widened in surprise. "Are you kidding me, man?" Boatwright—one of the wealthiest men in Atlanta—was "old money." His family had been in Georgia for generations; possibly, Swift thought, since before the Civil War. Boatwright was regarded as an eccentric philanthropist who gave sizable donations to black organizations and liberal causes. "Why?"

"The man is rotten to the core. Was." Fiorello's expression showed savage satisfaction over his use of the past tense. "I've been trying to make him for years. 'The Enterprise,' do you know what I'm talking here?"

"Yeah, I know." The drug distribution network with a lock on metro-Atlanta had been dubbed "The Enterprise" by the media.

"Boatwright. His shit killed thousands in this town, most of them black, the greedy bastard."

"Huh!"

"According to the colonel here, Andrew told him all about it, and I don't give a personal fuck why he decided to spill his guts. You understand me? The circumstances don't interest me at all, just what Boatwright said is all I care about. The fucker owned The Enterprise and thanks to Richardson, I'm gonna have that whole bunch of crackheads in jail before the sun comes up.

"*If* you butt out. So butt out!"

Chapter

9

Tuesday, April 27 • Denver, Colorado

WHEN JAMES TRIGGE HUNG UP THE TELEPHONE, HE ALMOST missed the cradle. "That was different," he mused, drifting to his feet but unaware of where they were taking him. It was as though his mind had moved him off the planet. He walked out of his office, down a short hallway, and into what had once been a guest room in the 1880s Denver mansion that had become NASP headquarters. The former guest room was now Frankie Rommel's office. He floated in like a sleepwalker and sat down.

"Trigge. Wake up."

"What? Oh." He was mildly surprised to discover where he was. "I just had the damndest telephone call."

Frankie glanced at her watch: It was after five o'clock, and she didn't really need the interruption. She was editing a Motion for Sanctions in a California case, trying to stay as current as possible. The governor's decision on the appellate judgeship was expected any day, and she wanted to be ready, just in case. "You may as well tell me about it."

"Did you see that piece in the paper yesterday about the drug bust in Weld County? Something about the ex–Marine in Atlanta who blew a big whistle, and it had a ripple effect that reached into Colorado?''

"It rings a bell." She continued looking at her screen. "Why?"

"They've charged the guy with a homicide but can't find anyone to prosecute him."

"You aren't making sense, Trigge. Not unusual."

"It could be you're not listening. Some war hero in Atlanta found out all about the local drug scene down there. He beat up on this prominent society type—guy's name was Andrew Boatwright the Third—kind of the Earl of Atlanta and there's a huge buzz over that, too. Back to the hero. He took notes, and all of it checked out: where the dopers got their stuff, who their suppliers were, numbers and locations of bank accounts, names of the people who ran it—the works. Big drug bust over the weekend, combined law enforcement effort. DEA even found some stuff in Denver, Topeka, and Billings earmarked for the Atlanta market.

"But our hero did some arm-twisting to get his information and the arm twistee—after having his arm wrenched about—passed on to his holy reward." Trigge laughed. "Needless to say, no one in the law enforcement community particularly misses him. In fact, the problem is, what do they do with the hero?"

"So you got a call from Atlanta? Isn't it past their bedtime?"

"Just goes to show there are dedicated public servants everywhere."

"Let me hear it again, okay? Go slow."

"What didn't you understand? Turn that damn thing off!"

"I just did." She also took off her reading glasses and set them next to the computer terminal. "Tell me again."

"Okay. Telephone call from the DA in Atlanta. He tells me that the war hero—Rambo—had a conversation with the Earl, let's make him the Godfather. Godfather spills innards to Rambo, telling him where records are kept and the names of a couple judges and cops on the take, and bad guys and so forth, then dies. Then Rambo tells the cops everything Godfather said. Huge raids in Atlanta, blowing the drug business to bits. There is no cocaine to be had.

"But the Godfather is dead, and it looks like Rambo did him. Somebody needs to prosecute the bastard, even though they'd like to give him a medal, and the DA can't because of a conflict."

"What's the conflict?" Frankie asked.

"Rambo made about a dozen cases. He could be a material witness in all of them. The DA can't prosecute the fellow for murder in one case and use him as a witness in the others."

Frankie was clearly intrigued. "How hard has he looked for a prosecutor?"

"We weren't his first choice, let me put it that way. They have a procedure down there for the appointment of special assistant district attorneys, but it didn't work. They couldn't find anybody. They even looked into getting a private special prosecutor—turns out Godfather's family is a very prominent set of folks who'd pay for it—but there's a court rule in Georgia against it now, and they decided not to try for a variance. Besides, how would it look if the prosecution, in the name of the state of Georgia, was financed with drug money?"

Rommel was impressed. "The rich can't pay for justice in Georgia? What a pity. Is Rhode Island the only place left?"

Trigge grunted. Private special prosecutors had long been a sore point with him. "You know, NASP has never been in Georgia, or Alabama, or Mississippi. The justice department is looking at us like they could use the money they spend on us somewhere else. We're supposed to be national, but we can't hook into Dixie, and Justice is tight-ass about it."

"I have this feeling that your idealism is about to be tested. And that it will lose."

"No one but me ever thinks of such things, but if we don't get funded, we cease to exist. And old Senator Foremaine is on the appropriations committee."

"In other words, you'd like those good ol' boys in Georgia to owe us one?"

"Damn straight. It would bring down a wall, and at the

same time we do them a favor. You did one in Texas, but nobody's been in New York yet, or the Deep South. We need it."

"Okay, boss, we need it. Why me?"

"All they want is someone to do the indictment, and you're all I've got. It sounds simple, no problem, something you could do before donning those judicial robes and converting into God, which will happen as soon as you become a judge." He glared at her in mock anger. "I won't send you down there if you don't want to go. What am I gonna do? Fire you? But give yourself a break before your transformation into Madam Holiness, babe. You don't need to finish up all this crap." He waved his hand at her desk. "Give us something to bitch about when you're gone."

"What do they want? Exactly."

"The DA would like the guy charged with something less than murder. That way Rambo can plead guilty and get probation. Then they'd be able to use him in all those drug cases."

"Why not give him immunity?"

"To murder? No way."

"Jim, what happens every time someone says 'No problem'? Huge, insurmountable complications suddenly erupt like volcanoes!" She started to put her reading glasses back on. "Send Davey down there with his bike. He'd love you for it."

"Davey's in New Mexico trying those Navajos. Besides, you know Davey. He really *would* turn it into a federal case." He stretched his feet out in front of him and watched them move. "I need this one, Frankie. What I said about funding? That's no joke." He settled his friendly puppy-dog blue eyes on hers. "Think about it, okay? Atlanta in the spring, warm days, cool nights, the scent of blossoms in the air—and the opportunity, before you go on to bigger things, to do one last grand and glorious favor for your good friend, your trusted compadre, perhaps one of the greatest living humans ever to grace this planet—to wit, me."

"Shit." She tapped her glasses against the desk. "Ricky and I broke up. Did I tell you?"

"No. The son of a bitch. What's wrong with him?"

"I wonder what this hero is like. Of course, we'd have to talk around his lawyer."

Trigge smiled at her somewhat wistfully. "Don't take up with someone too quick," he said. "Give yourself a chance to heal. The guy probably only looks good in a uniform anyway."

"I could take him out to the rifle range and show him how to shoot."

Trigge got up as though not wanting to think about it. "Come on. I'll buy you a drink."

Thursday, April 29 • Atlanta, Georgia

Frankie knew she would have time to change clothes when she got to Atlanta. She would lose two hours on the flight from Denver, and she had an appointment at 2:00 P.M. with the district attorney. So she put her working uniform on at seven o'clock that morning: a pleated cotton skirt and safari jacket—each in its own shade of khaki—a white blouse, and sensible shoes. "I have great legs," Justice Agnes Minorski of the Colorado Supreme Court had once told her. "But when I go trucking off to try a case, I always wear sensible shoes, because you never know how far you'll have to walk." Frankie long ago had learned the remarkable old jurist was right about how to treat her feet, as she was in most things.

After checking into her downtown hotel Frankie barely had time to get to the courthouse by two o'clock, but she made it and was introduced to Aaron Slade, the district attorney. She had met her share of DAs. In her book, they fell into two categories: those who were politicians and admitted it, and those who were politicians and pretended to be prosecutors. She couldn't make up her mind about Aaron Slade.

He was a large man, affable and courtly, who wore his five-hundred-dollar suit with the ease of a television anchorman. He had flowing silver hair styled a bit like a Hollywood cowboy. He stood up when she entered his office, eyed her with the steadiness of John Wayne, and walked easily into the center of the room to greet her. "I'm very pleased to meet you, Ms. Rommel," he said, extending his hand in a patrician manner. "Won't you sit down?"

He indicated a couch that stood away from a wall of books. On the opposite wall huge windows looked out toward the low, blue mountains to the east. The office—as big as any DA's office she had ever been in—spoke of prestige and power.

"Thank you."

"We have us a tiger by the tail," Slade said. "A most unusual situation. I don't mind telling you it's caused some real problems, and we're counting on you to help us out."

"Do you mind if I smoke?"

"Not a bit. I mightily enjoy the smell of tobacco. But I had to stop. Doctor's orders." He provided her with an ashtray and sat in a chair that angled toward her. "Are you familiar with the case?"

"I've read the materials that were faxed to us."

"And they included?"

"Police reports—readable, by the way, which is unusual—from a Detective Doug Swift. The transcript of an interview with this fellow Richardson, conducted by a Captain Al Fiorello, who obviously believes the defendant's excrement—if you'll pardon the expression—has no odor. A copy of the accusation that came out of your municipal court, binding him over to the grand jury. And newspaper articles."

Slade smiled cautiously. "I hope you don't mind my asking you a few questions?"

Damn right I do, Frankie thought. "Of course not."

"Jim Trigge tells me you will probably go up to the court of appeals. That's unusual, isn't it? Don't the appellate judges in Colorado serve in the trial courts before moving up?"

"Usually. But I've had lots of trial experience in many, many states, and I've written about it for *Colorado Lawyer* and some of the law reviews. I'm fairly familiar with the way things are done all over, which would be an asset on the appellate bench. Including California, I might add, which many lawyers don't consider a part of the United States." She let him laugh. "So I'm very hopeful."

"If circumstances were to break down, could you try this case?"

"I don't understand, Mr. Slade. I thought I was here to get an indictment, not try a case."

"Your appointment would be to prosecute Colonel Richardson for whatever crimes the grand jury might indict him for. The expectation is that he will plead guilty, but that would only occur if he were charged with manslaughter rather than murder—and even then it is possible he would want a trial. Your appointment is personl to you alone. Georgia law has no provision for the appointment of an agency such as NASP. If some unforeseen circumstance occurred that would necessitate the trial of the case, could you try it?"

"Do you think that will happen?"

"I personally don't. I have every confidence that—after your review of the situation—the grand jury will come back with a true bill charging Colonel Richardson with manslaughter, to which he will plead guilty. But as you know, glitches often develop. As a consequence, I will have to say it's possible."

Frankie inhaled a wad of smoke. "If I don't get the judgeship appointment in Colorado, no problem. But if I do, you'd have to get yourself another lawyer." She smiled at him.

"Well. I appreciate your directness. When will you know?"

"No later than the middle of May. Whoever receives the appointment starts the first of June."

"Assuming no glitch, you will certainly have the time. Have you experienced the grand jury procedure?"

"Many times. Although never in Georgia."

"There are local differences, of course, but you will have my office at your disposal if questions arise, and I'm quite certain you would have no difficulty. I must warn you that in Georgia the grand jury does not have to go along with the recommendation of the prosecutor. We've had maverick grand juries in the past, but this one looks fairly manageable." He smiled.

"I've had experience with maverick grand juries, too."

"They are like buses without a driver on occasion, aren't they?" Slade said. "In any event, your primary task as I see it will be to make a selection between voluntary and involuntary manslaughter. From my perspective, it doesn't matter which way you go, although involuntary might be preferred because it is a lesser offense. But an extremely serious problem would result if the colonel were to be charged with murder. He would never plead guilty to that, for the very good reason that under Georgia law he would be sentenced either to life imprisonment or death. He could receive probation, however, for manslaughter."

"Would he?"

"Presumably a plea bargain would be struck whereby he would be sentenced to probation."

"Will that be a part of my responsibility?" Frankie asked.

"Yes."

"How long will this take? I need to be in Colorado next week." She decided not to tell him why. She had some unused vacation time and had arranged to go scuba diving in Mexico.

"Well. Presumably you could go before the grand jury Monday. Can you be ready that soon?"

"If I'm motivated, it's amazing how fast I can do things. What about the defendant? Will he be ready to plead?"

"I am certain he can be. The defense lawyer—one of the best trial lawyers in Georgia, incidentally—is extremely anxious to have this matter behind him."

"Will there be a problem with the plea bargain? Will the judge agree to let this guy walk?"

"Richardson was awarded a Medal of Honor for gallantry in combat. That counts for a great deal anywhere but is especially meaningful in the South. He has no criminal record and has volunteered to assist law enforcement in the prosecution of the other cases. I have talked the matter over in the abstract with the judges in the criminal division who are most apt to be involved in the sentencing, in order to get their thoughts, and none of them foresees a problem." He smoothed a wrinkle out of his trousers. "In Georgia a defendant can withdraw a plea of guilty up to the time that sentence is pronounced. Our law in that respect is designed to facilitate plea bargains. If Fortanier—Richardson's lawyer—thought his man was prison-bound, all he would have to do is withdraw the plea."

"Well, Mr. Slade—"

"Aaron."

"All right, Aaron, you've got to know I can't commit to anything. But I understand your situation and am sympathetic. What more can I say?"

"Many of us in the South have learned never to trust a Yankee."

Rommel didn't know how much more she could take. "Don't trust me, then."

"Well, perhaps we can take the chance. You appear to talk our language." Slade smiled, but there were questions in his eyes, and Frankie saw a hardness she hadn't seen before.

"I don't like this," she said. "You don't want a lawyer. You want a law clerk." Instantly, she regretted her statement. The case meant too much to Trigge.

"You will do fine," Slade said, measuring her expression and then standing up. "I have talked with several people about you, Frankie. They assure me you are a sensible person who readily relates to the problems of prosecutors. I also heard that, ah, there is some question concerning NASP's ability to survive the appropriations committee in Congress. Of course, Senator Foremaine—who sits on that committee and has some influence—is particularly interested in the progress of these drug cases, as is any right-minded Georgian. It would be insulting of me to suggest, of course, that such considerations could have any bearing on your decisions." He smiled at her with thin lips. "In any event, I have the impression you'll soon leave the arena and consequently won't be too judgmental. But I quite naturally wish to make this situation as easy for myself as possible." Frankie inhaled deeply, glad her stomach had something it could chew on. "You see, I'm a politician. Politicians use people, and I'm merely trying to determine if you can be used."

Trigge, you son of a bitch, Frankie thought. This bastard is putting so much heat on I'd like to tell him to stick it where the sun won't shine. "Let me put it this way, Aaron," she said, standing. "You can trust me to do the right thing."

Slade took her to a small office down the hall. He introduced her to Traynor Jaynes, whom he had described as a "good man" and who would walk her through the special appointment procedure. He seems awfully young, Rommel thought, although it could have been the horn-rimmed glasses over his pug nose, or his smooth cheeks. He glowed in the presence of his employer, but his attitude changed once the door to his office was shut.

Jaynes inspected her figure with an openness she didn't like. "You ever eat Cajun?" he asked, bending over her slightly as he seated her in the chair in front of his gray metal desk. "There is this place out in Dunwoody serves the best Cajun."

"I'm flexible," Frankie said, "where food is concerned."

He quickly moved to his seat behind his desk and stretched, flexing his muscles. "You probably don't get to Atlanta every day. There's a lot I could show you." He raised his arms over his head as though stretching and flexed his muscles. The fibers in his short-sleeved linen shirt expanded to their limit.

"That would be nice." If he becomes a problem, Frankie decided, she would tell him she was gay. "My problem is I don't have much time. Let's get this case down first, okay?"

"Y'all done lots of murders?" He smiled at her. His thick black hair surrounded a comfortable white face like an ornamental buffer against reality. "I only tried about a dozen. 'Course, I haven't been here long, and they've all been pretty slam-dunk."

"I've tried a few."

"This one won't even be a murder case, will it? It sure would be slam-dunk if it was!" He looked craftily at her. "I'd like to see old Fortanier wiggle his way out of this one if it was filed as a murder. I'm glad it won't be me has to cut him a deal like that."

"What do you mean?"

"I'd love to go against Fortanier someday—especially on a case good as this. Hell, everybody in Atlanta knows

Richardson murdered 'em, plus you got some really grue-some exhibits—which I guess you won't ever need because he'd be a fool if he didn't plead to manslaughter.'' He took off the glasses and rubbed his eyes as though his over-worked orbs needed a massage. Then he flashed a profile, as though the act of taking off his glasses had transformed him from Clark Kent into Superman. "I'd love to take on that sleazeball and kick his . . ." He grinned at her.

"Ass."

The man laughed wickedly. "You said it, not me." He looked at his watch. "We're supposed to be in court in fifteen minutes. You'll meet the judge. Fortanier, too—he'll be there, sighting you in. You'll find him pleasant enough, but don't trust him.''

"Fortanier or the judge?"

"Good judge. Sam Driscoll, real Southern gentleman. Knows the law, too. Wrote the book on procedure. I mean he didn't write it, but he knows it. Recognized authority.''

"Helpful, or—"

"Fortanier won't be able to push you around, not with Driscoll presiding. Of course, we're just talking about a grand jury proceeding probably, so there isn't much he could do anyway, but that doesn't mean he won't try. He'd push you all the way to hell if he could, but Driscoll won't let him, so you don't need to worry. Judge Driscoll is old school. Fifth-generation lawyer. Fine old man.''

"Do you mind if I smoke?"

"Shouldn't have any trouble getting you appointed as a special prosecutor, even though it'll be the first time in the history of Georgia where somebody's come in from outside the state and been appointed as a special prosecutor pro tem. I've got all the papers drawn—took me a whole day to research it and tell the Supremes what they had to do, then write up the motion. We never even use a special prosecutor from another county in this office. Why? Becuase Mr. Slade don't believe in them. But this case is different. The fallout over this one—oh, sorry, honey. If you want to smoke, you have to go out in the hall.''

"Will it bother you?" Frankie asked, the unlit cigarette in her hand.

"Not at all, kitten, but it's policy." He turned on his masculine charm.

"Traynor, don't call me 'kitten' and don't call me 'honey.' I don't even want you calling me by my first name."

"What?"

"Now regarding this policy. Who sets it?"

"Mr. Slade. Gosh, Miss Rommel—"

"Then apparently things have changed in the last few minutes. I smoked in his office." She lit up. "Why not open the window if it bothers you?"

The young lawyer cleared his throat. He stared at her, somewhat bewildered, clearly at a loss. "You think that will be all right?"

Rommel had a thousand questions but had time for only a few before they went to court. She discovered that the ladies room was on the fifth floor and that the law library was down the hall, and she was introduced to Miss Anne, who would take her dictation. The woman peered critically at Frankie over a pince-nez on the end of her nose. Her blond hair had turned white, and her thin, capable hands were blotched with liver spots. "I hope you haven't felt a compulsion to take any nonsense off Traynor," she said from her chair.

Frankie fell in love with the woman. "No. It might take him a day or two to get used to my accent, though."

Miss Anne smiled. "I'll take care of you, hon. Whether you need me to or not."

On the way to the elevator Jaynes confided that Miss Anne had been Mr. Slade's personal secretary before he ran for office, as though to explain her impertinence. "If she's been with him from the beginning, she probably knows more law than he does," Frankie said.

They rode the elevator down to the third floor, then pushed through a pair of large doors off the main hall into courtroom D. "This is where you'd do the trial if there was to be one," Traynor Jaynes said, holding the door. "Driscoll's courtroom, otherwise known as Sam's sweatbox."

The courtroom was empty. It reminded Frankie of a country church. There was a wide aisle in the middle and high-back wooden benches on either side. The ceiling rose high above them, with electric lights encased in large reflector cups that hung from metal poles. The lights in the back of the large room were off, leaving the spectator area in relative darkness. The carpeted area from the railing forward was well lighted. The judge's bench rose above everything else in the room, like an altar, with the jury box and counsel tables strung out below. "It's huge," Frankie said, opening the gate through the railing known as the bar. "It's intimidating."

"You could have lots of fun here," Traynor said. "All the room you need to charge around in."

The door behind the bench opened, and a small woman carrying a court reporter's typewriter and tripod scurried into the room. "Hello," she said, setting up in front of the witness box. "The judge will be right here. You're Mrs. Rommel?"

"Yes. It's 'Ms.' "

"You're not married?"

"No."

"Then it's 'Miss.' "

Frankie started to argue when the door opened a second time and the court reporter jumped to her feet. "All rise," she announced. "Superior Court of Fulton County now in session, Honorable Samuel W. Driscoll presiding."

Two men entered, both laughing easily. The short, round, baldheaded man who walked quickly to the defense table was apparently Abraham Fortanier. To Frankie's surprise, Judge Driscoll was a black man. He trotted easily up the steps to the heights of his high-backed throne, gathered his robes under his knees like a woman with a full skirt, and sat down. "Mrs. Rommel," he said, nodding. "Mr. Jaynes. Mr. Fortanier. Please be seated. We are in order."

"It's 'Miss Rommel,' sir," the court reporter said.

Frankie started to correct the record, but Traynor Jaynes—who had remained on his feet—was already talking. "If it please the Court." He marched briskly to the large lectern by the jury box. "This is in the matter of the special appointment of Frances Rommel. It concerns that certain Bill of Indictment, a copy of which is attached to this petition, labeled as the State of Georgia against Randolph Richardson."

"Mr. Fortanier, where is Mr. Richardson?" the judge asked suddenly. "Should he be here?"

Fortanier looked around him as he got up. "I asked him to come, sir, but he's like most clients of mine and not very reliable when it comes to following advice." He faced the judge. "I don't think he needs to be here anyway. The presence of the defendant is only required during significant stages in the proceedings, and this isn't very significant. As a matter of fact, I don't believe you need me. I have chosen to attend out of curiosity." His voice was high but mellow, like Mel Tormé's. He was easy to listen to. "It's principal significance to me is that I will have the privilege of meeting the prosecutor"—he turned toward Frankie and smiled graciously—"which will provide me with the opportunity to drip all over this Yankee woman with Southern charm."

Frankie wasn't sure she'd heard him correctly. "Well! How kind of you, Mr. Fortanier," she said, smiling. "I am instantly charmed. Drip away!"

"Mrs. Rommel, I hope you can overlook Mr. Fortanier's antics," Driscoll said. "Those of us in Atlanta are used to him, but he may come as a shock to others. Mr. Jaynes, do you have an opinion?"

"As a matter of fact, sir, I think Mr. Fortanier belongs in a zoo." Traynor Jaynes spoke with vehemence, and his remark destroyed the undercurrent of good humor. "Whoever heard of—"

"Excuse me, Mr. Jaynes," Driscoll said. "My question is, do you have an opinion as to whether or not the defendant Richardson should be present at this stage of the proceedings?"

"No, sir, I don't."

"Mrs. Rommel, perhaps you can assist?"

Frankie faced the judge. "Actually, it's 'Ms. Rommel,' Judge. I'm not married."

"Then someone . . ." Driscoll hesitated and cleared his throat. "Well. I apologize, Miss Rommel. Can you tell us whether the defendant should be here?"

A moment of truth, Frankie thought. And it isn't worth it. "My appointment as special prosecutor is usually regarded as a pro forma matter. It is not ordinarily considered a significant stage. I might also point out that technically there isn't even a defendant at this stage, in that the

THE WATER CURE

grand jury has yet to return a true bill. I might further suggest that in any event, the matter can be waived by Mr. Fortanier."

"Mr. Fortanier?"

"I hereby waive the presence of Randolph Richardson," Fortanier said with great cheerfulness, waving his hand like a magician. "As a matter of fact, there have been occasions—and we are just beginning our acquaintance—when I have sincerely hoped he would disappear."

Frankie laughed. She noted that Driscoll smiled, although Traynor Jaynes looked shocked. "Is this a courtroom?" she heard him say.

"Very well. The presence of the defendant having been waived, you may proceed, Mr. Jaynes."

"Your Honor, preliminarily I should point out that this motion is brought pursuant to Official Codes of Georgia Annotated Section fifteen dash eighteen dash five, which provides that where a district attorney is disqualified from interest or relationship from engaging in a prosecution, the presiding judge may appoint a competent attorney of the circuit to act in his place. The words 'of the circuit' are somewhat troublesome, in that Miss Rommel has not yet been admitted to practice law before the courts in this circuit or in Georgia." He smiled with confidence at the judge, as though to say, "Just leave it to me." Then he continued. "By virtue of a letter from the Chief Justice of our Supreme Court that our office received today, and which I believe you will find in the court file, you have been empowered to admit Miss Rommel to practice law before this, the Atlanta circuit. Before proceeding any further I request that you do so at this time."

"Very well. Miss Rommel, will you stand and raise your right hand?"

Frankie did as she was directed. As the judge administered the oath the door to the courtroom opened, and a man of average height, thin and quite good-looking, poked in. Frankie turned her head enough to see him walk down the aisle. Who is he? she wondered. The man wore a brown plaid sportcoat over a yellow golf shirt. He had thick graying hair and a youthful face. She felt his energy, and something within her turned up a notch.

81

Randolph Richardson? she asked herself. She had expected a much larger man, a Sylvester Stallone or at least someone who more nearly fit the Rambo image. But whoever he was, everyone seemed to nod at him as though to acknowledge his presence.

"Congratulations, Miss Rommel," Fortanier said, following the oath. "A moment ago you were just a Yankee, but now you are one of us."

"Thank you," Frankie said. "I'll do my best to adjust my accent." It had to be Richardson. Fortanier had signaled a very clear "Where have you been?" to him, and in reply he had shrugged his shoulders and sat down in the front row behind the lawyer.

"Shall I go on, sir?" Jaynes asked, obviously annoyed by the interruption.

"Yes. Proceed."

"The Court should note that our motion sets forth the following facts: that Aaron Slade, the district attorney for Fulton County, is disqualified from engaging in this prosecution from interest or relationship, in that the defendant in this matter is a material witness in several other prosecutions that the district attorney has and will file. As a consequence there is a conflict of interest, et cetera, et cetera.

"The motion further sets forth that Frances Rommel—in addition to her presumed admission to practice before this Atlanta circuit—is a member in good standing of the state bars of Colorado, New Mexico, California, and Texas and has also been admitted to practice before various United States District Courts; that she is employed by the National Association of Special Prosecutors, a federal agency with offices in Denver, Colorado. References are made to the legislation that empowers the NASP lawyers to prosecute cases in state courts at the invitation and request of state and local authorities, and a letter specifically requesting the National Association to provide a lawyer in this case is also attached as an exhibit. The motion goes on to state that Mr. Slade desires to secure the appointment of a district attorney pro tempore to handle the violations, if any, committed by the defendant Randolph Richardson, in particular against the persons of Andrew Boatwright and Charles Williams, before the grand jury, and in the trial of any and all such cases in the event the grand jury returns a true bill. The motion goes on to suggest that Miss Rommel, due to her obvious disinterest in the matter and her equally obvious competence, should be considered for that appointment.

"And finally, Your Honor, there is attached to the motion an order appointing Frances Rommel as district attorney pro tem in the prosecution of Randolph Richardson." Jaynes nodded his head slightly, as though taking a bow.

"Miss Rommel, have you read over the motion and the order?" Driscoll asked.

"I have, Your Honor."

"How does it look to you?"

"Very adequate, sir. Longer than most of them. But I'm quite impressed."

"Mr. Fortanier?"

"Judge, I believe Miss Rommel should testify in support of the motion. I'd like an opportunity to cross-examine her."

"Well, I don't believe we need any testimony. The motion is verified. Miss Rommel, would you raise your—"

"I protest, Judge," Fortanier said. "Certainly I have the right to test the sufficiency of—"

The gavel banged down on the marble plate with the sound of a rifle shot. Everyone jumped except the judge. "Mr. Fortanier. As you said yourself, you don't even need to be here. You are here out of curiosity, not necessity. If your presence isn't required, how can you maintain you have the right to cross-examine your potential adversary?"

Fortanier grinned. "It would appear, Your Honor, that I may have miscalculated."

Driscoll's exasperation quickly disappeared, and he looked at Frankie. "Miss Rommel, please raise your right hand and repeat after me. I, and state your name, please,"

"I, Frances Rommel."

"Do solemnly swear."

"Do solemnly swear . . ."

The words were the same as those she'd repeated in different courts, before different judges, dozens of times.

The lot of the trial lawyer, she thought. The cases you'd like to try settle. It's the ones you go on that bore you to death. Wouldn't this one be fun to try? Atlanta, in front of a black judge, described by a priggish deputy DA as "a fine Southern gentleman" and "a fifth-generation lawyer." A defense lawyer like no one she'd ever met. For a defendant, a hero who had tortured two people to death, yet everyone wanted to give him another medal!

Oh, well, Frankie thought. Cut him a deal.

She felt something warm on her cheek, as though the curtain had been pulled back, exposing her face to the sun. She turned in time to see Richardson look away.

"So help you God."

"So help me God."

Driscoll picked up a pen and signed the order appointing her as a special prosecutor pro tem in the case of *State of Georgia* v. *Randolph Richardson*.

Chapter
10

WHEN FRANKIE TRIED TO OPEN THE DOOR TO HER HOTEL room the box with the Julia Downing Christmas plate fell to the floor. "Damnit!" She lifted her knee and applied body English to keep the other packages from spilling out of her arms, then fitted the key into the door and pushed it open, cursing her cheapness. For a dollar a bellhop would have carried the stuff up, and nothing would have happened. Now the plate—by Reed and Barton, one she'd been looking for for months—might be in pieces.

Her room was pleasant enough. The furniture was basic hotel 1990 desktop veneer. All of it was bolted to the floor: lamps, tables, television. She wondered why they took a chance with the towels. The bolts didn't show; it was done unobtrusively, as though to say to the guests, "Please don't hate us. We're just trying to save you from your inclinations." She dumped the packages on one of the two beds, then retrieved the plate. Holding her breath, she opened it. It had been packed in a box with wood shavings. The scene—a hearth hung with stockings and a tree—was not particularly original. But the style was so distinctive, the colors were so true, and the whole piece was so artistically done that it breathed with life. Frankie shut her eyes and sighed with relief when she saw that the plate was intact.

The collection filled an empty shelf in her living room, making it glow.

She glanced at her watch: almost six-thirty P.M. Fortanier had said he would send someone for her at ten of seven, which gave her twenty minutes to get ready.

She plopped on the bed beside the telephone. Trigge would want to know whether she had been appointed, and she telephoned NASP headquarters in Denver.

"It's wonderful," she said a few moments later. "I got the appointment. They call it special prosecutor pro tem. Everything is cool. This town is beautiful." She described the air, the trees that were everywhere, the blossoms and smells, and the shops. She realized she'd lost him when she got to the shops.

"Didn't you work today?"

"I didn't come here to work. That happens tomorrow."

"What about Mexico?" he asked, referring to her vacation.

"I'll work Saturday. They do that around here."

"In the sleepy old South?"

"Honey, this is Atlanta."

Then she told him what an asshole Traynor Jaynes was—although possibly she could civilize him—and how pushy Aaron Slade was, how surprised she was at having Sam Driscoll described as "fifth-generation lawyer" and "fine old man" without any reference to the fact he was black. She also described Fortanier's antics and how she was glad she didn't have to try the case against him, because she'd get whacked. He did everything right. In fact, if she didn't get the judgeship, she might marry him. He'd invited her to dine with him that night at his home.

"What about Richardson?"

"He's okay."

"Do you like him or what? Wasn't he there?"

I swear to God, Frankie thought, I'm having a hot flash. Maybe it's time I started taking estrogen. "He scares me," she said.

"What do you mean?"

"He's *very* attractive. We didn't get much of a chance to talk, naturally." What could she say, she wondered?

That he fulfilled all her girlhood fantasies? "I won't mind cutting him a deal."

"Do you really think you can do it in one week?"

"Why not?" The message button on the telephone began blinking. "A day with the cops, Saturday in the library putting it together, I get the indictment Monday or Tuesday, and he enters his plea Wednesday or Thursday. I can come back after my vacation and do the rest of it."

"You mean the sentencing hearing, where Rambo would be put on probation."

"Right. He doesn't look like Rambo, by the way. Do you ever watch old movies?"

"Sure," Trigge said. "I can't stand the new ones."

"He looks like"—she thought about it a moment—"he's somewhere between Errol Flynn and Stewart Granger."

"Katie bar the door. Is the grand jury in session now?"

"All of next week. They'll convene whenever I call them." She felt like Wonder Woman, smug in the knowledge that she could do it all. "Any word from the guv?"

"Don't worry, babe. The smart money's on you. How the hell am I gonna call you 'Your Honor?' "

"You will never call me Your Honor. I'm totally serious here. You are the only person I know who can keep me humble. Therefore, you will call me Your Holiness. Got that?"

Trigge laughed. "Gotta go, babe. Have fun."

"Right." She punched the message button. "Yes?"

"A Detective Doug Swift to see you, Miss Rommel. Shall I send him up?"

Frankie looked at her watch. "Can I talk to him?"

A moment later a pleasant, unassuming voice spoke to her. "Hi, Ms. Rommel, I was in the territory and thought maybe if you weren't busy, we could have dinner on the department. You know, kind of get acquainted before you go to work."

"I can't. I'm really sorry. I should have telephoned earlier to let you know I'd arrived."

"No matter. What time will we see you tomorrow?"

"The earlier the better. You tell me."

"Six o'clock?"

She laughed. "Don't call my bluff so quickly! I really don't function very well until nine."

"Make it nine then. Why don't I pick you up?"

"Fantastic," she said. "I'll meet you in the lobby."

The message light was on again.

"Miss Rommel? Mr. Abraham Fortanier's driver is at your service in the lobby."

"Isn't that nice of him? Tell him I'll be down in about ten minutes."

She shrugged off her clothes, showered, and put on a trim, fairly formal red dress. When she left twelve minutes later her room was a mess, but she was immaculate. She carried a dark blue stole rather than a coat. She enjoyed flinging the end of the thing over her shoulders.

The chauffeur—an impeccably uniformed giant who would not look at her, as though that were against the law—opened the rear door of a large white Lincoln Continental and helped her in. When he spoke to her in the car he would permit his eyes to touch hers through the intermediary of a mirror. "I hope the drive to Mr. Fortanier's home will be a pleasant one, Miss Rommel," he said. "My instructions are to treat you with every courtesy."

"I certainly hope so."

The ride through the rolling Georgia hillside was pleasant once they were off the interstate. "Do you mind if I roll down the window?" Frankie asked, searching for the right button.

"Of course not. Allow me." The window slid down.

"I'm very surprised at the quality of the air," she said. "It's as good—actually, it's better than Denver."

"Atlanta is a thousand feet above the ocean level, and it's somewhat mountainous," the driver told her. "This time of year the air is usually very good."

"Atlanta reminds me of Denver, and I can't think why."

"There are many similarities, Miss Rommel. Both cities are economic hubs. Both are gateways. And geologically, both are covered with red clays through which mountains made of granite poke."

"Really!" Frankie settled comfortably into the soft leather seat. "Tell me more!"

"Of course," he said, smiling. "Both were frontier

towns, full of rowdies and gold seekers. A region in both cities was even founded by the same man: a Cherokee Indian named Russel, who founded Auraria, first near Atlanta—the precise location is no longer known—and later another Auraria across Cherry Creek from Denver City." His smile grew larger. "Architecturally, there is much to compare. Both Denver and Atlanta really became cities after the Civil War. Both started more or less from scratch at that time: Atlanta because she had been burned to the ground, and Denver because she was new."

Ten minutes later he turned off a narrow paved road and onto a neatly graveled lane that led to Fortanier's house. Tudor-style, it looked like a replica of an old English inn, presiding over a beautifully landscaped lawn while nestled comfortably in a copse of trees. "I'm obviously working the wrong side of the street," Rommel joked as he opened the door for her and helped her out. However, his manner had become quite formal again. "I enjoyed talking with you," she said to him.

"Thank you, Miss Rommel." He handed her to a servant who ushered her inside, where she was warmly greeted by Abraham Fortanier.

The interior seemed as convoluted as Rommel imagined Fortanier's mind to be. Impish rococo designs permeated the marble foyer, and the living room—also rococo—had its large hall-like spaces converted into little circles and squares where guests could talk. Much of the furniture was French provincial, although the formal dining room—replete with heavy wooden surfaces—generated the atmosphere of a German castle. "This is definitely not Lander, Wyoming," Rommel said to her host as he took her arm and escorted her to a chair.

"My wife did this," Fortanier said, waving his arm at the furnishings and the house. "Then she died. But like a good little wife, she finished the job first." Rommel liked the ironic tone in his voice. "I haven't so much as changed a place mat in the dining room. Not out of reverence, even though I loved her dearly. Out of fear."

"Fear?"

"She told me it was perfect the way she was leaving it,

and if I were even to consider redecorating, she would come back and make me wish I hadn't.''

They found a comfortable conversation nook in the living room, with a mantel where Fortanier could stand and prop his arm while Frankie sat comfortably in a leather chair. A servant stood nearby, ready to fill the wineglasses. Fortanier entertained with Mayor Hartsfield stories—tales of the nationally known politician who successfully led Atlanta out of a racist past and into the future. "There was a time— right after World War II, way back in the 1940s—when the leadership in Atlanta actually erected steel barriers to prevent black people from moving into white neighborhoods. The barricades were photographed, of course, and appeared in publications throughout the nation. This did not happen during Hartsfield's administration. He had been the mayor during the war, after which he was defeated. Then he ran against the man who had beaten him. 'Never make the kind of mistake they can take a picture of,' he told his adversary. And then he beat him decisively, never again to lose.'' Rommel nodded her appreciation of the anecdote. "Hartsfield had an unparalleled facility for the one-liner. Some wags trotted a horse into his chambers— those were the days when such things were done—and when he saw the animal he said, 'This is the first time I've had a whole horse in my office.' ''

Frankie laughed. "That's almost too good," she said.

"Different times." Fortanier held his wineglass high, as though preparing for a toast. "In those days politicians were men of conviction instead of census takers, which is all we have today.'' Frankie selected a carrot stick off the elegant silver platter in front of her. "They were leaders with opinions who tried to persuade the electorate to do what was right. Not followers, who let the pollsters tell them what public opinion is, then jump on the bandwagon, even when it's headed over a cliff.''

"Hartsfield was such a leader?''

"Oh, yes. A huge man in his vision. For example, early in the 1950s, by mayoral decree, he discontinued the practice in Atlanta of forcing prisoners to work the streets in chain gangs. Of course, ninety-five percent of them were black. You can't imagine the furor that act of humanity created." Fortanier stepped forward, as though acting out a part. " 'All society has offered these men is a liquor jug furnished by profiteers,' " he declaimed, " 'followed by a bloody head at the hands of the police, then sweat off their brow from wielding pick handles furnished by the construction department. If the construction department can't get along without prison labor, its doors should close in shame.' " Fortanier smiled, relaxing against the mantel and resuming his identity. "The man had a savage integrity. He wrote a letter in 1944, when decent white people weren't supposed to have such opinions, to the parole board about a black man who had been convicted of murder." He lifted his glass and donned his Hartsfield voice. " 'If he had been a white man, and had a good lawyer, he would have been exonerated, with thanks.' "

"Didn't he run for governor against Lester Maddox?" Frankie asked.

"How did you know that?"

"I was here. Rather, not here in Atlanta, but in the South. I marched with Dr. King."

"Really, Miss Rommel. Did you become a prosecutor before or after your adventure as a radical?" He spoke with humor rather than rancor.

"After. This was in high school."

"He did indeed run for governor, at the age of sixty-seven, after retiring as our mayor. I heard him speak in the campaign against Maddox. A terrible speaker, one of those poor creatures who need notes, but when he'd get riled he'd let go of himself and belt it out. Some hecklers started in calling him 'nigger lover,' and he went after them." Fortanier put his glass down and moved away from the mantel. " 'Shut up! What do you want me to do? Put on a bed sheet and go out and burn a few crosses? Go dynamite a few houses? There is more than one issue. While you've been peddling hate and discord, my city has been moving ahead!' "

Rommel felt goose bumps on her arms. It thrilled her to relive, in a small measure, the days of her idealism. "He lost, didn't he?"

"I should say so. It was not particularly close. Maddox beat him by more than two to one."

"Whose side were you on, Mr. Fortanier?"

"May we dispense with the formality of last names?" Fortanier asked. "I understand you are called Frankie. May I call you that?"

"Please. And you're Abe."

"Thank you." He sipped from his glass. "I was a bigot in those days, one of the huge majority for Maddox. I was born and raised in Savannah. It was not until later I came to appreciate his greatness. That's what I mean about leaders."

"How would you compare him to Martin Luther King?"

He studied his glass. "You might say that Hartsfield was to King what John the Baptist was to Jesus. I hope you will not mistake this for sacrilege. But I often wonder if Hartsfield didn't pave the way for the messiah—Martin Luther King—in the same way that John the Baptist had paved the way for the earlier one." He drained the contents of his glass. "Sometimes I think the Second Coming has happened, but nobody knew it."

"What an unusual thought." Frankie was charmed by the man's odd view of the world. "Just in time for the New Order!"

"However, the Old Order marches on. Have you been in town long enough to hear of Maurice Brown?"

"No."

"A wonderful man. Truly a saint. Executed by white supremacists because of the color of his skin." He looked at the back of his hand. "There are times when I want to weep with shame over my whiteness. Absolute madness to kill a man such as Brown."

"Who was he?"

"A typical black man. No education. Typically imprisoned at an early age, typically beaten by the authorities and maimed in the process—and through it all, somehow, typically filled with true reverence for life.

"I say 'typical.' Typical of so many blacks I have known. But not whites." He glanced at his watch. "Do you suppose they're waiting for us to go in there?"

The dinner was superb in its simplicity. The entrée was roasted duck basted with orange juice and served with diced pineapple. The conversation continued to be about civil rights, but it took an unusual turn, Frankie thought. Fortanier quoted graffiti on the walls of the men's room at the courthouse. He explained how a dialogue would emerge, as though three or four cartoonists had done a comic strip, each doing only one panel. His favorite series:

"First writer: Niggers are absolute proof that gorillas have intercourse with buffaloes.

"Second writer: Gorillas and monkey are prima facie evidence that whites are mutants, unnaturally devoid of color.

"Third writer: Maybe so. But I'd rather be a mutation than the direct descendant of a buffalo.

"Fourth writer: Mutation! Hey, white motherfucker, what's a mutation? If you'd come from a line of ancestors with brains, you'd know it's a mutant!"

He smiled across the table at her. "When I retire, I believe I'll travel all over the land and record the graffiti—the folk excrement, if you will—of the nation. I'll compile it into a book and give it an appropriately outrageous title, such as *Come Squat with Me*"—they laughed—"and make more money than I've ever made representing miscreants like our friend Richardson."

"You seem to have done well enough."

"I've been very lucky."

The woman who had brought Frankie into Fortanier's house appeared. She waited for a lull. "Colonel Richardson is here to see you, sir."

Fortanier glanced at his wristwatch: nine P.M. "Those fellows are always right on time," he said. "I suggested he might come by around nine if he didn't have anything better to do. He's a military man, so he may have thought it was an order. It's precisely nine o'clock. I meant to forewarn you, Frankie, but became enamored of the sound of my own voice, and it slipped my mind. Do you mind his being here? Do you see a problem?"

Frankie was surprised but not suspicious. Oddly, she blushed. "No." She found herself touching her hair, wanting to look her best. "He won't confess to anything, will he? With you in the room."

"I really should have said something earlier, but quite frankly it didn't occur to me. However, if you're uncomfortable . . ."

"No, really. I wanted to ask you how much time you'll need between the indictment and the plea, but I'll forgo that. This will give me a chance to see what kind of witness he'd make if we had to go to trial."

"Show him in," Fortanier said to the woman. Then, to Frankie: "If the indictment is for murder, we'd have nothing to talk about, and it only takes five minutes to plead not guilty. If it's for manslaughter? Really not more than a day or two. We already know what we're going to do."

Richardson had not changed his dress. He wore the same yellow golf shirt and a brown coat. As he took her hand she wondered how he would look in a uniform. "Hello," he said diffidently. "Abe told me you might be here this evening, and as long as you'll be throwing stones at me soon, I thought I'd come by and try to make it worse for myself."

It's chemical, Frankie thought; something her body did on its own, without asking for advice. When she smiled at him she lost sight of Fortanier. "I'm not going to throw stones at you, Colonel," she said, unaware of the largeness of her smile. "I'm a fair-minded, impartial, totally objective prosecutor with the duty and obligation to seek justice at all costs, then hang you, if at all possible."

Richardson's grin was bigger than the remark warranted. "Hang me, I say. If you spring the trap looking as lovely as you do now, I'll go to my reward with a smile."

"Randolph, you big dummy," Fortanier said. "He's presumed innocent, isn't he, Frankie? Although one look at him is enough to bury the presumption."

"Meet my lawyer."

Frankie laughed. She could feel her pulse vibrating in her fingers and feet, the sensation warming her. "We need some rules, gentlemen," she said. "You all—how's that? Did I say it right?" She felt in control of the situation but could also feel the effects of alcohol; not numbing, but wonderfully exhilarating. "Did I say 'you all' the way they do in *Gone With the Wind?*"

"Actually, it's 'y'all,' " Richardson said.

"I'll work on it. Okay, rules. No cocaine, marijuana, heroin, ice, speed, or conversation about the case. I mean,

I know this isn't your ordinary situation, but we need some limits. Okay?"

"Okay."

Richardson had been born in Atlanta, and she loved the flowery way he talked about his town. It came in the form of a warning. She's deceptively simple, he said, like a painting by Gauguin, yet she's as intricate as an expression by Mozart. She smells like a woman who has dabbed herself with perfume in the mistaken belief the perfume smells better than she does. "And she is some woman. She is graceful where New York is frantic and cosmopolitan, where San Francisco is parochial and hospitable, where Denver is pretentious." When he smiled at her Fortanier might as well have been in another county. "Don't trust her. Ever."

Heroes aren't supposed to have nice voices, Frankie thought. But his had a magnetic urgency like a mating call. He sounded like Stewart Granger.

There didn't seem to be anything wrong in Richardson taking her to the hotel, rather than Fortanier's driver. "Colonel, this may seem a twist on tradition, but before I can let you—unless your lawyer wants to come along—I need his consent."

"Really? That's eminently interesting. Your intentions, perhaps? With luck, they aren't honorable."

She could feel the skin on the back of her hands as she brushed hair away from her ear. "Not that kind of intention," she said, then she rushed on, hoping no one noticed she had jumped to a particular conclusion. "Georgia has adopted the Code of Professional Responsibility, hasn't it, Abe?"

"She has," Fortanier said. "You won't take advantage of this man when you are alone, will you, Frankie?" he asked, a charming innocence spreading across his face.

"Would it be possible?"

"No. He is a rogue of the first order. You have my consent."

He dropped her off at eleven-thirty in front of the hotel. He wanted to walk her in, but she told him some newshound might see the prosecutor hanging on to the arm of the defendant, and it wouldn't look right. But when he asked her if he might show her the Smokies one day that weekend, she told him no. "Possibly when this is over with," she said. "Not before."

His hand had felt wonderfully warm when they said good night.

In her room she could recall—word for word—large chunks of their conversation. Odd how she continued to hear his voice in her ear. It touched her like the brush of a silky flower, and she listened again as he described his town. "She has beautiful skin, but if you look close enough, you'll find a few wrinkles."

"Are you drunk, Colonel?"

"No. Just cheerful."

"I want to hear about her wrinkles."

"She's not like you," he said, picking up her hand somewhat playfully and inspecting it, then replacing it on her lap. "You have lovely wrinkles. But hers have been etched in, with cruelties, and the code of the South."

"And mine?"

"I would say, with love. And not etched in, but folded. You dress differently than she does, too." His eyes had wonderful intensity, but it was as though they wouldn't fasten on what they touched. Rather, they seemed to surround and tug. "You dress with style and purpose, a bit as I imagine Joan of Arc might dress around her generals. But Atlanta dresses up like she's ready for a good time. And she's always ready to go dancing, even though in her heart she's an old-maid aunt."

"An old-maid aunt?"

"That's right." He looked at her with eyes that surrounded but didn't hang on. "She can explode into awful violence. But she aches for love."

So Atlanta is an old-maid aunt, Frankie thought as she washed her face and got ready for bed. The fifth adult at a family dinner, once filled with the exuberance of youth, who wonders whether life has passed her by.

Chapter

11

Friday, April 30 • Atlanta, Georgia

FRANKIE DRESSED QUICKLY, HER WORKING UNIFORM OVER a clean off-white blouse. It was after nine in the morning. She had dawdled in her room, as though on vacation, then rushed around, getting ready. She was certain Detective Doug Swift waited for her in the lobby.

She rode the elevator to the lobby and stood by the registration desk. A pleasant-looking man with steady, wide-open eyes detached himself from a chair and approached her. "Ms. Rommel?"

"Yes."

"I'm Doug Swift."

"Hello." She stuck out her hand and rather liked the friendly way he gripped it, then let it go. "I'm sorry I'm late." She wondered how he would feel if he knew it was because she'd been daydreaming about the defendant.

"Huh. You're the first lawyer I ever met who apologized for being late." He guided her toward the door.

Frankie was curious about Swift. She had read his reports and been intrigued by his writing style. She believed people revealed themselves in their writings, and Swift impressed her as a person with an original mind. Instead of typical police bureaucratese, in which individuals are identified as suspects, subjects, victims, or witnesses who depart from vehicles in a threatening manner requiring protective action on the part of reporting officer, Swift's language was cogent, precise, and readable. His reports even had a narrative pull, as though they were chapters in a book. "You served under Colonel Richardson, didn't you?"

Swift nodded. "He was my platoon leader."

"Was he good at it?"

"The best."

"Why?"

"Never thought why," Swift said, thinking. "He knew who he was. He had soul. He wasn't afraid to die." Frankie glowed at his answer.

When they reached the street she pulled a cigarette out of her handbag and lit it. She found herself liking Detective Swift. The waves he sent were friendly, tinged with respect, and nonsexist. "How long have you been in law enforcement?"

"Ten years." He nodded at the uniformed doorman, then opened the passenger door to his car. "Been a detective for four. I got passed over three times, even though I had the high score on the exams."

"Why was that?"

"Nobody trusted me. I did a lot of drugs after Vietnam."

"Now you're clean, I take it, and they do?"

"That's right. They shouldn't, but they do."

The drive to the police building was short. "This is the way I remember Atlanta," she told him. "Warm days, cool nights, and air that is breathable."

"You're been here before?"

"Oh, yes. Also in April, but more than twenty years ago. I came down for Doctor King's funeral."

Swift glanced at her. "You don't look that old." He steered into an assigned stall.

"I'm probably older than you. I'm forty-three."

"We're about the same." He jumped out of his car like a teenager. "You don't even have a briefcase, Ms. Rommel," he said, opening her door. "How's anybody supposed to know you're a lawyer?"

"They always do."

In the homicide division squad room she met Leon Webster, Al Fiorello, and Major Noah Ralston. They treated her like a visiting dignitary. "Don't trust these fellas," Fiorello told her. "They will lie, cheat, and steal. Trust me."

"Miss Rommel, this man is a spy," Ralston said, glaring at Fiorello. "He is probably recording everything we say. Me and my men are definitely on your side, but Al has his own agenda. If you need a confidant, I'm probably your best choice."

"This sounds typical," Frankie said, accepting a cup of coffee from Webster and sitting down. She thought she heard more, however, than good-natured banter. "I have the distinct impression that we will all pull in separate directions and wind up hating each other."

By the time she was on her second cup of coffee the male plumage-waving rites had been completed, and they were all on a first-name basis. After telling her that his department was at her disposal, Ralston left. But Fiorello stayed in his chair. "I got too big a stake in this thing, Frankie," he said. "I need the man as a witness. You see any problem with the accusation?"

"Let me make sure we're talking the same language," she said. "The accusation is what came out of the municipal court? Binding Richardson over to the grand jury?"

"Right."

In the accusation Richardson had been charged with the involuntary manslaughter of two men, Andrew Boatwright and Charles Williams. She shrugged. "Have I got a deal for you. But if that's what you want."

"Will the grand jury go along?" Swift asked. "After they see the evidence they might gag at manslaughter."

"What kind of grand jury is it?" Frankie asked. "Rubber stamp or runaway train?"

"They're straight, from what I hear," Swift told her. "They listen, but they aren't afraid to ask questions."

"They'll probably go along," Frankie said, "if we put it to them right."

"Okay, fellas?" Fiorello asked, standing and looking at his watch. "You gonna back-door me when I'm gone, go for glory? Or let this lady do her job?"

Swift and Webster glanced at each other. Swift seemed

to shrink, but Webster got larger. "Narcotics is getting all this great ink, as though you put together this whole deal, and my department feels ignored," Webster said. "That's all, Al. We just want them to interview us, too."

"I don't trust you, Leon," Fiorello said. "You've been squirrelly about this deal since before we worked it out. Is there a problem?"

"No."

"I'd beat your ass in poker, you know? Later, counselor." He left the door ajar.

Swift got up and pulled it shut. Frankie had hoped everything would go smoothly, but the room already felt smaller. She didn't like the way Swift and Webster smiled at her and wondered if she was in the middle of some bureaucratic struggle. "Where do we start?"

"There could be kind of a problem," Webster said. "It's a very sensitive situation. Can I ask a question?"

Here it comes, Frankie thought. "Sure."

"How locked in to this deal are you?"

"What do you want to know, Leon?" Frankie asked angrily. "Nothing has been signed in blood. But I don't do political bullshit, either."

Doug Swift moved his lieutenant out of the way. "Here's the problem," he said, twisting a chair around and leaning on the back. "Maybe there's a third body. We aren't sure."

"Wait a minute. Are you telling me he killed *three* people?"

"We don't know. But it's possible."

"Well, *tell* me about it."

Swift quickly told her about Maurice Brown: who the man was, where and when he had been found, how he had been killed. He told her it had the appearance of a racial killing and that one Harold "Happy Face" Munroe—a member of the White Patriots—had confessed to it and been indicted by the grand jury in Gwinnett County.

"What am I missing?" Frankie asked.

"We're having a problem with the confession."

"Why?"

"Happy Face is too wimpy," Doug said. "Whoever killed Maurice had to kidnap him first, and Happy Face couldn't catch a turtle. He couldn't shoot somebody in the head, either. Have to shut his eyes."

The situation made Frankie impatient. She didn't know whether to throw something or yawn. "Why Richardson?"

"Old German, the pathologist, has a feeling. He did the autopsy on all three of them and thinks they came out of the same cookie cutter."

"Really." Frankie could see how an experienced pathologist might see similarities leading to such a conclusion, just as a street cop can smell trouble. But then she thought about it. "Williams and Boatwright were essentially drowned, weren't they? Didn't you say this third man was shot in the head?"

"German says the ligature marks on Brown just like the ones he saw on the others."

"Ligature marks?" She remembered what she could of the autopsy reports she had seen. "Any burns on his feet?"

"No."

"What about water in Brown's lungs?"

Swift looked at Webster. "No water either. Just the ligature marks."

Frankie suppressed a yawn. "That's a bit thin, isn't it? I mean, is there anything inconsistent about Brown being tied up before he was shot?"

"Just that the ligature marks looked alike."

"What about motive?" she asked. "Was Brown a dealer? Into drugs?"

"No, he was really a good man. No drugs."

"Then what you have is a pathologist who thinks the similarities of ligature markings on the bodies go beyond coincidence," Frankie said. "Is that it?"

Swift and Webster looked at each other as though hoping for something more. "Yeah."

"Where are the bodies?" Frankie asked. "Have they been looked at by anybody else? For example, the expert in *Bundy* who did the bite-mark identification?"

"No. Brown and Williams been cremated," Swift said. "Boatwright's been buried."

Frankie smiled. "Photographs?"

"All kinds."

"I mean of the ligature markings. Something an expert could work with."

The two men checked with each other again. "Did German shoot them or just light them up?" Swift asked.

"Light them up with what?" Frankie asked. "A spectrograph?"

"He looked at them under a spectrograph but didn't take pictures," Webster said.

Frankie felt she had explored all the possibilities. "Listen to me. I have a reputation, and I have a conscience. So you can count on this: I'll be straight. That doesn't mean I won't try to figure out some way to bring this thing in as a manslaughter as long as that's what everyone wants. But I am not going to mislead this or any other grand jury. If he killed someone else—*two* bodies is hard enough to swallow. Three would push this deal too far.

"But you haven't given me a third body. I don't care how good the pathologist is. His feeling isn't enough to indict on, or to go to the grand jury with."

Webster nodded. "You're right."

"Is there something else here?" she asked. "I mean, doesn't everyone in Atlanta want to name parks after the guy? What's with you two?"

"Kind of sticks in my craw, Frankie," Swift said.

"After all he's done for law enforcement?"

"The man's a vigilante," Webster said. "It's probably reverse racism or something."

"What are you talking about?"

"Black people like the law, Frankie. Contrary to popular belief, we want it to work." Webster smiled carefully, as though not wanting to offend, but not willing to back away, either. "A lot of the time we need it when you don't."

After lunch Frankie slid into Swift's small car, and they drove to Rockdale Park and Flanagan's Auto Repair. She enjoyed the drive, partly because—unlike so many men— Swift was truly a considerate driver; but mainly because it gave her the chance to question him more closely about Richardson. "I admit I find him endlessly fascinating," she said. "What did he get the Medal of Honor for?"

"Gallantry and heroism in action, about all I know. He

came out of VMI—that's Virginia Military Institute, kind of the West Point for the Marine Corps—in the fifties, got shipped over to Korea as a second lieutenant. But he never told me what it was for."

"Can you find out?"

"Sure. Why?"

"I'd like to show them what an extraordinary man Richardson is. We wouldn't convict him of murder in a hundred years, and I'd like to lay that out for them. It might help them swallow the deal." She noticed the way Swift looked at her and smiled. "Don't worry. Nothing is set in concrete."

"Like if he did Brown?"

"You keep coming back to that," she said. "Did he?"

"I don't know."

"Could he have? Psychologically, is he capable of it?"

"He did Williams and Boatwright."

She could see no point in pursuing the matter of Brown and cut it off. "What is Richardson like?" she asked, putting her arm on the cushion behind Swift. "Your perspective."

"He's a soldier. Got the ethic and mentality of a professional marine, except he puts his own stamp on it."

"That sounds awfully simple. Shoot to kill?"

"Nothing very simple about shoot to kill," Swift said. "It's hard to kill. If it's easy, there's something going on that isn't simple."

Frankie nodded her head as though she understood even though she wasn't sure she did. "What is the ethic of a soldier?"

"When you go to war, win." She watched him smile and shake his head as he talked about it and wondered what else he was thinking. "The man loves war. That makes him different, because most people kind of tighten up when the shit starts to fly, but I swear, that's when Richardson feels the best."

Is that why I am so attracted to him? Frankie wondered. Am I the kind of woman who tingles over real warriors? "You make him sound like Clint Eastwood."

"No. He's not an act, for one thing. Besides, 'Make my day' is what Eastwood is all about. I see cops like that,

guys who twist their whole selves into a part, like a character in a movie. It's weird what people do to themselves."

"That's an entertaining bit of bullshit."

"Yeah. But what I mean about Richardson, he really
loves war. Not because he looks good doing it, but because
it's like a test to him, an exercise that makes him feel good.
You know how some people live to play games? He's one
of them, where war is this glorious game, and the only time
he's really alive is when he's playing it."

Frankie wondered if most men weren't afflicted with the
same disease. "Does he hate you now?" she asked. "I
mean, you were his friend in Vietnam, yet you're the one
who caught him."

"He's not like that. We're more friends now than we
ever were in 'Nam."

"Is he using you?"

"I don't think so. He doesn't use people. We weren't
friends in 'Nam anyway. He was field-grade soldier; they
aren't allowed to have friends. More like we were
comrades."

"What's the difference?"

Swift's eyes seemed to open to some proud moments.
"A friend is someone you like, someone you care about,
you know. But a comrade has to be another soldier. He's
someone you will die for on the battlefield, someone you
trust completely, but you don't even have to like the son
of a bitch." He blushed, which was nice of him, she
thought. "But if it's in the line of duty, you'll sacrifice
him."

She could feel the hair on the back of her arms. "That's
awful." Would I really want that man to touch me? she
asked herself.

They had been driving along a lush green parkway lined
with trees in full leaf. Suddenly it seemed to Frankie they
were on the moon. It was as though a hunk of South
Dakota badland had been dropped in the Amazon forest.
"This isn't real," she said. "It's a big ugly wart."

"Rockdale Park. Don't know much about it," Swift said.
"Used to be an industrial park. There's a railroad spur over
there somewhere"—he motioned with his hand—"and a
shantytown down at this end." They drove east along a

dirt road. "Some old buildings here kind of in the middle, and the only one that still has windows is Flanagan's Auto Repair."

Frankie remembered a ghost town in Montana called Antelope Butte Springs. Three or four old, dead buildings thrust their skeletons up off the prairie in the Judith Gap, scarring the horizon. Déjà vu.

They parked in front of the garage bay door. It had obviously been ripped and torn, then bent back into place. The building had been cordoned off with rope that hung from fenceposts that had been hammered in the ground, then locked up and bolted tight. Signs proclaimed "Keep Out— Official Police Investigation—Violators Will Be Prosecuted." Doug grabbed his long-handled flashlight, then jumped out of the car. "The electricity's off. Better lock your door." He fished in his pocket for keys.

They went through a side door into the interior of the auto repair shop. It was dark inside, like a cloudy day. It took a few minutes for their eyes to adjust, but they didn't need the light. "Here's where it happened. Just like we found it."

Frankie looked around the room. She had seen photographs earlier that day and compared what she remembered of them with the reality. "That's the rack?" she asked, walking to a warehouse dolly that had been modified with an ugly creosote pole planted in the dolly floor near the center. She shivered. "My God. It's ugly."

"I'll show you how it worked." Swift climbed on, resting his buttocks between the creosote pole and a backrest that angled between the floor of the truck and the push bar. He leaned into the backrest and clasped his hands behind it. "Pretend like I been handcuffed." His inner thighs gripped the pole, and he crossed his ankles, his feet hanging over the edge of the dolly. "Boatwright had on the cuffs when I got to him. His feet were buckled by those belts that are nailed to the end. His face was shoved into the shower stall, and some water was running over it."

"No fingerprints anywhere? The push bar, this table, the telephone, the lamp?"

"Got my palm print on the push bar," Swift told her.

"Nothing from Richardson. He was probably wearing gloves."

Frankie's mind jumped from topic to topic, as it always did when she first saw a crime scene. She didn't try to control it. "All these exhibits. Don't you need a guard?"

"No trouble so far. Got a trustee who sleeps here at night."

"What good would he be if some souvenir hunter came out here with a van and decided to equip a museum with originals?"

Swift put the flashlight down, hauled out a small notepad, and made a note. "I'll take care of it. Know just the place."

"The telephone isn't functional, is it? No outlet, and it isn't cellular?"

"No."

"What was it for?"

"Don't know, Frankie. Maybe just a prop."

"The ligature marks on Brown matched the ones on Boatwright and Williams?" She picked up one of the belts at the end of the rack. "I can see how they could be fairly distinctive." It bothered her greatly. She would have to talk to the pathologist. "But Williams and Boatwright had been drowned, right?"

"Yes."

"And Brown was shot. Here, or in Gwinnett County?"

"DA over there says it's his case because that's where they found the body. But if he was killed in Atlanta and dumped in Gwinnett, it would be ours."

"Is there any evidence to show the body'd been moved? Or that he was shot in Atlanta?"

"Only German. Maurice was tied up when they found him, wrists only, with rope. But German says that happened after he was dead because the bruise patterns weren't consistent with rope, and you can't bruise a dead man. He also saw some stuff on the man's ankles that looked like the bruise traces on Boatwright and Williams."

"Is he sure of it?"

"Yes. Absolute positive. But German's been wrong, and he watches 'Quincy' reruns."

"So you're telling me you aren't sure?"

"No. I'm not absolutely positive."

"Why didn't he get someone else to look and confirm his opinion? Or take pictures. Or something."

Swift shrugged. "Nobody told him to. About that time Harold confessed, and the DA in Gwinnett—see, they don't have any black people in Gwinnett County, and a year ago Oprah Winfrey did a big daytime TV show about a race riot over there when some blacks tried to move in. So the DA wants to prosecute a racist, show the world they aren't bigots." Frankie saw the muscles in Swift's jaw working as he forced a smile. "German gave it up."

"Who is Benjamin Smith?"

"You mean Dogwood? He's the pusher."

"He was found out here somewhere, wasn't he?"

"You can see where they found him out this window," Swift said, jumping off the rack and walking to a window on the north wall. Frankie followed him over. "See that little bush?" He pointed. "A little hole near it, kind of dug out with a spoon."

She stared at the bit of prairie in the middle of Atlanta but wasn't sure what he was pointing at. It didn't matter that much. "Can you put this thing together for me?" she asked.

"Started about a month ago. Richardson had a lover, a woman name of Melody Thralkin."

Rommel frowned at the detective. "Where have I heard that name?"

"She was involved in a big murder case in Tennessee ten years ago. Her father was the mayor of this hill-country town, and she testified against him."

"Bristol," Frankie said. "I remember now. He was charged with murder but not incest. Richardson is her lover? So what?"

"About a month ago she got whacked. She was a doper, tried to introduce a nark to Dogwood, and they killed her."

" 'They?' "

"The drug mafia. What Fiorello calls 'The Enterprise.' "

"None of this is in the reports," Frankie complained, walking toward the center of the room. "Is that why Randolph killed those men?"

If Swift noticed her use of the defendant's first name, he didn't make a point of it. "What do you mean?"

"His motive. Was it—I don't know—out of a sense of public duty? Or revenge?"

"All I know is she and Richardson were lovers, and she took a hit."

Frankie smiled. She appreciated the careful way the detective brought her back. "Then what?"

Swift told her. It seemed so obvious to him now, he said. Richardson knew—probably from Thralkin—who Dogwood was. After Thralkin was murdered Richardson captured Dogwood and dragged him to Flanagan's Auto. He probably worked the boy over on the rack, which is how he got the names of Williams and Boatwright. Or maybe all he got was Williams, and from Williams he got Boatwright."

"But he let Dogwood go? Why would he do that?"

"I don't know. Maybe Dogwood got away. Or maybe he let him go after getting what he wanted." He sat down on the rack. "When they found Dogwood he was in handcuffs. Had shoes on, but they weren't tied, and he was limping like he'd taken some burns to the bottoms of his feet."

"So the reason you came back here was that Dogwood was found near here?"

"Yes. I been kicking myself ever since. I should have realized this is where Richardson was doin' 'em, but other things were happening. That's about the time they found Maurice Brown."

She saw what appeared to be a metal skeleton in a corner of the room. "What's this?"

"The grille mount." Swift walked over to it. "It fitted over his car bumper and turned that old Chrysler of his into a tank so he could tear through walls. It was on his car the night he blasted through the door. Scared me to death. Thought I was gonna get all sizzled up by a dragon."

"Was it specially made for his car?"

"Yes. I've interviewed the man who built it, but his statement hasn't been transcribed yet. I'll get it to you."

"Can he identify Richardson?"

"He doesn't want to, but he will. He thinks the old man should get a medal."

"That grille mount interests me," Frankie said. "Did he have it built just for this?"

Swift nodded. "If he'd gone through that door without it, it probably would have broken out his headlights."

"In other words, he had the foresight to anticipate he might need it?"

"Man's been a marine all his life. He knows how things can turn to shit." Swift blushed. "Sorry."

"I've heard the term, Doug. Don't worry. Still, it seems—I don't know—so premeditated. Almost diabolic."

Swift shrugged. "Just second nature to a military man doing an operation. Contingency planning."

"An operation. Is that what this was?" she asked rhetorically. "Has GBI been through Richardson's car?"

Doug nodded. "It was super clean, they said. Like a boot camp barracks before inspection."

"Do they still have it?"

"Yes."

"Boatwright is easy. You found him there. But there is a huge hole in our case against Williams. How do we make him?"

Doug was caught by surprise. "What's the problem? Isn't it obvious?"

"Are you kidding me, Doug? It's obvious to the newspapers, but you should know better. We have to link him to Richardson. We have to put him in Richardson's car, or out here."

"German dug a splinter out of his ass." He blushed and grinned. "He told me about it."

"Great." Angrily, Frankie lit a cigarette. "He told you about it. What he didn't do was put it in his autopsy report. He'll have to do an addendum." She took a deep drag. "Has the splinter been matched?"

"You mean with the rack?"

"*Yes* with the rack!" She made herself settle down. Lawyers were supposed to think of such things. She shouldn't blame the cop. "Sorry."

"I'll get GBI to look at it. Might take them a while."

"Could you take it to them Monday? Some kind of preliminary comparison?"

"Probably."

"What about the dolly? Do we know where that came from?"

"Yes. He bought it from a warehouse supply store in Memphis about three weeks ago."

The enormity of what Richardson had done crushed in on her. "My God." She touched the rack and looked in the shower. "What does it feel like, to drown like that?"

"It wouldn't be an easy way to die."

She had a vision of a man's face trying to avoid a stream of water, fighting to keep from inhaling but eventually yielding. Coughing, twisting, turning, shaking, breathing again, gagging—and, at some point, giving up. And the other man, setting it all up, then watching it happen. "How could he do that? To anyone?"

"Man's a soldier."

"This is where he would have shot Maurice Brown," Frankie declared. "The shower."

"Yeah. I thought of that. I can't find anything."

"Have you checked the drains?"

"Huh! Hadn't thought of that."

"But why?" Frankie asked, not at all happy over the possibility that Richardson was responsible for Brown's murder and aware that she was losing her objectivity.

"He probably didn't." Swift spoke sympathetically, as though reading her mind. "Old German the kind of man who invents mysteries. Gives him something to do."

"What have you found out about the garage?"

"Richardson rented it three weeks ago for six months. We found the receipt in his town house when we searched it."

"You know something? I hate this!" Frankie declared. "All this planning: the grille mount, renting the garage, modifying a warehouse dolly. This is awful. He built a torture chamber out here, then kidnapped these people and tortured them to death." She was aware of Swift's patient eyes and thoughtful expression. "It's such an obvious murder case. Yet I'm supposed to bring it in as a manslaughter!

"I feel like a whore."

Chapter

12

DOUG SWIFT GLANCED AT THE CLOCK ABOVE HIS DESK. IT was after five, and he was tempted to ignore the jangling telephone and go, but he picked it up. "Detective Swift."

"Mr. Swift?" a timid woman asked.

"Uh-huh."

"Can I talk to you?"

We're not getting off to a good start here, he thought. "Sure. Go ahead."

"I mean not on the telephone. Like, I don't know. A bar, perhaps?"

"Don't I know you?" he asked. "Your voice sounds familiar."

"I'm Marilyn Smith. We met last Tuesday."

"We did? Where?"

"At my daddy's funeral."

"Are you one of Maurice Brown's daughters?"

"Yes."

"Okay. I got you now," Doug said, smiling and remembering. Her skin was the color of stained oak, and a couple of kids had been hanging onto her hands. She had the strong, thick build of a farm girl, with beautiful white teeth, a full mouth, and large eyes. "Except I thought your last name was Brown."

111

"My daddy was Maurice Brown but my husband—well, I'm in the process of divorcing him. Benjamin Smith?"

Doug sat up quickly. He didn't want to scare her away and waited long enough to make sure his voice would sound normal. "How you want me to call you then?" he asked. "I mean, all these options. Miz Smith, Miss Brown, Missus Smith, you know."

"What about Marilyn?"

"That's good. Marilyn, I got a little paperwork." He tried to sound casual. "Hour from now? I can come by and get you."

"I'd rather we met someplace, like near Marta?" She referred to the Metropolitan Atlanta Rapid Transit Authority.

"You don't want to be seen with me. Is that the problem?"

She laughed nervously, then cleared her throat. "Kind of."

"It's Friday. The bars'll be pretty crazy."

"A coffee shop, then. It doesn't matter. A hotel lobby."

"I know just the place." He told her how to get to the Hi-Lo Diner, within a block of the Broadway terminal.

"Thanks, Mr. Swift."

"Do you suppose you could call me Doug? It would make me feel easier about myself."

"Okay."

He got there early and watched her come in. She had on blue tights, a short-sleeved shirt with a high collar, and very little makeup. He stood up so she would see him, then sat down.

He had selected the booth at the rear of the diner, against the wall and away from the window. No one could get behind him, and he could see everyone in the room. He hadn't acted out of a sense of danger but wanted to give her a feeling of privacy as well as anonymity. "Hi," she said, smiling.

"You look nice," he told her. "Want some food?"

"The last thing I need is more calories." She slid into the booth and faced him. Her expression suggested she had already made up her mind to like him.

The waitress appeared, and they asked for coffee. Then

Marilyn changed her mind and ordered the peach cobbler with a slice of cheddar, after being assured it wasn't too big.

"So, your mom okay?" Doug asked.

"She'll make it. She has lots of family, lots of friends." Doug nodded sympathetically. "Everybody says good things about you, Doug. Even—well, some of the people my husband hangs out with."

"I can understand that," he said. "I'm a good cop."

"Did you know my dad?"

"I knew who he was." He looked at her. "I heard he got Christmas cards from those screws who put out his eye. Is that right?"

"Um-hum." She smiled, obviously relishing a memory. "One of them even came to his funeral. Nicest man you'd ever want to meet." She laughed. "Little tiny shriveled-up white man now. Said when Daddy first wrote him a letter it scared him to death. But he kept it up, and then one day he wrote back." Her hands fidgeted nervously. She tried to look over her shoulder.

"Nobody can hear you, Marilyn. Except me. No one behind you."

She flashed a quick smile. "Do you know my husband?"

"No. But I know a few things about him."

"Such as?"

"He's a pusher. His name is Dogwood. He's on the run." He glanced toward the aisle. "Here comes our order." They waited while the waitress poured coffee and put the cobbler on the table in front of Marilyn. "Thanks," Doug said to the woman.

"You're welcome."

"I didn't even know they called him Dogwood until six months ago," Marilyn told him, picking up her fork. "I've been married to the man three years and have two of his kids!"

"What did you know about him?"

Her eyes reddened, but it didn't affect her appetite. "Not very much. I didn't even know what he did for a living. He came across to me like, you know, somebody who wanted to be somebody."

Doug wasn't sure he believed her but kept his suspicions to himself. "Now you know better."

She nodded, putting cobbler in her mouth. "He knows some stuff."

"I'm easy to talk to."

"He can't come up. Everybody's after him."

"He could call me."

She chewed the cobbler. Doug found himself enjoying the immense complexity of the woman. While engaged in an important conversation she could savor the taste of food and be saddened to the point of tears. How could her body do all that at the same time? It was a miracle, he thought. Millions of miracles like it happening every second of every day. I am so glad I am alive.

"Is he in trouble with the police?" she asked.

"We're looking for him."

"Why do you want him?"

"We think he knows something about Richardson."

"That cowboy motherfucker." She put a piece of cheddar in her mouth. "Will the police do anything to him, the way he killed Charles Williams?" Her anger spread softly all the way through her body and ended in a smile. "I heard they were going to carve his face on Stone Mountain with those other heroes."

"Maybe he did Williams," Doug said. "But he let your husband go."

"He did not!" She looked quickly up, as though wondering if she'd been tricked. Swift was careful not to smile in triumph. "You knew he had Benjy?"

"Sure, we knew," Doug told her matter-of-factly. Ah, so, he thought. "He worked him over—put some burns on his feet, probably rinsed him out with water—then cut him loose. Why? What kind of deal did Dogwood cut with Richardson?"

"It wasn't like that." Her large brown eyes stared at the wall behind him, and Doug realized she loved the sucker.

He decided to turn up the heat. "A lot of people want to kill him, I guess. Is that why he won't come out?"

"He's so afraid."

"Don't blame him," Doug said sympathetically. "He

narked on Williams. I wouldn't want those dopers chasin' after me.''

She put her fork down. "What can I do?"

"Do you know where he is?"

"No."

"You've talked to him, though, and you will again?"

"Yes."

"Did he tell you to call me?"

She hesitated. "No."

"We want him alive, Marilyn. Isn't anything in this world that's one hundred percent, but if he comes to me, I think I can keep him alive.''

"Yeah. For how long?"

"Long enough to get him someplace where nobody knows him.''

She played with the fork, letting it rattle against the plate. He drank some coffee and looked at his watch. "Have him call me," Doug said, making a move as though to go.

"My daddy?"

"What about him?"

"Benjy saw Richardson shoot my daddy." Her lower lip started to quiver.

Swift reached across the table and took the woman's hand. She was in pain, and he wanted to help her. "Where?"

"That garage. Where he killed those others."

"Why? Your daddy wasn't a doper, was he?"

"No."

"Why would Richardson shoot your daddy?"

She put her other hand on the table, and Doug took it, too. "I don't know! But Benjy said he was walking around Rockdale by that garage and heard a shot and looked inside, and that's what he saw.''

Doug had to work hard to keep the skepticism off his face. "He told you that?"

"Yes."

"So Benjy was out in Rockdale by Flanagan's, and the door was probably open, right?"

"I—I guess so."

"And Benjy heard a shot, so he looked inside and saw Richardson shoot your daddy?"

"That's what he told me."

"What'd he do after that?"

"Then Richardson saw him, and he forced Benjy into the garage and tied him up. He's crazy!"

"Then what happened?"

"He tortured him! He burned his feet with cigarettes and tried to drown him!"

"How come he didn't?"

"Because Benjy got away."

"How'd he do that?"

"I don't know."

Swift let go of her hands and scratched his ear. "Did you ask Benjy what he was doing out at Rockdale? Kind of lucky for him to be wandering around out there just when Richardson pulled the trigger."

The woman pushed her way into the corner of the booth. "He told me you wouldn't believe it," she said, starting to cry. "I don't know why Benjy was out there, Mr. Swift. And I don't know how he got away either. But he told me that man shot my father. Why would he make it up?"

Frankie checked for messages with the hotel clerk before going to her room. The woman handed her three: from Fortanier, giving his office number; from Trigge; and from Randolph Richardson.

In the privacy of her room she called Fortanier first. It was almost six o'clock on a Friday evening, and she didn't expect to get him, but he was still there. "Thank you for calling me," he said. "I thought I'd try to find out if anything of legal significance happened last night between you and that crazy fool I represent. Did he confess? Or decide to get a new lawyer?"

Frankie recognized the bantering tone of voice, but she heard concern, too. "A full and complete confession, Abe. With details." She heard a small click. "Are we being recorded?"

"Oh, I'm sorry," Fortanier said. "There. I leave that dang thing on during the day and forget it's on."

"Abe, damnit, that makes me very uncomfortable," Frankie told him. "Are you setting me up?"

"My dear woman. I resent that remark mightily. Of course not."

Frankie thought for a moment. She was damned if she would apologize. "Will you be there a few minutes?"

"I can be."

"Let's start this one over. I have to call—"

"We can forget it altogether if you'd rather, Miss Rommel. I can be purely professional if you would prefer it."

"Look, I'm ..." She stopped herself from saying "sorry." "I need to talk to Jim Trigge a minute." Her voice had softened. "And I really do appreciate your courtesy and the dinner last night, and I want to talk to you, but Jim is hard to reach. Call you back?"

"Fine."

Be there, you son of a bitch, she said to the telephone as she dialed NASP in Denver. Six P.M. in Atlanta meant four P.M. in the Mile High City. "Damn you, Trigge!" she said when she had him on the line.

"Frankie? Uh-oh. A small problem?"

"This nice little vacation—this interlude—is turning to shit! I *knew* this would happen. Why did I let you talk me into coming here?"

Trigge knew when banter was okay and when it wasn't. "Am I to infer that the train has run off the track?"

"Remember that murder case Davey had in Colorado where the defense wanted a careless driving?"

"Of course. Davey won't let me forget."

"That's what this one is. It's awful!"

"Explain, babe."

In an emotional voice she described the scene at Flanagan's Auto Repair: the awful rack fitted with belts and buckles and a creosote pole: the shower stall where a stream of water washed over the victim's faces, eventually drowning them. "These men died during a slow, agonizing, brutal torture called the water cure. How can that be anything other than murder?"

"Presents a challenge, doesn't it?" Trigge said a moment later. She waited. "The victims weren't candidates for Citizen of the Year, were they?"

"No."

"What's the defendant like?"

117

"He's beautiful."

"Beautiful! What's that supposed to mean?"

"Just that. He's a Hemingway hero. He's articulate, sensitive, considerate, and very good-looking. He's who all us girls in Lander would love to cross the prairie with in a covered wagon."

"How do you know so much about him?"

"I had dinner with Fortanier last night, and Randolph was there too, and we talked."

"Randolph!"

Frankie blushed. "That's his first name. I didn't spend the night calling him 'Colonel,' for God's sake." Trigge said nothing. Frankie could feel the pulse in her temple. "He frightens me."

"It's that bad, is it?" Trigge asked.

"Yes."

"So what you have is a sexy defendant and villainous victims. If the case went to trial, you know as well as I do all the defense will need is a manslaughter instruction, and the jury would buy it. Right?"

"Probably."

"So think like a defense lawyer. How would you prove manslaughter?"

"I've tried and can't," she said. "Manslaughter here is either voluntary or involuntary. Voluntary is the old heat-of-passion kill, but it needs provocation, like catching your spouse in bed with your best friend." She laughed cynically. "Where is the provocation? He tied them up and burned their feet, then lost it because they refused to tell him what he wanted to know?"

"That might tend to stretch the credulity of your average juror."

"Involuntary is worse. Standard language in Georgia: accidentally whacking the victim while doing something wrong, like skiing out of control. But the bad conduct can't amount to a felony, and Richardson obviously kidnapped these people, then tied them up and tortured them! If I go that route, I am squarely in the middle of Georgia's felony murder doctrine."

"I've heard of this fellow Fortanier, Frankie. He's supposed to be very good. Very imaginative."

"He is."

"Why don't you ask him?"

It sounded so simple. She wondered why she hadn't thought of it. "Okay. Fine. Except . . ."

"What?"

"Is this the way the system is supposed to work?" she asked. "What does NASP stand for? It doesn't feel very good, Jim."

"I know." She waited for him to tell her what he knew, but he didn't. Instead: "This one time, Frankie. It's important."

"What are you talking about?"

"I've heard from Senator Foremaine. He's watching the case through a lens. If we don't get his vote on the appropriations committee, NASP is a thing of the past."

After hanging up she blew her nose and washed her face. "Damn." She telephoned Fortanier. "Your reputation reaches all the way to Colorado," she told him. "Jim Trigge says you're very imaginative."

"Never trust a prosecutor who calls you imaginative," Fortanier said. "I've heard that's a euphemism for 'liar.' "

"Not in this case," Frankie assured him. "Jim means it. He even thought I should ask you for advice."

"There is nothing that gives me more pleasure than giving advice to prosecutors."

"Then tell me. If you wanted an indictment from a grand jury composed of presumably intelligent people, against a man who—according to the evidence available to you—tortured two humans to death, but you want him indicted for manslaughter instead of murder, how would you do it?"

"My dear, you could be asking me to reveal my defense."

Does he want me to beg? she asked herself. "Knock off the shit, if you'll pardon the expression. You won't need the defense if we don't go to trial—and a trial is what I'm trying to avoid."

"You are such a delicate creature. I would dearly love to try this case against you! Challenging issues, a script like none I've ever seen—this case could be a real entertainment." He sighed. "Unfortunately, clients don't exist for the entertainment of their lawyers. Although Randolph is not the average client. I truly believe that even if his life was on the line, he would be entertained, too."

"Abe, dammit, are you going to give me some help or wave a red flag? It *would* be fun. But I've got other things to do."

"Randolph is here. Do you mind if he listens in?"

"Is he with you now?" She felt a surge of expectation. She knew her color deepened and was glad he couldn't see her. "Has he heard your end of it?"

"No. He's in another room."

She tried to control her breathing. "I don't care. Yes, I do. I don't want him listening in."

"He tells me he volunteered to show you the Smokies over the weekend, but you won't go with him."

"What does he expect? That I'll let him buy my dinner, then send him to prison?"

"I've tried to reconcile him to the realities of the legal profession. At the present time, however, he is inconsolable."

"Poor baby," she said, smiling. "Back to my problem, okay? Help!"

"Yes. You would like to know how to persuade the grand jury to indict for manslaughter."

"I don't see how I can ask them to do it."

"Let me suggest a couple of paths you might explore. In the first place, is it a problem? If the grand jury indicts for murder, you can always reduce the charge to manslaughter as part of a plea bargain."

"I can't do that for a lot of reasons, most of them political."

Fortanier sighed. "I forgot how mindful prosecutors are of appearances. No doubt you will try to persuade the public that any decision to indict for less than murder was purely the grand jury's. Right?"

"Of course. We're hard as nails, but grand juries are allowed to be soft in the head."

"You might try my side of the street, Frankie. The air is cleaner."

"Some other time. Another pathway?"

"Have you seen the *Gooch* case?"

"A Georgia case? Or federal?"

"Georgia. Within the last year; should be easy to find. Our Supreme Court has virtually told the trial courts to instruct on the law of manslaughter as a lesser included offense whenever the defendant requests it."

"Are you suggesting I tell them to indict for manslaughter because you'd get an instruction anyway if we went to trial?" She was doubtful. "That isn't enough. I need a theory."

"Do you know who Melody Thralkin is?" Fortanier asked the question in the manner of a schoolteacher helping a student to arrive at the answer.

"Yes. She and Randolph were lovers . . . oh." The light went on. "Provocation for manslaughter! She was murdered by the drug lords, so he killed them in the heat of passion!"

"Yes."

"Would that be your defense?"

"It might have been one of the less imaginative ones. But it ought to be enough to satisfy a Georgia grand jury."

"Wait." She thought it through. "There is one huge hurdle," she said, digging the *Georgia Annotated Code* volume on crimes out of her briefcase and opening it. "A month went by between the time she was killed and Boatwright's death. The statute says: 'However, if there should have been an interval between the provocation and the killing sufficient for the voice of reason and humanity to be heard,' then it's murder."

"You've left out the best part."

"I have?"

"Yes. It goes on to say: of which the jury in all cases shall be the judge.' "

Frankie laughed. "Of course! I've argued that statute, or ones like it, so many times to juries, too. 'One month, ladies and gentlemen? How many seconds in a month? Would you think in that one month of seconds that in one of those seconds bad-ass should have paused long enough to hear the voice of reason and humanity?' But you're right. It isn't a matter of law. It's up to the jury!"

"Do you think it's worth a try?" Fortanier asked.

"Hell, yes! With this defendant and that set of facts, all they'll need is a peg to hang their hat on."

That evening she took a cab out to Dunwoody and tested the Cajun restaurant Traynor Jaynes had recommended. Family-style meals were served on wood-plank tables in a rustic setting by maidens dressed in eighteenth-century gowns. The food was excellent. Frankie had a bowl of crab gumbo over long-grain rice, hot enough to twist steel rods. She sopped it up with wonderfully delicious fresh-baked French bread and washed it down with a beautifully textured cold pale ale.

Traynor obviously liked the place, too. He tried to hide when she saw him with an enthusiastic, young-looking bimbo, but she waved at him as she would at a good friend.

Saturday, May 1

The Fulton County District Attorney's office was not as active on Saturday as it had been the day before, but there were lawyers in the law library when Frankie got there at eight-thirty in the morning, all of them busy. It occurred to her that even though Slade was a politician, he had a real office.

It was fun preparing a case for the defendant. In two hours she structured a legal framework she believed would fly. She found the *Gooch* case and two others: *Rawlins,* which held that as a matter of law the provocation for homicide could occur more than a week before the killing, and *Bender,* which held that the defendant had the right to put forth his theory of the case as long as there was "credible evidence" to support it.

Back in her office she telephoned Al Fiorello. She knew he would be in because she recognized the type. He was a typical narcotics captain, a single-minded crusader, feverish in his desire to stamp out drugs. Probably he had seen too much. As she knew he would, he fell all over himself in his eagerness to help. Twenty minutes after her call he was in her office. "You are going to be my star witness," she said.

"You write the script, lady. I do great lines."

Their theory was voluntary manslaughter, she told him. Two killings in the heat of passion following the gangland-style execution of Richardson's lover.

"Heat of passion?" he asked. "I don't know, Frankie. You mean he tortured them to death while in the heat of passion?"

She laughed. "It will be a challenge."

"We can't lay it out he whacked people needed to be whacked and should get a medal?"

"That's what we really do," she said. "But we have to dress it up in a legal theory."

He pinched his lips together, which seemed to express his attitude toward law. Frankie wondered about her own. "You just tell me what to say, lady, and I'll say it."

They would begin their little dog-and-pony show at the most eloquent spot in order to make their case: the victims, who they were, and how they made their living. She prepared him as she would any witness, taking notes as he talked, offering suggestions on ways to better express an idea, and coaching him generally to tell it like a story. "You won't even be cross-examined," she said.

As she listened she assessed him as a witness. The term "war on drugs" had meaning to him; he was a soldier fighting an insidious, awful enemy with one hand tied behind his back. If she could tap into his commitment, he would be great. His style was anecdotal, and one of his best stories was how the drug organization got its name. "They got it from us!"

"You have to respect them," he said, describing their ruthless but businesslike efficiency. "Started out we called them enterprising little bastards, and wound up The Enterprise." When a reporter did a story after a series of execution-type murders, the label caught on. "Then *they* started using it."

It fit them well. Carefully tiered: salesmen, middle management, top management. "Honest to God, I think they done market surveys before they'd move into a territory." But once in an area they were absolutely ruthless in protecting it from competition and cops. "This be secret?" he asked.

"Yes."

Good. Then he could tell her things he didn't want the public to know. These guys were killers. In their rule book, the presumption of innocence didn't apply. If they suspected someone of narking—a Melody Thralkin—they killed. It happened to buyers, pushers, "route salesmen"— anyone. But they were also equal opportunity employers, Fiorello said. No discrimination based on sex, age, or ethnic origin. "Very commendable." And they paid well and rewarded loyalty.

"A very well-managed operation. But we couldn't get in." Three plants; three dead cops. That isn't to say they didn't know who the enemy was, because they knew. They even had movies of Williams and Boatwright and Sammy "the Pope" Warner and others they had cases on now, thanks to what Richardson did. But until Richardson showed up, no cases.

"How much of this did Randolph know?"

"You want the truth? Or what you want me to say?"

"Hold it right there," Frankie said. "The truth. You do not depart from the truth."

Fiorello shrugged. "Play it either way."

Two days after Thralkin's murder Richardson was in his office. A hard man to put out the door. Fiorello talked to him personally—an older man, former Marine, a way about him. "I told him, Colonel, we are doing everything we can, and there is nothing you can do. Except stay out of the way."

"Did he get the names of the victims from you?"

"No."

"Not even Dogwood's name?"

"Nothing. I was tempted after checking him out, finding out about the medal. But I didn't need a loose cannon, you know? I didn't think we could trust him with anything."

"Good. As far as our theory goes, his hatred builds, his provocation builds. What did he learn about The Enterprise?"

"He already had all the media hype. A long article in *East Wind*—local underground newspaper—couple of stories from the Atlanta *Constitution*, and some stuff he'd picked up in the library. Good stuff, some of it. One I hadn't seen, a doctoral dissertation, some woman joined the PD in Athens. Estimated profits two billion a year, number of murders, number of addicts, something about child abuse even. I can tell you this much, Frankie. He knew a lot, and he was hot.''

At four o'clock, after sandwiches at a stand-up counter down the street, Frankie thought she had it nailed. Fiorello would be her main witness before the grand jury. He could humanize Melody Thralkin: photographs, her story, what he knew of her addiction and her relationship with Richardson. ("We're weak here," Frankie told herself, knowing she could do Thralkin better with another witness.) Then— reluctantly—Fiorello would admit the woman had narked for his department and been executed.

At that point she would question him about The Enterprise. He would describe their operation, their murderous efficiency, their profits, and the misery—in terms of lives wasted by addiction and destroyed by crime—it caused. And the villains, Charles Williams and Andrew Boatwright? "Both barrels," she told him. "Lay it on thick."

He would finish his testimony by telling them what he knew about Richardson. There was no doubt the man knew, first, that his lover had been murdered, and second— in a general way—who the killer was. He would describe his conversation with Richardson and his background check. He would tell them what he had told Richardson, but also how the man's pain had been like a tangible force. He would finish by telling them what he knew of Richardson's amazing efforts: the seizures, drug busts, and arrests that the soldier had given Narcotics. "Work on that part," Frankie advised. "Tell them he didn't have to come in at all. Don't quit until they start cheering through their tears."

She felt good. She had "the peanut." Everything else, she knew, would fall into place: Doug Swift, who had investigated the "incidents"—preferred terminology to "murders" or "homicides," she would suggest—and who could provide the linkage between the corpses and Richardson; then end it with either the testimony of the coroner or his reports.

After giving them the facts—her version, at any rate— she would tell them what she thought they should do. For those who want to let him go with their blessing, she would say: "If you don't do something, you will have chaos. Otherwise dozens of private citizens will be out there playing cop." The thinkers who wanted to charge murder would be the tough ones. She would have to tell them they could, but in her opinion no jury would convict him of it, then explain why.

She glanced at her watch—fifteen minutes after four—and called Fortanier, hoping to catch him in his office. "Does everyone in Atlanta work on Saturday?" she asked when he was on the line.

"Only the wicked."

"I'm ready to go, Abe. My ducks are in a line. I can take this thing to the grand jury early next week for the indictment, and he can be arraigned right afterwards. Will you be ready?"

"May I ask what you are going to ask the grand jury to do?"

"You may. Indict for manslaughter."

"Good! Do you foresee any problems?"

She lit a cigarette. "A minor one. I'd like to be able to paint a nice, clean, rose-colored portrait of Melody Thralkin, so they can understand how her death created this powerful passion in your client. I need a witness who can do that. You know. A person who can wipe away the moles and warts."

"What about Randolph?"

"Are you serious?" she asked.

"Why not? There isn't any legal reason an accused can't testify before the grand jury if he wants to," Fortanier said. "No one can *force* him to bleed in front of them, but he can volunteer."

"It's worth talking about," she said.

Fortanier had to take a long-distance call. They quickly agreed to get together "sometime tomorrow." Since Frankie was free all day, Fortanier would make the arrangement and leave a message at her hotel that night.

Frankie was tired. She'd been "on" for three days without letup. She walked back to her hotel, thinking about a long bath and a good book.

What can go wrong? she wondered, satisfied that this one was in the bag. She decided the smart thing to do was not to wonder about it, lest she will a problem into existence.

Leon Webster had said black people like the law to work. She would like to feel better about what she was doing.

Chapter

13

Sunday, May 2

DOUG SWIFT KNEW HE SHOULD HAVE CALLED FIRST, BUT HE took a chance and drove over instead. He'd been up all night and had consumed at least a gallon of coffee. He was so wired he had to keep moving. He also thought it might be harder for the old man to say no to his face.

He pulled his car in front of Major Noah Ralston's wide green lawn in Buckhead. He sat a moment, watching the house for signs of life. But the sun had come up fifteen minutes earlier, and there was too much daylight to see lights on in the house. He looked on the lawn for the papers. He didn't see any. Maybe the old man was up and reading the paper.

He planned his strategy. He would tell the major that Dogwood was Maurice Brown's son-in-law, and Ralston would say "So what?" "It's a link, sir," Doug would say. "I don't know what it means, but I'll bet it means something." "You and your links," the old man would say. Then Doug would tell him how he had spent all day Saturday and most of Saturday night trying to find Dogwood, but the boy was really down. He would add what Marilyn Smith had said—all of it—and Ralston would grunt and hoot, but he'd agree that maybe Dogwood had seen something.

That would be the time to stick in the clincher. Doug had talked to Raleigh Ives—the deputy in Gwinnett who had the case—and Ives had told him he didn't believe it either. The "it" was Harold Munroe's confession. Too pat, Ives thought, in spite of the fact that he gave all the right answers. The papers had reported that Brown's hands were tied behind his back but hadn't described the rope. Munroe did. Perfectly. The papers inferred that Brown's feet had been tied, but Munroe knew they hadn't been. However, the SO's office in Gwinnett had more leaks than an old scow, Ives said. Happy Face Munroe was a hanger-on out there and could have found out.

The trouble with all that caffeine is it makes me cocky, Doug thought, jumping out of his car. He didn't see how he could lose. All he wanted was permission to reopen the Brown case. Then he could dig up the drain at Flanagan's and see what was in it. Nothing, he hoped. But if Richardson did Brown in the shower, which is where the lady prosecutor thought he'd have blasted him, there'd be something. Blood, brains, and gore would have splattered into the stall, and not all of it would have washed into the sewer. He punched the major's doorbell and, after the second ring, thought again that it might have been more politic to have called first.

It was too late. Ralston—wearing a robe—yanked open the door. He didn't invite Doug in.

The detective quickly discovered that Major Ralston had no difficulty in saying no to his face. "That case is solved!" Ralston boomed, interrupting Doug's carefully planned maneuver. It was obvious the major didn't appreciate being rousted out of bed on Sunday morning.

"Sir, if I can just have permission to dig up the drain and take a look, see if some brains or something stuck down there?"

"You'll need a damn plumber. An authorization from the DA's office. A work order so the lab can analyze whatever you gather up. Which will mean—"

"An authorization from the DA?"

"Right, dammit. The case isn't our case. It's solved! The

DA in Gwinnett has it. And if he wants some more shit, let him request it. We don't need the work!"

"Sorry to bother you, sir," Doug said happily. He had a plan. "I know it's early, but don't you sleep better knowing our boys in blue—that's me, sir—are on the job ferreting out crime?"

"Get the fuck out of here." Swift started to close the screen door. "Doug."

"Yes, sir?"

"Look under that cedar bush and grab the paper for me, will you? Little bastard tosses it in there every Sunday without fail."

Doug did as he was asked, then drove to the Marriott Hotel. Traffic was light, as always on a Sunday morning, and in twenty minutes he was in the lobby. If all that was needed was an authorization from the DA, he'd run the problem up another pole.

Frankie Rommel had the look of an early riser. He asked the hotel operator to ring her room, half expecting to see her trot through the lobby in a jogging outfit. There was no answer. He left a message for her to call Dispatch ASAP and made a mental note to make sure he told Dispatch where he was. He also checked the diner to see if she was having breakfast. The maître d' told him she'd been in at six-thirty, read the paper, drunk coffee, and gone out.

The bellman knew who she was when Doug described her. He iced Doug with a cold stare. "That Marine Corps hero-motherfucker picked her up just a few minutes ago," he said. "They certainly make a fine-looking couple."

Frankie had not expected that Richardson would pick her up. The message from Fortanier the night before had said: "An early breakfast? My driver will pick you up at seven-thirty. Please call and confirm. Abe."

"How nice," Frankie said, smiling as he held the door to the car. *He is such a hunk*, she thought, very aware of his muscled thinness. She looked in the back seat, expecting to see Fortanier. "Where's Abe?"

"He'll meet us there."

Frankie felt uncomfortable about traveling alone with the

defendant. However, Fortanier obviously knew about it. "Where is 'there'?"

"The Smyrna Hotel."

Riding with Richardson was not like riding with Doug Swift. There was a lazy recklessness to Richardson's driving, together with an attitude of playfulness, that kept her sitting up straight. He seemed casually unaware of what he was doing but managed to avoid a series of imminent collisions. Eventually she concluded he didn't need help but bore watching.

They were not in the heavy Chrysler sedan that had bashed through the door of Flanagan's Auto Repair. He drove a late-model Mazda sports car, about two inches over the road. Whirring along the interstate toward the Chattahoochee River was like tobogganing down a mountain near Vail. "You drive like a maniac," she told him comfortably.

"I *am* a maniac. Thank God for small favors. If I wasn't certifiable, you wouldn't be here."

"Don't flirt with me, Colonel," Frankie said, testily. "Not now." She realized she sounded like a real grouch. "At least wait until your lawyer can give his consent."

"I'll be damned! Is flirting covered by that damned Code of Professional Responsibility you lawyers live by?"

"Not exactly. Communications between a client and the lawyer for the other side are, though. I'm surprised Abe sent you to pick me up. He said his driver would."

Richardson glanced at her. She could feel his eyes. "Actually, this was my idea," he said. "You see, I'm an environmentalist. Not many people know that. In fact, you're the first."

"What are you talking about?"

"Two cars where one will do. It seemed pointless to have that black giant of Abe's drive all the way in and pick you up and drive you back out, just so we can breakfast at Abe's convenience, when I have to drive within spitting distance of your hotel to get there myself."

"How thoughtful of you." She really did not want to flirt with him but was aware of a teasing quality in her voice.

He nodded agreeably. "I didn't know lawyers worried about ethics." He slid into an inside lane and neatly avoided a truck that had slowed for a hill. "I thought soldiers and prostitutes were the only professionals with ethics." He has a nice smile, she thought. "Of course, there are ethical limits to what soldiers and prostitutes will do, but I thought lawyers would do anything. What do you need a Code of Professional Responsibility for?"

"I've wondered the same thing," Frankie said. Lighten up, she thought to herself. "It's important for us to have standards, because without them we couldn't go about suing one another."

He glanced over at her as though he needed to see the expression on her face to understand her words. "Are you referring to the economy?" he asked, smiling still. "The way lawsuits generate business?"

"Yes." Frankie didn't quite know what had gotten into her, but she felt like a hypocrite. "Soldiers do the same thing, of course. Destroy all of Saddam Hussein's tanks, then sell them more expensive ones."

Richardson laughed. "This is great fun, do you know that? Lawyers, if you will excuse the expression, tickle the shit out of me!"

They talked on. He is easy to talk to, Frankie thought as her mood changed. They drove for half an hour before stopping in front of a charming old brick building, protected from too much sun by huge green trees. It hadn't seemed to take half an hour to get there.

Fortanier had reserved a small room off the dining room. A white linen tablecloth was spread elegantly over an elaborately laid out table. A private buffet had been set up against the wall. Fortanier stood up as they came in the room. A black man in a red coat took the paper he had been reading off the table and stood by. "I hope you had a pleasant drive."

"Very."

The breakfast was superb. Freshly squeezed orange juice, delicious croissants, fluffy omelets made to order as they watched, jams, biscuits, grits and gravy. The coffee aroma was heavy enough to taste, and the coffee itself was thick enough to chew. Frankie loved it.

But the more they talked about Richardson as a witness, the less Frankie liked the idea. It had the look of collusion, as blatant as a coroner's jury; a deliberate wash. And too much could go wrong. What if a juror started asking questions Richardson shouldn't answer? She wasn't willing to allow Fortanier in the grand jury room while Richardson testified. To her mind, that would be too great a departure. It could result in delays while Richardson conferred with his lawyer, and there was the possibility he would have to take the Fifth. "You fellows are planning this little sortie like staff officers," Richardson observed. "Quite an education."

"Have you talked with Miss Thralkin's landlady?" Fortanier asked.

A shadow dropped over Richardson's face. Up to that point no one had talked about what his testimony would be, just whether or not to call him. Thralkin's name had not even been mentioned.

"No," Frankie told him, avoiding Richardson's blanked-out smile. "Who is she?"

"Perhaps she is who you need, rather than Randolph," Fortanier said, looking at his client. "Would you agree?"

Richardson shrugged as though not particularly interested. "She's a nice woman."

Fortanier had been fidgeting for the last few minutes, looking at his watch. "I hope you will excuse me, gracious lady," he said, standing. "I must leave you in the hands of this rogue. He has been instructed to take you back to your hotel and keep his mouth shut. He won't follow my advice, but as long as he pays his bills, I don't mind too much."

"You have to go?" Frankie asked.

"My wife's mother is still alive, and I am in the habit of taking her to the eleven o'clock service." He had a final sip of coffee. "Do you expect to get the indictment tomorrow?"

"Probably Tuesday." It felt odd, planning strategy with the defense lawyer. "I want to meet his new witness and go over the language of the indictment. Traynor Jaynes is making a couple of presentments soon, and I can go in with him as co-counsel and see how it's done here."

"Tuesday, then. Do you think we can have this miscreant arraigned Wednesday?"

"Or Tuesday afternoon. I can let you know."

"Good. You'll excuse me, then?"

"Abe."

"Sir."

"I would like to show this woman the Smokies."

"Well . . ."

"It's a beautiful day. She may never be out here again. Tell her it's all right." Richardson talked to Fortanier, but he watched Frankie.

"Allow me to be perfectly candid," the small man said.

"Shall we allow that?" Richardson asked Frankie.

"He's your lawyer."

"Quite honestly, I don't care. I don't see any harm in it now." He looked at his watch and started moving forward. "She has my consent—but has it occurred to you, Randolph, she might have something else to do?"

"Not for a second."

"I really must go. Thank you, Miss Rommel." Impishly, he picked up her hand and kissed it. "Old Southern tradition, borrowed from the French." He was gone.

Frankie daubed at her lips with her napkin. "We'd better go."

Richardson nodded at her and got up. A valet brought his car around, but Richardson opened the door for her. As they drove toward the freeway he asked again. His voice was like the gentle push of a cloud.

"Will my smoking bother you?" she asked.

He rolled his window down. "Not at all."

An hour later they turned east off the interstate and wound their way into the mountains of northern Georgia. They stopped for coffee at a roadhouse—"Talk Yankee, if you don't mind. It will make a more lasting impression"—and everything around her seemed to sparkle. The blueness of the sky was like the crystal-clear water at Cozumel, coating the sugar pine and the dogwood that reached up from the rising hills with exuberance. She felt like a mermaid in a very clear lagoon.

She enjoyed the sound of his voice. It invaded her nervous system somehow, seeming to send electric impulses into her brain, where they radiated out with each beat of her heart. She had the sense that her voice did the same thing to him, as though they connected. Even the smallest inflection—like the tilt of Leonard Bernstein's wand to the first violin—seemed to convey a totality of meaning, a universe of experience.

Then they were driving again. Richardson's driving adapted itself to her mood as well as his. Even though it was Sunday the roads were not crowded, and he knew how to focus on the scenery. Frankie gave herself over completely to the panoramic views. "This is beautiful," she said as the brilliant colors of spring grew toward her and surrounded her with life. "So different from the Rockies. The colors are so wonderfully vivid."

"Aren't the Rockies like this?" He stared at her with a look of sudden wonderment, then looked quickly away. He seemed so grateful to be driving in the mountains with her. "They're huge when you fly over them."

"They're huge, all right. They have grandeur. They are magnificent. I feel about them the way you do about Atlanta."

"They're an old-maid aunt?"

"No. That they can be personified. Are you ready for some bullshit?"

He laughed. "In the South we call it poetry. Let me hear it."

She would have liked to have taken hold of his hand, as though her touch could more precisely define her words. "At times they terrify with menace, like a woman suddenly confronted by a painted savage, who doesn't know whether she will be raped or touched with tenderness."

"You're right. Bullshit."

"But these mountains—we're in the Smokies, aren't we?"

"Yes."

"They're subtle. They have fragrance. They exude—I don't know—sensuality?"

"Now you are more in the tradition of the South. Even my mother would approve."

"The Smokies are like a woman, I think." She knew he didn't expect her to be deflected by his commentary, only entertained. "They are soft, sensuous, nicely molded, yielding. But the Rockies are like a man."

"Meaning?"

"Remote. Capable of brutality. But clean and wild."

They stopped for an early dinner at an old hotel in a picture-card Tennessee town. Their table—next to a wide window that overlooked a cobblestone street—was set with real china on a linen tablecloth. "Request permission to gaze into the lovely lady's eyes with tenderness?"

"Permission denied." But the little finger of her left hand, near her napkin, seemed to reach out on its own and hook his thumb. "However, you don't need to move your hand."

"I don't think I will." She could feel his eyes on her face, but they turned to the window when she looked at him. "When this is over I'll want to see you."

"What if I send you to prison?"

"Then more than ever. Before they throw away the key." She rather liked the way his hand lay still. It really seemed to respect her hand, in that it didn't try to take it by storm. "My generation of soldier never treated women very well. Maybe that's how it happened."

"Wait." She moved her hand. "I'm not going to let you talk about the case."

"This has nothing to do with that. I'm talking about Melody and me."

"Well, but—"

"My mother, God bless her, has tried to get me involved with any number of women. But when they find out I'm a retired marine, either they expect me to act like the Great Santini or they want to sit at my feet and hear war stories. Melody was different. I met her one night in a bar—not too auspicious a beginning, but I wasn't looking. I was brooding. So was she."

"Randolph—"

"Please. It's important to me that you know. I loved her in a way I've never loved. I knew nothing about her past and didn't care to find out, and she didn't know anything about mine. But I knew she was pretty, that she was genuinely attracted to me, and that her passion was real.

"I've seen death. In my business you see bodies galore. But when I saw hers at the morgue, unlighted, dead . . ."

136

Frankie pushed herself away from the table. "That's all. We go."

Richardson's expression shifted from bewilderment to sadness. "Sorry. Rules. I hate the fucking things."

When he pulled in front of her hotel he left the motor running and took her hand. The bellman saw his gesture and waited. "I'm former military, and my language is a bit rough at times, which seems essential to precision of expression. I want you to know that my love for Melody was different because she was a child. You probably think this impersonator is as full of shit as a Christmas goose. He's slathering all over me like he did her. He is definitely not to be trusted.

"This will be over soon. The sooner the better. I'll want to see you. I hope—God, how I hope—you'll want to see me."

When Frankie got up to her room she turned off the light and opened the curtain. She felt like an eye staring into the night. What did he mean? Thralkin had been dead not much more than a month. Was he trying to explain how he could feel love for another so soon? Or was she being set up by a real expert?

She turned the desk chair toward the window and sat down. I've known lots of men, she thought. I thoroughly enjoy sex. But when I'm with him that isn't what I think about. I just want to be near him, and hear him talk, and feel the violence and the tenderness of his eyes. The truth is, he makes me feel very old-fashioned.

Am I in love?

Chapter

14

Monday, May 3

DOUG SWIFT LIKED MISS ANNE WITHOUT KNOWING WHY. The thin, bent-over spinster lady never smiled and hardly ever looked up. Her tastes in people were the same as Doug's, only she was more open about them. She thought Traynor Jaynes was a pompous prick, although she might not have been that graphic in her description of the lad. But there could be no question that that was what she thought because of the way she treated him.

Doug thought Traynor was a prick, too.

Miss Anne was also disappointed in Aaron Slade. The man no longer carried a huge, burning torch for justice as he once had. Her feelings were apparent in her attitude. She treated her employer in the manner of a mother who knows her son is better than that.

Firing Miss Anne was unthinkable, although occasionally Slade would be riled to the point of action. He had moved her desk away from the lawyers', possibly encouraging her to retire. But she remained in his employ, always nearby like a conscience. She got along quite well with the investigators she was expected to work for and continued handling no end of administrative detail. Frankie had been installed in the small office behind Miss Anne's desk.

Doug thought Miss Anne was the perfect secretary for Frankie Rommel. Standing in front of her desk, he enjoyed a good, old-fashioned exchange of courtesies, after which he asked to see Frankie. "You just go on in, Mr. Swift. I know she'll be glad to see you."

"Hi, Doug," Frankie said, smiling. She took off her glasses, thrust a legal pad into her place in *Georgia Criminal Practice,* and shut it. "I like your tie."

"Thanks. Got to say you look real pretty this morning." She glowed, in fact, like a woman in love, but Swift didn't tell her that. He wondered about it, however.

"Sit down. Your message said ASAP, but the hotel operator blew it, and I didn't get it until this morning. Am I too late?"

He chose the chair in front of her desk. "No big deal. I got myself electrified on coffee yesterday, really just wanted to talk. Here." He laid a manila folder filled with reports and papers on her desk. "All the stuff you asked for. I stuck in a few other things, too."

"Thanks." She pulled it in front of her but didn't open it. "All you wanted was to give me this?"

"No." He got up and closed the door. "Need some help."

"What?"

He told her what he needed: an authorization to dig up the drains at Flanagan's. She had to be reminded it was her idea. He told her of talking to Maurice Brown's daughter over the weekend, and of learning she was married to Dogwood. Dogwood had told her he saw Richardson shoot her father at Flanagan's, in spite of the fact that Happy Face Munroe had confessed to shooting him somewhere else.

Frankie barely moved while he talked. But he watched the warm look fade from her face, replaced by a dispassionate coldness. She asked if the linkage between Dogwood and Brown meant anything, and he said he didn't know. But it was there.

"Do you know something?" she asked. The rhetorical

question did not call for a reply. "I think I've been had. What exactly do you want?"

"A letter telling me to dig up the drain at Flanagan's Auto and saying what to do with it."

"Ask Miss Anne to come in."

Miss Anne sat down carefully in the chair without arms in front of the desk. She had a stenographer's pad in her hand and adjusted the pince-nez on her nose, then looked over it at Frankie. "Yes?"

Frankie told her what was needed, and asked her if she wanted the letter dictated or if she would rather compose it. "I think I can manage, dear," she said, looking at her notes. "You'll want the drainpipe under the shower stall, including the trap?"

"Yes. Good point."

"The length of pipe to be determined by the investigator in charge?"

"That's right."

"And you will want these items transported without unnecessary contamination or delay to the Georgia Bureau of Investigation, there to be examined in its laboratories for traces of blood and other animal matter? And the results of such analysis are to be reported back to you without delay?"

"I couldn't have said it better myself."

"I will prepare it then." She struggled out of her chair. "Miss Rommel, Aaron has asked me to provide him with copies of any written material you generate or receive."

"Really!" Frankie leaned forward angrily, then calmed herself. "I don't want to put you on the spot, but you work for me. I'll take it up with him."

The elderly woman smiled. "I'm sure you will, dear." She left the room, shutting the door behind her.

"Once you have the letter in your hot little hand, how long until you have some answers?" Frankie asked, staring beyond him.

"Not long. My lieutenant was a plumber's helper. He's rounding up tools now." Doug swept some lint off his trousers, then settled back in his chair. He could see her disappointment and could feel her anguish. He wanted to encourage her but didn't know how. "It'll go through GBI pretty quick. Might have a preliminary analysis this afternoon."

"What about the splinter?"

"I can get that done this afternoon, too."

Frankie spun away from him, obviously thinking of something else. She opened a pedestal drawer, yanked out a tissue, and blew her nose. When she lighted a cigarette her hand shook. "Did you tell me Brown was cremated?"

"Yes. But old German saved some blood, a patch of skin, and hair samples."

"Good!" Frankie spoke with vehemence. "If you pull something out of that drain, we'll be able to match it." She blinked her eyes in momentary pain.

"How have you been had, Frankie?"

She took a couple of deep breaths. "I shouldn't have said that. Let's see what we've got before I jump off the edge."

There was a light tap on the door, and Miss Anne stuck her head in. "May I?"

"Yes. Please."

Once in the room Miss Anne handed Frankie the original of a letter and gave Doug a copy. The stationery carried a letterhead proclaiming Frances Rommel the Special Prosecutor Pro Tem in the Matter of Randolph Richardson. Frankie quickly read it. "This is perfect, Miss Anne. Thank you."

"You're welcome, dear. I wish you wouldn't smoke." She sounded concerned, as though giving motherly advice to the daughter of a friend. "I always tell young people if they need a vice, it should be sex."

"I'll remember that."

"Will you let me know whether Aaron is to get copies?"

"I can let you know now. He is not to get copies."

Miss Anne smiled at her, then shut the door. Doug got to his feet. "What Marilyn Smith said. Is it worth anything?"

"Not in court, if that's what you mean. It's pure hearsay."

"Do you want a written report?"

She shrugged halfheartedly, then nodded. "Yes. It's exculpatory. The DA in Gwinnett may want it."

Doug put his hand on the doorknob. "You know something, Frankie?"

"What?"

"You are one tough woman. A lot of us are glad you're here." He left, leaving the door slightly open.

Frankie didn't feel tough at all. She wanted to cry. She didn't know what to do now or what to tell Trigge. But she knew how to handle that asshole Slade. She yanked the telephone out of its cradle and called him.

She told him—diplomatically, she hoped—that Miss Anne could not give copies of documents generated during the course of the investigation to anyone because it could compromise the result. Slade was astounded by the call and insisted there must be a misunderstanding. Miss Anne had been requested to maintain a history of Frankie's work to be used in the event someone were to challenge its independence. But he scoffed at the notion that he intended to monitor it as it went along. Frankie ground her cigarette to bits. The man is such a good liar he probably believes his own bullshit, she thought.

She turned to the file Swift had dropped off. Reports, photographs and neatly labeled envelopes with newspaper clippings had been methodically arranged and tabbed in the folder. It would be an easy matter for her to insert them into her notebooks. "Richardson: Medal of Honor" grabbed her eye, and she pulled it out and started reading.

The citation was for "conspicuous gallantry and intrepidity at the risk of life, above and beyond the call of duty, in action involving actual conflict with an opposing armed force." Second Lieutenant Randolph Richardson, USMC, had received it for action during his first combat mission in Korea.

His regiment had been ordered to evacuate a position at the Chosin Reservoir. In the course of that maneuver the newly commissioned officer stayed at the rear with his platoon, visibly displaying himself to both the enemy and his own men. His example and continuous encouragement gave them courage. When his BAR rifleman was hit Richardson dragged him to safety, saving the man's life. Showing a maturity and command presence completely unexpected in so recent a graduate of the Virginia Military Institute, he

142

deployed his men in a strong defensive posture and calmly waited for further orders.

When an enemy battery began finding their range Richardson ordered cover for himself and advanced to a location behind it. He rolled two grenades into the bunker where the battery was established, thereby neutralizing its effectiveness.

He thereafter led his platoon in strategic withdrawal maneuvers, remaining at the rear guard position throughout the exercise. He singlehandedly inflicted severe casualties on the enemy through his skillful use of the Browning Automatic Rifle.

On several other occasions, until his regiment was evacuated at Hungnam, Richardson performed acts of conspicuous gallantry and daring. Every man in his platoon—including the dead and the wounded—reached the harbor. He was awarded the Medal of Honor at ceremonies at the White House in October, 1951. A five-by-eight-inch black-and-white glossy photograph of a beaming President Truman pinning the medal on the uniform of a handsome, expressionless young man was next to the citation. "He hasn't changed," Frankie heard herself say.

She thumbed through police reports on Andrew Boatwright, many of which she had seen, and opened the envelope containing newspaper clippings. She quickly became absorbed in a feature piece from the Atlanta *Constitution* titled "A Stranger among Us."

Andrew Boatwright III—in addition to his secret life as head of "The Enterprise"—had been one of Atlanta's leading philanthropists.

Boatwright's financial and business associates, as well as members of the Four Hundred Club—composed of Atlanta's most prominent families—were stunned.

As a fourth-generation Atlantan, his obvious wealth was questioned by no one. Most assumed he had built a hefty inheritance into a fortune through shrewd investment. In fact, he parlayed a small inheritance into a tightly controlled, absolutely ruthless, highly profitable drug empire. Had it not been for its flagrant illegality, his great-grandfather might have been proud.

There followed the disclosure that Silas Boatwright, the

builder of the Boatwright fortune, had been a carpetbagger. He acquired extensive property stretching from present-day Almond Park to the Chattahoochee. Frankie looked at a photograph of the man: black beard, thin hair, heavy features. After the Great War Silas became more southern than the rebels he had fought against, including active participation in the Ku Klux Klan. In spite of that, neither he nor his heirs achieved total acceptance in Atlanta society.

The Boatwright saga was Faulknerian in its depiction of a southern family, the journalist loftily stated. Boatwright's grandfather, through bad investment and the crash of 1929, lost everything except the Boatwright Building on Peachtree Street. Had he not been killed in an automobile crash in Europe in 1938 he might have lost it, too.

Boatwright's father, Andrew Jr.—reportedly a neurotic man who subjected his only child to frequent whippings—maintained the semblance of gentility by living off the proceeds of the Boatwright Building. He died of cirrhosis of the liver in 1953, leaving the heavily mortgaged property to Andrew III.

Young Andrew, raised in Atlanta during World War II, learned the perfect manners of the silver-spoon set. In addition to his father's beatings he was fed the normal southern diet of tradition, honor, and image. He responded by becoming a "flake." He never marched with Doctor King but appears to have supported the movement. He also experimented with drugs, but not to the point of addiction. Instead he managed the Boatwright Building, reducing its mortgage and paying the taxes, eventually selling it. Those profits were used to form the organization dubbed "The Enterprise."

Boatwright never married. In prep school he was nicknamed Toad because of a squat, penguinlike waddle. In later life he indulged a desire to be what he appeared to be: heir to the Boatwright fortune, the liberal-minded scion of an old Atlanta family committed to the future of the city. He contributed lavishly to black causes. The image provided a perfect cover for illegal activities. Relying heavily on legal advice and paying his taxes, he owned many legitimate businesses and established several large trusts for the benefit of "his town," leaving prosecutors in a dilemma with regard to possible forfeitures.

Not real hard to hate, Frankie thought as she flipped through the pages. She stopped at a report from Tom Nuchrist. A narcotics agent, he had interviewed Lemuel "Boy Jake" Watkins, one of the herd arrested after Richardson's disclosures. Watkins was trying to trade information for freedom.

Reputedly one of the organization's enforcers, he stated that on three occasions—the last involving "a white chick, not even a month ago"—Boatwright had been the executioner. He stated he wasn't a psychologist, but the man seemed to need it.

What an awful twist, Frankie thought. Was it true?

She turned to a magazine-section article on Maurice Brown, titled "Tribute to a Most Unusual Man." A photograph accompanied the story, showing a man with a patch over one eye and wearing a baseball cap. He was surrounded by children who clowned in front of the camera. Frowning, she started to read.

Born in 1920 in a house on Auburn Avenue, Maurice Brown was ten years old when Dr. King was born. The only child of stable, hardworking parents who knew the importance of education—his father worked sixty-hour weeks as a porter, and his mother made and sold uniquely designed pot holders and doilies—Brown was encouraged to do well in school and expected to go to Morehouse College. But he couldn't read. "Words on the page just wouldn't stay still. They jumped around like hot grease," he told a biographer. "So I made up for that little defect with action."

In the educational parlance of today Brown might have been diagnosed as a hyperactive child suffering from dyslexia. "But in those days I was just plain trouble." Tall, muscular, and cocky by the time he was fourteen, he broke his parents' hearts with fights, failures, and expulsions. At seventeen—without a high school diploma—he told them he didn't need them anymore and removed himself to Illinois. A year later he was in the Joliet prison for the attempted robbery of a filling station.

The bombing of Pearl Harbor and the commencement of

the war might have been an opportunity for him; others had their sentences commuted so they could enlist. But Brown was 4-F. "I had the ability in those days to draw beatings," he said. "I was an invitation to a club." Three guards "just plain satisfied me" in the summer of 1940, beating him savagely. The barrel of a pistol was punched into his right eye socket, disfiguring him and destroying the optic nerve.

He was released from prison in 1949 and came home to Atlanta. "It was like a miracle had happened. All I had was one eye, but it could read!" His father—"He lied about his age. Probably the only lie he ever told"—had enlisted in the navy, served as a steward on board a destroyer in the South Pacific, and been killed in 1945 by a kamikaze pilot. "My one regret is I never told him how much I loved him." But his mother was still alive, "and I didn't make that mistake with her." He moved into the home on Auburn Avenue and took care of her until she died in 1957.

Married at thirty to Linda Bates, a Spellman College graduate, Brown—over the years—had four children: three daughters and one son. One daughter died of a drug overdose in 1981, and their son was murdered in New York City.

But in spite of the many tragedies in his life, he exuded a sincere joy over "the experience." He became the subject of several articles and newspaper stories, not because he curried the favor of reporters, but because of his unusual observations and quotable statements.

When asked whether he bore animosity toward the men who had put out his eye: "I love them. If they hadn't done it, I would never have been able to read." Asked to explain: "Some doctor told me I had dyslexia. I looked it up. That just describes the symptoms, not the problem. What I had was two eyes, and each eye wanted to do it his way, and neither eye would give in to the other. Well, when those screws put one eye out, then the war was over. Now words stay on the page where they belong."

On the general subject of reading: "I am so glad I didn't learn how until I was thirty! Young minds are offered mountains and mountains of garbage and a few good books, but they don't have the experience to tell the difference. What a preposterous bunch of foolishness I was spared, until I was old enough to handle it."

Reading, writing, and talking formed a large part of his life. A construction worker, he devoted much of his free time to the teaching of illiterates and said, "I'm always ready to give advice." In later years especially, leaders in both the black and white communities sought his counsel. Frequently encouraged to run for political office, he firmly declined. "I'm too twitchy to be a leader and too picky to be a follower."

On racism: "It's a by-product of language. The truth is all of us are colored, but language makes it seem like there's whites and blacks. Well, look at yourself. You are no more white than I am black. You're kind of orange, and I'm kind of brown, but we're both of us colored." When asked if he had ever lusted after a white woman: "Sure enough. But I've loved more of them than I've lusted after, and the only woman I ever knew in the way you're talking about was my wife." On death: "I'm ready. Any time."

Brown attended many churches but didn't belong to any. He was welcomed wherever he went and often preached. He prided himself on an ability to give meaning to hard-to-grasp biblical concepts. "When you look out in a meadow full of grass, if you make yourself still, you can hear each blade singing its praises to the Lord. Why do they do that? It's because they don't know any better. All they do is feel the sun and soak nutrients out of the soil and enjoy the wonder that is life. Then, when some old cow comes along and eats them, they keep right on singing all the way into the creature's digestive tract.

"I'm like that. I just don't know any better. I didn't do anything to deserve to live, any more than that blade of grass. I am blessed by life and feel so sorry for my brothers and sisters, black and white, who don't have it in their hearts to accept the blessing. Instead they spend their time worrying about that old cow.

"It doesn't surprise me that every now and then there's an earthquake or a plague or some other catastrophe. That's what I'd do if I was God. I'd lose my temper."

Another favorite: "I got my own name for God. I call him Giver. That's what he, she, or it is to me.

"And I have a prayer. 'Giver, let me live with richness but die poor, knowing I gave more than I got.' "

He practiced what he preached. When Freedom Hall—the heart of the Martin Luther King, Jr. Center for Nonviolent Change—was planned, his $15,000 house on Auburn Avenue was in the way. Brown was out of work at the time, with a wife and three children to support. Nevertheless he gave it to the center for "ten dollars and other valuable consideration." When questioned by a reporter who wanted to make sense out of his motives, Maurice told him: "The roof leaked."

This is the man Abe Fortanier thinks so highly of? Frankie wondered, rubbing her eyes. The guy was a nut case!

Brown had opinions on a wide range of subjects, the article stated. The common cold: "The reason doctors can't cure it is because it isn't a sickness. It's a response. When your nose drips with mucus, probably the worst thing you can do is take a pill so it won't run anymore. When you get a cut, blood forms a scab. Is the scab a sickness? When the membranes in your face get hot and dry your body *needs* the mucus to cover them over so they can heal."

He also saw the connection between emotional disorder and arthritis and cancer long before the medical profession accepted the notion. "Fear can literally freeze the body, and hate can literally burn it up."

At the time of his death he looked—and acted—much younger than he was. Tall, broad-shouldered, and thin-hipped with a slightly protruding stomach, Brown always wore a hat, "even to bed." Retired and living on social security, he worked full-time as an editorial and research assistant for the Atlanta Centers for Disease Control.

"Maurice Brown is survived by his wife, two daughters, and seven grandchildren. He will be missed."

Frankie folded the article and put it back in the envelope. She didn't know what she had expected, but it wasn't that. Brown sounded more like a character than a saint. Her mind still churning, she found Swift's report of his interviews with the witnesses who had last seen Boatwright alive, and his synopsis of the events of that evening. She read them again.

The Atlanta Historical Society was one of the organizations to which Boatwright gave large donations. Possibly for that reason, he had been the speaker at an historical society dinner the night before he was murdered. Richardson, along with his mother, had also attended.

Frankie leaned back in her chair. When she and Randolph had dinner at that lovely old hotel in Tennessee he had talked about his mother. She had pictured Nancy Reagan—a thin, vain remnant of the past who called blacks "cleaning people," in case one of them was listening in. She lit a cigarette and continued to read.

Boatwright's speech had been on the historical accuracy of Margaret Mitchell's portrayal, in *Gone With the Wind*, of Sherman's march through Georgia. After finishing his prepared remarks, which put some of the attendees to sleep, he called upon Richardson for comment.

Exuding good humor and charm, Richardson rose to the occasion. He said his instructor in military tactics—a Marine Corps sergeant named Butler—assigned the book as a text. Butler maintained that everything in it was true and worthy of study. However, when the sergeant claimed to be a descendant of Rhett Butler—one of the characters in Miss Mitchell's epic—Richardson began to suspect the man's veracity. His joke apparently was well received.

The two men left the dinner together in Richardson's car in order to go drink some Wild Turkey. Boatwright's chauffered limousine had taken Richardson's mother home. That was the last time Boatwright was seen alive.

What kind of man is he? Frankie asked herself. The night before she had held his hand. She could feel its warmth now. How could he publicly joke with Andrew Boatwright—she didn't care how bad he was—then torture and kill him?

She was frozen with a thought. What if Boatwright told Richardson he had killed Melody Thralkin?

"I don't know what I'm going to do!" She wanted to hurl the file through the wall and go back to Denver. Instead she found an article on Charles Williams, the other victim.

It told the prosaic story of a man who appeared happily married and prosperous; a black product of the New South who lived in an upper-middle-class neighborhood with a beautiful wife and talented daughter. In spite of his political connections, however, his contracting business lost more money than it made. Information from "reliable sources" linked him to "The Enterprise."

"That's all there is to it?" Frankie asked no one in particular. She looked at the portrait picture of Williams's daughter and wife. They were more interesting to her than the story of the man's life. If push came to shove—and that was the way it was headed—she might at least have a couple of decent witnesses.

Her telephone buzzed. "A James Trigge of Denver would like to talk to you," Miss Anne said.

"Put him on, please."

"Frankie?" Trigge could scarcely contain his exuberance. "Guess what?"

"I'm really not in the mood for games, Jim."

"Well, la-de-da! You just got a letter from the Supremes, babe. Want me to open it?"

"No."

"Damn it, woman, this looks like the big It. I can fax it to you, but I have to open it first."

"Don't."

"You don't want to know? Hey. Maybe *you* don't, but the suspense is killing me! How about I call up the court? Or *you* call them?"

"Jim, remember that careless driving ticket you got a year ago, when you thought the cop was a dipshit and you defended yourself and lost?"

"Sure I remember. He was, and is, a dipshit. That jury never understood the significance of it."

"And so you spent two days trying it. Right?"

"Yes. I was pissed! I still am. What are you talking about here, babe?"

"You did it because of the principle involved, didn't you?"

"Uh-oh. What's going on?"

"I'll have to call you back, Jim. I really don't know what's going on. But I could be up to my ass in principles."

Chapter

15

Wednesday, May 5

DOUG COULD HEAR THE CHOPPER APPROACH. HE DIDN'T
want to get his hopes up. Probably the damn thing . . .

Something was seriously wrong. You can feel an
approaching helicopter because they vibrate, and besides,
it sounded like short bursts. . . .

It was the telephone. He hit it with his fingers, knocking
it off the bedside table. He found it on the floor. "Hello."

"Mr. Swift?"

"Yes." He got the light on, then shut his eyes to keep
from going blind. "Do you know what time it is?" he
asked.

"Don't know, man."

Doug got an eye open and looked at the clock. Three-
ten A.M. "Who is this?"

"Can we talk someplace, Mr. Swift, 'stead of the telephone? I got too much at stake."

The speaker was male, young, black accent. Doug was
wide awake now. He couldn't believe he had slept that
hard. "Give me a reason, man."

Silence. Then: "I saw some stuff Rockdale Park."

Dogwood. "We can get together. Name it."

"That diner, you know what I'm talkin'?"

"Yeah."

"I be outside." The phone went dead.

Doug dressed quickly. He stuffed a wallet-size tape recorder in his coat, brushed his teeth, urinated, and ran for his car. Fifteen minutes later he pulled up in front of the Hi-Lo Diner on Broadway.

The city at night was pretty. The modern buildings along Broadway radiated with power like holy men. Doug got out of his car and locked it, then stood on the sidewalk in front of the diner. He felt like a target as he let the lights from inside illuminate him.

He waited. There was very little traffic. Four people—not a group—appeared on the street from the Marta terminal, and he watched them walk by.

The door to the diner opened. The young man who came out walked painfully. "Swift?"

"Yeah."

"You alone, right?"

"I didn't have time to bring reinforcements."

"Let's get off the street. We talk in your car?"

"Sure."

It was Dogwood. Doug had seen his picture, and there was no mistaking the paper-sack-brown, green-eyed dope peddler. He unlocked the passenger door and opened it, then went around to the other side and got in.

"Let's be drivin'," Dogwood said.

Swift started the motor and headed for Martin Luther King Boulevard. He reached inside his pocket and turned on the recorder. Dogwood either didn't notice or didn't care. "You walk like a man with sore feet," Swift said. "Richardson?"

"Gonna waste that motherfucker."

"What do you want to do that for?"

"Huh!" Nervously he pulled out a cigarette, poked it in his mouth, and lit it. "Are you straight as they say?"

"I'm a cop. I don't know what they say."

"Serve and protect, right?" He pushed smoke out of his mouth. "Man, I carryin' too much."

"Hey, man. Maybe I can take some of the load."

They drove west, toward the Chattahoochee. When Dogwood started talking he couldn't stop. It was as though he had to tell someone—anyone—what he knew or go mad.

He told of getting jumped in the parking lot at Destry's, a bar in Little Five Points where he sold his stuff to friends. "Man, I still don't know what happen, it was so fast. Like a canvas bag drop over my head, big as a body bag, then cinched up tight, you know, pin my arms so I couldn't move! Then got a barrel in my ear, and the man say 'Wrists, please,' like he ax me for the ketchup, and I don't do nuthin'. Shit. He cock the motherfuckin' gun, and he say, 'Now.' "

After handcuffing him the man shoved him on the floor in the back seat. "Then he taken me someplace—I thought the white motherfucker gonna hang me to a tree—but when he let me out we're in this garage. He take the sack off. Had this old nylon sock over his face so I couldn't say for sure, but I knows it was Richardson."

He's on something, Doug thought, watching him sweat, twitch, smoke, and talk at the same time. He had rolled down his window even though it was cold out. "Motherfucker thought he was so tough." Dogwood spat, laughing and jeering. "I do something he don't like, and he start drop-kicking me all over that room, kung fu moves, shit." He snorted and took a huge gulp of smoke. "Then he plop me on that torture machine."

He hurt him bad, Dogwood said, almost killing him. He peeled off his shoes and put cigarette burns on his feet, then pushed him in a shower and tried to drown him. Dogwood's feet were swollen up like basketballs. "Man wanted names from me, but I wouldn't give him shit. Then it got so bad I just blurted out a name popped into my head, old Mr. Perfect, you know, the Saint of Atlanta. Huh!" He snorted contemptuously. "Gave him my wife's daddy, old Maurice Brown."

Dogwood believed everyone in Atlanta had heard of old Maurice, so the man had to know he was lying. But he handcuffed him to a pipe that stuck out of the wall, told him he'd better be telling the truth—and left. "Didn't leave me jack shit, man. No water, no food."

Then the next morning he came back into the garage,

153

Dogwood said. He'd go through this routine: close the bay door, face his car toward it, then put a steel cage over the grille. He still had that sock on his face. "Then he pull Maurice out of the back seat." Dogwood at that moment looked hunted, like a murderer who knows he will be caught. "I yell at the motherfucker, but nothing happen. I couldn't get no sounds to come out."

As Dogwood watched, the man put Maurice on the torture machine. "Maurice so scared, and he's prayin', like he knew he would die." Dogwood heard the questions. "Man axed him if he was in the drug business, and Maurice said no. Then did he know Dogwood, and old Maurice—I didn't know he knew my street name—said I sure do. Said he's my son-in-law. Said Dogwood pushes dope, so he's hooked into the system, which was too bad because the boy was really good, only he didn't know it." Dogwood glared harshly at Doug. "That old son of a bitch talk like that all the time."

They parked on a hill west of the Chattahoochee, overlooking the valley. The eastern sky—clear and bright—had faded into predawn lightness at the edges. Dogwood lit a cigarette from the one in his hand and kept talking, sweating and smoking. His high was still on him.

"Then the man act gentle. He get Maurice off that torture machine and stand him up in the shower stall and talkin' real nice, sorry for the mistake, you know, wait while I take off the cuffs, and Maurice nice and relaxed, then blam. Shit!" He snapped off a drag. "Why he do that to Maurice? Put that barrel near his ear—not too close, you know, like he knows all there is to know about blow-back—and blew him up." Dogwood's head sagged forward, and his haunted eyes wouldn't close. "That was so bad. Maurice drop down to his knees, and his face lean into the shower, but he won't die." Dogwood stared at Doug. "How could he stay alive with that hole in his head, man? Motherfucker wouldn't die! I could hear him gurgle and slurp, like eating soup."

The man knew exactly what to do next, Dogwood said. When Maurice quit making those noises the man stuffed his body in a trash sack, then hauled it out a ways and put him in another trash sack, then put him in the trunk of his car. He turned on the shower and washed down the walls and got everything clean. "Then he come back to me."

Dogwood knew it wasn't any use. The man knew who he was now. He might go get his wife next. "So I give him a name, Mr. Charles Hot-shit Williams, that black motherfucker." Dogwood spat out the name. "Treat me all the time like I'm his boy." Then he hung Dogwood on the same pole, took that cage off the front of his car, and went out again.

But this time Dogwood worked the pipe loose, he said, lighting another cigarette. "Got me some leverage on it and bent it back and forth, you know, till it broke." The handcuffs on his feet and wrists slowed him down, he said, but there wasn't anything that could keep him in that building. "I'd peed all over myself and when that po-lice found me, he kep' his distance. He taken me to the station house, and they break off the cuffs, say 'Stay out of trouble if you can,' give me five dollars, and push me out the door."

"What happened to the cuffs?" Doug asked.

"Said I could keep them. Said maybe they'd remind me about the trouble. I threw them somewhere."

Doug nodded. He'd come back to it if there was time but wanted to get the rest of it first.

"Who have you told?"

"Nobody, man. You're the first." He had to stay out of sight, he explained, because everybody he knew was looking for him. And he couldn't tell anybody anything. If his wife knew the truth, she'd blame him for what happened to her daddy. And if anybody knew he'd narked off Williams, he would be dead meat. "Everything changing now, but I'd still be dead meat."

"What do you mean?"

"Big scramble for the drug business, a new bunch all set to take over."

"Who are they?"

"Ain't gonna name names, man. Black dudes, mean motherfuckers, say they're gonna clean house, make some changes and do things right." That's what Dogwood had heard, anyway, he said. "So now what am I supposed to do, man? Got this smooth Ferrari, still at Destry's where that motherfucker snatch my ass, but they're probably watching it!''

Doug told him there was a lot he could do. "I can keep you alive, man. I can get you your car, too—I will make that my personal business—but it will cost you."

"What it gonna cost?"

"You'll have to come in, man. You'll have to testify to what you've seen."

"So Marilyn and all her family and everybody in town will know what I done?"

"So the hero who blew off Maurice's head will go down."

"I don't know, man."

Doug weighed the alternatives. He could arrest him, but then what kind of witness would he make? He would also lose the credibility he had on the street. "You're dead if you don't."

"I got to think about it."

Doug pulled out all the money in his billfold: fifty-seven dollars. "Here."

"Thanks, man."

"Want me to take you back into town?"

"No." He opened the door.

"Where will you be?"

"I know how to call you, man." He got out, standing painfully, then shut the door.

"Come in soon, man. I'll take care of you."

Doug drove out of his vision, then pulled out the recorder. The cassette had run to the end and stopped. He sped through the light early-morning traffic to the Police Building, ran up the stairs to Leon Webster's office, and burst in. Leon kept all kinds of high-tech equipment in his file cabinet and never locked it, as though daring someone to steal it. Doug found what he needed and spread it out on Leon's desk.

He made a copy of the cassette, put the original in an envelope, and worked off the copy. Dogwood had opened the window of Doug's car and smoked like a forest fire, bouncing around when he talked like a cat in a cage. The recorder had been too good. It soaked up everything it heard without focusing on meaning.

But Doug could make out most of it. He cranked paper into a typewriter and started transcribing while the words were fresh in his mind. He freely filled in the gaps of dialogue when traffic sounds blanketed their voices, tossing parentheses around those passages to indicate uncertainty, even though often he was more sure of what had been said when a truck went by than of words or phrases that required him to go back and listen carefully. By the time Leon arrived at twenty minutes after eight he was almost done.

Numbered pages were scattered on the floor. Leon picked them up, put them in order, and started reading. Doug had typed "Ain't gonna name"—when the tape stopped, emitting a low signal. Yanking the page out of the typewriter, he gave it to Leon.

"Where is he?" Leon asked when he was done reading.

"I let him go." Doug had been having second thoughts. The quick, sharp glance of his lieutenant did little for his confidence. "Maybe I should have arrested his ass."

"We know he's around," Webster said, shutting the door. "This puts the cap on, man. When did you get it?"

Doug told him.

Webster prowled around the room. "How do we handle this?"

Doug had been thinking about that, too. "Let's get a copy to Frankie before anyone—Fiorello or Slade or maybe even the Major—can sit on it. Then lay it out to the Major and tell him we need to pick up Dogwood."

"Ralston won't like being boxed in that way."

"Okay. Then I'll send a copy to Frankie, thinking that's what I'm supposed to do. You're a lieutenant, you know better, you go right to him and tell him what I've done."

"Bullshit." Webster dropped in his chair and rubbed his face. "No one—not even Ralston—knows about this until we've got Dogwood. The boy is at risk."

"We need to tell Frankie."

"Why?"

"She can order us to pick up Dogwood like he's a material witness. She also needs to know how to aim her case."

"I don't know, man." Webster's dark eyes appeared to

be trying to see through walls. "What's your read? There's something going on between her and Richardson."

"She's straight, Leon. She got Slade walking stiff-legged, and she gave me that letter. If it's there, she'll charge it."

"Will she keep it down until we got it? That's what the problem is now."

"Maybe she's too straight." Swift told Webster about the report of his interview with Marilyn Smith. "She said 'It's exculpatory,' going to make sure the DA in Gwinnett gets it."

"Uh-oh." Webster could think like a political bureaucrat, and Doug trusted his advice. "We'd better bring her in quick. But you tell her to wait until we've got a case before she passes out all that exculpatory bullshit."

"Are you worried about Richardson finding out?" Doug asked. "You think the old man'll go after Dogwood?"

"Richardson doesn't scare me half as much as Fiorello."

Frankie wasn't ready to talk to Fortanier. She ignored his messages but left one of her own with his secretary. It said a glitch had developed that she couldn't discuss. She hated the way she was acting, but there was nothing else she could do. If Richardson had murdered Maurice Brown, she couldn't possibly let him slide by on manslaughter indictments.

The report from the Georgia Bureau of Investigation had been inconclusive. No animal or vegetable matter had been found in either the pipe or the trap under the shower at Flanagan's. However, there were traces of an industrial solvent, evidencing a thorough and recent cleaning.

Also, the GBI specialist who compared the splinter in Williams's butt with some off the so-called "rack" had examined the dolly under a strobe light. He found a hair in the backrest, wedged into some grains of wood that hadn't quite splintered. Dr. Jolene Taggart, the hair and fiber expert with the bureau, identified it as human, probably male, probably from the head, but not Caucasian. She had tried to match it with known samples in the case with no luck, although she had been able to exclude one of the victims: Andrew Boatwright.

Frankie had called her up. In essence, Taggart could testify the hair could have come from either Williams or Brown, although the matching characteristics were slight, indicating it probably did not.

Who, then? Frankie wondered. Benjamin Smith, aka Dogwood?

She had spent that morning in the grand jury room with Traynor James. She had appeared, somewhat questionably, as his co-counsel. It had given her an opportunity to assess the grand jury. In the space of forty-five minutes Jaynes obtained two indictments for murder and no-billed a presentment for kidnap and robbery. The no-bill took most of the time. A high-school dropout with a record had taken five dollars from the daughter of a city councilman. He claimed it was a loan. In spite of what the girl told her father, it probably was. Frankie took pleasure in watching the system work. The grand jury could be a shield as well as a sword.

At eleven that morning she smiled at Miss Anne and opened the door to her office. "Are you all right, dear?" Miss Anne asked. "You don't look as though you are getting enough sleep."

"I'm fine."

Three messages were in the middle of her desk: two from Doug Swift to call ASAP and a third from Fortanier: "Anything you can tell me? My client is extremely anxious." There was also a sealed envelope from the Atlanta Police Department. She opened it, scanned the contents, then carefully read through them.

Afterward she sat for a moment with her eyes closed, listening, as Richardson compared her to Atlanta. She smiled at the memory, then dialed the police department and Swift's extension. There was an urgency in Swift's voice. "Did you read that interview?"

"Yes. I hate you. You've complicated my life."

"Can I come over? We need to talk about it."

"Sure, but what's wrong with the phone?"

"Just take me a second. I'll be right there."

She thought her head would explode, told Miss Anne she'd be back in a moment, and went to the restroom. She took two double-strength adult-size Tylenol and wished she carried something more potent, like a flask of Scotch. At least she knew what had to be done. There was no question in her mind she would do it.

When she got back to her office Swift was already there. "That was quick," she said. "Come in."

He followed her through the door and shut it. "Do you believe that creep?" she asked as they sat down.

Doug's reply took a moment. "Yes. But I keep hoping it wasn't the old man."

"What do you mean?"

"Dogwood said the man wore a sock. Maybe it was somebody else."

"You sound like a defense lawyer, but you'd better clear it up. Get a voice identification. Have him identify Richardson's car."

"We will, soon as we find him."

"You let him go?" She pulled a cigarette out of her desk drawer. "Why did you do that?"

"Just thought I should. Keep him on our side, you know. Everybody thinks I made a mistake."

She lit it, inhaling deeply. "We won't know that until later, but I can tell you this much now: It was dumb." She took another hit. "How could Richardson kill Brown like that, Doug? It's inhuman."

"Maybe he didn't think it was bad."

"I don't understand you."

"He didn't do it to Brown. He did it to Dogwood. Like he was at war. It's okay to do anything as long as you win."

"Even kill an innocent man?"

Swift shrugged his shoulders. "He needed some intelligence and was all done negotiating. So he sent the boy a message."

"That's crazy."

"Not if you think like a soldier. He did the same thing in 'Nam."

"What?"

"Those VC he cured, Frankie. The two gooks."

"What are you talking about?"

"It's in the reports, why I had this kind of hunch about Richardson. Didn't you see it?"

"No." This always happens, Frankie thought, digging out her notebook. "I think it's time we compared files." She pushed it at him. "Tell me what else I don't have."

Swift flipped through it quickly. "Uh-oh. Should be something in here about when Leon searched the old man's house."

"Did he find anything?"

"Yeah. An altar." Swift kept looking. "Not in here."

"An altar! What's that all about?"

Swift told her. She listened with fascination, feeling cold. "I need the report," she said. "It's getting easier."

She told him she had already sent a copy of the reported interview with Marilyn Smith to Gwinnett but would hold the one with Dogwood. "I can't go to the grand jury over Brown until we have a case. And we won't have a case until we have Dogwood."

"I screwed up."

She tried to make it easy for him. "A judgment call. You simply used bad judgment."

"What if Dogwood is gone?"

"Then we charge *two* murders instead of three."

She watched him go, then called NASP in Denver. "Hi, Frankie," Mary Gallegos said. The NASP receptionist, who did more work in less time than a Japanese automobile factory, sounded genuinely glad to hear her voice. "How're you doin'? Congratulations! Mr. T. hasn't come in. Want me to have him call?"

"He didn't open that letter from the Supreme Court, did he?"

"No. I wouldn't let him. But he knows what's in it. He found out."

Frankie didn't pursue the subject. "You have to do something for me right now, Mary."

"Sure."

"Prepare a very simple letter to the nominating committee withdrawing my application."

"Do what?"

"You heard me. Tell them I deeply appreciate their consideration, but after much soul-searching I don't think I'm temperamentally suited to the position." A second wave of relief washed through her. In a long-ago fantasy she had seen herself in mythic proportions, as Diana, goddess of the hunt. I don't belong on the bench, she told herself now. I'm too damn feisty.

"Shoot, Frankie," Mary Gallegos said. "I thought I'd get to know a judge!"

Chapter
16

Friday, May 7

FRANKIE WARNED SWIFT AND WEBSTER TO SAY NOTHING about the investigation into the murder of Maurice Brown. They did not need the warning. They had been afraid she would send a copy of the Dogwood interview to the DA in Gwinnett County. "No chance," she said. "You guys make the case. Then we fight them for it."

However, she couldn't mask her change in attitude. In a brief telephone talk Wednesday afternoon with Fortanier she was curt. The unexplained delay in going to the grand jury led inevitably to speculation. Had the special prosecutor changed her mind? Would she seek an indictment for murder?

Aaron Slade confronted her and demanded an explanation. When she refused to discuss it he concluded the rumors were true and told her that in his opinion he had been betrayed. It confirmed everything he already knew about Yankees, and he vowed to make her pay for her treachery. He started by billing her for office space and the services of Miss Anne.

Frankie made the best of the man's pettiness and allowed Miss Anne to talk him out of such foolishness. She remained in her office, and Miss Anne continued to take her dictation. She even continued to use the law library and to call Traynor Jaynes for quick answers. Her one hallway encounter on Thursday with Aaron Slade had been shrouded in civility.

She stayed in hourly contact with Swift and Webster, but the information was always the same: Dogwood hadn't been located. This in spite of the fact that Fiorello's men were looking for him, too. Webster had dropped a nugget, and Fiorello was searching for the vein: Dogwood knew the group within The Enterprise that wanted to take it over. He might trade what he knew for his life.

According to Webster, the hotshots in Narcotics should turn him up.

Earlier Thursday morning Fortanier caught her on the telephone. He told her he had talked to Slade and pressed her over the delay. As before, she said it was unavoidable. As a courtesy she informed him he should expect the worst.

Fortanier's manner changed abruptly. He told her that in fairness she should withdraw. If she stayed on the case, he would file a grievance against her for unethical conduct based on the intercourse—he implied it might even have been sexual—between her and his client. Frankie was outraged by the threat. "If anyone has a grievance, it's me," she retorted. "Take your best shot."

Not even an hour later Trigge called. He fired her over the telephone, no ifs, ands, or buts. "Pack your bags, lady. You're history." She told him no. He could fire her from NASP—not a bad idea; possibly NASP would keep its funding. But she had taken an oath to prosecute Randolph Richardson for his crimes, and she had no choice. "Come to Atlanta, Jim. You'll understand."

In a rage Trigge had banged down the telephone. But five minutes later—the longest five minutes in her life—he called back, said her request to resign was under consideration, and told her he'd be there in the morning. He faxed flight information, and Frankie arranged to have him picked up.

When Richardson called she hung up. He left messages, but she didn't return his calls. He tried to see her Thursday night, but she refused. She sent a letter from him back unopened. But she could feel his hand and hear his voice. She hated the way the memory of him clung to her and how it would unexpectedly touch her at odd times. She tried to stop it from happening but could not. Then she left it alone, letting the knowledge of what might have been come to her gently, like a soft smile.

Other than a story about her appointment when she first arrived in Atlanta, nothing had appeared in the media. There had been telephone calls, but Frankie instructed Miss Anne to return them with the advice: "The matter is under investigation."

However, rumors reached them, too. On Thursday a reporter from the *Constitution* waited two hours to talk to her—"I cannot comment at this time"—and on Friday, as she hurried to a meeting with the homicide detectives, a channel seven news team caught her in the hallway and poked a microphone in her face. She smiled graciously, a hostess greeting the guest of honor. "Thank you so much for your questions, but out of fairness to all concerned I cannot comment at this time." Her instructor at the prosecutorial training course on how to handle the media during the trial of a high-profile case would have been proud.

But she couldn't wait forever for Webster and Swift to make the case on Brown. The grand jury would only sit one more week. What's wrong with those guys? she wondered, knowing it wasn't their fault, yet determined to get some action. She jammed her way into the Police Building shortly before eleven for a meeting. The sergeant on duty waved her through, and she took the elevator to the fourth floor. Fiorello confronted her as she got off. "Lady, what the hell is going on?"

"Hi, Al. Not here." She pushed past him. "We can talk in Leon's office."

Webster motioned them in. When he saw the hostility in Fiorello's expression he stood up. Fiorello's face had turned red, as though someone had applied a tourniquet to his neck and then released it. "You in on this?" he asked, squarely facing the lieutenant.

"What?"

"Don't play dumb."

"Al, what the hell do you think you're doing?" Frankie asked, shutting the door.

"We talked a week ago, remember, counselor? What's the hangup?"

"Leon, would you mind leaving your office?" She smiled at him. "Al thinks he has a bone to pick with me, and—"

"I want Leon here." Fiorello sat down. "I want to know what's going on, lady. I don't give a fuck who you are."

Frankie took her time. She opened her purse, got a cigarette, and lit it. Then she took a chair opposite Fiorello. "Get a couple of things straight," she said, watching the smoke rise in a straight column from the end of the stick. "Don't call me 'lady.' I will answer to either 'Frankie' or 'Ms. Rommel.' And another thing; don't ever—repeat, ever—try to push me around. Now. Would you like to start over?"

Fiorello brushed at his scalp with his hands. His eyes stabbed at her angrily. "Randolph Richardson has done more for this town than Coca Cola," he said. "The man has singlehandedly destroyed a major drug distribution operation. Addicts are going wild. They don't have anything to put in their noses."

"Coca Cola?" Frankie asked.

"Atlanta's first big moneymaker. Frankie, I got seven cases he made. Seven bad people. I'm starting to think you want to let them go. Why?"

"That's ridiculous," she said, feeling herself being drawn into a long, pointless argument.

"Yeah. Well, they'll be gone, Frankie. Back out there doing their shit. But you think it's more important to nail Richardson for wasting a couple pukes nobody needs. Twenty-seven deaths in Atlanta last year directly attributable to cocaine. Measure that against two rotten pukes!"

"What if it's three?" Frankie asked, losing her patience.

"*What?* What are you talking about?"

She knew instantly she should not have said that. She stood up. "I don't like this. Leave."

"Wait." Fiorello placated her with a gesture, showing the bottoms of his hands and raising his eyebrows. Frankie waited. "Look, you're putting something out that's very serious. I haven't heard of any third person. Who?"

Frankie looked to Webster for help. "We've got some information we're checking out," Webster said. "Classified at the present time."

"There aren't any bodies!" Fiorello said, raising his hands in frustration. "I mean, some bums maybe, but I'd *know* about a hit. What gives here?"

The telephone interrupted. Webster picked it up and spoke into it. "James Trigge?" he asked Frankie, his hand over the receiver. "He's downstairs."

"From NASP," she told him. "I told him I'd meet him here."

"Let Mr. Trigge through," Webster said, then he cradled the telephone. "How much longer will you be, Al?"

Fiorello go up. "I guess I can take a hint. I don't get you, Frankie. I checked on you. Fact is, I'm the one who told Slade you were okay. The word I got back was you're tough, hate the pukes, and have good sense." He made an obvious effort to make the best of it. "Look. Keep the door open, okay?"

"It's always open."

"Later, *pal*," he said to Webster. "Didn't we start out working this together? I stuck my neck out for you even." He grinned as though to emphasize his own foolish trust. "Remind me the next time you need a favor." He closed the door quietly.

"I'm really sorry," Frankie said. "I fucked up."

"You sure did."

When Trigge's large, bearlike body appeared through the glass walls of Webster's office Frankie had an urge to run away. She smiled at him instead. His rumpled brown wool sport coat—comfortable in Denver, but in Atlanta more of a buffalo robe—fit him like hair. She tried to give him a hug when he came in the room, but he would have none of it. He held out his hand, and she didn't care what he thought. She gave it a squeeze.

After introductions she pulled her file out of her briefcase. Webster volunteered to leave, but she wanted him to stay, to fill in gaps and answer questions.

For more than two hours—Frankie doing most of the talking, and Webster amazed at her grasp of the facts— they went over the evidence and talked about the case.

Webster's stomach began growling shortly before one P.M., which all of them heard but chose to ignore. Trigge's questions were objective and dispassionate, giving no hint as to what he was thinking. But when she was done he sat back in his chair and grinned. "So the straw that breaks it for you is Maurice Brown?"

"Yes."

"You said something about principle?"

"I'll tell you later."

He nodded. "I apologize, Frankie. I've got some principles left somewhere. I should have trusted you."

Frankie had been drained of emotion. Otherwise she might have cried. "I hate this case, Jim. I hate what it has done to me and what it may do to NASP. But I love it, too."

"The name of the game. It's what you wanted, isn't it?" He rubbed sweat off the back of his neck. "You told me you'd like to litter the floor with ideas instead of bodies. Well, I see a few bodies down there. But some ideas, too."

"Jim, it's an important case. The issues are huge."

She was aware of the black man behind the desk who seemed to be smiling.

"Yeah. Like NASP." Trigge lumbered to his feet. "NASP will probably follow the path of your typical good politician."

"*That's* an oxymoron if ever I heard one!"

"No, there are such things. I admit they get knocked off fast. Maybe good agencies don't last either."

Frankie butted the cigarette she had been holding and looked at her watch. It was close to two P.M. She was starved. "I'm hungry. Let's go eat."

"You two go on," Webster said. "I've some catching up to do."

Frankie got up and stuck her hand in Trigge's arm. She knew it made him feel good. "Come on, Jim. He just doesn't want to be seen with a couple of lawyers."

The phone rang. Webster frowned as he picked it up. He had left instructions to hold calls except in an emergency. "Uh-oh," he said, then he gestured with his hand, holding Frankie and Trigge in the room. "How long will you be?"

he asked the person on the other end, then he nodded and hung up. "That was Doug. They found Dogwood."

Frankie had a premonition. "Are they bringing him in?"

"Yes. In a body bag. Damn!"

"He's dead?" she asked, rather foolishly.

Webster nodded. "They just found him in Gwinnett, by Sugarpine Creek, not far from Maurice Brown's body. Preliminary indications are a high-velocity gunshot wound to the head."

Tueday, May 11

It's chemical, Frankie thought. She was waiting at counsel table in Judge Driscoll's courtroom when she became aware of a feeling of anticipation. She knew without looking that Richardson had entered the room. When she saw him her face glowed and her whole expression softened. For a brief moment their eyes locked. She was certain he felt it, too.

Richardson smiled at her, nodded, and sat down next to Abraham Fortanier. I'd better get a handle on *that* little problem before the trial starts, she thought.

Though not packed, the courtroom was crowded. Word had spread that the grand jury had returned an indictment against Randolph Richardson for murder, and he would be arraigned.

Security precautions had been ordered, adding an aura of drama to the simple procedure. Seven uniformed sheriff deputies, creaking like saddled horses because of their leather holsters and large revolvers, were spaced around the walls. Frankie had her suspicions regarding the display of weaponry. "Street talk"—underground rumor—had it that Dogwood had been executed as an informant and that Richardson could be next. But Frankie suspected a publicity stunt engineered for the benefit of Richardson by Aaron Slade and Al Fiorello. She had seen both of them talking to reporters in the hall.

The court reporter scurried into the courtroom like a mouse that didn't want to be seen. She set up her stand in front of the witness box, sat down, and nodded at the bailiff. "All rise," the bailiff said. Judge Driscoll appeared and trotted up the steps to the bench amid the sounds of scuffling feet.

"The Superior Court in and for the County of Fulton now in session," the bailiff intoned. "Honorable Samuel W. Driscoll presiding."

"Be seated, please," Driscoll said. He waited for the room to settle down. "For the record, I note the defendant is here with his lawyer, Abraham Fortanier. The State of Georgia is represented by the special prosecutor, Frances Rommel.

"We are here in the matter of the State of Georgia against Randolph Richardson." He poured water from the pitcher on his bench into a small cup. "Are the parties ready to proceed?"

"Defendant is ready, sir," Fortanier said, standing quickly.

"Yes, sir," Frankie said, also standing.

Driscoll drank from the cup. "Mr. Fortanier, have you been provided with a copy of the indictment?"

"I have."

"Just so I'm straight. Are you entering an appearance only, asking that the arraignment be set later, so you will have time to file motions? Or do we take his plea now?"

"If it please the Court, it is my desire to enter his plea now. I intend to file one motion only, and I have it with me. It is a demand for trial at the earliest possible date and is designed to start the clock on speedy trial." He started to hand a copy of the motion to Frankie.

"Excuse me, Mr. Fortanier," Driscoll said. "I believe the demand should be filed after the arraignment. A technical point, but just to be safe."

Fortanier smiled with self-deprecation and nodded courteously at Frankie. "I've already given a copy to the prosecutor, Judge. Should she give it back?"

"No. We'll work it out. Will the defendant please rise?"

Frankie, holding the motion in her hand, sat down. The first thrill of battle, like a small electric shock, bit into her. Defendants often tried the tactic of delay, but these guys wanted to get it on.

Rather lazily Richardson got to his feet. He looked cool and relaxed, wearing a navy blue single-breasted suit with no vest. Frankie knew she wasn't the only person in the courtroom who could feel his charisma. He had some kind of star quality even the judge seemed to acknowledge. "Mr. Richardson—or Colonel Richardson— How should I address you, sir?"

"You couldn't promote me to general?"

Frankie joined the others in laughter, although Driscoll did not smile. "No."

Richardson apparently realized he had made a mistake. "Colonel Richardson, sir," he said respectfully.

Driscoll pushed his glasses back on his nose and picked up the document in front of him. "Thank you, Colonel. I will now read the indictment." He thumbed through it quickly. "It's somewhat lengthy. The first three counts go to Charles Williams and the rest charge crimes against Andrew Boatwright." The judge peered over his glasses at the defendant. "After each count, I'll stop to ask you to plead to that count. Do you understand?"

"Yes, sir."

"Very well. This is Georgia, Fulton County. The grand jurors selected, chosen, and sworn to the County of Fulton, to wit." He paused and glanced up. "Mr. Fortanier, would you waive the reading of the names of the jurors?"

"Yes, Judge, I will spare them that embarrassment."

Discoll frowned his displeasure at the small lawyer. "Continuing. In the name and on behalf of the citizens of Georgia, charge and accuse you, Randolph Richardson, with having committed the offense of murder"—a sound, a collective intake of breath, whispered through the room—"for that the said Randolph Richardson, on or about the twenty-third day of April of this year, in Fulton County, with malice aforethought, did cause the death of another human being, to wit: Charles Williams, contrary to the laws of the state of Georgia and the good order, peace, and dignity thereof." Driscoll stared over the document in his hand. "How say you, sir? Guilty or not guilty?"

Richardson turned to Frankie. She tried to look away but couldn't. She could see pain and something else in his face. Playfulness? "I wouldn't swear to the date, sir."

"Ask the remark be stricken as not responsive," Fortanier shouted quickly.

"Motion granted. Colonel Richardson, how say you, sir?"

Richardson seemed amused at the consternation of his lawyer. "Not guilty, sir."

Warily, as though not certain what to expect, Driscoll started reading again. "And the jurors aforesaid, in the name and on behalf of the citizens of Georgia, further charge and accuse Randolph Richardson with having committed the offense of murder, for that the said Randolph Richardson, on or about the twenty-third day of April of this year, in Fulton County, when in the commission of a felony, did cause the death of another human being, to wit: Charles Williams, contrary to the laws of the state of Georgia and the good order, peace, and dignity thereof." He looked at Richardson. "How say you, sir, and please confine your response to 'guilty' or 'not guilty.' "

Richardson appeared perplexed. "Begging the Court's pardon, sir, but that sounds just like the other one to me."

"There is a technical difference, Colonel. The first count is called 'malice murder' and this count is called 'felony murder.' I'm sure your lawyer will be glad to explain."

Fortanier whispered a couple of words, and Richardson shrugged as though bored. "Not guilty."

Driscoll appeared more comfortable. "Count three," he said. "And the jurors aforesaid, in the name and on behalf of the citizens of Georgia, further charge and accuse Randolph Richardson with having committed the offense of aggravated assault, for that the said Randolph Richardson, on or about the twenty-third day of April of this year, in Fulton County, assaulted Charles Williams with various objects, devices, or instruments which, when used offensively against the person of the said Charles Williams, resulted in serious bodily injury.

"How say you, Colonel. Guilty or not guilty?"

"Not guilty."

Frankie felt warmth to the left side of her body, as though the sun had broken through a cloud and shone on it. The heat came from the direction of Richardson. How can that be? she asked herself. He's twenty feet away!

Three other counts were read, charging the same crimes against Andrew Boatwright, on April 24. Richardson dutifully pleaded not guilty.

"Thank you, Colonel. You can sit down."

Other matters were quickly resolved. Frankie agreed to bail in the amount of twenty thousand dollars—extremely low for a capital case, but she knew she would lose any argument. "Mr. Fortanier, you have a motion?" Driscoll leaned forward with his hand extended, inviting the lawyer to approach the bench.

"Yes, sir." Fortanier quickly stepped around the table and gave a pleading to the judge. "So the record is clear, I am at this time filing a Demand for Trial, and I have previously given a copy to the prosecutor. In order to avoid misunderstanding I wish to put her on notice now that the defendant will stand on his right to a speedy trial."

"I see," Driscoll said. "Well. Do you want any time at all for the filing of motions, demurrers, or special pleas?"

"No, sir. It is our desire to proceed to trial as rapidly as possible. And in that connection, I would request that the Court order the prosecutor to make her election regarding the death penalty in one week. There is a new procedure now—"

"Yes, I am aware of it. Miss Rommel? Can you decide in a week?"

Frankie tried to sound as tough as Fortanier. "Yes, sir. The state of Georgia will make every effort to accommodate the defense in its desire for a speedy trial."

Court was adjourned. She tried to avoid Richardson's soft stare but couldn't.

The bastard winked at her.

Doug Swift picked Frankie up that night at seven and tossed her bags in the trunk of his car. Her flight to Denver would leave shortly before eight. The air felt warm, and the sky was clean. She had already missed her vacation and didn't feel like scuba diving now anyway. She would like to remain in Atlanta.

"When will you be back?" Swift asked, turning onto the freeway.

"That will depend on Fortanier. He said he wouldn't, but he still might file something fancy that'll require a hearing. I hope so."

"Why?"

"Because if he doesn't, we might find ourselves in trial in six months."

"You'll be here then, won't you?"

She smiled at him. "Wouldn't miss it."

As they drove in silence Frankie looked out the window and saw her reflection on its surface. She liked the mouth, but not the smile. It was the determined smile of an old-maid aunt.

"Some fancy footwork going on?" Swift asked, slowing to let a car pull in front of him.

"Or lack of it." She stared past her image toward the line of hills in the western sky. "He wants us on the defensive, which is different. Usually the prosecution attacks, pushing for trial, while the defense covers and protects. But I'm in no hurry. And Fortanier is."

"Why?"

"Randolph is this huge hero." She realized that again she'd called Richardson by his first name. Swift didn't seem to notice. "They want to try him fast, before the public finds out he has clay feet." She rolled down the window and lit the cigarette in her hand. "We're on the slow side, hoping for a break. Like some solid evidence on Brown."

Swift glanced at her. "What do you think, Frankie? Does he have clay feet?"

"You know him better than I do," she said. "You tell me."

"Talk to you real?" he asked. "Like in 'get real?' "

"If you want."

"The way he looks at you and the way you look at him, I think you know him pretty good."

Frankie stared quietly out the window. Apparently he'd heard her slip after all. But his voice was gentle and full of understanding, and she wanted so much to talk to someone about it. "He's an attractive man."

Swift waited for more. "To you, maybe," he finally said. "He's got too much cheekbone for my taste."

Frankie laughed. But it didn't feel right; she couldn't say anything else. She took a short drag on her cigarette and folded her arms, feeling alone.

"You know something?" Swift said, his voice not much more than a whisper. "This thing with Dogwood gonna keep me awake at night. That boy would be alive if I had good sense."

"Don't do that to yourself. You don't know." She looked toward him and tried to sound tough. "No great loss to mankind, Doug. He isn't worth your sleep."

"What do you know?" Swift asked her, speaking sharply. His rebuke surprised her. "Sorry," he said a moment later. "Ever wonder why you do what you do? I'd like to know how come I'm a cop."

She laughed, feeling better. "Easy money?"

"Must be it. What can you do about Brown now?"

"Nothing." She inhaled slowly and deeply, thinking about it. "All we have is the uncorroborated hearsay statement of a dead man. That isn't enough for an indictment. For all we know, by the time we go to trial old what's-his-name—Harold 'Happy Face' Munroe?—will have been found guilty of Brown's murder."

"Could that happen?"

"My dear. Be serious."

"But we've got that tape. If Happy Face gets a lawyer, won't his lawyer get a copy? And what about Fortanier? What's he gonna do when he finds out about it?"

"We don't tell Abe Fortanier anything. Under Georgia law he has no right—at least at this point—to that information. If he knew we suspected Richardson of *that* one, he might get right in the middle of the investigation and muck it up."

"Abe spoke at Maurice Brown's funeral." Doug looked at her. "You know, if he thought Richardson killed him, I think he'd dump the old man down the toilet. He and Maurice were close."

"*That's* an interesting wrinkle. I could drop a hint." She smiled at her reflection. "Am I that rotten? Yes!"

"Can you do that?"

"I could, but I won't." She fiddled with the door latch. "My trouble—yours, too, isn't it?—is that I believe in what I do. The system works, if you let it. I'm a white hat. I believe in the rules and play by them."

"Instead of 'white hat,' how about 'good guy?' I mean, if you want me on your team?"

She hadn't realized what she had said. "I'm sorry."

"Some system, too. Didn't you almost deal it down to manslaughter?"

"Yes."

"But you didn't because he killed Maurice Brown, just that we can't prove it?"

"That's right, too."

"So we bring him to justice over what he did that we can't prove?"

"You should have been a lawyer, Doug. You ask good questions."

"And we don't even tell him the real reason?"

"Damn." It could have been, she thought. Her eyes reddened, and she looked away, hoping Swift wouldn't see and knowing he would, because the man saw everything. She worked the wetness into her skin.

"Talk real again?"

"Go ahead."

"Your feelings. Will they get in the way?"

Once again she thought she heard understanding. "I don't know," she said. "I don't think so."

"Should you be trying this case, Frankie?"

"Yes." She flipped the cigarette out the window and rolled it up after taking a sudden wave of cold air. "If I don't do it, there won't even be a trial."

"How come?"

"Because a new prosecutor would have to be appointed, and Slade will give a litmus test. The next person will have to agree to cop Richardson out to a manslaughter."

"Would that be bad, Frankie? I mean, this case is strange." He looked perplexed. "I don't understand my own feelings. I'm not a head-knocker. I'm not the kind of cop who wants to nail everybody's ass to the cross. I love the man, too. But I want him for murder."

"You should." She saw him peer at her over his shoulder. "This one goes beyond the simplicity of 'did he or didn't he.' Look at the real issue. Does the end justify the means, or doesn't it?"

"As important as all that?"

"Yes." Frankie tried to articulate how she felt. It was more than a head game. Her guts were in it, too. "So many people want to forgive him. God knows I did. I wanted to wink at what he did, but that would be so wrong." She remembered, long ago, imagining how Joan of Arc felt when leading her troops into battle: filled—consumed—with gratitude for the opportunity to fight for what was right. Frankie had been so proud of the fact that she was a lawyer. "We tell ourselves there is this war on drugs that we must win," she said, angrily brushing at a tear. "It's so easy to slide into a war mentality—you know? Like 'All's fair in love and war'—even when we're not really at war at all! That is so wrong. It's one step from totalitarianism."

Swift smiled. "Kind of like 'God is on our side?'"

She nodded, understanding him perfectly. He had that good, healthy democratic doubt that the good old USA is all about. "You got it."

"What if Richardson didn't kill Maurice, Frankie? What if old Happy Face is telling the truth? Would you still go after Richardson for murder?"

"Yes." She looked at her reflection in the window again and saw pain. "It's the principle, Doug. It wouldn't be the first time the right thing was done for the wrong reason."

"I don't know," Swift said. "You're tougher than me."

"What about Dogwood? Didn't Richardson kill him, too?" Angrily she brushed at her skirt. "That was so phony in court today. All those cops hanging off the walls, ready to leap into action at the blink of any eye. It was an armed camp in there!"

"The tip was real, Frankie."

She turned toward Swift, watching him carefully. "He didn't do it? His life really is in danger?"

"Richardson was on the golf course when Dogwood was hit."

"He could have had it done."

"I don't think so. Not his style."

"Then what's going on?"

"A big void in the drug world right now, and it's filling up. This is very confidential."

"Don't worry."

"There's a new group establishing themselves, and the word on the street is they're showing their muscle." He slowed to let a car with a blinking signal turn in front of him. "What they say now is if you don't get Richardson, they will."

Part
Two

Part

Two

office had obtained guilty pleas in two of the

Chapter
17

Monday, October 25 • Atlanta, Georgia

FRANKIE SAT ALONE AT COUNSEL TABLE WAITING FOR THE trial to begin. Fortanier had been as good as his word. He had carefully jumped through all the procedural hoops erected by the law of Georgia to compel a speedy trial, and it was now or never.

There had not even been one pretrial skirmish. At the very least Frankie had thought there would be a challenge to the sufficiency of the indictment. But Fortanier had done nothing. No *Brady* motion for discovery. No motion for a *Jackson-Denno* hearing. No motion *in limine,* to limit the prosecution's proof. In a headlong rush to stand on their right to a speedy trial Fortanier had decided not to ask for anything that could cause delay.

It was a gutsy maneuver, one Frankie had seen work before. She had seen cases lost by prosecutors who were rushed to trial, then found they weren't prepared. She had spent the last two weeks scrambling to get this one ready.

The tactic bestowed other benefits on the defense. The Fulton County district attorney—although neutral in his press releases—was obviously on Richardson's side. Slade's office had obtained guilty pleas in two of the seven drug cases attributed to the Marine war hero; three of the remaining five were expected to plead guilty. Drug-related crime and drug-related deaths, according to the media, were measurably down. Richardson's actions were cited by authorities as the reason. The climate could not have been more favorable to the defense. Three of the five people pictured in a recent newspaper opinion poll did not think the state should prosecute.

Frankie was also appalled regarding the murder of Maurice Brown, which she still believed Richardson had committed. Yet in Kafka-like fashion, Happy Face Munroe pled guilty, and his plea had been accepted! She provided a copy of Dogwood's statement to Munroe's lawyer and the prosecutor. What more could she do? Swift and Webster had quit working the case because there was nothing to work on.

Uniformed deputy sheriffs were spaced at intervals around the walls of the courtroom, acting with courtesy and authority, a mix between theater usher and crowd control. The first three rows of benches immediately behind the bar had been reserved for prospective jurors. They were spotted by the court clerk as soon as they came in the room, then escorted to front-row seats like privileged patrons of the arts at the opera. Apart from those rows, all other sitting space was filled.

The crowd seemed expectant and quiet. The noise level was less than a break between acts, but more than a funeral. It seemed to Frankie like the soft murmur of a theater crowd before the performance begins. When Richardson appeared wearing a light brown plaid suit and a solid green tie the room grew still. As he walked down the center aisle whispers and gestures trailed along behind him like shadows.

Frankie hadn't talked to him since before the grand jury indictment. She monitored her feelings. There was no surge of anticipation, no giveaway glow or blush. She looked at him easily, acknowledged his nod, and broke off the contact.

Doug Swift dropped into the chair next to her, his muscled body hidden under a sky-blue suit. Frankie smiled, genuinely glad to see him. She had come to rely on his quiet competence and trusted his judgment and instincts. "How're you doing?" he asked.

"My normal pretrial jitters," she said. "I've been bolted to a railroad track, and here comes the train."

"You don't look it. You look cool."

Abraham Fortanier struggled down the aisle carrying a briefcase and some books. He looked somehow like an American flag: solid red tie, silver-white hair, and dark blue suit. Swift—always the gentleman—jumped up and opened the gate for him. "Thank you," Fortanier said. He nodded to Frankie. Their last few exchanges had been heated, but he showed no anger. "You look very nice, Miss Rommel," he told her. "Far too nice to be a prosecutor."

"Thank you," she said, smiling pleasantly. "What are all those books for? Did I forget something?"

"I hope so."

Many times in the last few days Frankie had tried anticipating the defense. Obviously Fortanier would put the victims on trial; she had heard the lawyers joke that Boatwright and Williams were lucky they were dead. But what would be the peg the defense would offer the jury to hang its hat on? What would be the legal excuse offered for a defense verdict? And what was the defense really after? An acquittal? Manslaughter?

More and more people crowded into the room, and at five after nine the last of the prospective jurors were seated. Frankie felt their eyes upon her and tried to act normally. She had deliberately chosen an off-white tailored dress suit that reached over her knees. Trigge called it her "suit of shining armor," and she knew she wore it well.

The entrance doors were shut, and a deputy stationed himself in the hall where he could tell the curious there was no place to sit. Frankie was amazed at how courteous the jurors were. No one had shoved or pushed; people had made way for others. A kind of gentility resonated throughout. She had a sense of quiet humor and spoiled dreams. The women—black and white—appeared content to be women, although many of the men stood out like symbols. Some of them seemed literally to have transformed their bodies into statements. She saw the quintessential college professor, the quintessential handyman in bib overalls, even the prototypical fuck-up with a coat that didn't fit, a loose tie that didn't match, and the grin of a clown.

Which of them would make better jurors for the prosecution, she wondered? The men—some of whom looked like cartoons—or the sensible-appearing women? To further complicate matters, she had filed a Notice of Intention to Seek the Death Penalty in an effort to turn up the heat. Now she was stuck with it. Instead of a "normal" jury—of course, there was no such thing—this one would be death-qualified.

The little court reporter bustled into the room and set up her box on top of its tripod. Frankie could not understand why the woman annoyed her so much, but everytime she saw her she wanted to grab her by the rib cage and rattle her teeth. The court reporter nodded at the bailiff.

"All rise," the bailiff announced. "Superior Court in and for the county of Fulton is in session, Honorable Sam Driscoll presiding."

Driscoll trotted briskly up the steps to his chair behind the bench, told everyone to take a seat, and sat down. He adjusted his glasses and opened the file that had been placed on the polished wooden surface of the bench. He began announcing the case before people were seated like a Catholic priest rushing through mass. "Georgia versus Randolph Richardson, and it comes on this day for a trial to a jury." No one in the back could have heard him, but the court reporter took it all down. Her fingers appeared to move slowly to the cadence of the judge's voice. "I note the defendant filed a demand for trial," Driscoll said, "and that at previous terms of court juries were impaneled and qualified to try the defendant. The defendant has been present and announced ready for trial every time, but the state announced not ready.

"Miss Rommel, you are here to prosecute this case on behalf of the State of Georgia?"

Frankie stood up. "I am, Your Honor."

"It is my duty to advise you that if the state is not ready, I will have no alternative except to discharge and acquit the defendant. Are you ready for trial?"

The acrimony between the lawyers was not untypical for a capital case. In the past Frankie had enjoyed it, but not this time. She had the impish temptation to avoid the ensuing battle by making the simple pronouncement of not ready. She smiled. "The State of Georgia announces ready for trial, Judge."

"Mr. Fortanier, is the defendant Randolph Richardson ready?"

"Most assuredly," Fortanier said, not quite standing. "As he has been for several months." He dropped back into his chair.

"Very well. I note an array of jurors is present"—he nodded at the prospective jurors seated in the first two rows—"and the clerk is prepared to read their names from the list." In a loud voice: "Ladies and gentlemen, as your name is called, please stand for a moment so the lawyers can see you."

Fortanier swiveled around in his chair and smiled at the sea of faces as the clerk read from her list. Rommel, feeling a bit like monkey-see-monkey-do, did the same. Swift agreeably did as the others were doing, but Richardson appeared reluctant. He needed a poke from Fortanier before turning and facing the people seated behind the bar.

Frankie felt a twinge of something for the man. Compassion? Whatever it was, she quickly buried it. Tall, thin, casually graceful in his movements, he had the aspect of a king brought to trial in a foreign land. If he was aware of the fact she looked at him, he didn't show it.

As their names were called the prospective jurors stood for a moment, then sat down. The lawyers quickly compared the faces with the names on their list. Frankie liked the balance. Half were black, half were women, and the age mix ranged from eighteen to seventy. She smiled at the ones who looked at her as though they were being introduced. She wanted to know them and had enough confidence in herself to want them to know her. But Richardson's peers? she wondered—then she ordered herself not to think about it. Fortanier knew these people better than she did. She couldn't let herself worry about the man. She also had the uncomfortable feeling that the trial—this trial—could be lost in jury selection.

"Will there be a challenge to the array?" Driscoll asked, directing his question at Fortanier.

The small man stood and faced the judge. "The array of jurors is to be composed of intelligent and upright citizens, isn't it, sir?" he asked in his soft, penetrating voice. His manner suggested a serious problem. "I observe *most* of them look all right, but I saw a couple in there I'm not sure of."

There was some laughter, although it was apparent that Driscoll was not amused. "Mr. Fortanier, I can provide you with the opportunity to challenge the array in private, sir."

"That won't be necessary, Judge," Fortanier said, preparing to sit down. "We do not challenge the array."

"Counsel will please approach the bench," Driscoll ordered.

Frankie quickly walked to the bench, where she huddled with Fortanier and the judge. Driscoll spoke softly, not wanting even the court reporter to hear him. As he spoke he kept his head and eyes down so no one could know whom he talked to.

"Mr. Fortanier, this is a court of law," he said. "You will refrain from your comedic efforts. I deem it an attempt to ingratiate yourself with the jury and consider it unethical. Do I make myself clear?"

Fortanier smiled benignly and stared at the floor. "Perhaps we should be on the record, if it please the Court," he said in the same low tone. "I feel the Court may try to intimidate me. If successful, that could deny my client his Sixth Amendment right to representation by counsel, and a record should be made."

"Intimidate you, sir? That will be the day! I merely point out to you that effective assistance of counsel does not carry the right to ingratiate yourself with this jury or turn this trial into a performance. I am putting you on notice at this time that I will resist any such efforts on your part, and I believe you know what I mean."

"My apology, but I must request we go on the record, sir," Fortanier said. "I have to know exactly what you mean."

"You will have your opportunity, Mr. Fortanier. However, at the present time we will get on with it. Please resume—"

"When, if it please the Court?"

"When there is time. Please resume your chairs."

Frankie was nasty enough to enjoy watching them fence with each other. She also sent body signals of support to Judge Driscoll and frowned at Fortanier in a nonverbal effort to tell the judge she approved of his desire to conduct a fair trial. She wanted him to know she would join him in thwarting the defense lawyer, who was bent on tipping the scales to favor his client—which, of course, was his job.

Fortanier smiled benignly. "Thank you, Judge," he said aloud. To everyone else in the courtroom it looked as though he had won the argument. Then, with courtesy, he ushered Frankie to her chair.

The little fucker is *good*, Frankie thought, wondering what she would have done if he'd held the chair for her.

"Will all those persons whose names were called by the clerk raise their right hand?" Driscoll requested. The prospective jurors lifted their hands, and Driscoll swore them to truthfully answer all questions put to them. He went on to explain that the questions were to determine their suitability to serve as jurors in the case. When Driscoll introduced the lawyers and the defendant Frankie stood gravely a moment, then sat down.

It is like live theater, Frankie thought, watching them. So far they seem to like the play. "Miss Rommel?" Driscoll asked, turning the stage over to her.

Frankie had familiarized herself with Georgia trial practice, in which the prosecutor reads the indictment to the array of jurors. Standing and smiling nicely, she turned the lectern around so it faced them. "Ladies and gentlemen," Frankie said to them from behind the lectern. "The defendant, Randolph Richardson, has been charged with the murder of two persons." She spoke pleasantly and confidently, knowing her voice carried through the room. "The indictment is in six counts." She showed them the copy in her hand. Here and there she made eye contact. "The first count charges that Randolph Richardson committed murder, in that on or about April twenty-third of this year, in Fulton County, with malice aforethought, he caused the death of another human being, to wit: Charles Williams, contrary to the laws of the state of Georgia and the good order, peace, and dignity thereof."

At first the words were merely words, and her part in the play was simply to recite them. But she wondered at their impact on the array. "The second count . . ." As she continued the mechanical quality lessened, and the reality of the situation took hold. How civilized all this is, she thought. ". . . assaulted Charles Williams with various objects, devices, or instruments . . ." When she reached that point she always seemed to reach. The reading of the indictment stopped being a performance. She knew what the words referred to. She could see the rack and watch a man's body as it twisted in a futile effort to avoid a "cure." "The fifth count . . ." Her voice was charged with quiet outrage. Even Fortanier sat riveted by the obvious depth of her conviction.

Murder is monstrous, the woman in her seemed to shout. She could feel the electricity in her body and the intensity of the vibrations that radiated out. This handsome, clean-looking gentleman is a murderer, her heart and soul said—and she glared toward him.

Richardson—still as a statue—stared at the floor.

Frankie liked the approach to jury selection provided by the statutes in Georgia. It was not a task that would consume weeks, as it could be in California. Even in a capital murder case, where the jury had to be death-qualified, one might be selected in less than a day. And in Georgia the combatants didn't "select" a jury. They would "strike" one from the array, as a sculptor might cut a statue out of a block of marble.

She read the statutory questions to the prospective jurors, letting the language soak through her mind and body. She loved its cadence, knowing it to be rooted in their consciousness, as was the Bible and, to a lesser extent, *Gone With the Wind*.

"Have you, for any reason, formed and expressed any opinion in regard to the guilt or innocence of the accused?" she asked of all of them—and many of them admitted that they had. She would like to know which way they felt, but the rules didn't permit her to ask. She would have to guess.

"Can you lay aside your impression or opinion and render a verdict based on the evidence presented in court?" They said they could. "Have you any prejudice or bias resting in your mind either for or against the accused?" Oh, no. "Is your mind perfectly impartial between the State and the accused?" Yes, of course. "Are you conscientiously opposed to capital punishment?" A few of them were. At that point Driscoll would take over the questioning.

"Mrs. Buchanan, you have indicated you are conscientiously opposed to capital punishment?" he asked a matronly looking woman in her late forties.

"Yes, Your Honor."

"Is your conviction such that you would not vote for the death penalty under any circumstances?"

"Well, Your Honor, I'm not sure I know what you mean." She spoke very thoughtfully.

"I am reluctant to suggest examples, Mrs. Buchanan. However, I note some hesitation on your part. Are your reservations about capital punishment such that you could not under any circumstance vote to impose the death penalty, regardless of the evidence and instructions of the court?"

"My goodness. If Mr. Richardson had set off a bomb at Falcons Stad—"

"Excuse me, madam. I must interrupt. I hear you say you might be willing to impose it in the right circumstance? That your reservations are not such that you would absolutely refuse even to consider it?"

The woman thought it over carefully. "I would consider it. But it's very unlikely that I could vote for it."

The State of Georgia is in a box, Frankie thought. I am asking for the death penalty but don't want a panel of flag-wavers. I want thoughtful, intelligent people who believe in the exercise of law—like this woman. Yet she may be excused because she doesn't believe in the death penalty! She felt Fortanier's benign smile and resisted the temptation to look at him. He's in a box, too, she thought. Instead of thoughtful, intelligent people who know what reasonable doubt means, he wants super-patriots who have total faith in the military solution. Most of them are all for the death penalty, but would never vote to execute a man like Richardson. All Randolph has to do is wear his Medal of Honor to court—

He's not 'Randolph' anymore, she thought, glaring at the defendant. What is wrong with him anyway? He won't even look at me!

"Will counsel approach the bench?" Driscoll asked.

When the attorneys were before him he asked whether either of them would challenge the juror for cause. "I have no basis, unfortunately," Fortanier said. "What can I say? She isn't competent because she can't vote to execute my client?"

"Miss Rommel?"

"I like her," Frankie said.

Driscoll recognized the dilemma both lawyers faced. "We might strike a jury in record time," he said. "Miss Rommel, are you prepared to put evidence on today?"

"That would be awfully hard, Judge. I'm still working on an opening statement."

"Abe?"

"Judge, my secretary is in the process of finalizing a motion I intend to file today. I will need a ruling on it before opening argument."

"Is it something we should take up before we get a jury?"

"No, sir. As a matter of fact, for tactical reasons, I won't file it until after we've struck the jury."

Driscoll avoided looking at Frankie. Both of them knew a defense motion at this stage could keep them up all night. "We won't start until tomorrow, then. Do you want to go on record regarding my alleged attempts to intimidate you?"

Fortanier smiled. "That was just for exercise, Abe," he said. "I just wanted to feel like I was in trial."

What a lovable little bastard, Frankie thought when they went back to work. The first thing Fortanier did was exercise one of his "peremptory" challenges and excuse Buchanan.

Shortly after noon Driscoll called a recess until one-thirty P.M. Frankie walked with Doug Swift across the street to a hole-in-the-wall of an old building called the Greek Diner. "I heard lawyers are temperamental, like actors," he said. "Do you want to sit by yourself so you can rehearse your lines?"

"No!" she said. "I want company. Where's Leon?"

"He'll be back after lunch. He went to get the rack."

Frankie shuddered as she thought of the wooden slab to which Richardson had lashed his victims. "Don't let him bring it into the courtroom," she said. "Not while we're striking a jury. We could have a mistrial if one of them sees it."

"There's a little room between the judge's chambers and the courtroom," Swift told her. "Judge says put it in there."

Frankie ordered a Greek salad and pita bread; Swift a huge salad and a baked potato. Frankie took a sip from her cup of coffee. "I don't need this stuff," she said. "I'm wired now."

"Nobody would know that."

"How do you like the jury?"

"A couple you don't need. That guy Jensen has a gleam in his eye." Swift referred to an elderly white man, a retired engineer from Massachusetts. "He looks at Richardson like a disciple looking at Jesus, you know. Kind of worshipful."

"This is weird," Frankie said. "I'm satisfied with a lot of defense types, and Fortanier wants convicters!"

"He does?"

"Look at Jensen. An older man, wonderfully conservative, who wants to preserve what he's worked for all his life. He's itching to take a bite out of crime. Add his background. Engineers *think* right as far as prosecutors are concerned. They are rational rather than emotional. Their world operates in cause–effect terms. It helps them see a relationship between crime and punishment." She jerked the coffee toward her mouth for another sip, spilling some. "I've never tried a case where he wouldn't be perfect for me—until this one. And you're right. It's because of that gleam in his eye."

"All that go through your mind with each juror?"

"It never works, either. I'll get people who are perfect,

only to find out later they *hated* me because I reminded them of their husband's second wife!''

"What about Buchanan?" Swift asked, referring to the woman who would have had difficulty voting for death. "Fortanier kicked her off. I thought you would."

"Another example. Too much intelligence for the prosecution." She smiled at the irony. "She could obviously make distinctions and have doubts. A perfect juror for the defense." She drew a line down the water glass through the moisture. "But *I* want her in this case because she's smart enough to understand what's really at stake, and woman enough to appreciate the horror of murder. So he kicked her off." She fiddled with her fork. "I won't get the death penalty anyway."

"Why did you ask for it?"

"We're playing hardball. Also, I don't want the jury to feel absolutely awful if and when they convict him. They can give him life in prison."

"You know as good as me what prison will do to him, don't you?" Swift asked.

"Oh, good. You're telling me if we win it will kill him." She smiled. "I know. I hate it."

"A suggestion about the jury?"

"Sure."

"Get as many blacks as you can."

The waiter arrived, spreading food on their table. "I've had that feeling," Frankie said, putting cheese in her bread. "Why?"

"The dumbest black in Atlanta is intelligent when it comes to understanding what the law is about. Isn't any of us who don't want the law to protect us from vigilantes."

"Black women, too?"

"Black women mainly." Swift poured ketchup on his potato. "My mom was a cleaning woman, told me that's how come she was so smart. When you're on your hands and knees scrubbing somebody else's kitchen floor you've got time to think."

"We're being a bit dramatic, aren't we?" Frankie asked, stabbing lettuce with her fork.

"Maybe. But it's good advice."

"I have a problem with it, though," Frankie said. "Doug, do I talk down to you?"

"No. I mean, if you do, I'm down there where I don't notice it. Why?"

"I hate to say this, but what if I am prejudiced and don't know it?" She didn't tell him about her experience as a civil rights activist, when she'd been raped.

A flicker of irritation showed on Swift's face. "Who isn't?"

"The question is, do I relate well to black people? The trial could last weeks."

"Don't worry about it," Swift said. "You'll do fine."

How odd, Frankie thought. This man reminds me of my grandfather.

Every state is different, Frankie found. In Georgia the lawyers were not allowed to question jurors hypothetically about the facts of the case. As a prosecutor, Frankie approved. She had seen too many cases where voir dire was converted into a long-drawn-out minitrial and the jurors were brainwashed like political prisoners. Any advantage to the state was balanced by granting the defendant the right to challenge and excuse more prospective jurors. The defense had twice as many peremptory challenges as the State.

Frankie had ten peremptories, Fortanier twenty. Frankie—who huddled with Swift at each opportunity—used all of hers. Fortanier—who couldn't seem to arouse his client's interest—used eighteen of his. At four P.M. a jury had been struck from the array: twelve members and two alternates. Of the twelve, seven were black: four women and three men. Of the five whites, three were men and two were women. They ranged in age from twenty to fifty-eight.

The jury was sworn, admonished, then placed in the custody of the baliff. Very few spectators had stayed in the courtroom through jury selection, and the few who remained left when the jury did. "Is there anything further?" Driscoll asked before recessing. He looked at Fortanier.

"Yes, sir," the small man said. He looked as relaxed as

though he'd spent the day at the movies. "Request permission to file a motion."

"Granted. Let me see it. What's in it?"

Fortanier strolled easily up to the bench and handed Driscoll a fifteen-page document. "It's for an affirmative defense," he said, giving Frankie a copy.

Frankie was tired. She wanted to kick off her shoes and spread her toes. But she got to her feet impatiently, glancing at the thing, ready to object. "Miss Rommel?"

"An affirmative defense in this case?" she asked. "Doesn't the concept refer to such things as self-defense, or killing in the defense of another?"

"I am as curious as you are, Miss Rommel. It hardly seems appropriate. However"—he adjusted his spectacles—"perhaps we should read it." He frowned, concentrating momentarily on the first page. "What is your request, Mr. Fortanier?"

"As the Court well knows, before a defendant in Georgia can prove up an affirmative defense he must first make a prima facie showing that he is entitled to one. We are asserting here that Colonel Richardson was justified in his conduct. Of course, I can't put on evidence to show he was justified until it is my turn, but I need a ruling at this stage so I can argue the point in my opening remarks to the jury."

Frankie was heartened by the skeptical smile on Judge Driscoll's face. She smiled, too, as their eyes met. A typical bullshit motion we have to wade through, his eyes seemed to say, before getting to the guts of the case. "Well, I'll read it tonight," Driscoll said, "and we can take it up in the morning. All right?" He stood up. "If there's nothing further, we are adjourned."

As Frankie stuffed the motion in her briefcase she realized she had expected more from Fortanier than some last-ditch maneuver that seemed destined to fail before it started. What could possibly be the legal justification for the murder of two men who had been tied up and tortured to death? Often a case will break apart for a defense lawyer, she thought, and in desperation he will try some of the dumbest tricks. She wondered if that had happened to

Fortanier. She felt genuinely sorry for him and wished the ice would break so they could at least talk.

Leon Webster banged into the courtroom, looked around until he spotted Frankie, then charged down the aisle. He broke through the gate in the bar, a trickle of sweat running down his cheek. "Can we talk a minute, counselor?" he asked.

Webster did not want to be overheard. They moved over by the jury box, and Frankie's eyes touched those of Richardson. He nodded with courtesy, then looked away.

"How important is that splinter?" Webster whispered.

"Don't tell me. You've lost it."

"Not quite. I mean we don't know exactly where it is, but—"

"If you can't find it, it's lost. What happened?" She had the sudden vision of losing the entire case involving Williams.

"Frankie, that isn't the problem. Dr. Riposa, the expert? The guy who can identify the splinter?"

"Yes. What about him?"

"He had a heart attack. He's in intensive care."

"The jerk!" Frankie exploded. "Why didn't he take better care of himself?" She realized how she sounded. She and Webster burst into laughter.

Fortanier—shoveling books into his briefcase—glanced at them with disdain. Richardson looked toward them with a question. "What happened?" Swift asked. "Leon, did you finally get a punch line right?"

"Abe," Frankie said, walking across the room. They hadn't been on a first-name basis since the grand jury indictment, and she corrected herself. "Mr. Fortanier, something has come to my attention you need to know about."

"Apparently."

"Dr. Riposa, our sliver expert? He's suffered a heart attack."

Fortanier smiled. "How very unfortunate. I will instruct my secretary to send a get-well card. Or is it too late?"

"He's alive. He's—where, Leon?"

"Mercy Medical."

"Can we enter into a stipulation regarding his testimony?" Frankie asked.

"My dear woman. Of course not." He snapped the case shut. "Miss Rommel. I have never been so outraged at the conduct of an attorney in all my life. Perhaps it's because my expectations—after our first meeting—were high. But—"

"Abe." Richardson's voice had the unfathomable ability to interrupt anything, even a presidential debate. It goes with the medal, Frankie thought. "You don't know what you are talking about," he said.

"There. You see? Ask my client, Miss Rommel. Or should I say our client. I'm sure he'll stipulate to whatever you wish."

"I don't need this," Frankie said.

"Nor do I." Fortanier blasted through the gate. "Randolph, are you coming with me or—"

"Wait." Richardson's quiet voice once again stopped the world. He looked at Frankie with warmth, an expression she remembered from their day in the mountains. His eyes surrounded her and seemed to hold her without hanging on. "Abe talks too much, Miss Rommel, even for a lawyer. Please accept my apology on his behalf."

Chapter

18

Tuesday, October 26

"JUDGE WANTS US IN CHAMBERS, FRANKIE."

She had been sitting at counsel table concentrating on her notes, having shut out the sounds of the courtroom. When Leon Webster touched her shoulder it took a moment for his words to register. "What for? That bullshit motion?" she asked, turning her chair and sliding out from under the table.

"Something else." Webster glanced around as though not wanting to take a chance on being overheard.

"Where are Fortanier and Richardson?"

"They're in there."

Frankie led the way. She hated the turn her relationship with Fortanier had taken. She liked him and knew that under other circumstances, trying a case against him would have been fun. But the formality he had imposed was awful, as though that was the only way he could control his rage.

She wondered if it was part of his battle plan. Possibly it was simply a very good act. If that was the situation, fine, she could deal with that. And if that's what it was, sooner or later she'd smell it.

197

Webster reached in front of her and opened the door. Judge Driscoll, Fortanier, Richardson, and Doug Swift were seated around the conference table. The large piece of furniture—usually snubbed up against Driscoll's desk—had been pushed forward so everyone could sit around it. She nodded a greeting at Driscoll and Mrs. Hanks, the court reporter, whom Frankie had dubbed "the bird lady." Richardson—perhaps to spare her embarrassment—avoided her quick glance, and Fortanier shot her a look filled with contempt. Swift sat at the arced end of the table. "Hi, Doug," she said, surprised—and glad—to see him. At least one friendly face, she thought. She and Webster sat down.

Driscoll nodded at Mrs. Hanks. "We're on the record," he said. "This is the State of Georgia versus Richardson, it's eight fifty-five A.M. Tuesday, October 26, and we're in chambers. Present are the following persons," and he named them. "A serious problem has come up. Miss Rommel, did you know that threats have been made against your life?"

Frankie jerked her head up from the notepad in front of her, very aware of a stab of fear. "No, but I'm not surprised." She straightened her back, smiling and fighting to avoid the bunker mentality that prosecutors often develop. "I won't say I'm used to it, Judge, but it happens. Usually"—she knocked on the wood surface—"it doesn't mean anything."

"Am I to infer you aren't concerned?" Driscoll asked.

"I'm very worried. Is that why Doug's here?"

"Yes." Driscoll rubbed a hand over his mouth as though to wipe off a particle of food. "Detective Swift approached me a few minutes ago. Apparently Swift and Colonel Richardson have also talked about it, as have Richardson and Mr. Fortanier."

"*That* could be awkward." Frankie questioned Swift with a frown. "I'm sure it is all well-intentioned, and I don't mean to sound ungrateful, but I would not be thrilled by a headline that said 'Defendant Saves Prosecutor's Life.'"

Richardson and Swift smiled, but Fortanier could not. "I will instruct my client that under no circumstances is he to save your life."

You unrelenting little shithead, Frankie thought. But at least his hostility was out there where it could be seen. "He's your client."

"Is he?"

Driscoll sagged wearily. Frankie could read the demeanor of his body because she'd seen it before, in judges and mothers. It said something like "Are these guys going to act their age or fight like two-year-olds?" "We need to find out the extent of these threats and decide what to do," he said.

Swift told what he knew: two death threats had been received in the district attorney's office the preceding afternoon. The operator who took the calls had been able to engage the caller in dialogue, in accordance with security procedures. Much of the conversations had been recorded. Swift had heard the tapes and thought they were the same person. That wouldn't be known, however, until a computer comparison—kind of a voice fingerprinting procedure—had been completed.

The best guess at the moment: dialect and voice patterns were those of a male, middle-class, middle-aged, white Georgian. The caller was on the line long enough for a telephone trace to start, and the general location of both calls was Stone Mountain. In view of the emergency Swift asked the defendant to listen to the tapes. He could not identify the speaker but provided names of individuals who had contacted him since the indictment—he termed them "droolers"—who fit the general profile.

Driscoll called for a discussion of options and offered one: postpone the trial until the caller could be identified. "I will object to a postponement," Fortanier said. "I would regard that as a denial of my client's right to a speedy trial."

Frankie didn't think there should be a postponement either. "I don't believe in clearing the building every time there's a bomb scare." She also observed that the defendant was under a similar cloud, and they talked about that: reports of the so-called street talk in recent newspaper articles. A new group of drug dealers had risen from the ashes of the defunct "Enterprise," according to the reporter. They even had a name: the Dead Poets. They were waiting for the trial to finish before meting out their own brand of justice on the life of Richardson.

A direct and provable threat on the life of the prosecutor was more serious, in Driscoll's view, than the rumors that formed the substance of a newspaper reporter's fantasy. "That stuff goes on all the time," he said. Nevertheless, he suggested trying the case where security might be better: another courtroom, another building, another county.

Webster stuck up his hand like a student in a classroom who wanted to talk. He said the sheriff's department had done some fairly elaborate planning for the trial based on its taking place in courtroom D. Moving the location would require new plans. Frankie added that she felt safe there, safer than on the street, but she requested permission to carry a concealed weapon and asked that Webster and Swift be allowed the same privilege. Driscoll told her it was up to the sheriff, but he would recommend it.

"What about my client?" Fortanier asked. "As Miss Rommel noted, his life, too, has been threatened."

"Allow the defendant to carry a gun?" Driscoll shook his head. "No. The sheriff won't go that far."

Richardson smiled at the table. Am I just a cynic, Frankie asked herself, or is that a bulge over his left rib cage?

She additionally asked for modification of the rule regarding sequestration of witnesses. The state was allowed one advisory witness in the courtroom during testimony, and she had designated Leon Webster. She requested that Doug Swift be allowed to remain in the courtroom, too.

Fortanier objected. No defense witnesses—except the defendant, if he chose to testify—were allowed to hear testimony other than their own. Why should the state be allowed two? Let the police department furnish more bodyguards if they were needed.

Driscoll imposed a compromise. Both men could remain in the courtroom, but they had to be the state's first two witnesses. Additionally—because each would carry a concealed weapon—they had to be as watchful of the defendant's welfare as of the prosecutor's.

Frankie did not enjoy the humorless exchange. At least

the jury won't be subjected to the spectacle of the lawyers hugging and kissing during the breaks, she thought.

"Anything else?" Driscoll asked, glancing at his watch.

Frankie brought up the problem that had developed the previous day: Riposa's heart attack. She handed out a motion that would authorize the substitution of yet-to-be-designated expert witness. The testimony concerned the identification of a sliver of wood found embedded in the buttocks of one of the victims, she told the judge, and—although of a perfunctory nature—was critical to the prosecution's case. Mr. Fortanier had been notified immediately, would not be prejudiced by the substitution, and had refused to enter into any stipulation regarding the testimony.

Driscoll granted the motion over Fortanier's objection, with conditions: the state would have to disclose the witness's name as soon as possible, make the person available for interview before testifying, and provide the defense with copies of any written reports. How sporting we are, Frankie thought. Rules for knights, to insure that neither side has the high ground.

"My motion regarding justification?" Fortanier asked.

"You'll have to wait, Abe. You haven't even given Miss Rommel an opportunity to respond."

Frankie pulled out a five-page document she had thrown together that morning labeled "Opposition to Defendant's Motion for Affirmative Defense." "I can file this now," she said, handing the original to Driscoll and pushing a copy across the table to Fortanier. "It isn't as polished as I would like."

Driscoll picked it up eagerly and told the court reporter to note it had been filed. He skimmed through it quickly.

When writing it, the hardest part for Frankie had been taking Fortanier's motion seriously. She had almost succumbed to a temptation to ridicule it. How can a court of law allow evidence to show that murder is justified? she rhetorically argued. On the telephone with Trigge the night before she had told him it shouldn't take the judge more than five minutes to make up his mind on *that* one. "This should be very helpful, Miss Rommel," Driscoll said, nodding at Mrs. Hanks and starting to stand. "We'd better get started. We've kept that jury waiting long enough."

"If it pleases the Court, can I have a ruling before the prosecutor makes her opening statement?" Fortanier asked.

"No," Driscoll said. "I won't be pushed into a ruling." He smoothed the back of his head with his hand, as though he needed to rub himself back into a judicial frame of mind. "I expected it to be an easy call, Abe. But it isn't. I'm having trouble."

Frankie stared at the judge with astonishment. The motion read well. In some respects, the argument was brilliant. But a hard call? Incredible!

"I appreciate the care this Court in particular takes with its rulings," Fortanier said. "However, there are a host of tactical decisions and strategies that hinge on your decision. My timing with regard to an opening statement, for example. Do I give it today or wait until the state has put on its case? I suggest to you that—given the present state of the record—I could have a denial of effective assistance of counsel issue here."

"You can't expect a decision that quick, Mr. Fortanier. Miss Rommel got your motion yesterday afternoon. You could have filed it well in advance of trial."

"No, sir, if it please the court. For several reasons I am not privileged to disclose."

"In any event, Miss Rommel has filed a reply—I don't know how she did it overnight, but she did—but I haven't had a chance to read it and am in no position to make a ruling." He took his robe off the coatrack and began putting it on. "Let's get started. We've kept that jury waiting long enough."

"May I suggest we argue the motion before bringing them in, sir?" Fortanier said.

"If it appears a ruling is needed before you put on your defense, we'll take it up. But—especially considering that the motion was just filed—it is my judgment that you do not need a ruling at this time."

Fortanier smiled at his client, then struggled to his feet. "Trust me, Randolph," he said. "If I don't do this correctly, sue me for malpractice. Or direct the executor of your estate to sue, in the event you are executed."

* * *

The courtroom—jammed with spectators and festive as a circus—grew quiet as the parties filed into the room. Five deputy sheriffs, in uniform and wearing pistols, were evenly spaced around the walls. I hope the caller isn't one of *them*, Frankie thought. Webster sat next to her as an advisory witness, and Swift drifted toward the back of the courtroom.

Fortanier and Richardson took their places, and Mrs. Hanks set up her little stand.

Judge Driscoll entered quickly, trotted up the stairs of the bench, and sat down before the bailiff had the chance to announce him. "All rise," he said, somewhat lamely. "Superior Court in and for the County of Fulton now in session."

"Be seated," Driscoll said. "Bailiff, you may bring in the jury."

It took a few moments for them to fill the box. In spite of Driscoll's hesitation, she wasn't worried about the motion. She gave herself over to a feeling she loved: the thrill that comes after the preliminaries are over and the trial itself is about to begin. It makes one's hands sweat and will bring a smile to one's face; like sex, for the first time, with a new lover.

"Clerk will please call the roll."

The names of the jurors were called. Each one responded, indicating presence. When the defendant's name was called there was no answer. Richardson was staring at the floor between his feet and hadn't heard. Fortanier pushed him with a hand. "What do you want?"

"Are you here?"

"Yes."

Driscoll watched Mrs. Hanks record the defendant's response, then turned toward the jury. He spoke loudly enough to be heard throughout the room, but his voice wasn't normal. "Members of the jury, we are about to begin the State of Georgia versus Randolph Richardson." He sounded like an amateur performer. That will change once he gets into his part, Frankie thought, knowing it would also take time for her to ease into her role. "In a few moments the lawyers will present their opening arguments." It's so much like a play, she thought. It takes place on a stage, and the actors pretend there isn't an audience—then when it gets going, the audience disappears. She wondered if theater people had the same experience. "You should bear in mind that what they say to you is not evidence in the case. It is merely an outline of what they expect their evidence will show."

Right, Frankie thought. I only worked on mine for five hours, and when I am done you will want to hang him on the spot.

"You should also bear in mind that the defendant is presumed to be innocent of the charges, a presumption that remains with him throughout the trial. You are not to form an opinion as to his innocence or as to his guilt until all the evidence is in, and you are not to form an opinion based on opening arguments." Frankie let her eyebrows lift as though to tell them "You don't have to believe everything this nice man says." "At the conclusion of the case you can only find the defendant guilty of the charges if you are persuaded as to his guilt to a moral certainty and beyond a reasonable doubt." He stopped long enough for a drink of water.

"The defendant may or may not give an opening statement at this time. He may prefer to wait until the state has put on its evidence and then give his opening remarks before presenting to you his evidence. And that, generally, is the procedure we will follow: opening arguments, the state's case, the defendant's case, then closing arguments, after which I will instruct you as to the law. You will then make your determination as to guilt or innocence.

"A further observation. In the course of the trial both sides may find it necessary to make objections. You are not to draw any inferences from the fact that the lawyers object or from the ruling on the objections." Frankie could feel the hair on her arms and legs, even the soft hairs that grew along her spine. It felt wonderful. I am so glad I didn't become a judge, she thought. "The lawyers have not only the right but the responsibility to make objections, so don't worry about them or speculate because of them. Your job is to concentrate on the evidence in the case—the evidence that is lawfully admitted—and not on objections.

"It is also possible that during the course of this trial

you will be asked to disregard evidence that you may have heard or seen. You will do so. The only evidence you are to consider is evidence that has been lawfully admitted.

"There should be a small notebook and a pencil on the floor under your seat." He waited for the ones who didn't already have notebooks on their laps to pull them out. "Please take a moment now and make certain there is nothing written in them." They flipped dutifully through the pages. "You may, of course, take notes if you wish." He looked toward the lawyers, relegating the jury to the status of Greek chorus. "Are counsel ready?"

"Ready," Frankie said.

"Ready."

"Miss Rommel, you may address the jury."

Frankie had worn a a light yellow suit over a gold blouse. She wanted to look the way the case made her feel. So what if it's bullshit, she thought, wondering if anyone else would get it. She wanted them to see her as a flame. "Thank you, Your Honor." She moved to the lectern that had been positioned in front of the jury box. "Members of the jury, as you already know, I'm the prosecutor. I am here to present the evidence against the defendant, Mr. Richardson." As she acknowledged him their eyes touched. She was surprised by a rip of regret. She chopped it off. "My name is Frankie Rommel, and I am from Colorado. I'm here because your elected district attorney, Mr. Aaron Slade, had to disqualify himself. I'm a special prosecutor, and this is what I do for a living.

"Judge Driscoll told you the defendant is cloaked with the presumption of innocence. I ask that you give me the benefit of a presumption, too. Please presume my good intentions. No two places are quite alike, and everywhere I go is different. Small differences usually that don't mean very much. But if I should—well—belch when I shouldn't belch, or fail to respond properly to a custom of yours, I hope you will understand. Please believe me. There is no desire on my part to offend."

She spoke with sincerity, even though the introduction to her speech had been given countless times before to countless juries in countless states. Even the belch analogy was deliberate. She wanted to tell them in advance what they would find out soon enough: that she might be rough-hewn around the edges and was not genteel, but she meant what she said. She turned toward the judge. "With the Court's permission, may Mr. Webster be permitted to bring in a piece of evidence?"

"You are at your peril, Miss Rommel," Driscoll told her. "If it isn't admitted, there will be a mistrial."

"If I can't get *this* in, Judge, I'll lose anyway."

"Very well."

Webster—wearing a dark blue lightweight suit tailored to hide his stomach—walked quickly to the anteroom to get the rack. Frankie had not realized how big he was until he walked in front of her. "Ladies and gentlemen, the defendant has been charged with the murder of two persons," she said, her voice electric in its intensity. "We will show you that those deaths did not occur gently."

She heard the unoiled wheels of the heavy modified dolly as Webster pushed it over the thin carpet into the courtroom. She watched the eyes and expressions of the jurors as it came into view. She wanted them to see it for what it was: an ugly, vicious instrument of death. The large creosote post thrust up from the middle, and the belts and handcuffs—fixed to the wooden, splintery surfaces—seemed to wave and clank. "Those deaths occurred in the course of torture. A torture known as 'the water cure.'"

She walked to the rack. "Two human beings were placed on this instrument of torture." She held one of the belts and showed it to them. "They were lashed and handcuffed to this rough surface." She put down the belt and touched the wood. "Head at this end"—she pointed—"and feet down here. Their legs were wrapped around that huge pole, and they were belted in and lashed down—by that nice-looking man over there." She watched them appraise Richardson. "At some point he removed their shoes and burned the soles of their feet with cigarettes. They were quite helpless, unable to move. All they could do was endure the pain and possibly smell their own flesh as it burned." She waited for an objection, but Fortanier didn't move. "That was for starters. Then he administered the water cure."

The gloves are off, she thought, moving back to the lectern and loving every second of her performance. She didn't want them to wait for the evidence to make up their minds. Do you see what he did? her body asked. Make them up now.

"Mr. Richardson had rented an abandoned garage in Rockdale Park. It had a shower stall inside that still worked. We will show you pictures of the garage and the shower. That nice-looking man would turn it on and push his victims under it, letting the water drip into their faces. If you can imagine—"

"Objection," Fortanier said, showing surprising agility as he jumped to his feet. "She's pushing pretty hard, Judge." He smiled. "I don't mind her talking about the evidence, but I don't believe she should ask the jury to start imagining things."

"Sustained. Proceed, Miss Rommel."

Frankie sensed the jury was with her and let herself burn with righteousness. She faced them again, using his comment about evidence to highlight her indignation. She hurled the word back at him like a spear. "The evidence will show that the cause of death in both cases was water. The evidence will show that these victims were cured all the way to death. The evidence will show that both victims drowned, not in the relatively quick way of most drownings, but cruelly and slowly.

"Dr. Eric Mueller, a pathologist, will explain the difference. He will tell you about a valve in your throat. When opened one way it admits air and directs it to the lungs. When opened the other it sends fluids and food to the stomach.

"He will tell you—the evidence will show—that when a human being is under water past the time he can hold his breath the air valve will open, and he will pull water into his lungs as though it was air. A person's lungs will literally pack with water. If there is such a thing as an easy way to drown, that's it. But when a person fights for air, as one will who can't swim, before he goes down for the third time"—she made eye contact with some of the jurors—"or as one will who is having water splashed in his face, it happens much more slowly. The person will choke and gasp for air as more and more water goes down the wrong

WARWICK DOWNING

pipe, slowly filling the lungs, destroying their ability to process air.

"Not an easy way to drown at all, you will learn from the evidence. The evidence will show you that the agony of these painfully drowning human beings, who were lashed down to this rack and forced to spend their last moments in a shower stall, was orchestrated and presided over by"— she extended her arm toward Richardson, as though introducing him as the main speaker—"by this fine-looking man who sits at counsel table before you."

She had worked as hard on what not to say as on what she would tell them. She did not mention motive at all. Let the starkness of his actions burn in their minds without explanation as to why. Her tactic was to show the killings, unsoftened with shadow. Force the defense to justify what he had done, then counterattack in rebuttal with Melody Thralkin.

"That, substantially, is the case the State of Georgia will present. I am confident that at the conclusion, after you have had an opportunity to hear all the arguments and review the evidence and talk it over, you will do your duty and uphold the law. Thank you."

She sat down.

"Mr. Fortanier?"

"Thank you, sir." Fortanier smiled congenially at the jury, then ambled to the lectern. "And thank you, Miss Rommel, for those stirring comments. Especially for reminding this jury that when the evidence is in and they have the opportunity to review it and talk it over, they must do their duty and follow the law." He found a glass on the shelf beneath the angled wooden surface of the lectern and poured water into it. He drank some, put the glass back, and smiled.

"In the twelve-month period that preceded the deaths of these—well, the prosecution has characterized them as 'human beings,' and perhaps that characterization is accurate—approximately two thousand other human beings also died in metropolitan Atlanta. The deaths of each and every one can be traced directly to drug usage. So the evidence will show."

Frankie shot to her feet. "Your Honor, I protest—"

208

"*Since* the demise of these two unfortunates," Fortanier boomed, "our evidence will show—"

The gavel cracked against the marble plate on the bench, sounding like a rifle shot in a canyon. "Mr. Fortanier," Driscoll commanded, glaring at the friendly faced, silver-haired saint who gazed back in wonderment, as though surprised at the interruption. "You will refrain from any further comments along those lines, sir. They are totally inappropriate at this time."

"But Your Honor, I have raised the affirmative defense of justification. It is provided for in our statutes and is as much a part of our law as the laws against murder. And I have every expectation of proving—"

The gavel cracked again. "Enough, Mr. Fortanier. Members of the jury, I am afraid you must be excused until a question of law has been resolved. Bear in mind my previous admonishments, in particular that you are not to discuss the case even among yourselves at this point, or to form any opinions." The bailiff stood up. "Mr. Bailiff, they are in your custody."

The man is a genius, Frankie thought as she watched the jury file from the room. I've never tried a case against a genius. He has given the judge a chance to screw up. He knows him—how he operates, how he feels—and now the trial has started. A mistrial could result in double jeopardy.

Driscoll angrily got up. "Counsel, we will meet in chambers," he said, and he started down the stairs.

"For what purpose, may I ask, Judge?" Fortanier asked. He smiled his most charming smile.

"Because . . ." Driscoll controlled the emotions in his face, then stopped and stared with civility at the small man in front of him. "In order to consider how to proceed now, sir."

"If it pleases the Court, and I must regretfully observe that it may not please the Court, I respectfully request that any consideration be done in open court. My client is entitled to a public trial. There are also members of the press present who are part of the public. They have a stake, if it please the Court, in order to insure their right—the public's right—to a free press. Sessions in chambers are not conducive to—"

"Mr. Fortanier." Driscoll spoke softly, but his voice carried through the room. "I am directing the parties to meet me in chambers for conference. I have the inherent power to do that. Please attend, sir." He moved quickly down the steps and disappeared.

As Frankie stood up she listened to the silence in the courtroom and glanced at Webster. "Let's go," she said.

An icy but ever-gracious Fortanier opened the door to the judge's chambers for them. "I hope this is enough excitement for you, Miss Rommel." It was the first time he had volunteered a comment to her in four months. Frankie decided the encounter must have put him in a pretty good mood.

"I am enjoying myself immensely," she lied.

As Mrs. Hanks set up her box Frankie realized that Richardson wasn't there. "Judge, we need the defendant," she said.

"He has chosen not to attend," Fortanier said, sitting down. "My client and I seem to get on better when we are in different rooms, so I didn't discourage him."

"I don't know, Abe. Don't we need him here?" Driscoll asked.

"No, sir. His right to be present is personal to him. He can waive it."

When Mrs. Hanks nodded Driscoll recited the time, place, and persons present for the record. He added that Richardson had voluntarily absented himself from the conference and requested Fortanier to confirm his statement.

"That is correct."

"We will proceed without him." He slouched in his chair and rubbed the back of his head. "You're getting to me, Abe," he said.

Fortanier couldn't have been more genuine. "I'm sorry for that. But I truly believe I have not asked for nor done anything improper."

Frankie forced her way into the conversation. "Is he like this all the time?"

"I don't know about all the time. But I can vouch for the last ten years." Driscoll pounded the top of the table with his fingers. "Is there any chance of a plea bargain?"

The camaraderie that develops between combatants during the intervals when they were not on stage dissolved. Fortanier—who for a moment behaved as though he could tolerate the sight of the prosecutor—withdrew into his shell of civility. "Perhaps the Court has heard the rumors," he said. "There had been—I can't call it an agreement—but an understanding regarding a plea bargain. For reasons unknown to me, following what may one day be revealed as a most serious ethical breach of conduct, the prosecutor has chosen to pursue a murder charge."

"Any time Mr. Fortanier wishes to inquire into my ethics, he is welcome," Frankie retorted angrily. "All he's done so far is attack with innuendo. How can I defend against that kind of crap?"

"My dear woman, I'd file a grievance against you if my client would permit it. But he won't."

"It's possible he has a reason!" She exchanged looks with Webster, who knew what she meant. Can I help it if he hasn't told his lawyer the whole story? she asked herself.

But it didn't sound that way at all.

"I'm confident he has a reason," Fortanier said.

Driscoll listened attentively, trying to understand what was beneath the surface. "Well," he said when it became apparent that nothing more would be said, "I had hoped for some way out of this dilemma. But I guess there isn't anything to do except bite the bullet and rule."

Fortanier is so good, Frankie thought. He doesn't even tell the judge "I told you so."

"Miss Rommel, I must tell you I am inclined to grant it."

She stared at him. "You're not serious, are you, Judge?" She knew she was on thin ice even in an informal setting. "How can there be justification for murder? In spite of the brilliance of his argument, and I agree it is very original, how can it be?"

"Believe me, it goes against every grain in my black body, but I see his point. There is no reason, in principle, that the law of justification cannot be extended to include this case."

Frankie was stunned. "My God. There's no reason in

principle that elephants can't fly!'' Everyone looked shocked, especially Leon Webster. ''Obviously, Judge Driscoll, I wish I hadn't said that.''

He grinned at her. ''Your point is well taken. We'd better have some argument. How much time do you need to prepare?''

''I don't want the jury to forget my opening statement before he gives his,'' she said. ''Half an hour?''

Driscoll looked at the clock on the wall. ''It's a quarter after eleven. I'll tell the bailiff to take them to lunch. We'll hear argument as soon as you're ready.''

Chapter

19

FORTANIER LEANED ON THE LECTERN, WHICH HAD BEEN aimed at the bench rather than the empty jury box. It was ten minutes before noon. There couldn't have been more than thirty spectators in the courtroom. As the moving party, Fortanier spoke first.

"Your Honor, the defense of justification is available to those who have been driven—one might say, righteously driven—to homicide." Frankie knew if she were to turn her head, Richardson—who was watching her—would turn away. "It is customarily raised where a person kills in defense of himself or others, or in defense of his home, or in defense of property. But Georgia law does not confine itself to those situations. It can also be raised, and I quote from the Official Code, Georgia Annotated, 16-3-20 (6): 'in all other instances which stand upon the same footing of reason and justice as those enumerated in this article.' "

He frowned as though thinking his argument through at that moment. "In order to fully appreciate what is meant by 'other instances that stand on the same footing as those enumerated in this article' we need to go back to the common law. That is because the specific defenses articulated in the article are merely particular instances of a general principle that's been around since King Arthur.

213

"That general principle has been phrased in various ways. Georgia law uses a cumbersome phraseology that talks of the right of a person to defend against serious threats to his personal well-being or the well-being of others. But other states, and the common law, often speak in terms of the right to avoid harm by inflicting harm, or to avoid injury by inflicting injury, or a choice of evils. What it comes down to is this: In a proper case, a person in this country has the right to fight fire with fire."

Fortanier poured himself a glass of water and took a small swallow. "Because Georgia law uses the terminology of defending oneself against serious threat, I will use that terminology here. My evidence will show that this man, Randolph Richardson, knew of such a threat. It threatened not only his well-being, but the well-being of others, and I refer to the citizens of Atlanta, the state of Georgia, and the United States. That threat is the harm inflicted by the drug cocaine.

"Our evidence will demonstrate that this man, as well as the public at large, has been terribly harmed by the distribution and use of that drug. It is no longer confined to adults. Young people and even children are being devoured by this national addiction that is virtually destroying our state and nation.

"Our evidence will further establish that this man had every good reason to believe that nothing—or virtually nothing—had been done to stop this destruction, this awful cancer that threatens the lives of us all with serious disruption and even death. The police have the best intentions in the world, but their efforts don't even begin to contain the spread of this cancer. It rages through the land like a fire out of control."

The man has magic, Frankie thought. His argument on the cold page was good; here it was alive. She watched him take the time to put his hand on his hip and stretch his lower back. "Pardon me," he said. "My doctors tells me I've got some arthritis down there somewhere."

"Take your time," Driscoll said.

"Thank you. Now, I've detailed some of the points our evidence will show, such as who these victims were. They committed and were responsible for the commission of far more serious crimes, of course, than this defendant. All of that is spelled out in my motion."

"You don't need to repeat it, Mr. Fortanier," Driscoll told him. "I've read it over a few times."

"Allow me to emphasize this much. Georgia's law of justification derives from the ancient common-law defense known as the defense of necessity. In ancient times, no distinction was made between public and personal. If the threat of injury or the harm to be avoided was imminent, that was the threshold question. Hence the first element to be established by one who seeks to invoke the affirmative defense of justification is this: a showing of the imminence of the injury.

"Second, according to the cases, there needs to be a showing that there was no reasonable alternative to the action taken to avoid the injury. In other words, the defendant must demonstrate that the only way to avoid the harm was the action he took.

"Third, he must establish a reasonable nexus between the actions taken and the harm avoided. That language refers to the linkage he needs to establish between the harm and the action.

"Judge, our evidence—which will be presented in large part through experts—is sufficient to show each of those elements." Fortanier had emphasized his points in such a quiet, compelling manner that Frankie found herself rooting for him. "There *was* an imminent injury to be avoided: the deaths of two thousand persons per year, the infliction of misery and abuse on wives and children, the ever-expanding social and economic tragedy we see every day. The well-being of our fair city, our state, and our nation *was* in imminent danger of destruction. Cocaine can be 'free-based'—converted into 'crack'—with increasing ease. In that form, it is used by children! What can be more imminent than that?

"The second element concerns alternatives. Our evidence will show that our borders are sieves and that traditional police methods do not work. Captain Al Fiorello of Atlanta's police department—grudgingly, perhaps—will so testify. But the direct and forceful action of this man?" He tried to touch Richardson on the shoulder but couldn't

215

reach him. "Well, sir, that worked. We hear time and time again that we are losing the war on drugs. And it *is* a war, and it is time we used the strategies and techniques of soldiers to fight it!

"Third, our evidence will show not only a *reasonable* nexus between what Richardson may have done and the harm he avoided, but a *provable* one. The linkage between cocaine usage on one hand and misery, addiction, and death on the other is self-evident. Our experts will show there has been a significant interruption in cocaine usage in Atlanta, which translated directly to a significant decrease in death and misery. Captain Fiorello, in his praise of this man's effort, stated publicly that Colonel Richardson had done more for Atlanta than Coca-Cola."

Fortanier let his eyes fall away from the judge as though he had lost his train of thought. "Seems like I'm forgetting something," he said, fumbling with some papers.

"You'll have a chance to speak again," Driscoll said.

"That's true. I'll stop now." He sat down.

"Miss Rommel?"

Frankie got up. She didn't know exactly what she would say, but she knew the law and how she felt. "Mr. Fortanier spoke of the 'efforts' of the defendant in this case. Those 'efforts' weren't homicide, Judge. They were murder." She spoke with immediate intensity. "He has characterized the deaths of two human beings, in the course of torture, as 'efforts.'

"The law of justification, or the defense of necessity, was never intended to justify murder! Homicide, yes. But this case is murder!

"What Mr. Fortanier is asking on behalf of his client is a license to kill. A *legal* license to kill. He wants to exempt his client from the laws of Georgia that proscribe *murder*. He wants the right to prove his client was some kind of superagent, above and beyond the law, a James Bond or a Dirk Pit. He wants to turn reality into a movie!"

"Miss Rommel, let's back up a moment," Driscoll said. "Are you drawing a distinction between murder and homicide?"

"Yes!" she said. "That is where his argument breaks

down. There is a huge difference between murder and homicide. Self-defense, the defense of one's home, even the defense of property can occasionally justify a homicide. But that isn't what we have here. Those situations come up suddenly. The actor doesn't have time to plan a strategy or devise and implement a course of action. He reacts. There is no malice, implied or otherwise, in his action. He simply responds to a threat and commits a homicide. There is no similarity, in fact or in law, between those situations and the one we are presented with here.''

Driscoll frowned as though he didn't quite understand her argument. She didn't want to lose him. How could she make him see? "Judge, our evidence will show that the defendant conducted *research* into this so-called problem. He developed a plan that called for the deliberate kidnapping and torture of the victims. He had the foresight to specially design a grille mount for his car. A military tactic, I'm told, so he could avoid being trapped in the garage where these killings took place. These people were killed in the course of torture. How in the name of law and order can that kind of 'effort' be classified as a *homicide?*''

Frankie turned toward Fortanier and saw Richardson. She had no difficulty in identifying his expression, but it startled her. His open, sensitive eyes were those of an adult who had just learned to read, or of a previously deaf person listening to music for the first time. What kind of ploy was that? "Mr. Fortanier speaks of a threatened destruction of society by the proliferation of drugs. Isn't there a greater threat to society he wants this Court to employ? Shouldn't our law be a barricade against people who take upon themselves the role of God?

"Surely this Court is aware of the awful excess of vigilante 'justice,' those terrifying times that followed the Civil War and ruled the South. Lynch-mob justice. The arrogant exercise of force by self-appointed heroes. How does this situation differ from that? Are you ready to make a ruling that could provide others with the legal apparatus to justify cold-blooded murder?''

Frankie was heartened by the approving nods of Judge Driscoll. Maybe I've brought him back to his senses, she thought, knowing it was time to quit. But she had to make one further point.

"Your Honor, there is a fourth element to this common law of necessity that Mr. Fortanier appears to have forgotten. He mentioned it in his brief, but not his argument. That element is this: The harm to be avoided must be greater than the harm inflicted." She stopped long enough to focus clearly on what she wanted to say. "I agree that drugs and drug usage are awful. But the alternative chosen by the defendant to avoid that harm—legal justification of torture and murder—is a greater harm. Wouldn't it be more dangerous to the citizens of Atlanta to hand out licenses to kill to self-appointed heroes than to tolerate drugs? Such soldiers, however noble their intentions, simply cannot be given permits to cut down those they have determined to be criminals."

She hated her inability to read Driscoll's face. "I submit, sir, that the harm he would inflict is a much graver threat to our society than is the threat of cocaine."

She tried to avoid looking at Richardson as she turned and walked back to her chair. Damn you, she thought, watching him duck away from her gaze and stare thoughtfully at his hands. What are you doing?

"Rebuttal, Mr. Fortanier?"

Fortanier sought her eyes and smiled at her as he walked to the lectern. When the press are present, she thought, he can be very nice. "I knew I forgot something." He faced the judge. "Miss Rommel honed right in on it, too. The fourth element to the defense of justification—and she's right. Well, right enough. It isn't really an element to the defense because it came into the law from a different direction, but it's there. She stated it fairly, too, whatever it's called.

"She said, and I wrote it down, 'The harm to be avoided must be greater than the harm that is inflicted.' "

Thoughtfully, he drank from the water glass on the shelf below the lectern. "If I may borrow an analogy from the medical profession: What do doctors do when they are faced with cancer?

"Those cancerous cells are alive, and one might say they are entitled to rights. Perhaps they should be given their rights under *Miranda* before they are questioned." He appeared perplexed for a moment. "I am probably mixing in some other analogies here, and maybe some metaphors, and to be honest I never could tell the difference between a metaphor and an analogy, but I trust this Court can follow me as I wander through this jungle of my own creation."

"I'm capable of it so far. Mr. Fortanier."

"Doctors don't consider the rights of cancer cells before removing them from the patient," Fortanier said. "Thank God they have more good common sense than that. They just cut them out.

"And there was a time in the history of this country when we did the same thing. Now, I am not referring to those terrible days in the South when blacks were lynched indiscriminately. This court knows me better than that. I am talking of Montana in the 1870s, when gangs of cutthroats terrorized that frontier. Of San Francisco, when thieves and criminals took control of that city and had to be eliminated. Of New York City when similar actions were taken—and applauded.

"Extreme times call for extreme measures. The vigilantes rose up, and when the emergency was over the vigilantes—the good citizens—receded back into the population of good people from whence they sprang.

"There were excesses, of course. But there are always excesses. There are excessive verdicts now, we are told, verdicts of millions of dollars where perhaps hundreds of thousands would do.

"But do those verdicts destroy our law? Of course not. That is the beauty of our law. It isn't a perfect instrument, because who is there among us who can say when a verdict is perfect? The widow who receives the million dollars, or the insurance carrier who must pay it?

"Our law is *fair*. It permits defendants to put on their cases, no matter how outrageous they may seem to others. It permits a defendant his day in court.

"That is what I ask here, Judge. I am not asking for, nor do I believe that you would be giving, a license to kill. I am asking you to allow this man, in this case, his day in court. Let the jury decide whether they were homicides or murders. Let them decide if there was justification. Don't take that decision away from the jury.

"Be fair to this man, sir. Let him have his day in court."

Fortanier slowly closed the file in front of him, wandered back to his chair, and sat down. Driscoll—his palm holding his face—watched. "I don't know," he said. Frankie stared at him, appalled. She wanted to shout, "Judge, *think* about it!"

Driscoll straightened up. "Well. I'm not going to agonize over it. I've read the briefs, done some research on my own, and considered the argument. Thank God we have appellate courts to correct our mistakes.

"The burden of proof the defendant must carry in order to establish an affirmative defense is not a heavy burden, Miss Rommel. He need only make a prima facie showing of entitlement, and I refer to that *Milton* case, and also *Hagans,* both of which are cited in Mr. Fortanier's brief. Now if I make a mistake here, it will be in favor of allowing evidence in.

"I will note the defendant will give up two valuable rights in order to put on an affirmative defense. The first is obvious. He will have to testify. Am I correct, Mr. Fortanier?"

"Yes, sir."

"The second right is not as obvious. In most states the prosecution opens and closes final argument. But in Georgia the defendant has the right to the last word—unless he puts on evidence of his own. The right to open and close the argument is a powerful weapon. By putting on an affirmative defense—which of course will require him to put on evidence—he gives up that right. He will have to fight his battle without that weapon."

He's going to let them do it, Frankie thought. This hero now has a peg to hang his hat on. What chance have I got?

She answered her own question: all the way from zero to none.

"The issue is not 'Shall the defendant be acquitted as a matter of law?' Rather, the issue is this: Does he have the right to present evidence to support an affirmative defense? I believe he does. After all, jurors are not stupid. I think we should let them see this evidence. So I will permit it.

"We will leave it to the jury."

Chapter
20

AT FIVE MINUTES AFTER TWO THE JURORS FILED SOLEMNLY into the box. "Clerk will call the roll." Frankie sat next to Leon Webster and watched the jurors respond. She tried to look alert and ready for battle, as though she had won, but she heard her stomach growl. She realized she'd forgotten to eat lunch.

Webster perked his head up as the unidentified sound caught his interest. The jerk, she thought. She whispered in his ear: "My stomach."

Driscoll told the jurors that the defendant's lawyer would now continue his opening statement. They were not to concern themselves over the cause of the interruption, he added, or with what had happened outside their presence. He reminded them that the defendant's opening statement was not evidence, any more than the state's had been, and thanked them for their patience. "Mr. Fortanier?"

Fortanier approached the lectern. He arranged his notes on its surface with great care, like an artist doing a preliminary study of patterns. "A rotten day for sitting in a courtroom," he confided to them, pouring himself a glass of water. "Seems to me when I was a boy we had days like this all the time. Have they become a rarity, or is it that I don't see as well?"

He took a sip of water. "I hope you will not think it ungracious of me if I start over. The fireworks happened so quick that last go-around, I don't remember if we were introduced. I'm Abraham Fortanier of Atlanta. As all of you surely know by this time, I've been hired to defend Randolph Richardson."

Frankie marveled at the instant rapport he generated. The jury loves this gentle-looking man, she thought. Who wouldn't? His eyes—vividly alive, humorous, full of self-mockery—were as innocent as those of a mischievous boy. "The law is a peculiar animal," he told them. "She sees things differently than any of us. Yet she has this glorious capacity to see what all of us do. I don't know how she does it, to tell the truth.

"Take this case as an example. Miss Rommel had you watching a man—presumably the defendant—stretch another man on that dolly over there and tie him up and push him into a shower. You would think this law animal would perceive that in only one way. As murder.

"But she may not be quite so narrow as all that. She can see, perhaps, where it might not be murder at all, but what in law is called justifiable homicide. Which—if we get that far—is what I expect our evidence to show."

What a gambler, Frankie thought. Before he can give them a peg to hang an acquittal on, he has to admit that Randolph killed them.

"Under our law, every murder is a homicide. But it doesn't work the other way around, because not every homicide is murder. Homicide is a generic concept. It includes all the different ways a person can die, and murder is merely a particular instance." As he spoke his hands shaped a large hole. He made a fist and stuck it inside.

Frankie had to admire his advocacy. He made, of murder, a little thing that fit within something larger. She wondered how far she could let him go before objecting. "There are occasions—I won't say large numbers of them, because human life is sacred in this state—but there are a variety of situations where killing a person is justified. And that is what the law of justification is all about."

Even Driscoll looked impatient. Frankie stood up. "Your Honor, I think—"

"Yes," Driscoll said. "This isn't argument, Mr. Fortanier. Please confine your statement to what you expect the evidence will show."

"Thank you," Fortanier said, as though Driscoll had paid him a compliment. "With the Court's permission, may I outline the elements of justification? So they'll know what I'm talking about?"

"All right."

He faced the jurors. "I don't want to try your patience any more than is necessary, so I'll do this quickly. There are four elements my side must prove to your satisfaction before you can acquit this man of killing the two humans the prosecutor says he killed—which assumes, of course, that the prosecutor proves to your satisfaction he killed them. The prosecutor may do that. She seems capable of doing that. But—and this won't come as a surprise to any of you, I'm sure—she won't get any help from me."

"Mr. Fortanier—"

"I'm getting there, Judge."

"Then *get* there, sir."

Fortanier nodded, as though in total agreement with the judge. "Now Judge Driscoll will give you the precise law at the conclusion of the trial, but he has permitted me to outline it to you so you'll understand our evidence when it comes in. In order to justify the killing of these two human beings—and of course, the prosecutor will have to show that these drug dealers were human beings—"

"Your Honor, I object."

"To what?" Fortanier asked, his angelic countenance registering surprise. "Did I misstate something?"

The gavel came down. "Mr. Fortanier. Do not make a mockery of this proceeding. Do not mock me, or the law, or the victims in this case, or Miss Rommel."

Fortanier seemed to realize that even in the eyes of the jury his halo had slipped. "I apologize, sir. And I extend the same apology to Miss Rommel. May I continue?"

"You may."

Frankie could have killed him. She watched him change from mischievous little boy testing for limits into cracker-barrel poet. What might have been a dull explanation became an entertainment that sparkled with humor and wit.

He brought the elements of the law of necessity to life. Each element was like an archetype that personified a southern myth. With a few bold strokes Fortanier sketched them. Then with the skill of a Toulouse-Lautrec he completed the poster, quickly adding statistics and other evidentiary shadow to make his point.

When he had finished the jurors had the picture of an evil empire—"The Enterprise"—controlled by an arch-villain, Andrew Boatwright. Arrayed against that evil was one man, the defendant, Randolph Richardson. This hero knew what had to be done in order to save Atlanta, and possibly the world, from destruction. His methods may not have been pretty, but they worked; and, miraculously, he was able to do it.

Frankie watched Fortanier sit down. She wondered if the jury had a glimmer of the significance of the case. It was no longer simply a man on trial for his life—as though that wasn't enough. The law itself had become the defendant. Can this man persuade these twelve good citizens of Georgia that she is such a forgiving creature—Fortanier had even personified the law into a woman—that she can justify the infliction of cold-blooded murder in order to accomplish an end? Or can I hold them to the principle that gives this woman her life: The end can never justify the means?

"Miss Rommel, you may call your first witness."

"Call Douglas Swift."

As she watched him approach the witness box she felt totally inadequate. Swift didn't look like a detective, either. Wearing a dark blue suit and red tie, he looked like a salesman or a cab driver or a heavy equipment operator dressed for a meal at a good restaurant. "Your name, please, for the record?" she asked him after he'd been sworn in and seated.

"Douglas Swift."

"Will you tell us what you do for a living?"

He did: a detective for the Atlanta Police Department, a job he'd held for several years. "And are you the investigating officer in this case?"

"Yes, ma'am."

"In that capacity, have you come in contact with the defendant, Randolph Richardson?"

"I have."

"He is a man you had known before, isn't he?" she asked, knowing the form of her questions was off center. She wanted to get a sense of how far Fortanier would let her stray.

"Yes, he is."

"And is he here in court?"

"He's sitting over there next to his lawyer." Frankie watched them smile at each other.

"I ask the Court to note the identification of the defendant."

"So noted."

"Detective Swift, it's my understanding you served under the defendant in Vietnam. Is that correct?"

"If it please the Court," Fortanier said mildly, "object to the question as leading." He smiled apologetically at Frankie, who had her answer. He would hold her fairly close to the line.

"Sustained."

"When did you first become acquainted with the defendant?" she asked, rephrasing the question.

"Vietnam, 1966."

"Where in Vietnam, and what were the circumstances?"

"It was near Da Nang. I was a replacement, and he was my commanding officer."

"You were a marine?"

"Yes, ma'am."

"I take it the defendant was also a marine?" She was pushing again, but Fortanier let it go.

"Yes. He was my captain."

"Did the two of you become friendly?"

Swift glanced at Richardson, who watched with mild interest. "Don't know if 'friendly' is right. We didn't go on liberty together, you know. But we talked a lot, and I got to know him about as good as I've ever known anybody."

"And he became acquainted with you?"

"I think so."

"What did you think of this man, your captain?"

Fortanier started to stand, but Richardson put a hand on his arm.

"Thought he was somebody. About the toughest and best marine officer over there."

"Were you in combat with him?"

"Lots of combat."

"Was he—I don't know if 'good' is the right word, but was he good at it?"

"The best."

"You respected his ability as a soldier?"

"Had great respect for him. Still do."

Frankie poured herself a glass of water. "That doesn't mean you respected every little thing he ever did in Vietnam, does it?"

Fortanier was on his feet. "If it please the Court, I object to the question. Whether this man did or did not have respect for my client in 1966 in Vietnam can have no conceivable relevance to this case. A small point, perhaps, but—"

"Yes, Mr. Fortanier, I agree with you." Driscoll had through gesture tried earlier to interrupt. "Sustained. Continue, Miss Rommel."

Frankie felt as ragged as the face of a cliff. She could not think of a smooth introduction for the next line of questions, so she smashed her way in with a sledge. "In your tour of duty in Vietnam, when you served under the defendant, were there occasions when prisoners were interrogated?"

"Yes. That happened."

"Often?"

"Twice that I saw."

"That you saw. Was the defendant there?"

"Yes."

"Did he take an active part in the interrogation process?"

"Yes."

She had expected Fortanier to be on his feet screaming. He had to know where she was headed. The general rule of evidence won't permit a prosecutor to show the defendant committed crimes other than the ones he'd been charged with—yet Fortanier's feet spread lazily under the table. It would take a massive effort for him to stand and object.

226

"Directing your attention to the first time. Would you tell the jury what you saw?"

In a flat voice—from which the emotions had been sucked out as though to prevent them from getting in the way—Swift described the scene. He couldn't remember if the village had a name. All it consisted of was a scattering of thatched roofs near Dac To. "Daytime. Morning, I think. I remember how hot it was and knowing it would get hotter."

Fortanier suppressed a yawn. It helps to know the judge, Frankie thought. He must know Driscoll will accept my argument that the testimony comes within an exception to the general rule. Instead of heightening its impact by objecting and arguing and losing, he'll try to minimize it by going to sleep.

"Nobody being very careful when my squad moved in. We knew it was secure because the captain was already there." Swift nodded toward Richardson. "He was with two ARVN officers, and they stood around this boy, looked like he was on a stretcher. I thought he'd taken a hit and they were waiting for a helicopter, except his pants were dark blue like the VC wore, and he wasn't on a stretcher. He was tied to a couple of poles."

Frankie made him tell what the initials stood for: Army Republic of Viet Nam, "our side," and Viet Cong, "them." He also described how "the boy" was tied down: poles running along the outside of his legs beyond his shoulders, arms behind his back, lashed in tight.

"How old was this boy?"

"I don't know. He sure was little. Anywhere from fourteen to forty."

"What happened to him?"

"The ARVN officers could speak English, so they ask questions in Vietnamese, then tell the captain what the boy said." He gazed at the backs of his hands. "Long question, short answer, kind of a sneer. So the captain knelt down, had a cigarette in his hand, he kind of smiled at the boy, then touched the hot part against the bottom of his foot."

"Did he have boots or shoes on?"

"No." Swift did not appear to be breathing. His voice

had become hollow, words spoken while in a meditative state.

"What did the captive do?"

"Screamed."

"I see. How long did he hold the burning cigarette against the captive's foot?"

"Long enough to smell."

The boy was easier to talk to after that, Swift said. His answers were longer, at least. But they administered what the captain called "the water cure" because he wouldn't tell them what they needed to know.

"Describe this water cure, please."

"Had a hose hooked to a pump—you could hear the motor chug from somewhere—and they passed it around, splashing water in his face. They'd catch him when he was breathing, you know. He'd try to jerk his head out of the way and cough, and you could hear him suck and get panicky." Swift's eyes appeared to be stuck open. "Hard to watch. Then the captain'd move it and say, 'Ask him again.' "

He remembered how Richardson turned it into a joke. "He was kind of talking to us, you know, explaining what was going on. Some of the men even laughed. He told us the little gook had a disease—the loathsome disease of dishonesty—but water would cure him." Swift glanced toward the defendant.

Richardson, hands folded on top of the table, met his gaze directly. He appeared to be listening carefully, as appalled by Swift's words as were many of the jurors. If they wanted to hate him, what would they like him to do? Frankie wondered. Smirk and laugh? Instead they saw a stricken man as sickened by what they were hearing as they were. Fortanier had not overlooked a thing.

"And then?"

"The boy stopped talking. They held the water on him a long time, and he thrashed around on the ground, then went limp. But he could still breathe. The ARVN untied him, got him up, took him behind a hut, and shot him." Swift looked toward the door almost wistfully, as though he would like to go for a long walk. The courtroom was still. "So the captain said, 'Well, I guess the doctors decided he was contagious.' "

A month later they caught another Cong soldier hiding in a hooch, trying to look like a staw mat. "Captain gave Corporal Myerson the detail. Man came off a farm in Oklahoma, could make do with anything, you know. He and his men had to locate a hose and a water pump, hook it all up, get the thing to suck right and blow out water. Myerson squirted it around, you know, kind of drenched his team, making sure it worked. Then the captain took it to the prisoner.

"The boy's eyes were too much." Swift had started to sweat. "They darted all over, real quick movements, seemed like they saw so much, like the meaning of life." Frankie waited for an objection, but Fortanier appeared to have gone asleep. "An hour later, after they shot him, his eyes were covered with flies."

"Before they shot him?"

"Okay." Odd details had been embedded in his mind: the heat, the incredible blue of the sky against the building clouds, the smell of fear, the color of the wooden beams the prisoner had been lashed to. "Captain just watched that time as one of the ARVN burned his feet. I remember watching the boy's face. He didn't scream. Got all twisted up with hate and pain."

Then came the water cure. "The man gasped, coughed, you know, he really fought for air. Captain held the hose on him most of the time, complimented him even when he made a good move. Captain acted nice about it, you know, kind of like calling a game. Had some of us laughing."

"Did you laugh?"

"No."

"Did the captive talk?"

"After a while he did."

"Then did they let him go?"

"No. They shot him, too."

"Did the defendant shoot him?"

"No. He said he couldn't do it because he needed a moving target."

"Did some of the men laugh at that?"

"Yeah." Swift shut his eyes. "I did, too."

Richardson shook his head slowly and sadly. What an actor, Frankie thought. He's so good I almost believe him myself. Angrily she turned to the next page in her notebook

"Do you recall Friday, April twenty-third of this year? The early morning hours, right after midnight?"

Swift frowned. "Is that when I went over to the Williams residence?"

"You have to tell me, officer."

He looked at the file on his lap. "Okay if I look in here?"

"It won't bother me, sir," Rommel said. "I can't speak for Mr. Fortanier."

Swift glanced in the direction of the defense lawyer, who was hunched over his legal pad, scribbling notes. He opened his file. "Yes."

Frankie quickly drew the testimony she wanted out of him. She showed him photographs of a man who appeared to be sleeping on a lawn, which Swift agreed were true and accurate depictions of the scene he investigated. He described the man as black, early forties, good-sized, well-proportioned, wearing sports clothes "like he'd come off a golf course," and nice-looking. He had no pulse, nor was there any sign of life, in that there was no movement of any kind, not even a twitch.

Swift later talked to a woman who identified herself to him as "the dead man's widow." She lived at the residence with her husband and daughter. Both mother and daughter were visibly upset, but the mother—Mrs. Roberta Williams—was coherent. Swift described the dignity and grief of the women. "Was the person you saw on the lawn a human being?" she asked, hoping the jury remembered Fortanier's jibe during his opening statement.

"Yes."

She nodded and glanced toward the defense table, inviting the jury to do the same. Fortanier smiled cordially at her, and Richardson gazed easily beyond.

She turned back to the witness. "Directing your attention now to the following morning—that is, Saturday, April twenty-fourth, at approximately 2:37 A.M. Where were you?"

"In Rockdale Park, near an old garage called Flanagan's Auto Repair."

"What were you doing?"

"I was staking it out."

"Did you have reason to suspect the defendant might be in the vicinity?"

"Yes, I did."

Fortanier rather graciously had risen to his feet, as though ready to make an introduction. If he knows what he will lose, Frankie thought, he probably knows what he will win. "Without going into your reasons, would you tell us what happened?"

Fortanier nodded courteously at her and sat down.

Swift talked easily with the jury, gesturing naturally with his hands as he spoke. Frankie let herself be drawn into his story, even though she'd heard it enough times to gag over it in the last few days. Swift articulated his hunch that someone was in the building even though he didn't know for sure. He was making a mirror out of a whiskey bottle when the garage door blew out and a large passenger car hurtled down the road.

"Did you recognize the car?"

"Yes, I did. A big Chrysler sedan I'd seen the day before. It was Colonel Richardson's car."

She showed him a photograph of the car, which he identified. It was admitted without objection. "Did you see the driver?"

"Not a face, but I knew who it was."

Fortanier watched alertly but stayed in his chair. "How could you know who it was without seeing a face?" Frankie asked.

"His moves. The shape of his head. The way he sat behind the wheel."

"On that basis you knew who it was?" Frankie made her voice sound incredulous.

"Yes, ma'am. I've seen him in front and back, moving and dodging. I knew who it was."

Swift's eyes had drifted away and Frankie waited until he looked at her. "Who was the driver of the car?"

"The defendant, Colonel Richardson." Swift looked at his old commander. "The man sitting next to Mr. Fortanier."

Judge Driscoll broke the silence that followed. "The

Court will note that the witness has identified the defendant."

"Thank you, Your Honor. Officer Swift, please tell us what you did next?"

Swift told of finding the body of a man inside the garage lashed to the rack—"that big thing over there," he said, pointing to the dolly, which was still in the courtroom. It, too, was identified, marked as an exhibit, and offered into evidence. There was no objection.

Frankie showed him photographs of Boatwright's corpse spread obscenely around the pillar that thrust off the bed of the dolly like a huge erection. One showed his feet, shoes off, burn holes through the socks. Another showed his wrists and how they were tied. The third showed his face and the front of his tuxedo, wet and disheveled-looking. They, too, were received in evidence. "Was this person a human being?" she asked.

"Yes."

She glanced again at the defense table. Richardson appeared bored, and Fortanier smiled nicely at her again. "Did you subsequently determine the identity of this human being?"

"I did. His name was Andrew Boatwright."

Frankie made a quick decision. Plaster casts had been taken of the tire prints in front of the garage, establishing that the tires from Richardson's car had been there; don't bother with that, she thought. Don't wear them out with details they don't need. But she selected five photographs of the bleak interior of the building, and four of its exterior. She wanted to show the remoteness of the building to all habitation, and to emphasize the point she asked Swift to estimate those distances. The photographs were received in evidence without objection.

"Did you see the defendant later that morning?"

"Yes, ma'am."

The questioning quickly set the scene in Fiorello's office. Frankie saw the satisfied expression of Fortanier and knew that not only would he allow her all the latitude in the world, but he would take advantage of the opportunity on cross-examination. So be it, she thought, knowing it would come in sooner or later. Swift testified that Richardson claimed to be there to report a conversation he had over-heard that morning between Andrew Boatwright and an unidentified person. The name Charles Williams never came up.

She was finished with Swift, but she didn't want to leave off the questioning at that point. The juror's minds were in the police building, with Richardson helping the cops. She wanted them to focus on what he had done. "Your Honor, can Mr. Swift approach what has been referred to as 'the rack?' "

Fortanier, smiling pleasantly, got up. "Hasn't it also been called 'dolly?' "

"Yes. Well," Driscoll said, looking at his notes, "it's Exhibit 14." There was some muffled laughter. "We will refer to it by exhibit number." He glanced at Frankie. "For what purpose, Miss Rommel?"

"To demonstrate the position and attitude of the body of Andrew Boatwright when the witness first saw it."

"Mr. Fortanier?"

"Goodness, Judge. She isn't particularly subtle, is she?"

More laughter. "Do you object, Mr. Fortanier, or don't you?" Driscoll sternly asked.

"I have no objection, Judge."

Frankie left Swift on Exhibit 14 longer than she otherwise would have. She took advantage of Fortanier's obliging nature and soon had Leon Webster hovering over Exhibit 14 also. He simulated the handcuffs and buckled Swift onto its rough surfaces, exerting all necessary force. At Frankie's request he took off Swift's shoes.

By the time she said "Your witness, Mr. Fortanier," no one was laughing.

"Are you comfortable now, sir?" Fortanier asked when Swift resumed his chair in the witness box.

"Yes, I am. Thank you."

Fortanier fumbled with some papers for a few moments, giving the jury ample time to erase the previous vision and build up another set of expectations. He even felt around his hips, as though he'd misplaced something in a pocket. "Oh." He located a paper, which he placed on the lectern. "I imagine this is distasteful to you, isn't it, sir?" he asked. "Giving evidence against your former captain?"

"Yes, it is."

Frankie prepared herself for a bath. She could make strenuous objections and look foolish or simply get wet. She chose to get wet. Swift answered questions about Richardson with obvious respect. He knew of the Medal of Honor—everyone in the regiment did—but Richardson, in all of their talks, never mentioned it. Frankie objected mildly and good-naturedly when Fortanier tried to have Swift describe some of Richardson's battlefield heroics, and she was sustained. But when Fortanier questioned him about Andrew Boatwright she toughened her stance. Most of what Fortanier wanted—agreement that Boatwright headed the billion-dollar organization known as "The Enterprise"—was hearsay to Swift, and she kept it out. It would come in later through other witnesses, but she decided not to be *too* nice.

However, there was nothing she could do when Fortanier questioned Swift about the arrests, seizures, and convictions that flowed from Richardson's disclosures to the narcotics division. She solemnly nodded her head as though to say, "Of course."

When Swift was excused, Driscoll ordered a recess. "It could have been worse," Frankie said to Webster after the jury was out of the room. "He could have had Richardson levitate."

"He didn't ask him any questions about Williams," Webster said. "Did he forget?"

"That's right. He didn't." Frankie could think of a whole line that might have been asked to show Williams was a profiteer, too, among other things. "I wonder why."

When court convened Frankie called her next witness: Lieutenant Leon Webster, Homicide, Atlanta Police Department. He was also introduced to the jury as her advisory witness.

Webster's testimony went in smoothly and quickly. He identified a sliver—barely visible in a clear plastic bag—as having been given to him by Dr. Eric Mueller, the pathologist who performed the autopsy on Charles Williams.

Webster then told of searching Richardson's residence on Sunday, April twenty-fifth, persuant to a warrant. Richardson was in custody at that time. Webster identified a receipt found in a desk in the study. It was from Orson Cosgrif to Marlin Pike, evidencing a rental payment of several hundred dollars for the premises known as Flanagan's Auto Repair in Rockdale Park. Frankie next pulled three large photographs from one of her files. She allowed her attitude to reflect curiosity and questioned him about the scene they depicted.

"This was behind a Japanese-type screen in the living room," Webster said, examining them and speaking matter-of-factly. "It appeared to be a homemade altar of some sort."

She asked him to describe it in words. He did: an old Navy sea chest, upended and covered with the Stars and Bars, an old Confederate flag. A sword of the kind the Crusaders like King Richard might have used had been pushed through the top, with the hilt and part of the blade exposed. It formed a cross. There was a Bible, an antique-looking musket, and the color photograph of an attractive woman on top.

Frankie requested permission to pass the photographs to the jury, and the judge allowed it. Frankie knew she had the jurors' attention. "The person in the photograph on the sea chest. Was she identified?" Frankie asked.

Webster paused, as though to give defense counsel time to object. "Yes. The woman was Melody Thralkin."

"What can you tell us about Melody Thralkin?"

"She had been murdered, in Atlanta, on April third."

"Thank you," Frankie said. "No further questions."

"Mr. Fortanier?"

Fortanier didn't even stand all the way up. "No questions, Judge."

Frankie didn't know where they were, but it didn't matter. She and Doug Swift were having dinner somewhere. It was reasonably dark, and they sat in a cushioned booth in the smoking section, and the hors d'oeuvres were simple but tasty: potato skins dipped in a cheese fondue.

Because of the death threats the Atlanta Police Department had moved Frankie into a luxury two-bedroom apartment near Atlanta University, in a neighborhood that was primarily black. Swift had explained to her that because the threats were probably from white extremists, she would be safer there than in any other part of town. If she agreed, he would stay in the other room, but if she preferred a woman officer, they'd get one.

"Are you housebroken?"

"Yes. I clean up my own mess."

"Can you shoot straight?"

"Good enough."

"Fine. You're hired."

Sitting in the dark restaurant with a cigarette in one hand and a drink in the other felt wonderful to Frankie after a full day in court. It would be fun to tease Doug about his status—a paid escort or a bodyguard?—but she truly enjoyed his company and didn't want to create little tensions that could interfere with what she wanted most: comfort. She thought she could trust him, but why take the chance? "Exactly what I need," she said, avoiding his air space with her smoke. "I've been up since five o'clock."

"Long day."

She ordered lamb, and it was delicious: moist, tender, not overcooked. The peas were fresh, and the long-grain rice perfectly seasoned. They managed to avoid talking about the trial until Frankie brought it up halfway through the meal. "I've been thinking about their case," she told him. "They will claim this private war cleaned up Atlanta, right? But isn't the city back where it was before he started? Aren't drugs handed out just as easily as they were before Richardson's little campaign interrupted the pipeline—just different faces?"

"Not according to Fiorello," Swift said. "Al says there was a long hiatus. Drug-related deaths are still down, crime still down. Narcotics division still has a handle."

Swift was one of the few men Frankie had ever known who really liked salad. She wondered what he smelled like. "Is he right?"

"It isn't easy to argue with the captain of the narcotics squad, but you could ask him about the Dead Poets."

"How in the world did they get that name? It's a movie with Robin Williams, right?"

"Yeah, could be that's where it came from. The media

named them. Some newspaperman called them poetic because of the way they whack people."

"Give me an example."

"They killed a lawyer—one of Boatwright's who was cooperating with the police—then put a wig on him, like an English barrister. They put a bar of soap in a woman informant's mouth. The word on the street is they'll drown Richardson."

"Why would they do that? My God. They're dopeheads, aren't they?" She pushed away her plate and reached for her purse, looking for a cigarette.

"So was Edgar Allan Poe."

"What does that mean?"

"People think if you're a doper, your brain's been fried. You're some kind of crazed zombie, you know, prowling the streets with a machine gun, looking for victims to rob and kill so you can get more dope." He grinned at her. "Right? They're all fiends?"

She lit her cigarette, back in the case. Her stomach tightened, and she didn't even think about dessert. "So. The truth?"

"They're people. With imaginations, senses of humor, a lot of them with plenty of smarts. Even the killers."

There is nothing better than a cigarette after—hmm. Her initial thought was interrupted by another: after sex. "If Fortanier does his defense the way he outlined it in his written motion, he'll call Fiorello." She tapped off an ash.

"Al will be a witness for the defense?"

"Yes." She thought of something. "Where are we on the killing of Maurice Brown?"

"Harold Munroe is waiting for space at the penitentiary. That one's solved."

"I need to know, Doug. Did Randolph kill him?"

Swift didn't answer immediately. "I don't know," he said after swallowing the food in his mouth. "But I've been over that tape of Dogwood and me a dozen times, and I remember how he was that morning. He told me what he thought was the truth."

After dinner he drove them to the luxury apartment her bags had been moved to. She quickly walked through, telling Swift it was "really nice" and making sure they hadn't left anything in the hotel. Then she holed up in her room and tried to get ready for day three. At midnight she crawled into bed. She was exhausted but couldn't sleep and rolled over on her shoulder and stared out the window. Randolph wasn't a wacko, yet her tactic in court had been to paint him as one.

She thought: I will be so glad, a year from now, when you are out of my mind.

Then, as though he was in the room with her, she asked: Did you stand that man in the shower and in cold blood shoot him through the head?

She wondered if she would ever really know.

Chapter

21

Wednesday, October 26

FRANKIE WOKE TO THE SMELL OF COFFEE. SHE LOOKED AT her watch—7:42 A.M.—and jumped out of bed. Her robe hung on a chair in the middle of the room, and she put it on, opened the door into the hallway, and peeked toward the bathroom. The bathroom door was closed. "Are you in there?" she yelled.

"What?" Swift's voice came back. She heard movement at the other end of the apartment, and a moment later Doug Swift—fully clothed—looked at her from the living room. "I was in the kitchen."

"Well, next time, when you're done in the bathroom, leave the goddamned door open." She marched in, shut the door behind her, and turned on the shower. Fifteen minutes later, wearing a dark brown skirt and a light brown satin blouse with pearl buttons, she appeared in the kitchen. "The coffee smells good. Can I have a cup?"

Swift—seated at a small table and reading the paper—looked up. "Sure. The cups are in the cabinet, and the coffee is on the stove."

Frankie laughed. "We will get along fine."

Frankie didn't know where they were, but it wasn't far

from the courthouse. Swift negotiated the drive in under twenty minutes, and they didn't get on any freeway. On the way he gave her the address of the apartment—"It could happen you'll have to take a cab"—and a set of keys. He also gave her a loaded semiautomatic .25-caliber pistol, small enough to fit in her purse. "Hope you can shoot," he said as she examined the weapon.

"Don't worry. I'm from Wyoming, and I used to hunt elk and bear. I even shot a moose. I don't anymore. This thing looks like it might kill a goldfish if the shot was good."

"That's all I could get. It makes lots of noise. You could scare somebody to death."

With Swift leading the way she stopped by her office on the way to the courtroom. "You look lovely this morning, my dear," Miss Anne said, smiling at her. "Those colors are quite becoming—although a little green around the neck would look nice. I have just the thing." She opened a drawer and pulled out a soft cotton scarf. "May I?"

"You may."

Miss Anne arranged it loosely around Frankie's neck, tucking it under the collar of her coat. "That's for luck, dear," she said with affection.

Frankie didn't care how it looked. She would wear it all the way to hell. "Thank you, Miss Anne. If Jim Trigge calls, tell him I'll get back during the noon recess."

Five minutes later she and Doug walked into the courtroom. Swift positioned himself at the rear, near a guard, and Frankie walked up to counsel table. Neither Fortanier nor Richardson was there, but Leon Webster—looking more like a lawyer than she did, in a dark blue pinstripe suit and satin shirt—watched her from his chair as she arranged her files. "Hi."

"Leon, we could finish today," she said. "Who is doing the sliver?"

"Oh!" He jumped up and found a scrap of paper in one of his suit pockets. "I forgot. The guy's name is Leonard Chessman."

"Come on. We go tell the judge."

They hurried into the back hallway and found Driscoll in his chamber. The sliver was in evidence. Frankie got an order allowing its withdrawal and examination by the expert. "Are we really going to finish today?" Webster asked as they waited for Mrs. Hanks. The sliver, with the rest of the evidence, was in a witness interview room, and Mrs. Hanks had the key.

"Happens all the time," Frankie told him. "Months of planning, and then *varoom!* The testimony goes in like it was greased." She lit a cigarette to calm an attack of the jitters. "Especially when the defendant puts on an affirmative defense."

"What does that do?"

"That's where the defendant says 'Sure I did it, but I had a reason.' So the prosecution doesn't have to do much more than go through the motions to prove the crime, because the defendant will admit it anyway."

"Couldn't you save time by stipulating?"

"I don't want to save time," she told him. "I want that jury to know what it felt like." She dropped the cigarette on the floor and ground it out. "Here comes Mrs. Hanks. She'll squeal on me."

Mrs. Hanks made the magical notations, and Webster stuck the plastic bag containing the sliver in his pocket. "You'll have to give that to the expert," Frankie said. "Can Doug corral the witnesses for me?"

"Yes. They're all here except for Mueller. In the hall."

"Is Mueller on call?" she asked.

"Right. Although I told him tomorrow."

"Better get word to him he may go on this afternoon."

Frankie was worried. She had a lot of witnesses, but Fortanier might simply wave at them. When he walked into the courtroom Richardson and Fortanier were there. The room was packed. Looking at the crowd and knowing she would soon be onstage, Frankie wished she'd finished her cigarette. She avoided looking at Richardson—he made it easy by staring at his long, slender hands—but had to talk to Fortanier, which meant enduring his disdain. "You intend to call an expert today who is examining the sliver now?" Fortanier asked.

"Yes."

"Rather sure of yourself, aren't you?"

"You can always stipulate."

"Ask my client."

Angrily, Frankie jerked away from him. She saw Doug—standing against the wall in the back—and motioned him up. He had a coat on, but no tie. They sat down, and she wrote out the list of witnesses, telling him what had happened to Webster. "Make sure the witnesses stay in the hall until they are called," she said, giving him the list. "Then bring them in. Okay?"

"Don't I get to sit up here like Leon and take notes?" he asked, teasing, as though trying to settle her down.

"No, dummy. Not without a tie."

Moments later Mrs. Hanks came in and nodded at the bailiff, who said, "All rise," and everyone got up. The judge beamed at all the people and spoke some lines, and they sat down. It ran through Frankie's brain like a string of disconnected TV bytes. The jury came in, the clerk called the roll, and everyone—even Richardson—answered on cue. It seemed like seconds later when Frankie—on her feet by the lectern—called her next witness. "Roberta Williams."

Frankie had only talked briefly with Charles Williams's widow. She had seemed a nice enough woman who was not at all eager to testify. Frankie tried to read her attitude now. She wasn't dressed like a widow. She wore a tasteful earth-red dress with a wide belt tied around her waist accentuating her nice figure. "Your name, please, for the record?" Frankie asked.

"Roberta Williams."

From her tone of voice and the straight-on way she glared, Frankie sensed contempt. Witnesses frequently wore a hostile attitude like a coat of armor, as though to protect their egos from the arrows of the lawyers. Perhaps that was all there was to it, Frankie hoped, exuding friendliness and respect in an effort to draw the best out of the witness. After a brief introduction she started the exchange about the night Mrs. Williams found her husband's body on the lawn. Beneath the layer of contempt Frankie saw loneliness. She hoped the jury could see it, too.

She avoided asking Mrs. Williams any more questions than were necessary. The woman told of plans to have dinner out with her husband and daughter Felicia on the night of the incident. However, he telephoned shortly after seven and said he would be late because a reporter from the *Constitution* wanted an interview. "That was that mess with the city and his uncle Marcus." She and Felicia waited until after nine o'clock, then drove to a relative's house and watched a movie on the VCR. When they came home they found his body on the lawn.

Frankie showed her a photograph of Williams. It showed a large man who could have been asleep stretched out on grass. "Yes, that's him," the woman said, after being prodded to do so. She worked to keep her face under control.

"Thank you." Frankie moved away from the lectern. "You may examine."

"No questions."

The judge looked down at the witness, who obviously expected to play a bigger part. "You're excused, Mrs. Williams. Thank you. Call your next witness."

Frankie had expected some cross-examination, too. As it was, she didn't even have the chance to sit down. "I'll call Felicia Williams," she announced.

Doug Swift somewhat diffidently stuck his hand in the air, then walked down the aisle toward the rail. "Your Honor, can I have a moment?" Frankie asked.

"Yes."

As Roberta Williams left Doug whispered to Frankie: "You don't want Felicia. She's stoned."

Frankie made herself breathe twice, then nodded at Doug. "The guy from the newspaper," she said in a low voice. "What's his name?"

"Dave Larkin."

She turned around. "If it please the Court, rather than Felicia Williams, we call David Larkin."

Larkin—a well-dressed man whose suit did little to hide the thickness of his body—touched Richardson on the shoulder as he walked past him to the witness box. Obviously the two men had met. After sitting down he leaned forward earnestly and presented a look of great sincerity to the jury: sandy, thinning hair and a mass of wrinkles over his eyebrows.

"Your name, please?" Frankie asked.

Larkin projected care and accuracy in his testimony. He

was the city editor for the newspaper. In that capacity he knew who his reporters were, and—on any given day— what their assignments were. It was always possible one or more might be running a project without his knowledge, but very unlikely. To his knowledge, on the day in question, no reporter from his newspaper had been assigned to interview Charles Williams.

"Thank you, Mr. Larkin. You may examine," Frankie said.

"No questions."

When Larkin left the stand Frankie adroitly got between him and Richardson. She occupied him nicely, ushering him beyond the rail. She didn't need the spectacle of the city editor stopping to chat with the defendant.

"Your next witness, Miss Rommel?"

"Shelley Dyer."

Frankie took as much time as she could with the next three witnesses. They were offered to show planning and deliberation on the part of Richardson before committing the homicides.

Shelley Dyer—a plumpish woman in her mid-forties— was the bookkeeper and office manager for RBM Industrial Supply, Memphis. She clearly remembered selling an industrial dolly to the defendant. She even blushed and smiled shyly as she pointed him out, as though hoping he remembered her, too. After locating an imprint stamped into the metal band around the bed of Exhibit 14, she identified it as having been manufactured by her company. She climbed back in the box and described the transaction. The defendant paid cash and wheeled the industrial dolly out the door, where it was loaded onto a pickup truck. She had given him a receipt, a copy of which she produced, made out to "Mr. Robinson" for $247.00, which she signed and dated.

"Any objection, Mr. Fortanier?" Driscoll asked when the document was offered into evidence.

"No, sir."

The next witness—Orson Cosgrif—sold and managed properties in Atlanta and surrounding communities. One such property was Flanagan's Auto Repair, Rockdale Park. On April twelfth, according to his records, he had leased the building to a Marlin Pike for two months for $800. It was a cash transaction, which didn't excite his curiosity because the man's explanation was quite satisfactory. Mr. Pike explained he was retired and wanted a location where he could work on antique cars.

The defendant could have been the man, although Cosgrif would not positively say so. After all, he had only seen Mr. Pike on that one occasion. However, he recognized the receipt Frankie showed him, which had been found in Richardson's study. It was made out to Marlin Pike, but the handwriting was his.

Wayne Fulbright took the stand. A short man with a massive chest and huge forearms, he did business as "Wayne's Welding." He hunched in the witness box like a bus driver over the wheel, peering out a vast window at traffic. Frankie asked him to identify the grille mount that had turned Richardson's car into a battering ram. He did so reluctantly. His general manner told Frankie he didn't think much of her or the prosecution.

Fortanier smiled at him warmly, but—as with the previous witnesses—asked no questions.

"May I approach the bench?" Frankie asked.

"You may."

She and Fortanier huddled with the judge. "This has gone much, much faster than I expected," Frankie said. "I have two witnesses left. Both are experts, and neither of them is here."

"Who are they?" Driscoll asked.

Before she could answer they became aware of a mild commotion at the rail. The bailiff obviously didn't know what to do. A grinning young black male, no more than ten years old, was having his hand shaken vigorously by an obviously proud Randolph Richardson. "Good for you, Freddie! What did I tell you?" Richardson said.

"You said I could do it."

A hush descended over the courtroom, and the two of them became aware that everyone watched them. The boy became very shy. "Go on now," Richardson told him. "Go sit down. I'll talk to you later."

The youngster scampered down the aisle to a row in the

back and took a seat next to his mother. Richardson waved at the beaming woman, then sat down.

Most of the jurors were smiling. The pride and affection Richardson showed in the young man was unmistakable. It warmed every heart in the courtroom, except for Frankie's. She watched the performance with a grim face. "What— Judge, can I say something about what we've just seen?"

Driscoll kept his head down to hide a smile. "Yes."

"I don't know what that was all about, but I suspect theatrics. Perhaps the jury needs a special instruction."

"Oh, I'd object to that," Fortanier said. He reflected the general mood of the courtroom: warmth toward a touching scene. "That would imply the use of a stratagem of some sort, and I deny it." Still smiling, with eyes that shone as had those of the boy, he looked at Frankie. "I would like to take credit, Miss Rommel, but can't. I don't know any more about it than you."

"Frankie, would you like to make a record?" Driscoll asked.

Richardson, seated and facing them, appeared the picture of courtroom decorum. His hands were folded and resting on the table. He examined them quietly, although he continued to smile like a proud parent. Several of the jurors watched and smiled with him.

Frankie didn't want to draw the jury's attention to the incident any further. "No. I'd ask that Mr. Fortanier be directed to caution his client about any further performances in front of the jury."

"Do you have a problem with that, Abe?"

"That's the first intelligent thing he's done. But I'll talk to him about it."

Frankie worked her sneer into a smile. She tried to make the best of it but knew when she'd been had.

"Your name, please, for the record?" Frankie asked.

"Leonard Chessman."

Frankie hated putting on witnesses she'd never seen, but she didn't have a choice. She could have put the pathologist on, then talked to Chessman during the noon recess. But she wanted Mueller as her last witness. Fortanier agreed to the procedure even though he hadn't talked to Chessman either. She wasn't certain, but she might have seen a gleam in his eye.

View it as a challenge, she told herself. "What is your occupation, Mr. Chessman?"

"I'm a lab technician with the Atlanta Police Department."

The young black man wore his hair in a platter cut and had on thick horn-rimmed glasses. His expression was one of total disdain. Frankie suspected his arrogance was a cover for nervousness. "Do you have a specialty?" she asked.

He did: the examination and identification of real evidence, by way of example, hair, fibers, firearms, bullets, and soils.

"Does that include splinters, slivers, and wood particles?"

"I don't see why not."

An alarm went off in Frankie's head. She asked for a moment and bent down over Webster. "Has this turkey ever done a sliver?" she asked in a whisper.

"No."

She smiled at Webster and put her hand on his shoulder, as though thanking him for the good news. Obviously Chessman couldn't qualify as an expert in wood particle identification, so she tried it his way: an expert in the examination and identification of real evidence. Unfortunately, there was no such category of expert.

She could sense the acute interest of Fortanier in the witness.

"How long have you been with the Atlanta Police Department, Mr. Chessman?"

"Seven years."

Frankie made the most of his qualifications, which were impressive: training at the FBI academy at Quantico, a degree in criminalistics from Louisiana State, correspondence courses from two accredited universities, a master's thesis on the workup of bite-mark identification. She even got him to state that, in principle, the examination and identification of fingerprints, bite marks, and wood particles was all the same. "With any form of real evidence you proceed from the general to the particular. Or in the words of an identifications expert, from class characteristics to individual characteristics." He had loosened up by this time and fed the jury the stock analogy of a heel mark found on the scene of the crime. "If it says 'cat's paw,' well, then you have a general classification. You then look for particular nicks and cuts—individual characteristics peculiar to the heel you wish to identify." Frankie took a deep breath and offered him up.

"As what?" Judge Driscoll asked.

"As an expert in the examination and identification of real evidence."

"I see," Driscoll said. "I believe we will excuse the jury at this point. I anticipate an objection, and some argument." The jury left the courtroom. "Mr. Fortanier, do you have any questions of the witness?"

Fortanier got up but didn't even bother to go to the lectern. "Just one. Mr. Chessman, in the course of your career, how many wood particles have you examined?"

"One."

"And that was done this morning, for this case?"

"Yes, sir."

"I see." Fortanier smiled at the judge. "If it please the Court, I object to an expert opinion regarding the identification of wood particles from this witness. It is no reflection on the general qualifications of Mr. Chessman, but this appears to be the first time he's ever done it, and I do not believe he should get his training in a capital murder case."

Frankie refused to give up. She reminded Driscoll of his previous comments that jurors were not stupid, and that they could evaluate evidence. "Mr. Chessman has a specialized knowledge, Judge. He can assist the jury in understanding what weight, if any, should be attributed to the splinter."

Driscoll agreed! Frankie felt like the greatest lawyer since Clarence Darrow. But when the jury returned and questioning resumed she discovered Chessman had not even looked at the work of the earlier expert, Dr. Jerry Riposa. She wanted to kill him.

Chessman testified that even though he had never worked in the field of wood particles he could still render an opinion—with reasonable scientific certainty—regarding the origin of the wood particle in question. She asked him the question all the jockeying had led to: "In your opinion, did this splinter come from Exhibit 14?"

"I wouldn't swear to it," Chessman said, "but I think so."

Frankie smiled at him and said, "Thank you. Your witness." His answer was horrible. She thought she would like to place her face one inch from his and instruct him in the art of expert testimony. Rule one, she would scream, is this: If you can't swear to it, don't take the fucking stand!

She wanted to crawl in a hole and die when Fortanier took him on cross-examination. Instead she smiled her encouragement at the jerk. Fortanier cordially greeted the man, complimented him on his scholastic achievement, but established in front of the jury what he'd already shown the judge: that Chessman had never been called upon to make a wood particle identification until that day. "You have testified in court numerous times as an expert, have you not, sir?"

"I wouldn't say 'numerous,' Mr. Fortanier. It's only been three times."

"Well, I'll call that numerous," Fortanier generously allowed. "It's more than once. But I'm curious. Have you ever qualified as an expert in real evidence identification before?"

"Not in those words."

"It's always been something like firearms identification, hasn't it? Some specialty?"

"Yes, sir. Fact is, that's my specialty."

"I see. And in that specialty—firearms identification—there are manuals, aren't there, with which you are familiar?"

"Yes, there are."

"They show photographs of various guns and describe the general characteristics of those guns?"

"Yes, sir."

"Now, there are manuals to which a wood particle expert can refer that will do the same thing, aren't there? That show the grains of different woods, such as oak or pine?"

"I'm sure there are."

"Did you consult any such manuals before testifying?"

"Actually, no. Didn't have the time. Our regular man—"

"Then your answer is no?"

"That's right."

"Now, a wood particle identifications expert should be able to tell—from the grain and the density and perhaps the color—what kind of tree a particular particle has come from?"

"I'm sure they could do that."

"Can you do that?"

"No, sir."

Fortanier nodded agreeably at the witness, letting him know that was perfectly all right. "Now, when you consider Exhibit 14, there are three distinctly different kinds of wood on it, aren't there?"

"I don't know what you mean."

"Well, there's the planking." Fortanier ambled over to the rack and touched it. "This part here. The bed. Then there's the backrest." His hand brushed along the backrest. "And finally there is this pole. Now, I'm no expert, but they appear to be different kinds of wood. Would you agree with me that they appear to be different?"

Chessman stroked his chin, then nodded. "Yes."

"The particle in question. Which one of these sources did it come from?"

"Well—I really couldn't say."

"Is it fair to say that in your opinion it could have come from any of them?"

He nodded again. "Yes."

"For that matter, it might have come off a park bench?"

"I guess it could have."

"I see." Fortanier moved back to the lectern and looked over his notes. Then he smiled at the witness. "Thank you very much for your candor, sir, and your honesty here today. I mean that sincerely. No further questions."

"Redirect, Miss Rommel?" Driscoll asked.

"No," she croaked, thinking, That's as bad as it gets.

"Very well. The witness can step down." Driscoll looked at the clock on the wall. "We'll adjourn for lunch."

*   *   *

"Dr. Eric Mueller."

The short, stocky pathologist that everyone called "Cherman" had no neck, laserlike blue eyes, and chopped blond hair. Frankie watched him climb into the witness box. His shirt was too small, and the top button didn't close. The knot of his necktie pressed against his chest rather than his Adam's apple.

"Your name, please, for the record?"

Mueller was her last witness, and she wanted him to be good. She wanted the jury to go back to the hotel with a sense of outrage. She wanted to emphasize the brutality of the torture, the pain of slow death.

"How many autopsies have you performed?"

As she went through the formality of qualifying him as an expert she wondered if the jury could ever know him. He looked like a product of a Hitler youth camp, but they had lunched together, and Frankie knew the depth of his commitment to the ideal of law. He told her of life in Germany after World War II and of his father, who had been in Hitler's army. Mueller had square shoulders and stiff mannerisms, but his soul had been tempered with the experience of history.

Fortanier tried to stipulate to Mueller's qualifications, but Frankie refused. She wanted him to stay up there long enough for the jury to get used to him before turning him loose.

In time they got to the good stuff. "In the course of your employment, on the twenty-third of April of this year, did you perform an autopsy on the body of a person identified to you as Charles Williams?"

"I did."

He identified Williams from photographs so there could be no mistake.

"What was the purpose of the autopsy?"

"Primarily to determine the cause of death."

But there was much, much more—all of it relevant to the charge of aggravated assault. She started with the burns to the soles of the feet of the victim. Mueller testified as to their number, their exact location, and the size and depth of each. He showed photographs he had taken. They illustrated that the burns had been inflicted on living tissue, among other things. As he went along he defined his terms with great precision.

Frankie asked to discuss the length of time a cigarette would have to be held to the bottom of a person's foot to produce burns such as the ones depicted. She asked him to describe what it would do to skin, to blood vessels, to bone, to nerves. She was informed of nerve placement on toes as opposed to soles, of relative thickness of skin at different parts of the foot, of the difference between coagulate and sear, of the likelihood that pain would not be felt immediately, but once felt would continue like the slow, deliberate dragging of a knife.

She suggested the obvious: that when pain of that kind is inflicted on a body there would be involuntary movement and avoidance. Had he found anything to suggest restraint?

Mueller had. However, because of the darkness of Williams's skin, the photographs of his ankles, wrists, and inner thigh did not reveal trauma as they would in a lighter-skinned person. But Mueller's examination revealed bruising in those areas—again, to living tissue rather than dead tissue. He had also used a spectrograph on Williams, which quite clearly showed the trauma. Unfortunately, no photographs of the spectrographic enhancements were taken. He did not have the necessary equipment.

"The following day—that is April twenty-fourth of this year—did you perform an autopsy on the body of a person identified to you as Andrew Boatwright?"

He said he had. She ran him over the same road—uglier pictures of a man's cigarette-burned feet, because Boatwright's skin was lighter, older, and not as well conditioned. Additionally, photographs showed abrasions to Boatwright's ankles and wrists.

As Frankie watched the jury she tried to monitor the impact of Mueller's testimony. Some sat forward and listened intently throughout. Others slumped in their chairs from time to time, putting their hands on their faces as though to shield their imaginations from further onslaught. Most of them glanced at Richardson with varying expressions: amazement, horror, distress, increasing harshness.

The official cause of death in both cases, Mueller said, was asphyxia, meaning death caused by lack of oxygen.

Both autopsies revealed a most unusual process. As he talked his accent seemed to peel away. He was like the Tin Man in *The Wizard of Oz:* a human being covered in thin metal sheets whose heart had been allowed to show itself. Frankie was struck, then stricken by her perception of his pain. How could he do what he did for a living?

The autopsies showed violent aspiration as well as massive and convulsive efforts at expulsion of water, which induced vomitus to collect in the trachea and bronchial tubes leading to the lungs. He found little sacs of water in unusual places: in the diaphragm, even in the intercostals, between the ribs.

Boatwright's autopsy revealed atelectasis, a condition often referred to as collapsed lung. Because of hyperventilation or "air hunger"— that panicky feeling of suffocation that often precedes deep, rapid breathing—air had forced its way between the layers of tissue that surrounded the lungs, deflating them, preventing their normal expansion.

But the lungs of both men inhaled increasing amounts of water, eventually filling to the point where oxygen could not be processed, resulting in their asphyxiation. "Very different from ordinary drowning," Mueller said, "although the cause eventually was water. There were small, useless air sacs in the lungs." He shook his head sadly. "Oxygen could not reach into the body. Most terrifying." He shook his head. "Most terrifying."

Fortanier sat through his testimony like a student at a lecture, using his brain, taking notes, obviously intent on intelligently digesting the information. Frankie knew he wanted the jury to follow his lead. His example said to them, Isn't this interesting?

Richardson sat at attention through much of it, then seemed to lose interest.

She faced the witness. "Were the conditions you found these bodies to be in consistent with water, as from a shower, having been splashed in their faces over an extended period of time?"

"Yes." He smiled at her sadly.

Before turning him over for cross-examination she asked for a moment to confer with Webster. "Anything else?" she whispered.

"The sliver."

She had forgotten it. With a minimum of questions Mueller identified the sliver Chessman had examined as having come from the buttocks of Charles Williams.

"Your witness, Mr. Fortanier."

"No questions."

It was three-thirty in the afternoon of the third day of trial. "The State of Georgia rests," Frankie said.

The jury had been sequestered for the duration of the trial. Frankie did not know or care where the bailiff took them—presumably to a downtown hotel—but once Fortanier warmed up she knew she would rather be with them than in courtroom D, fighting to keep one half of her case.

"This Court has known me several years," Fortanier said. He stood easily behind the lectern, his small, plumpish frame commanding the attention not only of the judge, but of the reporters and others who stayed in the courtroom after the jury had been excused. "In that time this Court has had ample opportunity to observe some of the devious, manipulative, and on occasion preposterous tactics and stratagems I have employed. But I sincerely hope this Court will agree, one, that I have never been guilty of chicanery or unethical conduct, and two, that on those rare occasions when I am sincere, I mean it."

Driscoll nodded but said nothing.

"Your Honor," the cherublike man said, leaning forward with intensity, "I mean it now. Miss Rommel has rested the case of the State of Georgia against my client. Tomorrow I am charged with the responsibility of putting on his defense. Before we start there is a serious, serious question to resolve. How much, in law, should he have to defend against?"

Fortanier went on to apologize that his motion was not in writing but explained he had not expected the State to finish its case so quickly. "This motion is brought pursuant to OCGA 17-9-1. It is for a directed verdict of acquittal as to three of the counts in the indictment."

"It doesn't have to be in writing, Mr. Fortanier," the judge said tolerantly. "Go ahead."

"I won't waste the Court's time with nonsense. I will

not pretend there isn't enough evidence for the jury to find my client guilty of those counts involving Boatwright. But Mr. Williams is a different matter. I ask and urge this Court to direct a verdict of acquittal as to counts one, two, and three."

Frankie didn't need to look at the indictment to know what Fortanier was talking about. Counts one, two, and three alleged malice murder, felony murder, and aggravated assault against Charles Williams; four, five, and six against Andrew Boatwright. She had seen it coming. Fortanier, in his cross-examination, had brought out some of Boatwright's history but had not asked anything about Williams. Rather than risk an answer that might link Williams to Richardson, he had avoided the subject of Williams entirely.

"The law on directed verdicts of acquittal is quite clear," Fortanier continued. "If there is no conflict in the evidence, and the deductions and inferences demand it, it should be granted. Judge, the evidence is not in conflict on those counts. What is more, the deductions and inferences demand it."

Isn't it strange, Frankie thought. Fortanier wore a soft blue suit, and his face—even his ears—burned red. He looked like the flame she had wanted to be the day before. Did he have the same intense belief in his cause that she had in hers?

"Surely my client should not be convicted solely on the basis of autopsy reports. Yet where Charles Williams is concerned, there is no other evidence!"

Frankie felt the sudden tension of Leon Webster. She also heard rustling behind her: movement as reporters hunched over notebooks and started taking notes in earnest.

"There is not one witness who saw my client with Mr. Williams. There is not one witness who can say my client ever asked about Mr. Williams. There is not one witness who has even hinted at the possibility that Mr. Williams might have asked after my client. There is absolutely nothing that has been offered by the State in this case that links my client to Mr. Williams except autopsy reports!"

He paused, perhaps to free the judge from the lock of his eyes. "There was a sliver, which brought forth an effort

by the State to show it came from this plank over here."
He moved to Exhibit 14 and touched the bed. "Or did it
come from the backrest portion of the device? Or the pole?
The expert didn't know. It is apparent that backrest wood
is distinctly different from the creosote pole, and that neither one is at all the same kind of wood as the planking
that forms the bed.

"Finally, Mr. Chessman had to admit the sliver could
have come from a park bench!" He moved back to the
lectern.

"Judge, the law in Georgia is crystal clear. Where evidence is circumstantial—and as it concerns Mr. Williams,
that is all it is—then they must exclude every other reasonable hypothesis save that of the guilt of the defendant.
Well, I say it is perfectly reasonable to suppose that the
splinter in Mr. Williams's buttocks came from a park
bench!"

Fortanier knew when to quit. As though in anger, he
moved away from the lectern toward his chair. Before sitting he asked, "Will I be given the opportunity to rebut,
Judge?"

"Yes, of course."

He sat down as Frankie stood up. As she approached
the lectern her eyes met Richardson's. He appeared more
than anything to be curious. But he also nodded
encouragement!

What kind of military tactic is that? she wondered. "If
it please the Court, first, there *is* evidence that the splinter
came from Exhibit 14. Mr. Chessman said—and I remember it clearly, because"—she caught herself. She didn't
know the judge well enough to say "I could have strangled
him"—because I would have preferred something a bit
stronger. He said, 'I wouldn't swear to it, but I think so.'

"Who wouldn't think so?" she asked. "A splinter isn't
something one will leave in one's buttocks. One will
remove something like that at the earliest opportunity. The
fact that it was still in him shows he never had the chance
to take it out!

"The evidence also shows Mr. Williams had been tied
up and tortured. True, that came in through the autopsy,
but it's corroborated by what they found at the scene. If a

person were tied to Exhibit 14 there would be marks on his wrists and ankles like those found on Williams—especially if someone was burning his feet—for the very obvious reason that the person would be bouncing around violently to avoid the pain.

"And so of course the expert thought the sliver came from Exhibit 14."

"Miss Rommel, you didn't need an expert to tell us what you have just told us," Driscoll said. "I will grant the sliver may be entitled to some weight here, but it isn't because of Mr. Chessman's testimony."

Frankie nodded agreeably. "Assume then that the sliver in Mr. Williams's buttocks—in and of itself—is not enough to connect the defendant with the death of Mr. Williams. Surely when it is coupled with the autopsy it is."

She had a sudden sense of futility. The judge had already made up his mind. She felt like a barking dog on a leash. All that barking wouldn't make any difference, but if that's what you do, she thought, it's hard to stop. "Isn't it also obvious from the condition of these two bodies that they were killed by the same man? Both had feet with cigarette burns, both had similar markings on wrists and ankles and virtually identical causes of death. Both sets of lungs showed the same slow death, consistent with having water splashed in their faces."

Perhaps in some odd way Richardson's tactic had worked. She didn't really care whether she won or lost. "Thank you, Your Honor." She sat down.

But Fortanier cared. "Judge, let's assume the State had tried these cases separately. Would the evidence have linked my client with Mr. Williams? There would be a body found on a lawn miles away from Rockdale Park. Exhibit 14 would not even enter into it! There would be *one* autopsy showing cause of death to be asphyxia and so forth. And a splinter that could have come from anywhere. And that is all the evidence they would have!

"Would that have been enough to go to a jury? No! Not in this state! We're tough, but we aren't *that* tough!"

His hand even shook with passion as he poured himself some water. Frankie wondered if it was part of his act. "What they are using here is the other autopsy. I guess they want to say it's a common plan, scheme, and design or modus operandi. But surely they should not be allowed to use as evidence an event that occurred *after* the crime they allege!''

Are you going to buy that crap? Frankie asked herself. What about confessions? Aren't they events that happen after the crime?

''What they have on my client might look good to a newspaper reporter, but there is a vast difference between what is good enough for them and what is good enough in a court of law. I ask you: Should my client be judged by the standard of the media? Or should he be judged by the standard of law—that very law Miss Rommel seems so intent on protecting?''

Frankie watched as the judge nodded in apparent agreement. *C'est la* fucking *guerre,* she thought.

''The consequences here are extremely serious to the defendant. As the Court knows, my client must take the stand in order to establish his affirmative defense. He will be cross-examined regarding what he knows about Mr. Williams. Surely it would not be fair for the prosecutor to ask him such questions if the Williams counts shouldn't be there.

''The other side of the coin—the prosecution's case—would not be so drastically effected. My client will still have to face two murder counts and one aggravated assault count.

''There can be no doubt that if my client had been charged only with counts one, two, and three, the State would not have gotten home. The standard should be the same, Judge. If you would have granted a motion for a directed verdict of acquittal in that situation, you should do so now.''

Frankie watched the judge rub his head, then scratch his jaw. She knew what he would say and didn't care. It was as though she were a spectator rather than a player. As she sat happily on the sidelines it had no more effect on her than watching the umpire make another bad call.

''It would be so easy for this Court to say, 'This is a close question, so let the jury decide,' '' Driscoll said. ''I believe I would be upheld by our Supreme Court if I took that tack.

"But what Mr. Fortanier says strikes home. If it weren't for the Boatwright counts and all the evidence that the State has legitimately put before this jury to prove them up, there would be virtually no evidence to show that this defendant had anything to do with Mr. Williams. Our statute says in effect that where the evidence demands it, a motion for a directed verdict of acquittal should be granted. The standard Mr. Fortanier suggests—what would happen if the counts had been tried separately—seems to me to be the correct one.

"I would be less than honest if I didn't admit that nonlegal factors have entered into my decision here. If a mistake is made, who will suffer the most? The damage to the State's case by a mistake in favor of the defendant is nowhere near as great as the damage to the defendant if I make a mistake in the State's favor.

"One further observation: If any man is entitled to a fair trial, this man is.

"It is therefore my ruling that a directed verdict of acquittal be entered as to counts one, two, and three of the indictment. As to the defendant Randolph Richardson, those counts are hereby dismissed."

Chapter

22

Thursday, October 27

FRANKIE'S LACKADAISICAL ATTITUDE CONTINUED INTO THE next day. She knew how men could be led to the gallows with unconcern. It wasn't that they didn't care; they were all used up. She tried to rouse herself when Fortanier made his next move. Before bringing in the jury he moved for a mistrial.

"Judge, the jury has heard too much about the death of Williams. They have seen his widow. They have listened to Dr. Mueller describe his feet and the slow way he died. They have seen pictures of his body. No curative instruction can possibly cleanse their minds. In the interests of justice and fairness this Court should declare a mistrial with respect to the counts that remain and set them for trial at a later date."

Driscoll may have expected it, too. He denied the motion without even asking Frankie to respond. "Mr. Bailiff, you may bring in the jury."

It was a wonderful feeling, even though she knew it wouldn't last. She felt euphoric, untouchable—a cloud of ice crystals drifting prettily above Denver during rush hour.

She could barely hear the honking horns and couldn't feel the frustrations of all those hurrying people.

But when Fortanier called his first witness—Dr. Gregory T. Fox, Jr.—the bubble broke, and she was back.

The small, thin-haired man with thick horn-rimmed glasses was hard to dislike and impossible to disbelieve. He exuded warmth, sincerity, and compassion for the human condition. As a clinical professor of psychiatry, Neuropsychiatric Institute, School of Medicine, University of Alabama, he was affiliated with the National Institute on Drug Abuse. He helped to establish DAWN (Drug Abuse Warning Network) and had extensively studied, experimented, and lectured in the field of cocaine abuse. He qualified as an expert on the effect of cocaine ingestion as well as the epidemiology of drug abuse.

Frankie knew his testimony would be devastating, so she did what she could about it. She smiled.

"Define some terms for us, if you will."

They make a great team, Frankie thought as she watched the two of them kill her: Fortanier with his patrician, courtly manner bringing the very best out of Dr. Schweitzer. He explained the difference between use, abuse, and addiction. The taking of a drug within acceptable societal limits is "use." When one goes beyond those limits it is deemed "abuse." He agreed that "use" in Aspen, Colorado might be "abuse" in Des Moines, Iowa. But addiction, he said, is usually easy to spot. "That is when the drug has control of the user. It occurs where the procurement and use of the drug dominate behavior." By way of example he invited the jury to consider the three stages of alcohol: moderate equates to use, heavy is like abuse, and alcoholic equals addiction.

Fox then described the effect of cocaine on the user. "Usually it will lift your spirits, change your mood. It fills the user with a sense of exhilaration and well-being, loosening his inhibitions, evaporating tensions." His eyes lighted as though he were experiencing those effects. "Feelings of inferiority melt away. Fatigue disappears. He will have illusions of limitless power and energy." His hands dropped in his lap, and he faced the jury as though he had returned to reality. "The drug is often used by so-called 'self-medicaters' to treat such difficulties as perceived obesity, lack of energy, depression, shyness, and so forth. It is very seductive. It can quickly become a way of coping."

He next gave a short course on the three methods of cocaine ingestion: through the nasal membrane, directly into the bloodstream, or directly into the lungs. "The terms 'snort' and 'toot' describe the practice of sniffing the powder into the nose through a straw or rolled-up dollar. 'Shoot up' and 'mainline' refer to intravenous injection, and 'blow' and 'freebase' mean to breathe the drug directly into the lungs." He strayed from his text from time to time, little planned digressions and asides Frankie allowed because she didn't think she could shut him up. He told how snorters and tooters, who tried to confine their use to social occasions, often progressed to becoming mainliners.

"In Atlanta, to snort was chic, trendy, fashionable. After all, much of the potency of the drug is lost in that manner of ingestion. Snorting says—to the user, if no one else— 'You see? I am not an addict.' Derelicts and addicts, who need all the potency available, resort to mainlining, and the use of crack was confined to the young."

On the subject of progression Fox told the jury that the best predictor of cocaine use is prior use of marijuana. The most accurate predictor of marijuana use is prior use of alcohol and tobacco. "Dr. Sidney Cohen, an eminent authority in the field, has articulated this as what has come to be known as Cohen's Law. Accordingly, drugs that produce intense and immediate effects tend to displace those that provide slower and more moderate effects. And so the user moves up the ladder from the mood alterations produced by tobacco and alcohol to the most effective 'hit' or 'blast' of all: mainlining or freebasing cocaine."

When asked whether cocaine was more addictive than heroin he replied the medical evidence indicated that if not more addictive, it was certainly more. dangerous. He launched into a comparison of stimulants and opiates, the two general classes of drugs. Cocaine was a stimulant and heroine an opiate. "Experiments with animals demonstrate that unlimited access to opiates will rarely cause the animal to overeat the opiate, so to speak. The animal will self-regulate its intake. But unlimited access to cocaine usually results in compulsive ingestion and early death."

In layman's terms he explained the reason. "The crash that follows a stimulant is a very deep hole. An intolerable depression of mood follows the stimulation. The only way out is to go back up."

Frankie objected when Fox was asked to give an opinion on whether or not the drug should be legalized. Fortanier argued it went to the issue of whether or not there was a reasonable alternative to the actions of the defendant. Driscoll allowed Fox to give his opinion, and Frankie once again had to smile with nothing to smile about.

Dr. Fox admitted that several prominent persons, including William Buckley and Mike Royko, at one time advocated its legalization. In his view, however, it would be a mistake. In the United States there were seventy million current users of cigarettes, 110 million users of alcohol, and six or seven million users of cocaine. If legalized, it would become as available as cigarettes, and the number of users would rapidly ascend. "Cocaine is not a drug people can control." He believed in the Churchillian definition of democracy: It is a terrible form of government whose only virtue is that all others are much worse.

When Fortanier finally sat down Frankie wondered if the ironies of a prosecutor cross-examining such a witness occurred to the jury. She agreed with virtually everything he said. Still, she tried to make a couple of points. "You talked of Cohen's Law, Dr. Fox?"

"Yes."

"His law deals with the progression of drug abuse, beginning with legal drugs and moving on to those that are illegal?"

"Yes."

"Then doesn't it follow that legal drugs should be made illegal in order to control the spread of cocaine?"

Fortanier cleared his throat with impatience but did not object. "Yes it does," the witness answered.

"However, you don't believe persons who 'deal,' if you will, in tobacco and alcohol should be eliminated, do you?"

"Objection, Judge," Fortanier said mildly.
"Sustained."

Dr. Martha L. Simpson, a research scientist at Centers
for Disease Control, Atlanta, ponderously made her way to
the stand. A dowdy-looking black woman with bloodshot
eyes and the doleful expression of a beagle, she quickly
qualified as an expert in the epidemiology of drug abuse in
metropolitan Atlanta. It took no time at all for the tough-
ness of her mind to become apparent. Frankie knew, when
the time came for cross-examination, that she should not
touch the woman with a pole.

Quickly, clearly, and authoritatively she painted the dev-
astation caused by cocaine in Atlanta and presented the
facts that resulted in those consequences. For the proceeding year the DAWN system reported 117 deaths medically
attributed to cocaine—"the tip of the iceberg"—because it
did not include deaths due to suicide, accident, needle-
sharing, or criminal activity. The tabulation of such other
cocaine-related deaths was outside DAWN, but she had
undertaken its reportage. According to her data, a conservative estimate of the deaths in metropolitan Atlanta that
could be attributed principally to the usage of cocaine: two
thousand and fifty-seven persons.

Frankie wanted the woman to go away.

Dr. Simpson explained that the purity of the drug had
increased at the same time the price had gone down. She
agreed Atlanta had kept pace with the nationwide trend:
Cocaine had escalated to become the highest-ranked primary drug of substance abuse. Obvious consequences of
such eminence, Dr. Simpson stated in her flat and deadly
manner: In the preceding year Grady Memorial Hospital
reported over 600 emergency-room cocaine-caused episodes. Eight central city hospitals reported more than 400
such episodes in the same period. Statistics from DUF—
an acronym for Drug Use Forecasting, a federally funded
program—presented an alarming picture. Their findings:
From fifty to seventy-five percent of persons nationwide
arrested for felonies were contaminated with cocaine.

Frankie sat up straight, making certain that her expression reflected an appropriate amount of horror. She toyed

with the notion of taking the woman on, however. That statistic struck her as suspect. But she thought better of it. Dr. Simpson was obviously loaded for bear. It would be smarter not to give her one to shoot at.

"Epidemiology is the study of epidemics, is it not?" Fortanier asked.

"It is."

"Had the abuse of cocaine, as evidenced by those factors you have testified to here—deaths, emergency-room episodes, and felony arrests—reached epidemic proportions in Atlanta prior to April of this year?"

"Most certainly."

"Have you, at my request, developed information to show whether or not there has been an interruption, so to speak, in that epidemic as of April of this year?"

"I have."

Here it comes, Frankie thought. "Please tell us what you have found," Fortanier asked.

She did. The number of deaths medically attributed to cocaine had fallen sharply, down to twenty-seven. Suicides attributable to cocaine increased slightly in May but fell off. AIDS deaths due to needle-sharing remained constant. Homicides were significantly down. Most surprisingly, the actual number of felony arrests in metropolitan Atlanta had decreased. Grady Memorial Hospital also showed a dramatic decrease in cocaine-related ER episodes: 110.

"Most interesting," Fortainer allowed, gathering up his notes. "Your witness, Miss Rommel."

"Thank you very much, Dr. Simpson. No questions."

Kenneth P. Ryder, formerly a Deputy Assistant Secretary of State for International Narcotics Matter, trotted toward the witness stand as the next witness for the defense. He had the good looks—even to a lopsided grin—of a 1950s matinee idol, but he acted the way the average person might expect a DEA agent to act. He leaned forward as he spoke, using his hands like a conductor. There was nothing shy about the man at all.

Fortanier brought out another aspect of Ryder's background: former agent for Drug Enforcement Administration (DEA). The man qualified as an expert in two areas: national and international narcotics policy development, and narcotics enforcement. When Frankie saw him she knew she had met him before.

According to Ryder, there were three distinctive problems: supply of the drug, demand for the drug, and trafficking in the drug. The criminal activity surrounding each problem had to be separately addressed.

On the supply side, he told the jury that the coca leaf from which the drug is manufactured is grown primarily by Third World farmers in South America. Interdiction at the source of supply sounds easy but isn't. "For one thing, when you push an arm down, a leg pops up." Pressures on farmers in Colombia and Peru brought some success at first, but in the long run it spread out the problem. "Now the plant is grown in Indonesia and the Philippines." Still, more than seventy percent of it winds up in Colombia, he said, where it is processed—through the application of chemicals—into cocaine.

On the demand side, he told the jury that in the United States the number of users is expanding. "More than five thousand people a day try the drug for the first time. Six to seven million people can be termed users, although the estimates are that twenty-five million have experimented with it." The U.S., of course, is not the only market. Cocaine use is spreading—not only through the countries that produce it, but into Europe and Africa.

Ryder professed difficulty in blaming farmers for raising a crop that gave them a living. "Most of them can't afford it themselves." There were only two feasible ways of interdicting the supply at the source: herbicides to eradicate the plant—not attractive at all to environmentalists—and aid in providing the farmers with alternative crops. "Both solutions require international negotiation, diplomacy, and trade-offs. In other words, they require time—and there is no time. We are being destroyed by the drug now."

On the demand side: "How can you blame an addict? Take the man with the great job who gets hooked. He loses the job, sells his car, house—he'd sell his wife and kids if he could. Do you think he wants to do it?" But in a free society, how do you keep people from doing what they want to do? In his opinion, he did not know if the demand could ever be controlled; but if it could—through education, interdiction, and severe punishment—that, too, would take time.

The most culpable players in the equation, those least deserving of consideration, were the traffickers. In Ryder's view, they were the real criminals. He testified as to the enormity of their profits—billions of dollars—and of the corrupting power of that kind of money. Frankie considered objecting on the grounds of relevance, but it would give Fortanier the chance to make a speech. She decided against stepping into a quagmire.

But when Fortanier asked, "In your opinion, sir, are we winning or losing the war on drugs?" she had to object.

She requested permission to approach the bench. Granted. There, knowing the jury watched and hoping they couldn't hear, she argued her case. "What 'war on drugs?'" she asked. "Among other things, the question assumes facts that are not in evidence. It assumes as fact that which can't be characterized as fact at all. It is a rhetorical question designed to prejudice the jury and probably aimed at making me look foolish for objecting to it."

"Miss Rommel, if I may say so, you look splendid," Fortanier said.

It took a moment for the implications of the remark to settle in. The obvious sexism, masquerading behind the facade of Southern chivalry, would be known to Fortanier as the kind of jab that could inflict real pain—which made it a beautifully executed riposte between duelists, the perfect poke. "You are incredible," she told him, smiling in sincere admiration.

Take that, she thought.

Even Driscoll felt better. "I'll sustain the objection."

Fortanier focused as much attention on the ruling as he could when he returned to the lectern. "Thank you, Mr. Ryder," he told the witness. "You will not be allowed to answer the last question, and I have no others."

Prosecutorial paranoia, Frankie told herself. They aren't glaring at me in hatred, she made herself think as she arranged a few notes on the lectern. That little bastard. He didn't even give me a chance to sit down. "Mr. Ryder, have we met?"

"Yes, but I didn't think you remembered. You spoke at a NIDA conference I went to—National Institute on Drug Addiction? You told us how hard it is to prosecute drug cases."

Oh my God, Frankie thought. I have just stepped into a fresh cow pie. "Oh, yes," she said, as though delighted. "That was in Buffalo?"

"Yes. You were very entertaining."

Frankie did what she could to blunt his testimony. She got him to agree that the three sides he identified—suppliers, demanders, and traffickers—could also be characterized in purely economic terms as producers, consumers, and—for want of a better term—middlemen. "And traffickers are middlemen?"

"Yes. Although somehow—" she could have interrupted his answer but knew it would look bad to the jury, so she nodded at him, allowing him to go on—"somehow it's hard for me to think of Noriega or Andrew Boatwright or members of the Medellin cartel as retailers."

Frankie laughed along with everyone else. "You also testified as to the difficulty of controlling the demand for drugs in a free society, right?"

"Yes, I did."

Squirm, you little bastard, Frankie thought, glancing at Fortanier to see whether he was preparing to stand. "Free societies are based on principles, aren't they?"

Now Fortanier had to decide whether to object or let it in. "Yes," Ryder said.

"And if those principles aren't maintained—let me back up. As a former Deputy Secretary of State you've seen countries where the principles upon which a free society is based simply don't exist, haven't you?"

Fortanier got up. "May we approach the bench, Judge?"

"I wonder." Driscoll glanced at the clock. "It's almost noon. Can I ask where this line of questioning is headed, Miss Rommel?"

"I'd like to ask the witness whether, in his opinion, the baby should be tossed out with the bathwater."

"Oh, Your Honor," Fortanier said, as agreeably as he could. He even managed a smile. "I object."

*   *   *

Robin V. Mancusso, an attorney at law with offices in Atlanta who had formerly been agency chief, Atlanta Division, Drug Enforcement Administration (DEA), took the stand after the noon recess. He looked more suited to his role in life as a lawyer, Frankie thought: overweight, large head, bushy eyebrows, seven-hundred-dollar suit. He qualified as an expert in narcotics enforcement with special knowledge concerning metropolitan Atlanta.

"May we approach the bench, Your Honor?" Frankie asked.

"Yes," Driscoll said.

"Judge, this is the first departure from the order of witnesses set out in Mr. Fortanier's motion," Frankie whispered after they were secure in their little bubble. "I thought he was going to put this witness on last and have Al Fiorello and the defendant in front of him."

"Mr. Fortanier isn't bound by any particular order, Miss Rommel," Driscoll said.

"Agreed. My question—which is asked to expedite the trial—is will he call Fiorello? I know he doesn't need to answer it."

"Let's see if he will. Abe?"

For the briefest fraction of a second Fortanier looked at Frankie with respect. "Well. I can honestly, conscientiously, and completely respond to the question, Judge. I don't know." He beamed at them, possibly not aware of the fact that his smile could be seen throughout the courtroom. "It will depend on how far I get with this witness."

"Does that help, Miss Rommel?" Driscoll asked.

"If I can ask another question, sir. I assume Captain Fiorello is in the hall, under a defense subpoena?"

"That's correct," Fortanier said.

"Judge, I'd ask you to order Mr. Fortanier not to release the subpoena until the trial is over. If that's a problem, let Mr. Webster slip out there now and give him one for the State."

"I see," Driscoll said. "Apparently you have a line of questions for Fiorello, and you're afraid he'll get away. Is that it?"

"Yes, sir." She didn't add what was also apparent: that

Fortanier had anticipated it and might suggest to Fiorello that he get lost.

"Abe?"

"You have my word. But under these circumstances I'd feel better if she put the paper on him."

Frankie whispered instructions to Webster when she sat down, and Fortanier resumed his comfortable stance behind the lectern. "Now, Mr. Mancusso."

Mancusso testified to a host of details that—according to the motion—would have been brought out by Fiorello. Because of Mancusso's special knowledge of the narcotics network in Atlanta, coupled with his law degree, he had been retained by the DA's office to advise in the prosecution of the drug cases the defendant had made. Sure, Frankie thought, suspecting he'd been put on to keep any of them from hiring him.

He sat in the witness box with his elbows propped up, his fingers joined at the tips. He tapped them together judiciously, a banker considering the loan application of a first-time borrower or a lawyer making certain his client understood the importance of the situation. The organization was known as The Enterprise, Mancusso said, and the drug lord, or head, had been Andrew Boatwright.

Mancusso interrupted his narrative to inform the jury that Mr. Slade and others in the DA's office knew he was a witness for Randolph Richardson. They did not believe he would compromise those prosecutions by testifying. Only two appeared headed for trial; the other five resulted in guilty pleas. Great, Frankie thought. Now the jury knows what a hero Richardson is, and that the DA supports him. She smiled.

Boatwright was indeed a trafficker, Mancusso said. From the information available—and he expected to be extensively cross-examined with respect to its sources—he would conservatively estimate that Boatwright had profiteered to the extent of twenty-five million dollars a year. He had a virtual lock on the metropolitan area, draining the resources of Atlanta and destroying lives in the process. Frankie let him talk. She didn't want him to know what she was like.

THE WATER CURE

The Enterprise, according to Mancusso, had been completely dismantled by the raids earlier that year. Those raids, of course, would not have occurred but for the information provided by Randolph Richardson.

"To your knowledge, has the flow of narcotics—cocaine in particular—been interrupted by the dismantling of that organization?"

Frankie allowed the question. She hoped it would open the door. "It has," she heard Mancusso reply.

Fortanier didn't pursue the point. Too late, Frankie thought. You can't shut the door. There followed a series of missiles, each calling for an opinion—and Frankie had to let the questions be asked before shooting them down. In your opinion, is there a significant danger to the well-being of others because of the distribution of the drug cocaine? Objection, Judge. Sustained. In your opinion, is anyone in Atlanta safe from the consequences of the distribution of the drug cocaine? Objection, Judge. Sustained. Dear me, let me ask this, then. Where a society is being destroyed by the availability of cocaine, and where the only reasonable method of stopping that flow of drugs is to go after the trafficker, in your opinion, are military methods legitimized to accomplish that goal? Objection, Judge. I hope that is all, Mr. Fortanier. Sustained.

Fortanier smiled angelically at the jury. "Well. It appears that the laws of evidence won't allow me to continue. Your witness."

If *I* were the judge, and you were in *my* court, I would have you executed, Frankie thought. "Thank you," she said. "Hi, Mr. Mancusso," she offered in her friendliest manner, setting up at the lectern.

"Good afternoon, Miss Rummel."

She listened to him mispronounce her name. He's already been to a defense lawyer training seminar, she thought. "It's 'Rommel,' " she told him, amazed at the effectiveness of the ploy. If you do that again, I'm going to throw this lectern at you. "I believe you testified that the flow of narcotics had been disrupted significantly, didn't you? When the organization called The Enterprise was—well—toppled?"

271

"Yes, I did. Resulting in the saving of hundreds of lives, I might add."

She could move to strike the answer as nonresponsive but didn't. She wasn't about to get sidetracked. "However, trafficking in narcotics is still going on, isn't it?"

"There has been a significant reduction."

"Yes or no?"

He opened his hands. "Yes."

"As a matter of fact, a new organization is in place, isn't it?"

Mancusso glanced toward Fortanier as though asking for help. "So I've heard."

"You've done more than hear about it, haven't you? The fact is you've been actively involved in the investigation of this new group."

Mancusso pursed his lips as though considering his options. He glanced at the judge. "Yes."

"They are called the Dead Poets, aren't they?"

"So I am told."

"Their name has some reference to the—well—poetic manner in which they dispense with people?"

Mancusso glared at Fortanier, inviting him to object. "So I am told."

"For example, an informant was found with a bar of soap in her mouth, and a lawyer's body was adorned with a barrister's wig?"

"Yes."

"Why do they kill that way?" Frankie said, knowing she was pushing Fortanier all the way to the wall.

But he didn't move. "We characterize it as a management technique," Mancusso said.

"Explain."

"Oh, many of these drug people are impressed with flair and so forth." He laughed, finally realizing that—for whatever reason—Fortanier wasn't going to save him. "I suppose they are intimidated by theatrics."

"Thank you, sir." Frankie gathered up her notes.

"You're welcome, Miss Rummel."

She had wakened at night, bursting with lines of questions to ask, and had written them out. She had rehearsed in front of the mirror, refining and tuning them. She had always known that to win she would have to destroy him when he took the stand, and two days ago she had been certain she could do it.

But now—knowing he would be her witness in half an hour—she wasn't ready.

Richardson sat in the jury box, his thin face pointed in the direction of his lawyer. "Your name, sir?"

"Randolph Richardson."

They had not called Fiorello. Richardson would be the last witness. Frankie had never felt this way toward the end of a case. She could not shake her sense that the law itself was on trial, that she had to win. She wished she could hate him, but she wasn't even close.

"You are the defendant here?"

"I am."

She tried seeing him the way the jury did, still needing the key to open him up. He spoke softly, but everyone in the room could hear. If you didn't know his past, you wouldn't suspect it; but knowing it, she thought, you see it in him.

"Tell us a bit about yourself."

Centuries ago, it seemed, Swift had said: "He has soul. He isn't afraid to die." On the stand that quality shone. He seems so quiet to have been a soldier, she thought, yet it fits. As she listened to him avoid any mention of medals and battles she tried to see him the way he saw himself. Suddenly it came to her: Sir Knight. The sense of strength he projected was not that of a bully. He saw himself as a protector. Gotcha, she thought triumphantly—until their eyes touched.

I don't hate you, Randolph, she thought. Not at all. She looked away.

She knew Fortanier would be as brief with him as he could. He wouldn't have put him on except that he had to. He had to show that Richardson knew of the drug problem before he launched his campaign, and Frankie wondered how they would work their way around Melody Thralkin. They had to know she would paint his motive as revenge. And they would talk about torture and death hardly at all.

They started with his interest in the drug problem. It

273

was something Richardson had not even thought about until earlier that year. But the woman with whom he was romantically involved came to him with a problem. She had been caught with drugs in her purse. The authorities told her they wouldn't press charges if she would help them.

Frankie didn't object. The testimony would help her more than it would hurt. "What did your woman friend do?"

"I wanted her to see a lawyer, but she wouldn't," Richardson said. "She did what they asked. They call it 'narking.' She introduced the man who sold drugs to her to an undercover policeman."

"How do you know?"

"I watched." His hands were cupped on the wooden rail in front of him, and he laced his fingers together. "No one knew I was watching. Not even Melody. I've had experience along those lines. I wanted to be there in case something went wrong."

"Did anything go wrong?"

"No. Although nothing went right, either. The agent was a bit of an oaf. He didn't fool the fellow with the drugs at all. No arrests were made. The pusher—they call them 'pushers'—just drove off."

He has such a nice, easy manner, Frankie thought, letting herself smile at him along with everyone else in the courtroom. But under it there was a current of electric tension. You don't know what will happen if you plug him in, she thought. Will he play soft music or fry you?

"Then what happened?"

"Nothing for a day or two. Then they murdered her." Richardson studied his hands, and Fortanier didn't move. "I suppose at that time I realized drugs were a problem."

"Your friend's name was Melody Thralkin?"

"Yes."

"There was testimony about her earlier, as I recall. The State even introduced a photograph of her." He excused himself a moment and found a five-inch by eight-inch photographic portrait of an attractive woman among the papers on his table. "Approach, Judge?"

"You may."

He showed it to Richardson. "Is this she?"

"Yes." Richardson smiled at it with fondness.

The photograph was put in evidence and passed to the jury. Richardson told of his reaction: hurt, dismay, hatred. He spoke of his intense desire to do something about her death. He wasn't interested in simple revenge. He wanted to destroy the institution that had killed her.

"And so what did you do?"

"I went to the library." He had read everything he could get his hands on and learned, essentially, what the jury might have understood that day. Atlanta—the nation—was literally being destroyed by drugs. But because of the limitations of the law, nothing could be done about it. He gave titles and names of authors and produced a library card issued in April.

"Did you ever contact the police?"

"Yes."

"What was your intention?"

"To see what I could do to help."

"What came of that contact?"

"Nothing. They told me what I already knew. They could do nothing."

"And so what did you do?"

"I developed a plan of my own."

Fortanier shuffled his feet and looked down at them, as though curious about something they had done. "On Friday, April twenty-third of this year, did you attend a dinner sponsored by the Atlanta Historical Society?"

"Yes."

"Who was the main speaker that night?"

"Andrew Boatwright."

"Were you acquainted with the man?"

"No."

"Did you know who he was?"

"I'm sorry, Mr. Fortanier. What do you mean?"

"There has been testimony here in court that Andrew Boatwright was a drug lord, a trafficker in drugs, the head of an organization known as The Enterprise. At the time you attended the dinner, did you know those things?"

"Yes."

"In fact, that's the reason you went, isn't it?"

"Yes."

Fortanier looked at his feet again. They seemed to continue to puzzle him. "While at the dinner that night, did you talk with Mr. Boatwright?"

"I made it a point to."

"What did you talk about?"

"I invited him to go with me after the speeches and have some Wild Turkey."

"And is that what you did?"

"We left together, but we didn't go drinking."

"I see." He gathered up his notes. "Your witness."

The abrupt ending caught Frankie by surprise. She did her best not to appear discombobulated. "Well," she said, standing at the lectern and looking at him, "you stopped just when it was getting good."

It was not a question, and Richardson didn't reply. He smiled at her gently. Lancelot meeting Guinevere.

"After the dinner you took Mr. Boatwright to Rockdale Park, didn't you?"

"Yes."

"To a garage, which you had rented, called Flanagan's Auto Repair?"

"Yes."

"What time did you arrive?"

"I think around midnight."

This is so flat, Frankie thought. I wish I could question him without looking at him. "And there you tortured him?"

"Yes."

"You burned his feet with cigarettes?"

"That's right."

"Did he squirm?"

A soft quietness settled in his eyes. "I don't recall."

This is awful, Frankie thought. The jury doesn't want to hear this. They already know it. "He cried, didn't he?"

"No."

"He screamed in pain?"

His eyes are so expressive, Frankie thought. "No. I believe he passed out."

"You enjoyed killing him, didn't you?"

"Not at all."

"Oh, come now, Colonel. In your view, he was responsible for the death of Melody Thralkin, right?"

"That's right."

"You hated him, didn't you?"

Richardson dropped his eyes. He will try to deny it, Frankie hoped. "Yes." He looked at her again. "I hated him."

"How much?"

"I would say with every cell in my body. I hated his fat face, those piggy eyes, those stubby and bloated hands." Frankie said nothing, feeling like a miner who had just found gold. "He looked like a cartoon, an evil caricature of a human being."

"You killed him out of hatred and revenge, didn't you?"

"No. I didn't want him to die."

"Pardon me?"

"I wanted him to keep talking."

I don't like doing this, she thought. "Colonel Richardson, the truth. You idolized Melody Thralkin, didn't you?"

His expression questioned her. If he suspected a trap, he didn't show it. "No."

"Surely you loved her?"

"Yes, very much."

"The truth is you were sick with love for her and filled with intense rage when she was murdered. Isn't that the truth?"

He smiled. "No. I was in a lot of pain, but there was nothing sick about it at all."

"Quite rational? Very sane?"

"Yes."

She walked to the table where the exhibits had been placed. "Yet you built an altar to her, didn't you? As though you were a knight, and she had been your lady?" She found the photograph of the sea chest draped with the Confederate flag and pierced with the sword. Thralkin's photo was on it.

"Miss Rommel, we come from very different traditions."

"Sir, isn't this an altar dedicated to the memory of Melody Thralkin? And didn't you swear vengeance against those who had murdered her?"

"Not at all. May I explain?"

Frankie knew the rules of cross-examination as well as anyone. Never let a witness explain an answer. Ask only

WARWICK DOWNING

leading questions, keep the witness under control, never let a witness get away from you.

But you play it to a jury. If his explanation didn't come in now, it would come in later. "Go ahead."

"May I see that?" he asked, reaching for the photograph. She handed it to him, then moved back to the lectern. "Let the record show I gave the witness Exhibit 9," she said, thinking to herself: I've just been sandbagged.

He examined the photograph. "I was a soldier preparing for war," he said. "It sounds strange perhaps, but there are well-recognized traditions and rituals to which warriors adhere in preparation for battle."

Maybe not, Frankie thought. This sounds insane.

"That is a warrior's altar, Miss Rommel. It had very little to do with Melody."

"A warrior's altar?" she asked, as though amused.

"Yes. Filled with symbol. Something to pray to." He smiled a bit defensively.

"Tell me how it works."

"For example, the sword in the middle—a Japanese *katana*—is a cross, symbolizing 'mission.' The musket— actually it's a harquebus—pointed at my heart when I knelt in front, to symbolize my willingness to die. Melody's picture symbolized what the mission was all about."

"It was all about revenge, wasn't it?"

He looked at her with disarming openness. "No. I agree if she hadn't been murdered . . ." He shrugged. "But the purpose of a warrior's altar isn't revenge. You use whatever is available to mold your body and your will into a single purpose. I wanted to destroy this organization called The Enterprise. I didn't want them killing anyone else."

"You prayed in front of it?"

"Yes, with great intensity." The jurors appeared to be trying to make up their minds. "General Douglas MacArthur, for example, used the device. There is a history of superb fighting men who have done it. You try, deliberately, to turn yourself into an instrument, a weapon whose sole function is the accomplishment of the mission. It's a form of self-hypnosis."

All of the jurors were absorbed—fascinated—by the narration. But what were they thinking? Their attitudes didn't provide any clues. "Then it is your testimony that this is just a military technique?"

He smiled. She wished he didn't look so damned sane. "Not for everyone. But essentially, that's all it is."

"This technique will enable you to do anything, won't it?"

"Well, I've never been able to fly."

The smattering of laughter angered Frankie. "That isn't what I mean," she snapped, then she made herself lighten up. "It will excuse torture, for example." She smiled at him. "It will allow you the absolute freedom to inflict pain, even kill."

"The 'freedom' you allude to isn't a freedom at all. It is a discipline. It can only be exercised in the accomplishment of the mission."

She felt his integrity. She knew the jury could feel it, too. She had never anticipated the questioning would take her over a cliff. "Let's suppose you had to kill other people in order to accomplish your mission. Would you have done so?"

Fortanier seemed to drift to his feet. "I must object. The question calls for conjecture."

"Sustained."

Frankie kept her eyes on the witness. "There was testimony from Officer Swift earlier in this trial regarding your use of torture in Vietnam. Do you recall that testimony?"

"Yes."

"Enemy soldiers were tortured and killed?"

"Yes."

"That was done in order to accomplish your mission?"

He didn't appear proud of himself, but he didn't avoid the answer, either. "Yes."

The way their eyes touched was sensual. She knew there was much more she could do. She could show him the pictures of Boatwright and ask questions about them, stand him next to Exhibit 14 and make him look like a ghoul, grill him about his plan. The tried and true techniques of the prosecutor—although in this case they could backfire.

They would miss the point, too. Why make it easy for the jury?

She sat down.

"Redirect, Mr. Fortanier?" Driscoll asked.

"I think not, sir," Fortanier said. "The defense rests."

The judge turned toward Frankie. "Any rebuttal, Miss Rommel?"

It always ends so quickly, Frankie thought. "No, sir."

"Well." The judge looked pleased. "It's been a long day."

"How come you didn't call Al?" Doug Swift asked, driving Frankie to the apartment. "He sure wanted to testify."

"That's the reason." Frankie was worn out. After the jury had been excused they'd argued over the instructions. Tomorrow they would argue the case. "He'd like nothing better than to zing me. But I got what I needed out of Mancusso."

"Which was?"

"The fact that there's a new drug organization in place. What do we do? Commission Richardson to take it out, too?"

"Huh. Speaking of Mancusso, better stay away from him." Swift's eyes crinkled with amusement. "He could blow up."

"You heard something," Frankie said. "Tell me."

"Poor Abe got a bomb on his hands. That old fat man let Abe have it in the hall. He wanted to know how come his lawyer left him hanging out there, you know, him without a shield, having to answer all those questions about the Dead Poets. Like, 'Hey, Abe. I didn't sign on for *that*.' "

"And?"

"Abe told him he knew what you'd do. If it didn't come in from him, you'd call Fiorello, and that would have been like playing with a loaded gun."

Frankie leaned her head against the cushion. "What a crock," she said. "Lawyers trying to outsmart each other."

Chapter

23

Friday, October 28

WHEN THE ALARM WENT OFF FRANKIE HEARD IT BUT DIDN'T move. She realized she was fried. Until then she had convinced herself her emotions weren't involved, only her head. If you play the game any other way, she told herself—if your gut takes over during a trial, and you try too hard—you'll be like a novice golfer who swings mightily at the golf ball and misses it.

As she dressed—her flame outfit for final argument—part of her wanted to bury her face in her hands and cry. Another part wanted to wander around the castle like Ophelia, strewing flowers on the parapet. She cared too much and hadn't even known it—right side for the issue, left side for the man—and the conflict in her heart had used her up. In the kitchen she drank three cups of coffee, hoping they would jack up her heart. As Doug drove to the courthouse, and she listened politely as he told her he didn't care what happened that day, he was just glad he knew her. That's nice of you, she thought, but hurry up. I have to pee.

She could barely squeeze her way into the courtroom. Knowing all those people had come to hear the final argument ought to have affected her pulse, but it hadn't. Leon

Webster was seated at counsel table, and for the first time he stood up and greeted her before she sat down. Fortanier's nod was close to pleasant, and Randolph—chivalrous to the end—was kind enough to look the other way.

Some form of oriental martial art, she thought. His way of slamming me to the ground.

Usually she enjoyed final argument, the chance to put things right, nail it down. But this was different. The defendant admitted killing the victim, and there was no need to hammer away at the obvious. The question was simple and profound, she would tell them. Do you let him get away with it or not?

She didn't remember getting to the lectern, and when she first addressed the jury her mouth worked away on its own. So much of what she told them came out of a can anyway: thanks for your attention, the importance of what you do, da da, da da. She guessed her gestures were right—none of them appeared shocked. She wondered if she sounded sincere. She went over the evidence and the law and showed how they fit together like a hand in a glove. There was no way to make them care about the victim—she tried to get them to care about the law.

"Nothing can justify what he did." She made eye contact with several of them, as she had been trained. "If the law is to work, it must protect *all* of us." She leaned forward like an actress, evidencing an intensity she didn't feel. "It was a brutal, vicious murder committed in the course of the torture of a human being. Nothing can avoid that monstrous fact."

Maybe I'll warm up on rebuttal, she thought, reaching for more eyes to impress. "The question for you to resolve is really quite simple." My feet hurt, she thought, moving toward her table. "Do you believe in the law, or don't you? Is the law for everyone, or do we carve out exceptions for heroes?"

Fortanier got up slowly, as though he had been transfixed by her oratory. "That was really quite good."

Oh? Frankie thought. I don't see any tears in your eyes.

It took him a moment to surround the lectern. "My friends, I will have only one opportunity to address you in this case, so I hope you will forgive my intensity.

"This man is not a murderer." How does he do that? Frankie wondered, watching him hold all of them with his eyes and wrap his arm around his client from twenty feet away. "Look into your hearts. If this man is free to walk the streets of Atlanta, are any of you in any more danger? Will the public suffer as a consequence of your verdict of not guilty?

"What do you know of this man? A true war hero—a Medal of Honor winner, although to get him to talk about it is like pulling teeth. You also know him to have a true, honest, wide-open heart, don't you? Isn't that what you saw as Miss Rommel cross-examined him? A soldier, my friends, in the best tradition of that word. Not a murderer.

"Nor will you—as Miss Rommel so eloquently phrased it—'carve out an exception for a hero' if you choose to acquit. He does not want you to change the law for him. He wants you to follow it. And it is there for you to follow."

He is so good, Frankie thought, admiring the power of his advocacy. He took them through the law of justification with an eloquence that was stunning. Then he dressed the principles of law with the evidence his experts had brought out. The statistics were no longer numbers. They became lives.

Over and over, but each time as though for the first time, he stressed the utter hopelessness of the situation as it had appeared to Richardson: an epidemic of drugs, out of control, like a cancer ravaging a young woman. "It must be contained. It must be stopped if she is to live."

Yet how could it be stopped? He reminded them of the three-sided nature of the problem. "The experts agree that the supply cannot be interdicted. Or if it can, because of the international implications, time is required. The experts agree that the demand cannot be interdicted. Or if it can, because of the nature of the problem, time is required.

"But my friends, there is no time. The patient is dying. We must operate—now. We must interdict—now. The only interdiction that can occur is at the level of the trafficker." He paused, letting them feel his contempt. "Scum. Profiteers. Destroyers of lives. They are not deserving of the protections of the law. We owe them nothing. The law owes them nothing. If we allow them to continue, the patient will die."

His manner changed into that of a professor of ethics who wants to get to the bottom line. "Where a society is literally being destroyed by the availability of cocaine, where the only way to save the society is to attack the trafficker, are not military methods legitimized to save the society?" Frankie recognized the question. It was the same one he'd asked his last expert during the trial. The rules of evidence didn't allow an answer, but this was argument. "Confront it head-on, my friends. Do it now, for me, because if you don't do it now, you will be asked to do it by the prosecutor. Does not the end—the salvation of society—legitimize torture?"

He can't read them either, Frankie thought, absorbed now in her craft, watching him watch them. He paused long enough for water. "When I first practiced law I would look upon a jury—to borrow an analogy with which all of you are familiar—as a federation of sorts, as opposed to a union." He glanced at Frankie and Judge Driscoll as though one or the other might object. "I hope the prosecutor and the court will indulge me in this." Once again he faced the jury. "A federation is a collection of entities, you might say. An aggregate of bodies. But they have not been welded into one thing.

"Later, it seemed to me that a jury was more like a union. Perhaps I only tried to stay even with the progress in the South and the remarkable achievements of Dr. King. But as all of you know, a union has a singleness about it that a federation lacks. A union is one thing, welded together by history or by adversity, or by volcanic eruption in the case of rocks"—he smiled—"or by temperature."

He had some water. "Well, I was right the first time. Because you are not a union, my friends. You are a federation. Under the law, you are a collection of independent minds. And each of you, individually, must be persuaded of the defendant's guilt—beyond a reasonable doubt and to a moral certainty.

"Each of you, individually, must believe in your heart and beyond a reasonable doubt that Colonel Randolph Richardson is a murderer. Each of you, individually, must believe there was no legal justification for his actions. You have heard the evidence. You know of this cancer. You know of this man's efforts to interdict.

"Was it unpleasant? For him, as well as for everyone? Ask yourselves this question. When a doctor operates, can he do it without getting blood on his hands?

"The jails—the prisons—are for criminals. Not for men like this man." He sat down quickly, before Frankie could object to his final remark.

Frankie let her voice fill with the anguish she felt, the conflict in her heart she had tried to bury. Let it out, she thought, standing by the lectern. They know it's there. "As all of you know, punishment cannot enter into your deliberations." She started where Fortanier had stopped. "And as Mr. Fortanier has told you—and I believe him—his client is not after a break. He doesn't want you to give him a special deal because of his medals. All of us want you to follow the law."

That's a crock, she thought. Then another thought: I'm back. Thank God. I'm okay. "I must tell you, ladies and gentlemen, that this has been an extremely difficult case for me. I have such tremendous admiration and respect for these men. But think carefully over what you have heard here today.

"Mr. Fortanier is so gifted in his use of analogy. But don't be misled. Because there is such a vast difference between analogy and reality.

"There is a difference between a doctor operating on a patient and what this man did. There is a difference between getting blood on your hands and deliberate torture. There is a difference between stopping the spread of cancer and the cold-blooded, analytical, reasoned murder that occurred here."

She walked over to Exhibit 14. "Understand totally what he did, then ask: Can our law ever, under any circumstances, justify that? He rented an old garage, equipped with a shower stall, isolated enough so that screams could not be heard, big enough to hold this." She touched the rack. "Can our law ever, under any circumstances, justify strapping a man to this? Can it justify holding lighted cigarettes to another person's flesh, burning holes in living tissue? Can it justify the deliberate, painful, slow suffocation of life with water?'' She was appalled and let it show. ''My God. Think about it. Our law simply cannot, under any circumstances, justify such things.''

She moved back to the lectern. ''Are drugs really destroying our society? Please don't misunderstand me. I do not want to minimize the awful nature of addiction or its consequences in terms of human suffering.

''But is our country really in such extreme peril? Or is the real peril the absolute and complete suspension of law by a person who—for his own reasons—has proclaimed the peril?''

She had no idea how she sounded, but she felt like a flame. You must believe me, she could hear her soul shout. You must.

''Ladies and gentlemen, no one has the right to take the law into his own hands. No one has the right to set himself above the law, to establish his own rule and impose it on others. That is totalitarianism. That is the very antithesis of what our law is all about. That is the military solution.''

You are twelve people from all walks of life, she thought, who spend five hours a day watching television. Do you know what I'm talking about? All she could do at that point was hope they did.

''Our society is not the fragile, delicate woman with cancer Mr. Fortanier would have you believe. She is free, and that freedom is her blood. Don't drain the blood away to save the patient. Our country is alive, and it is a thriving, healthy life that will last—who knows how long?—as long as we preserve the blood of freedom. She laughs and cries, she make awful, tragic mistakes, but she makes up for them.

''If you give her the chance to heal herself, she will, because she is healthy enough to shed disease. And give her a flu shot from time to time. Toughen the laws, of course. Do those things.

''But don't medicate her to death. Don't kill her to alleviate a symptom.''

She felt herself running down. Let them wrestle with the rest of it, she thought. Time for the wrap. ''Our society can survive drugs,'' she told them. ''And you know why.

Because we are free. We allow people to make awful mistakes with their lives, but without that freedom our society will truly die.

"If we adopt a war mentality, which would allow self-appointed saviors the right to torture and kill—*that* will destroy us."

When she sat down she felt the flame go out. She tried to follow along as Driscoll charged the jury with the law and after the instructions had been read, did her best to appear alert. She watched the jury leave the courtroom with the bailiff. When asked by Driscoll if she had any objections to the charge, she stood like a sleepwalker and said "No." She wasn't quite sure when Driscoll declared they were adjourned but after he was gone, she sat down.

When she looked toward Richardson, she realized he and Fortanier were gone.

Some moments later she got up, surprised to find people still in the courtroom. She thought of all the things she had forgotten to say. But she saw respect in the faces of those who seemed to want to talk to her: Webster, Swift, even Traynor Jaynes and others she'd never met.

As she struggled down the aisle, she felt a tug on her coat and turned around. "I just wanted to tell you, dear," Miss Anne said, smiling up at her. The small woman had been crying. "You were superb."

Chapter

24

THE JURY HAD BEEN SEQUESTERED AT THE BEGINNING OF the trial, in accordance with Georgia law in a capital case. After their final instructions they were sent to the jury room to deliberate. They returned after dinner and worked until midnight. Then they were loaded into a county prisoner van and bused three blocks to their hotel.

The following day—a Saturday—they began their work at 8:30 A.M. They asked that lunch be sent in, often a sign of an imminent verdict. But they lasted until 5:30 and dinner. Then they returned to their labors at 7:00 P.M. and worked until midnight.

Waiting for a jury verdict was never easy, especially in a foreign land. Fortanier could disappear into his office a few short blocks from the courthouse, but Frankie had nowhere to go. She was not welcome at the district attorney's office, even though Traynor Jaynes continued cheerfully to answer her questions, and Miss Anne maintained her files. She felt awkward hanging out at the Atlanta Police Department and didn't enjoy sitting alone in the courthouse. But Doug Swift told her to stay at one of those locations, or he would lock her up.

She settled on the courthouse. The security was good on the weekend. No one could get into the building without authorization. She found a book by John Dunning and, even though she knew she couldn't concentrate on anything other than the mistakes she had made, immediately lost herself in a mystery informed by the fascinating world of the rare-book business. When the jury retired for the night a cheerful blond female patrol person drove her to her apartment and escorted her inside. Dunning's book kept her up until two in the morning.

She slept until eight, had breakfast with Doug in the apartment, and picked up a Clive Cussler paperback in a nearby shop on the way to the courthouse. The detective stayed with her for half an hour, which was all of him Frankie could stand. It was apparent he had other things to do. "Beat it," she said. "You're getting on my nerves." She resumed her vigil.

This time she disappeared into a modern-day search for an ancient Saracen library. She didn't quite know why it had to be found, other than that the fate of the world depended on it.

The jury sent out for lunch again. The bailiff, Tom Bowie, said, "They ain't even fightin' with each other, Miss Rommel, but they're sure hung up on something." He disappeared back to his station, an anteroom next to the jury room, where he waited for that fateful knock on the door. Frankie went back to her book.

At four o'clock Fortanier stuck his nose into the courtroom. He saw her and tried to leave, but—aware that he'd been seen—entered. Frankie marked her place with a bookmark, closed it, and watched him come down the aisle. "Hi."

He nodded at her. "You haven't seen my client, have you?" He avoided calling her by name.

"No. Is he lost?" Frankie smiled, hoping Fortanier might lighten up.

"Is the judge around?" he asked, pushing through the gate. "Perhaps he knows."

Frankie was puzzled. It really did sound as though Richardson was gone. "The judge went home. If we get a jury, Tom will call him. He only lives—"

"Yes. I know how Sam does things."

Fortanier sat down at the other table. "Well. I seem to

have lost touch with him. Probably nothing to worry about."

Frankie wanted to be helpful. "It's a lovely day. Doesn't he play golf?"

"That's a possibility. You would think he'd let me know."

"He is different." She wished she hadn't said that.

"Why did you do it, Frankie?" Fortanier sat with his elbow on the table, propping up his face with a hand.

His pose was not that of an accuser, and Frankie thought, Thank God. He wants to talk. Maybe we can clear the air. "I'm sorry, Abe, I don't know what you mean. Why did I refuse to withdraw from the case? Or why did I get a murder indictment rather than manslaughter?"

"I'm glad Randolph isn't here," Fortanier said in a pleasant tone of voice. "He's far too much of a gentleman to tolerate what you are about to hear. You are a bitch. A conniving, scheming, manipulative, deceitful, cunning bitch. Have you ever married?"

Frankie was floored. "You little prick! What are you talking about?"

He sat up, smiling angelically. "As a liberal lawyer with a modest criminal practice, I have developed a certain standing as a spokesperson for the underdog. In this community that includes women's political organizations. Until meeting you I sincerely believed I was not a sexist. I have worked diligently for the passage of the ERA, and I applaud with deep sincerity the manner in which women have come into the professions.

"But either I have been totally wrong about myself all these years, or you are a disgrace to your sex. I believe you have used your sexual charms to manipulate and destroy the will of my client. He is a fighting man, and you have employed your smell or something—in the old-fashioned manner of a temptress—to suck him dry. Do me the courtesy of not denying that which is so patently obvious!"

She literally felt as though she'd been bucked off a horse. "You miserable little bastard," she said, touching her face. "What are you talking about?"

"My client has behaved during this trial like a smitten

adolescent, and everyone—even those uniformed idiots who have adorned the walls to protect poor little you—has seen it. What has happened in this courtroom is a farce. How can a defense lawyer possibly obtain justice for his client when the man is so obviously in love with the prosecutor?"

"He is *not* in love with me! That is absurd! I can't—" She stopped to feel her face again, too angry and shaken to continue. She felt naked, violated, stripped of all sense of worth—deliberately so—by a man whose sense of decency she had trusted. She felt seventeen and in the back-seat of a car, a passionate believer in the cause of civil rights who had just been raped by two blacks.

"He killed Maurice Brown."

"I beg your pardon?"

"He kidnapped Maurice Brown, took him back to Flanagan's, stood him in the shower stall, and shot him through the temple. We had a witness who saw it!"

"What tripe! You have—"

"I listened to you. Now you listen to me." Without awareness she stood over him. "I believe in what I do. I believe in law. He believes in war. Might makes right on the battlefield, but it has no place on the streets of Atlanta. The military solution to civil problems is wrong!

"He's a vigilante. A Charles Bronson. He has nothing in mind but the accomplishment of his goal. An engineer, an executioner, who can kill without pity—anyone—to accomplish his end." Abruptly she turned away from him, reaching for control. "When I first got into this case and was told to go for manslaughter I didn't like it, but was willing to do it, perhaps because all of us do a little whoring now and then. But there is a difference between an occasional fling and living in a brothel. When I learned what he'd done to Maurice Brown I couldn't do it. I could never have looked at myself in the mirror again—even looked at my shadow—if I had let him get away with that."

Fortanier had slumped back into his earlier posture. "You really believe that, don't you?" he asked. "You are wrong, of course. But if you truly believe as you say . . ." He shrugged. "I suppose I could find it in my heart to understand some of your less blatant behavior."

She faced him. "I'm not wrong, Abe. I have a tape—"

"Of Doug Swift talking with Maurice's son-in-law, a boy named Dogwood? I've heard it. It doesn't mean a thing."

"You know about it?" Frankie asked, totally surprised.

"Of course." His mouth twisted into a tight little grimace. "This situation is not without irony. Did you know that I was a particular friend of Maurice Brown?"

She found her chair and sat down. "I knew you gave his eulogy."

"He was without question the finest man I have ever known. He had a deep spiritual sense. He truly believed in the power of goodness. He believed in the power of the body to regenerate itself through giving—and believe me, it seemed to work for him. He was in his seventies but acted and moved and talked like a man in his forties.

"He would say, 'That is the real message of Christ. And when these rich assholes in charge who are screwing everything up finally get it, when some medical doctor proves in a scientific experiment that a man will live longer when he learns how to give himself away, *then* you might see some changes on this planet.' A most amazing man."

"How do you know Randolph didn't kill him?"

"Because the stupid little idiot who confessed to it actually did it. He's sublimely happy now, incidentally. For the first time in his life he has status."

"That isn't a reason. That's a belief."

"My dear woman, I reviewed the evidence carefully with his lawyer before advising him to take the deal. Munroe's confession was replete with detail that had not been leaked to the press and that he could not have known unless he had been there. Further, he owned a .357-caliber magnum. The medical evidence was perfectly consistent with that as the death weapon."

"He had sources in the sheriff's office. He could have found out all he needed to know."

"Possible, but not likely. I also talked it over with Randolph. There were these awful rumors, and—well, I conditioned my representation of him on his replies. I am not a polygraph machine, but I've had some experience in these things. Randolph doesn't lie. He is so thoroughgoing military that he cannot. He can kill in the line of duty, but he can't lie."

"Why would someone—I don't understand. Why would Dogwood make it up?"

"According to my sources, the Dead Poets made him do it. They wanted to destroy Randolph's reputation. It is widely believed they killed Dogwood in the same way Randolph was supposed to have killed Maurice in an effort to frame Randolph for Dogwood's murder."

"Why didn't my people tell me this?"

"They may not have known. Fiorello cut them out of his loop."

The bailiff trotted into the room. "They have a verdict," he said. "I'll call the judge."

Frankie couldn't keep up with her feelings. What an awful irony, she thought, knowing she would not have tried so hard to win if Randolph hadn't murdered Maurice Brown. But when the bailiff said, "They have a verdict," sweat rushed into her hands and blood pushed into her head. It always happened. She could try a drunk driving case and it would happen. "Abe?"

"Yes. This might be rather awkward."

She was going to suggest a drink afterward but realized that—with a client who had chosen that moment to disappear—Fortanier had other things on his mind. "I'll help you stall," she said. "I'll help you find him. Let's call Doug."

He sat without moving, staring at the wall. "Can I tell you something in confidence? Lawyer to lawyer?"

"Of course."

"I drew up Randolph's will. Not a large estate, but more than a pittance."

Oh, no, Frankie thought. "He didn't leave it to me, did he?"

"No, nothing as romantic as that. He set up a trust fund for the benefit of Maurice Brown's grandchildren." He looked at her. "Randolph wouldn't play favorites, and there are seven so far. Who knows where it will end?"

"Are you telling me he knew Maurice Brown?" Frankie asked.

"No. But he met the family. I introduced him to them last June, partly so they could see for themselves the kind of man he is. They had heard the rumors, too, and I wanted them to know the truth.

"One young man in particular—Frederick—was raised by Maurice. His father was killed in some foolish brawl, and who knows where the mother is?" He got to his feet. "Isn't it strange? Randolph and Frederick became pals. He took the boy fishing." Fortanier smiled at her.

"Why are you telling me this?"

Fortanier shrugged. "The musings of an old man who may soon have his head handed to him on a platter."

Frankie scoffed at him. "You don't really think they'll convict him, do you?"

"I don't know. But I'm terribly worried. The Dead Poets promised to drown him. I just hope to God he's safe."

At 5:34 P.M., before calling in the jury, Judge Driscoll called his court to order. The only persons present in the courtroom were the court reporter, the bailiff, the clerk, the lawyer for the defense, and the prosecutor. Leon Webster sat alone behind the rail.

"It is my understanding the jury has reached a verdict. Is that correct, Mr. Bailiff?"

"So I have been informed."

"Mr. Fortanier, we obviously need your client."

"I don't know where he is, Judge," Fortanier said. "He was to keep me informed of his whereabouts and promised to check with me on the hour. He was like clockwork until three o'clock this afternoon. At shortly before four I telephoned his mother—the last location I had—but he wasn't there. I have not heard from him since that time."

"Well. For the record, I will state that the defendant, who is on bail, has the responsibility to stay in touch with you. He knows he can't avoid a verdict by disappearing."

"I'm quite certain he knows that, sir."

Driscoll wiped his nose. "A defendant has the right to be present at all significant stages of the trial, of course, and certainly this is a significant stage. But as you pointed out once before, Mr. Fortanier, the right is personal to him, and he can waive it. Unless you show me some law to the contrary, or give me a good reason, I'm going to bring that jury in and take the verdict. It will be this court's position that his failure to be present is a voluntary waiver of that right.

"Miss Rommel, what do you think?"

Frankie got up. "Might I suggest, sir, that the reputation of the defendant for honor is very good, and he has made all other appearances." She was not used to arguing on behalf of the defendant and found herself stuttering. "I know Mr. Fortanier hasn't asked for anything, but I believe the police are looking for the defendant, and his family and friends are, too, and I feel confident he'll show up. I wonder if—I know Fulton County isn't made of money, but perhaps—if the jury goes to dinner and we reconvene after dinner? There is probably a simple explanation."

"Juries have been known to change their minds, Miss Rommel, if they are kept waiting too long. Mr. Fortanier?"

"I appreciate the sensitivity of the State. Can I ask what the Court would do if the jury were to acquit my client?"

"You mean if we did it now? With him not here?"

"Yes, sir."

"I would discharge them with thanks, of course. Then I would undoubtedly direct a few judicious remarks in your direction, and discharge the bond."

"If he were convicted?"

"Issue a bench warrant for his arrest."

Fortanier took a deep breath. "There is the possibility of unavoidable detainment on his part, sir. I am very much in favor of the police continuing their search, but if he is acquitted, presumably that search would be called off. For that reason, may we do as the prosecution suggests?"

"What are you implying, Mr. Fortanier?"

"He could be in some danger, sir."

Driscoll shook his head with judicial fatigue. "This trial has been more of an adventure than most of them. I will do as you suggest. Mr. Bailiff, please advise the jury there has been an unavoidable delay and arrange to feed them. We will reconvene at 8:00 P.M. But at that time, Mr. Fortanier, we will take a verdict whether the defendant is here or not."

"The clerk will call the roll."

Frankie looked at the clock on the wall: 8:05 P.M. Her hands were covered with perspiration.

The jurors dutifully answered "present," but when Randolph Richardson's name was called there was no answer. Several of the jurors smiled uncertainly at one another.

"Randolph Richardson?" the clerk called again. She waited a moment. "The defendant does not answer the call."

Fortanier sat erect at counsel table looking at his fingers. "Mr. Fortanier?" Driscoll asked.

"If it please the Court, I must report that I lost contact with my client at three o'clock this afternoon."

There was some commotion on the other side of the rail. Five or six media representatives had heard a verdict had been reached and had been admitted to the courtroom.

"We discussed this previously. Do you know where he is or, more to the point, why he isn't here?"

"No, sir. I can mention several places he is not and have no idea why he isn't here."

"Very well. It is the Court's position that the defendant has voluntarily absented himself from his trial, and we will proceed without him."

"For the record, sir, I object."

"Objection noted. Mr. Bailiff, has the jury reached a verdict?"

"It has, Your Honor."

"Will the foreman please give the verdict to the bailiff?"

A small white man in the front row stood and handed the form to the bailiff, who gave it to the judge. Driscoll looked it over. "I will note initially that I had previously ordered a directed verdict of acquittal as to counts one, two, and three. The defendant is hereby acquitted of the malice murder, the murder in the commission of a felony, and the aggravated assault charge contained in those counts, concerning Charles Williams." He adjusted his glasses. "Please attend to the reading of the verdict as it concerns Andrew Boatwright.

"The People of the State of Georgia versus Randolph Richardson, defendant. Count four. We the jury find the defendant, Randolph Richardson, not guilty of the offense alleged, to wit: murder, with malice aforethought, of Andrew Boatwright."

Frankie felt Leon Webster's body tighten.

"Count five. We the jury find the defendant, Randolph

Richardson, guilty of the offense alleged, to wit: murder, in the commission of a felony, of Andrew Boatwright.''

The word "guilty" came out powerfully and loudly. Webster's body relaxed.

"Count six. We the jury find the defendant, Randolph Richardson, guilty of the offense alleged, to wit: aggravated assault against the person of Andrew Boatwright." He laid the form down. "Ladies and gentlemen, is this your verdict?"

Some of the jurors said "Yes," the others nodded.

"Mr. Fortanier, do you wish to poll the jury?"

"Yes."

The remaining business was taken care of quickly. A bench warrant for the arrest of Randolph Richardson was issued; no bail was allowed. Fortanier requested that the time for filing motions and notices be stayed until the defendant was found. Frankie should have objected, but she didn't. Driscoll said he would take the request under consideration but told Fortanier he should be prepared to follow the time limitations set forth in the statutes.

The judge hurriedly left the bench to avoid reporters, and Fortanier ducked out of the courtroom. Frankie wondered if she would ever see either of them again.

"Come on, counselor," Webster said, smiling down at her. "You were great. I'll take you home."

"Where's Doug?"

"He got called out."

A reporter caught up with them in the hall. "What was the difference?" she asked. "They convict him of murder in the commission of a felony but acquit as to malice murder. Aren't those inconsistent verdicts?"

"I don't know the law in Georgia that well," Frankie said, "but I doubt it."

"Care to elaborate?"

She lifted a shoulder and made a face. She was in exactly the frame of mind her instructor on high-profile murder cases had warned against, but she didn't care. "I guess the jury didn't think he had murder in his heart," she told the woman, "but they still wanted to follow the law."

Chapter

25

LEON WEBSTER—SWEAT POPPING OFF HIS FOREHEAD, abruptly stopped his solid blue police car in front of her apartment. The police band was on. The dispatcher had ordered Webster to report in ASAP. He was needed to coordinate the search for Richardson. The word on the street: the Dead Poets had him.

Webster started to open the car door, but Frankie put her hand on his arm. "Go!" she told him, jumping out of the car and slamming the door. "I'll be all right."

"Thanks, Frankie," Webster said, the car microphone already in his hand. He shot away.

But when she walked into the living room she sensed immediately that something was wrong. The place had been touched: a missing chair at the dining table, the newspaper not where she had left it. She remembered the story she'd read recently in Denver of a murdered network anchorwoman.

She stopped, mentally gauging the distance to the door, and opened her purse as though searching for a lipstick. She started to reach for the small pistol Swift had gotten for her.

"Put the purse on the floor," a familiar voice said.

It really frightened her. She spun around and saw him

sitting in a chair near the coat closet. He held a pistol in his right hand. "Ever go to the movies?" he asked. "There's a great scene in *Butch Cassidy*—"

"What are you doing here?"

"Put the purse down, Frankie," Richardson said. "Fat lot of good that pea-shooter will do if you can't even find it."

She thought of throwing it at him and bolting, but he stood up and blocked the door—not in a threatening way; more like a sheepdog. "Five minutes. Then I leave."

"You bastard!" She was shaking. "Break in here and scare the shit out of me! Put the gun down!"

He did, on the chair seat, stepping away from it. But she knew he could get there first.

In an odd sort of way she felt relief. The face she saw was as familiar as that of an old lover. It wasn't some super-patriot in a hood carrying a shotgun. "I should have you arrested!" she said angrily, pissed off rather than threatened.

He laughed. "You probably should." Gently he took the purse away from her and put it on top of the television set.

"How did you get in? So much for security!"

"You don't want to know."

"Did Doug let you in?"

Richardson laughed. "It wasn't Dudley Do-Right. In fact, he's out looking for me now, if he's worth his salt. I dropped them a clue."

"What did you do?"

"I called in the name of one of the Dead Poets and told them where I planned to meet with the fellow."

"They believed you?"

"Of course. Would I lie? I won a Medal of Honor!"

Frankie sat down. "What do you want, Randolph?" She spoke harshly. "You've heard about the verdict, haven't you? You know about the bench warrant?"

"Yes. Congratulations." He smiled cheerfully. "The thing I would like most in this world right now is a cup of coffee."

She sighed, got up, and went out to the kitchen. "It will have to be instant."

"You were right, Frankie," he said.

Her hold on the jar of instant coffee loosened, and she almost dropped it. "Sorry, Randolph. No confessions."

He followed her to the kitchen and leaned against the doorjamb, watching her. She felt oddly domestic, filling the glass coffeepot and putting it on the stove. She pulled one cup out, hesitated a moment, and took out another one. "Not a confession, Frankie," he said. "An awakening. I can't tell you what I've been through."

"Then don't."

His eyes can be so soft, she thought. His smile can be so gentle. She had read somewhere that Billy the Kid was like that. "I have to," he said. "It isn't over."

"What isn't?" All she could think of was what he had said on the stand: how a warrior prepares for his mission. She could see more bodies. "Randolph, don't kill anyone else. *Please.*"

They stared at each other. She really felt stupid. She wanted to hold him. "The water's boiling."

"Oh."

She found a teaspoon in a drawer under the sink and measured the powder into the cups. She wondered how long she could keep him. Long enough for someone to realize he might be with her? "Sugar?"

"No." Their fingers touched when she handed him the mug.

"Careful. It's hot."

He laughed.

"What's funny?"

"Here we are. You've just prosecuted me for murder, and if I'd been on that jury, I'd have hanged me in a second, but it took them two days. If the gendarmes knew where I was, they'd be gathering out there in force, but I'm in here trying to explain why I've broken into your quarters. Then you tell me to be careful because it's hot." He lifted his mug in a mock toast. "Don't you think that's funny?"

"I don't know."

"Mud in your eye. You've changed my life."

She glanced involuntarily at her watch. "I've changed a lot of lives."

"They won't get here in time, Frankie. I sent them out by Stone Mountain."

She glared at him. "I don't like that. It sounds like a threat."

"It isn't." He sipped some coffee, then sat at the table. She sat near him, wondering what to do. He seemed sad in a way, and she wasn't afraid, but she knew, too, that he was capable of anything. "I just want to talk."

"Then talk."

"Rotten coffee." He looked into the cup. "In war you don't know people," he said. It seemed to her he could talk as long as he didn't look at her. "You just kill them. It's easy. They stick their heads up"—he watched a head go up, then pulled an imaginary trigger—"and you blow it off. If someone sees you do it, you get a medal.

"I wonder how many Maurice Browns I've killed."

No one could blame her now if she let him talk on, she thought. Possibly she should try to change the subject— but then he might leave. She held the cup to her mouth, hoping her silence would keep him talking.

"I didn't believe that fellow Dogwood for a second when I worked on him. But do you know? He had some stomach muscle. He even spit on me. He said, 'I'm gonna give you AIDS, mothah fuckah.' "

It was so ordinary. She watched him smile and smiled with him, a married couple gossiping about the neighbors. "I didn't know who Brown was. I had no idea. To me just a black fellow who drove a Pinto and fetched doughnuts for the people he worked with." His eyes had that peculiar expression they had worn through much of the trial: a deep sadness. She had thought it was a ploy. "But I knew what to do. I've always known exactly what to do. If Dogwood watched him die, he'd break. It worked, of course."

"That isn't what you told Abe."

"You've talked with him about this?"

"Yes." She didn't go into details.

"You're right, it isn't." He smiled at her. "I lied to Abe. That's something they teach in the military, believe it or not. The honor code? You get that first. Then you take a graduate course in look-'em-in-the-eye lying, in case you have to in order to accomplish your mission.

"I just wish the son of a bitch hadn't introduced me to Maurice's family."

He made it sound bad. "What was so awful about that?"

"I got to know them." He smiled at her, but the focus of his eyes slid around her. "Freddie especially. Cute little bastard. One of Maurice's grandchildren."

"And?" she prompted.

"Possibly it's because I've never had children of my own. Of course, Freddie is black, but he could be mine. Don't tell my mother. He's all boy, and he thinks I'm special, and . . ." Richardson stopped talking, as though out of breath.

Frankie remembered the young black Randolph had been so obviously proud of in front of the jury. She had thought the scene had been staged for the jury's benefit.

"Maurice raised him," he continued conversationally. "They tell me he's just like his grandpa." She was suddenly aware of his intensity, as though he had come to the point of the story. "Maurice was no hero. But he was worth ten of me."

For a moment all Frankie could do was stare. She could feel his pain.

"I had to tell you," Richardson said, putting his cup down. "So you won't spend the rest of your life in a nunnery, you know, blaming yourself."

"What?"

He laughed—gently—at her confusion. "I wanted to congratulate you, too. You accomplished your mission. Democracy is saved."

"You're not making sense."

"I'm not?" His voice regained its customary teasing quality. "You proved the ends don't justify the means. Bully!"

"Randolph—"

"I don't give a rat's ass about democracy, personally." His head leaned to one side, and he peered at her. "Don't you see?"

"See what?"

"I can't abide myself any longer. In my absolute and utter arrogance I killed a man who . . ." He stood up.

Frankie masked the alarm that rang inside her. Is he going to kill himself? she thought. "You're not at war now, are you?'' She moved comfortably, as though there was all the time in the world.

"Nope. War's over.'' He looked around him, then saw the pistol on the chair in the other room and moved toward it.

"Wait.'' She touched his arm. "I don't get it.'' She tried to think of something to ask, then asked the question that troubled her the most. "How—well—I don't believe you. We've talked. You're not a monster. How could you do it? Torture and kill?''

"You don't torture and kill people, Frankie. It's the enemy.'' He sat down again. "Back in the days when I was a hero I didn't feel bad about it. In war it's what you do.

"I have never felt death as a loss. That's strange, I know. Good friends, people I'd been drinking with the night before, and I see their faces in death, but it doesn't bother me. I don't block out battles, either. My mind plays them back, all the bloody details, but the gore doesn't bother me. I see courage, or the valor of my men. Although sometimes I'll be surprised by a recollection of sudden panic.'' He smiled, obviously entertained by the memory. "There is nothing like it in the world. You are moving on the battlefield, in control, everything working, when you realize you've been tipped upside down.

"But there's no pain in my head over it, like those fellows that get traumatized or whatever it is that happens. Any more than there's pain in a movie reel. A good night's sleep—one a week—and I'm fresh as a daisy.''

The poor man, Frankie thought. Something Swift had said made sense: If it's easy to kill, there's something really wrong. "That's awful.''

"Not anymore.'' He got up again and walked to the chair his pistol lay on. "I'm not a hero now. I've been turned into a person.'' He stuffed the pistol in his belt.

"Randolph, stay. Don't go.'' The words jumped out of her mouth. She really meant it. "I've got some Wild Turkey,'' she said, jumping up to get it. "Let's get drunk.''

"No.'' He smiled at her. "Do you know something, lady?''

"Randolph, listen to—''

"You'd have been fun to go to Nepal with."

He was gone before she could stop him. She ran to the telephone. Nothing worked. She tried direct-dialing Webster, then realized the telephone line was not in the wall. The bastard! She plugged it in and tried again, but no one answered. She ran an emergency number for Swift and was put on hold. She dialed 911. "Hello. This is Frankie Rommel, and I'm calling from my apartment. Randolph Richardson was here not more than five minutes ago!"

"Yes, of course," a professionally trained voice replied. "Are you in immediate danger, Miss Rommel?"

"No! He's wanted, and he's getting away, and I don't know what he's going to do!"

"I understand you completely," the woman's soothing voice said. "Your address, please?"

Doug Swift was in front of the others. Pistol drawn, he pushed the palm of his other hand downward, telling those behind him to go slow.

At night the old garage—in the wasteland of Rockdale Park—looked like a shipwreck. But through a few of the cracks in the window covering, and under the bay door, they could see the soft yellow glow generated by a light bulb.

Doug didn't know three of the five uniformed officers. One of the responding patrol units—jockeyed by a real cowboy—had approached with siren blaring until Swift had ordered him over the air to cool it. A big black storm trooper, he wanted to charge the building like it was part of the set for *New Jack City*. "No," Swift told him. "We want cases, man. Not corpses."

He outlined his plan. Four officers deployed to windows, two on each side of the building. The fifth officer—the only woman—positioned herself near the bay door. If anything came roaring out, her instructions were to shoot the driver if possible, then the tires.

Swift approached the side door. At his command the men at the windows—armed with carbines—were to break them out and hold the occupants inside, letting them see the barrels. They were to shoot only if necessary. No bullhorns; no warning to those inside. A tipster had said Richardson was in there, and they wanted to rescue whatever was left of him.

He tried the door. It was not locked. Cautiously pushing it open, he halfway expected a fusillade of bullets and stood out of the way. He cracked it an inch and peeked inside—nothing. No voices, no movement. Taking a deep breath and letting some of it out, he banged the door open and jumped in. "Freeze!" he shouted, crouched low with his gun aimed at the center of the room. "You're under arrest!"

No one was there. He heard the splinter of glass as the four windows broke out and barrels poked through. Shots were fired from one of the apertures. "Hey!" Swift hollered. The man was shooting at him "Hey!"

The black cowboy. "Swift?" he hollered.

"Chill out! Shit!" Swift hollered.

"Sorry."

When his heart settled down he heard the soft gurgle of water. He ran over to the shower stall.

Someone had put a curtain over it. "Captain?" Swift asked, wanting to rip back the curtain but afraid of triggering a booby-trap. His heart had fallen into his stomach. He knew what was back there. "Captain?"

He pulled it back slowly. Richardson—lashed to a long plank of wood—had been stripped and leaned against the wall, feet over his head. Water from the spigot washed over his face and into his nose. "No." Swift turned off the water in one fast twist and dropped to his knees. "No."

Richardson's open eyes stared at nothing. There were several cigarette burns on his body, including on his penis.

"You found him?" the woman officer asked. He could hear the others moving around but couldn't see them.

"Yeah." He couldn't hug the old man. Still kneeling, he stared at the dead face and hugged himself. "Call it in, okay?"

It was after midnight before he could get to a telephone. He found one in a shop off Martin Luther King Boulevard. "Frankie?"

"Doug! Did you find him?"

"Yeah."

"Is he all right?"

Doug looked up quickly, eyes wide, to keep tears from forming. He saw the Big Dipper. "No. He's dead."

He could hear her breathing. "That stupid man," she said softly. "Where?"

"Flanagan's. Don't know why I didn't think of that sooner."

"God." He heard ice tinkling in a glass. "I'm so sorry."

"Me, too."

"The Dead Poets?"

"That's the way it looks. He's drowned, and . . ." He couldn't say any more. An awful rage closed off his throat.

"And what?"

"They beat him up pretty bad. Even burned his feet."

"Doug, I'm so sorry. Will you be okay?"

"Yeah. How about you?"

"I'll be fine."

A tear dropped off the end of his nose. So long, Captain, Doug thought. "Keep the door locked, okay? I don't know how long I'll be."

Sunday, October 30

It was so strange. As Frankie waited for her flight at Hartsfield International, there was no one to say good-bye to. The verdict in the case, followed by Richardson's murder and the hunt for his killers, had entirely absorbed the cops and the media. It might even have been nice if a newscaster or reporter had found her, she thought. At least then there would have been someone to talk to.

After telling her to lock the door Doug seemed to have forgotten about her. He hadn't returned the night before or even called. She hated leaving without seeing him. But it occurred to her that he might blame her. Possibly he just didn't want to see her. So she called his number and left a message. She hadn't been able to get Leon Webster either. She talked briefly with Miss Anne but couldn't possibly go by the DA's office. She even called Traynor Jaynes but was glad when he wasn't there.

The flight for Denver left on schedule at 10:06 Eastern Daylight Time. It would get her home midafternoon. Good old Trigge had said he would pick her up.

She had a window seat and stared at clouds through

much of the flight, watching them make faces and ignoring the man who sat next to her. Then she started a long personal letter to Abe Fortanier. She knew he would find out that Richardson had come by the apartment. She didn't know what she would tell him about it but knew it wasn't going to be the truth.

When she saw Trigge, rather unexpectedly she started to cry. "Hey," he said, hugging her. "Don't do that. I hate it when women cry. It makes *me* cry."

"I'm sorry."

"It's okay, babe." He held her hand and broke out a handkerchief. "You don't want to use this one," he said, wiping at his face.

As they waited for her baggage she stood close to him and was glad he understood and didn't move away. "Oh," he said, reaching in a pocket. "Forgot." He gave her two handwritten notes Doug Swift had faxed. "He telephoned, too. Told me you should not have gone to the airport by yourself and said when he sees you you're going to jail. Then he said something about how he's been rounding up dead poets, whatever that means."

"Really." Frowning, Frankie started to read. The letter from Doug was on top. "Damn you, girl, for leaving me that way without saying good-bye," it said. "We didn't finish at Flanagan's until two this morning. I found this letter from the old man when I got back to the PD. Tape was right where he said—not the one on his stomach—and the DA says we've got some good cases.

"You better call me before I have to call you. Okay?"

The other letter was also handwritten in a large, bold hand, like a proclamation. It filled the page.

Dear Little Mac,

Go to Flanagan's, son. There you may find my remains, as they are euphemistically known—although these fellows aren't known for their gentility. I could be scattered all over town.

Be that as it may.

Look in the grease pit. You will find a trash sack in a corner that looks as if it was blown in there. Be

WARWICK DOWNING

careful with it. Expensive sound-activated recording equipment is inside.

You never know how a campaign will go. But the Dead Poets appear to be a romantic bunch of miscreants with a weakness for poetic endings. It helps to know your enemy's weakness. I have a hunch they will get real satisfaction out of doing unto me what I have done unto them, if you can tolerate a brief biblical reference. As a precaution, I've taped a recording device over a favorite scar on my stomach.

I'll draw them out for you fellows: names, places, plans, other crimes. I've had some experience recently on the subject.

What a way to go, right, old fellow? Although at least I'll know how it feels to die.

Semper Fi.

About the Author

Warwick Downing was born and raised into the law. His father was a lawyer, as was his grandfather. Both his brothers are lawyers, and his sister is married to one.

Downing is a former Deputy District Attorney (Merced, California), Assistant United States Attorney (Denver, Colorado) and District Attorney (22nd Judicial District, Cortez, Colorado).

He is also a novelist. In addition to the NASP series he has written three suspense books and one book for young readers.

He presently lives in Morrison, Colorado.

The chilling new tale of psychological terror by
an acclaimed and brilliant mystery writer

FRANCES FYFIELD

"Frances Fyfield is remarkably thorough in her
psychological profiles...she certainly understands
the pathos of those people who are caught up in
their dark mischief."—*The New York Times*
This is the spellbinding tale of suspicious characters and potent chemicals that will keep mystery
and suspense fans turning the pages. You'll be
up nights wondering if a mysterious death was
really murder and if a grieving husband is really a
cold blooded killer in

Coming In Hardcover In March 1992

POCKET
B O O K S

Courtroom drama that invariably yields "crackingly dramatic scenes and some surprising turns."
—*L.A. Times Book Review*

RULES OF EVIDENCE

A NOVEL BY

JAY BRANDON

AUTHOR OF FADE THE HEAT

Delve into a world of drug dealers, informers, crooked cops, and racism and discover a first-rate reading experience that lingers long after the verdict is read and the last page is turned. You won't want to miss a word of the spine-tingling tale of courtroom suspense.

Coming in Hardcover in March 1992

POCKET BOOKS